SHE SMELLED WONDERFUL, LIKE LILACS AND POWDER.

Olivia's hair, released from the braid it had been in, lay spread against the white pillow, making an elaborate frame for her face. The top two buttons of her gown were open and the hem was raised to her thighs in a very modest invitation to Spencer.

"What happened to your braid?" he asked, lifting a long strand and letting it slink through his fingers. Livvy's hair was soft and silky, and just the feel of it across his palm made drawing a deep breath harder.

"I thought—" she began, then stopped herself. "I could do it now if you want."

"Leave it." Spencer's voice sounded gruff to his own ears. More softly he added, "You can tie it up later."

He turned to face her, knowing that sooner or later he had to get started, and his leg slipped between hers as if by its own accord. Before he could pull it back, her hand rested on his thigh. It was, perhaps, the boldest thing Olivia had ever done.

He had meant to tell her he was too tired. He had thought to put her off until tomorrow or the day after that, or when he might feel more in control. But now, as he grew hard against the roundness of her hip, he tried to concentrate on things he could control in the hope of stopping things he couldn't.

STEPHANIE MITTMAN

The Marriage Bed

A DELL BOOK

Published by
Dell Publishing
a division of
Bantam Doubleday Dell Publishing Group, Inc.
1540 Broadway
New York, New York 10036

ISBN: 0-440-22182-X

Printed in the United States of America

Published simultaneously in Canada

May 1996

10 9 8 7 6 5 4 3 2 1
OPM

This book is gratefully dedicated to my critique partner and friend, Sherry Steinfeld, who read every word and asked me to change only a few of them. Thank you for making me replace ordinary phrases with ''Mittmanisms,'' for keeping me honest, and for liking my books. Thanks also for coming to my rescue at the drop of a hat, offering always to listen, and giving me good advice. I'm so glad we're friends.

And, as always, to Laura, who is the best editor a woman could ask for—always available, encouraging, and supportive. But I still liked the line about the old maids being like vultures.

To all my friends and supporters on AOL—a bouquet of roses, which I can't figure out how to do, and a ;-).

And last, but never least, my incredible family, each of whom, at one time or another, was called upon to convince me one more time that I am really a writer.

I hope I've done you all proud.

Prologue

He lay on the old oak bed in the darkened bedroom listening to the thud, thud, thudding of his heart compete with the sound of his new wife's ragged breathing, and stared through the window at the last two stars in the Big Dipper's handle. How did that little rhyme Kirsten had taught the children go? *Star light, star bright, something about the first star at night . . . wish I may, wish I might, have my wish come true tonight?*

Nearly that, anyway.

I wish . . .

He glanced over at the woman nestled beneath the covers just inches from his side. Outside, the few dried leaves that still clung tenaciously to the dormant lilac bushes scraped against the glass panes. Wind whistled through cracks in the painted white frames of the windows.

I wish . . .

She shifted slightly, the mound of covers moving like a snow drift in the wind, and a tiny whimper escaped her lips.

I wish I was dead.

"Olivia? You all right?"

"I guess," she answered softly. She sounded bewildered, confused. Of course she was. So was he.

"I'm sorry," he said, grateful the room was too dark for her to see the rush of embarrassment that heated his cheeks.

Not that she needed to see him to know how mortified he was. He told himself once again it was just too much wine, too many toasts drunk to a newly wedded pair.

The white mound moved again as she extricated a hand to lay softly against his arm. "Don't apologize," she said, sidling up closer to him. "It's not your fault. When a man and a woman . . . that is, a husband and wife . . . well, I knew it would hurt. I didn't mean to cry out. I'm fine now, really."

"I'm sorry about it hurting you," he said, annoyed with himself for being so lost in his own distress that he hadn't even thought to apologize for the pain he had caused her. "But, then," he said. "After . . ."

"After?"

Could it really be that she was unaware of what had just happened between them? Or was she simply being kind? Could she be so naive she actually thought that what they had done was all there was? No, she must have felt him suddenly grow soft inside her. Mustn't she?

"So then I guess I'm really, finally, truly your wife now."

He couldn't help but hear again her choked scream as he had broken through the thin barrier that separated a maiden from a wife. With no small amount of regret, he conceded as much. "I guess you are."

"I thought it would feel, I don't know, different."

So had he. Certainly it had been different with Kirsten. Hell, with a few minutes' rest in between, he had taken her over and over on their wedding night. He'd expected to get through it at least once with Olivia. After all, it had been more than two years since he had lain with Kirsten.

And it had started out well enough, considering it was Olivia's first time. He'd been gentle, slow, giving her time to get over the initial pain before setting up a rhythm between them.

In truth, it had been all right. Better, maybe, than just all right. But then she'd started to respond. He'd heard that same little moan from deep in her throat that he'd heard a hundred times, no, a *thousand* times, escape Kirsten's lips. And suddenly he'd been unable to go on. The sadness just welled up in him and ended his wedding night almost before it had started.

"I waited a long time for this," she said, admitting quietly what he and everyone else in Maple Stand already knew. "To be your wife and have you love me. Do you suppose we might have made a baby?"

"A baby?"

"Mmm-hmm," she said dreamily, squeezing his arm. "Do you think we did?"

It was as if she were looking for something good to have come out of the mess he had made of their wedding night. A mess of which, thank the good Lord, she seemed blissfully unaware.

"I . . . I don't know," he choked out, choosing to lie rather than admit to her that there was no chance of it.

At least there was that to be grateful for. There would be no child from their aborted union. And, given Olivia's lack of experience, if he was very careful, and he swore he could be, *would* be, there might never be any children.

Oddly, the idea gave him solace and he warmed to it, even in the face of his failure. "The odds are against it."

"But it could be, couldn't it? I mean we've done it and—"

"Not everyone gets with child on their wedding night, Olivia. Surely you must realize that, at least."

"But it could be," she said more strongly, her voice betraying the hope she felt. "Spencer, we could have just made a baby."

No. We couldn't have. "It's not a good idea to get your hopes up. Lots of couples don't have any children at all."

"But not us. That won't be us. After all, you've been a father. Peter and Margaret—"

He interrupted her. "Peter and Margaret are dead, remember? My children are dead and so is my wife."

"But I'm . . ." she started, then put the back of her hand to her mouth to stifle a sob. In the dim light of the quarter moon he couldn't make out her features, but he didn't need to see her to know that she was biting the back of her hand and crying silent tears. It was Olivia's way. The way she had cried when her mother died. The way she had cried soon after that when he'd told her he was marrying Kirsten.

He could have apologized. He could have simply rolled onto his side and pulled her against him. He considered both options and thought better of them. Best not to fill up her heart with false hopes or her head with silly dreams. "It's late, Olivia. You're tired. It was quite a day of celebrating. Go to sleep. We've got a lot of work to do come morning."

She turned onto her side, away from him, her chestnut braid whipping his cheek as she settled herself. It smelled faintly of lilacs, and he fingered the soft ends as he moved it away from his face.

It was silent for a minute or two, and then, quietly, tentatively, she asked, "Was it . . . was I . . . all right?"

Funny that she should be asking him, when he had failed her so miserably. The least he owed her was some reassurance. "Perfect," he said, patting her back gently through the layers of quilts their friends had given them as wedding gifts. And truly, she had been perfect. Softer than he had expected, her breasts fuller, her arms more willing.

And innocent. Completely innocent of what had happened and of the plan that even now was forming in his head. The plan that, ironically, would surely restore his manhood. Just knowing that he would never leave his seed within his new wife was settling the hackles that had risen on the back of his neck. He could withhold his essence just as he was withholding his affection.

And Olivia need never know.

Oh, but her innocence was a blessing. Another woman would have known that his groan had been born of frustration and not satisfaction, as Olivia must have assumed. Another bride would have known that his trip beneath her nightdress had been cut short before his mission was complete.

Surely Kirsten would have known, for theirs had been a perfect union. They had soared like the eagles together, even from the first.

But then their little blond eaglets had faltered, and all his dreams and hopes had been dashed against the rocks and lost. Diphtheria, they had called it, as if giving it a name could make sense of the senseless.

His little Margaret had been the first to go, her skin so flushed with fever that she was still warm long after her little chest had ceased to rise and fall. Beautiful, delicate Kirsten was next, he and Peter struggling to keep her alive even after her tongue was furred with slime and her throat had all but closed, long hours after the doctor had said there was no hope. Then, before she was gone, Peter, too, had succumbed to the fever. And all Spencer could do was stand by and watch as everything he loved was put into the frozen ground and covered with cold clumps of the pale frostbitten earth.

A tear escaped from the corner of his eye, trickling silently down his temple to the pillow beneath his head. He made no effort to wipe it, but swore silently that it would be the last he ever shed.

Beside him, Olivia released a shuddering breath. If there had only been another way, he'd have taken it. But Olivia's brother, Remy, had been right. The farm was too much for one person to handle, and he couldn't go on there alone.

And Olivia was so willing, so eager. Despite all his misgivings, he'd finally had to give in. He'd taken another wife.

But married though he might be, this time he was going to protect himself. He could make sure that he never lost another child because he would see to it that he never had another child. And he would never lose another woman he loved, because, quite simply, he would never love another woman. Not even sweet, innocent Olivia.

And that would keep him safe.

Chapter One

Maple Stand, Wisconsin
April 1897

Olivia loitered in the corner of Zephin's Mercantile where the United States Post Office stood, the letter in her hand.

"Mail it," her sister-in-law, Bess Sacotte, urged, nudging her less than gently toward the counter where Emma Zephin waited. "Send it and deal with Spencer later, when there's nothing he can do about it."

"Will you stop it," Olivia whispered, brushing at Bess's hands and then straightening her coat in an effort to restore her dignity. "This is not like sending for a new pair of commonsense boots, you know."

"It's sending for a whole new life, Olivia Williamson, and it's high time you did it. Why, if I could fix all my troubles by sending away for something, don't you think I would?" She rubbed at her ample hip and grimaced. "Bet it'll be quite a storm tonight."

"You're too young to be telling the weather with your bones, Bess," Olivia said. "It isn't fair."

"Married to Spencer Williamson and you talk to me about life being fair? Seems to me the snow is calling the ice cold."

Olivia said nothing. What was there to say? Bess would never understand that Spencer didn't mean to be unkind. He was still just hurting. If Livvy could give him the time he needed to heal, she didn't see why her sister-in-law, and everyone else in Maple Stand, couldn't be more patient.

"Can I help you ladies?" Emma asked, still standing behind the counter, her feather duster poised in midair so that she wouldn't miss a word. Emma was Charlie Zephin's oldest daughter. His other girls had all married and were raising families of their own. But Emma, who was even uglier than Charlie's other daughters, was an old maid.

"Mail that for you?" Emma asked, reaching across the counter for the letter. Olivia couldn't seem to let the envelope go, allowing it only enough leeway to slip inch by precious inch through her fingers. "Mrs. Williamson?"

"Yes," Bess said, pushing Olivia's arm toward the counter like a puppeteer. "She wants it to go out today, if possible."

"That right?" Emma asked Olivia, who nodded, then looked at her sister-in-law, disgusted.

"He isn't going to like this."

"He doesn't like anything," Bess said sharply, and Emma let a snicker escape her lips before quickly covering her mouth with her hand.

"How are you doing anyways, Emma?" Olivia asked, anxious to change the subject. "You over that cold?"

"Finally," Emma said. "I think it was that spring-green soup of yours that did the trick. My papa swears you spent the whole winter curing other people's children since you haven't—" Emma's hand flew again to her mouth as if she wanted to pull the words back in.

"It's all right," Olivia assured her.

"I didn't mean to hurt your feelings or anything. I suppose Papa's right and there's just no hope for me. Often as not, I seem to say the wrong thing."

"Don't worry, Emma," Bess said, patting the woman's hand gently but looking straight at Olivia. "You can't hurt

Olivia's feelings. She's plum numb. And it's time she got thawed out and started living.''

No feelings. Is that how she seemed to all of them? Just because she refused to break down and cry at every last little thing? Why, she had so much feeling inside sometimes she thought she'd just burst apart from the pain of it all. But there was enough sadness in her house. Spencer had the rights to all the misery there. With what he'd been through, most of her little dissatisfactions seemed petty and unimportant.

All except one.

And that was why she was standing in Zephin's Mercantile when she should have been baking Belgian pies for the church and getting a jump on her spring cleaning. There wasn't much hope that the problem would just take care of itself. After all, they'd been trying for three years and she wasn't getting any younger. She felt that today, especially.

It was hard to swallow around the lump that formed in her throat. No babies. Even if taking a new wife hadn't made Spencer happy, surely a new baby would. A new baby to replace the pain he carried like a newborn against his heart.

And so she was doing the next best thing. If there wasn't any hope for children of her own, Olivia didn't see any reason for denying the pleas of her brother-in-law any longer. With her sister, Marion, dead almost three years, Julian had found it impossible to take care of their children alone. Of course he was right not to try to move across the entire country and get resettled with three little ones in tow to look after. Who better to raise the children than their Aunt Olivia and Uncle Spencer? Her sister's children were bound to need her love almost as much as she needed theirs.

''Olivia?'' Emma said softly, fingering the edge of the envelope that lay on the counter beneath Olivia's sweaty palm. ''You want me to send it?''

''Yes,'' Bess said with determination, as if she could will Olivia the courage to do it.

"Yes," Olivia said to Emma, and then turned a bright smile to her sister-in-law. "Yes. Send it. Right away. Today. As soon as possible."

"Quick," Bess said. "Before she changes her mind."

The three women laughed and Charlie Zephin looked down at them from the ladder on which he was perched counting cans. "What are you three witches cackling about?" he asked good-naturedly.

"Just cooking up a little magic, Mr. Zephin," Bess said, then rubbed her hands together like an evil witch.

Olivia felt a chill run down her back. This plan could blow up in her face, she knew. Spencer could hate the children. Hate her for bringing them. Lord, he seemed to hate everything else these days.

"Magic," Charlie said. "Well, you be careful there ladies. We sure don't want the devil in Maple Stand, do we? They may not be burnin' witches anymore, but they sure ain't too popular 'ceptin' on Halloween." He laughed at his own joke, nearly lost his balance on the ladder, and then righted himself. "Well! No need to kill me off, ladies. Your secret's safe with me."

"Speaking of secrets," Emma said in a loud whisper, "I hear there's talk about that railroad spur again. Hear they might even be paying money for the land it's gonna run through since they've got to get to Sturgeon Bay. And they're sending an agent." This last detail was acompanied by a flush to Emma's cheeks.

"Well," Bess said as she sighed and rubbed again at her aching joints. "Don't suppose that'll matter much to us out on the outskirts. I'd about give my whole cherry orchard for a hundred dollars cash."

Olivia tsked at her and laughed. "That's my family's farm you're giving away, my dear. I'll thank you to take better care of it!"

Bess nodded but the smile was gone from her face. It

made Olivia think, only for a moment, that perhaps she really meant it.

"Guess we'd better be getting home," Bess said after they had traded banter a few moments longer. "I got three little boys and one big one that'll be clamoring for supper before I get my own front door full open."

Olivia knew what was waiting for her at home and was in no rush to get there. For a moment she considered taking the letter back from Emma and forgetting the whole idea.

"And they'll all be wanting hugs and kisses as much as bread and butter," Bess added, as if she knew just what Olivia was thinking and could feel that extra encouragement she needed.

Children waiting for her who would want hugs and kisses. She sighed and caught herself, realizing how foolish a woman of her age must look daydreaming in the middle of the mercantile.

"You send that letter," she said to Emma as she tied her hat ribbon beneath her chin.

"Atta girl," Bess said, and looped her chubby arm through Olivia's thin one. With their woolen coats on, it was a tight fit.

"That's easy for you to say," Olivia said as they headed for the door.

"Oh, no, it's not," Bess said more solemnly. "I don't know where I'll put the four of you if comes to that."

Olivia stopped in her tracks and even Bess's bulk wouldn't budge her.

"It won't come to that," Bess reassured her. "Don't worry so. It'll all work out."

Bess had promised her that before. When, after more than a year of marriage, Olivia still hadn't conceived, Bess had assured her that time would take care of everything. But it hadn't. And now Spencer hardly touched her in bed, as if he believed there was little point in it. And in some ways she was glad for his lack of attention. If there wasn't any hope of children, she'd just as soon never be intimate with her husband again. Each union left her strangely bereft, as if her body was as sad as her heart. And except for that moment on their wedding night when she had begun to feel a heat that spread from her most private places, she had never felt even remotely warmed by what they were doing.

In fact, despite the intimacy of the situation, she felt lonelier when they were making love than at any other time in her life. And lately it had gotten worse. Now Spencer didn't just collapse against her and moan. Now he got up and left the room, claiming a good cigar relaxed him and helped him sleep. As far as she was concerned, all it did was stink up their home.

And so he left her alone in their bed, lying perfectly still in the hopes that his seed would take root within her. Left her to wish on stars in the darkness, with only the moon and her hope to keep her company.

She stopped for just a moment at the edge of Sacotte Farm by the wayside shrine her father had built for her mother after the house and barn had been miraculously spared in the great fire, and promised the Blessed Virgin that she would remember to bring the delphiniums as soon as they bloomed. Just as it had when she was a child and had helped her mother tend the little chapel, so it calmed and comforted her now.

And calm and comfort were surely what she would need, she thought, as she rose from her knees and headed toward her home. That and a healthy dose of strength and courage.

She went over her news one more time in her head as the farm came into view and her husband's form loomed on the horizon. *Heavens. There's going to be the devil to pay.*

"You what?" he asked, staring at his wife for any sign that she was bluffing. She sat serenely in the chair across from him, her hands folded in her lap as if sending for three children without even telling her husband was as ordinary and normal as taking a stroll by the lake. But if this was a stroll by the lake, she was in over her head. In her heavy boots. With her hands tied behind her. And it was going to take more than that Houdini magician fellow to get her out of this mess.

"I told Julian to send the children," she repeated, so calmly that he was tempted to reach out and check her forehead for signs of a fever. Spencer knew firsthand the kind of man Julian was, and only for the sake of Olivia's sister, Marion, had he held his tongue for all these years. Now Olivia had invited the man's children into his home.

"Without asking me?"

She shrugged and he saw the edge of her lower lip disappear between her teeth.

"You just got it in your head to go to town and send that brother-in-law of yours a letter telling him to put his three children on a train and send them to my house—"

"*Our* house—"

"*My* house," he repeated, thumping on his chest for emphasis. She hadn't been the one to put up the house, log by log, brick by brick, just the way Kirsten had wanted it. She didn't pay the mortgage, work the soil, chop the logs. . . .

One of her eyebrows lifted. She sat ramrod straight. Her eyes scanned the room silently, but the only sign of her hurt was the hard swallow he watched in her neck.

New curtains framed the windows in the kitchen. A new cloth covered the table. The cows were milked, the chickens fed, and all of it because of Olivia. He had married her to keep his house, to cook his meals and wash his clothes, to tend his garden and take care of his livestock while he did the work in the fields. He hadn't asked for the hundred other things she did, and all with that damn smile on her face, but he was grateful she did them.

"Our house," he conceded honestly.

She nodded at him as if she had followed his thoughts and appreciated his conclusion.

"I didn't just 'get it in my head,' " she said quietly. "It was time."

"Time?"

She nodded, opened her mouth, but nothing came out. After all, what was there to say?

"Well," he said, and looked up at the clock on the mantel, squinting despite his glasses. "Too late to do anything about it today. We'll send a wire tomorrow and tell him they're not to come."

"They're coming."

"They're not!" he shouted, not happy at all with her highhandedness. It wasn't like her to defy him. What had happened to the agreeable girl he had grown up with, the one who had followed him around and hung on his every word? What had happened to the woman he had married who had sworn that all she wanted was to see him happy again?

"What have I asked from you, Spencer? In all this time?" She picked at a thread on her sleeve, then looked at him guilessly. "Nothing. I've asked you for nothing. But now I'm asking."

He studied her. Over the years her face had softened so that there wasn't an angular line to it. Her lips were full, overly so, perhaps. Her cheeks, too, were fleshed out, especially where he thought he ought to see her bones. And her nose lacked any fragility, as well. Not at all like the fineness of Kirsten's tiny face, Olivia's was more like some painting of an exotic woman from far away, her dark eyes watching him from beneath her only fine features, two thin, nearly straight dark brows. While not one to turn a man's head, he supposed plenty of men would find her chestnut hair and olive skin pretty enough.

In all truthfulness, though there was none of Kirsten's frailty about her face, she did have a sweetness that the years hadn't managed to dim. And to her credit, despite a long and severe Wisconsin winter, there was still a warmth in those soft cheeks, and her dark eyes met his with a new determination.

"Isn't there something else you'd like?" he asked. "A new range? A pretty dress?"

She was right, of course. She had asked for nothing, and that was exactly what she had gotten in return. It wasn't her fault she wasn't Kirsten, didn't have Kirsten's long blond curls, her sweet high voice, fine bones, girlish smile. But then again, it wasn't his fault, either.

"Been a long time since you got a new dress and we did something special, huh, Liv? Would you like that?"

"You know what I'd like, Spencer. You know what I've wanted from the day we married."

"Ask me for something else, Olivia. Something I can give you. Anything else." *Just don't ask me for a child. Don't ask me to bring another child into a world full of disease and danger and misery, because I won't.*

"They're all I want, Spencer. I can't seem to have them myself, that's hard enough to live with. But these children . . . Spencer, I know I'll love them like my own."

All right, he was selfish. He knew that. He was cowardly. He knew that, too. But he was saving them both from true heartache. It was disappointment only that drove Olivia to tears each month when her time came. She didn't know real despair. She hadn't ever lost anything as precious as a child.

"They'll be a help to you, Spence. The boy is old enough now to help in the fields." She thought for a minute and then nodded. "Yes, I'm sure Neil is nearly ten. And Louisa is eleven, at least, or twelve. She could be a blessing around this house."

"There's another, isn't there?" He knew there was. The one that had been born on the day her mother died. A baby that couldn't be more than two or three. "That one gonna be a help, too?"

Olivia looked wistful and embarrassed as she smiled at him. It hurt to see the hope shining so brightly in those dark eyes, so he studied the edge of the tablecloth. "She's gonna be the biggest help of all. She's never known a mama, Spencer. Josephina is gonna make my wishes come true."

"Three children!" He struggled for a breath, but couldn't seem to draw one. Christ! Children in the house again. How could she expect him to bear it? "Do you realize what you're asking?"

"I'm asking for a life for us, Spence. A family. I can't give you one . . . it doesn't seem. So I'm asking you to let me do the only thing I can."

He took his forehead in his hand, his elbow resting on the table. "How many times are we going to have this same damn conversation, Olivia? How many times do I have to tell you I don't want any more children? That I didn't marry you to have children?"

"What *did* you marry me for, Spencer?" she asked. "For a warm meal every night and a warm bed once a week? For help with the cows and the chickens? Is that the good life you promised me?"

He examined the blue cloth as if it held the answers to her questions. "I promised you a roof over your head and food in your belly. I promised you someone to grow old with."

She shook her head sadly. "I thought that meant *someday*, Spencer. I didn't know you planned to start getting old so soon."

"Well, you were wrong."

"Seems I was wrong about a lot of things, but that's neither here nor there, is it?"

"Sorry you gave up taking care of old Mr. Larsen? Sorry that instead of reading to that blind coot all day and going home at night to Remy and Bess and your pa that you're stuck in this house with me?" He waved his arm at the sheer size of the kitchen, which was big enough to accommodate all the children he and Kirsten had planned on having. "If you liked being an old maid so much, how come you went and married me?"

"Because I thought I could make you happy," she said so honestly that he felt ashamed of himself for asking. "But I can't. Not the way things are going. That's why I've got to do this." She reached out, her hands so soft when they cradled his cheeks, her voice so tender, that it pierced his heart in a way that harsh words never would. "I know what Peter and Margaret meant to you and I know how much you miss them. Hard to believe the trick fate played on you—first taking your children and then giving you a barren wife to replace the one you loved. . . ."

"Don't do this," he begged her, pulling away from her touch. Her warm softness was more than he could bear. "Don't do this to yourself and don't do it to me. I don't want more children, Olivia, truly I don't. Not my own, not anyone else's."

"But . . ."

"But you do."

She nodded, almost guiltily, as if she were the one being selfish. As if her wanting a family wasn't the most natural thing in the world. Hadn't he wanted one? Hadn't he thought nothing on earth could make him happier? Did he have the right to deny her that chance?

"Why now, Olivia? Why today of all days?" Didn't she realize that it was just five years ago to the day that Margaret had come down with the fever? That his whole world had turned upside-down and never was righted again?

"It's my birthday," she said simply. No accusations, no display of temper. But that was Olivia. Kirsten would have made a party for them all and baked some genoise to celebrate. Olivia just sat there quietly. "I'm twenty-eight."

"I know how old you are," he said, more than a little

annoyance creeping into his voice. "You could have reminded me. I'd have gotten you something if you'd told me."

"You know what I want, Spencer. And I've already sent for them." She tried to make the words sound final, as if she had the authority to simply send for her nieces and nephew and that there was little he could do. If she could only stop her lip from quivering and the tears from pooling in her eyes, he might have been convinced.

As it was, he knew that all he had to do was tell her that his answer was still no and that would be the end of it for another few months. The subject would go away as it had before, only to resurface again sometime in the future. If he was lucky, it would disappear forever.

But there she sat, the woman who traipsed out to the fields in the rain to bring him a cup of hot tea and a dry towel, the woman who washed his sheets with lemon because he once told her he liked the smell, the woman who wished on stars for his happiness. She sat there with her hope pasted on her face like a treasure map to her heart and he knew he had no choice.

"Happy birthday then, Olivia." His voice cracked and he wasn't sure she understood him until she looked up. Beneath the tears that threatened to spill over her cheeks, he saw a tiny, tremulous smile. "When are they coming?"

"I told him to send them as soon as the threat of snow is past, since they'll have to take the stage from Milwaukee. Is that all right?"

He snorted. "Well, I guess that means I've got a little time to get used to the idea, anyway." He kept his disgust to himself. Julian Bouche's children in his house. Jeez. Any children would be bad enough, but Julian Bouche's? The man had tried to run away from his responsibilities all those years ago when Marion had found herself carrying and her father had found Julian at the train depot with a ticket to California. The bank was happy enough to let him go, the hint of scandal clinging to his fancy suit all the way to the job Henri Sacotte had arranged for his new son-in-law in Chicago. Now Julian wanted to dump his kids and head for greener pastures. And he wanted to leave Olivia's family holding the bag again.

They'd all managed to shelter Olivia the first time, pretending that the wedding of Marion Sacotte and Julian Bouche was something to be celebrated. Spencer hoped no one was going to expect him to shelter her again.

"So maybe a month from now? June, don't you think?" Olivia asked, stretching up to the top cupboard to put away the few supplies she had brought back from town. She was a good size for a woman, not so small as to be delicate, like his Kirsten had been, but not big and bulky like John Delisse's wife, who could probably whip half the men in Maple Stand if she was of a mind to.

No, he had to admit that Olivia was a good, good size, her shoulders ample, her hips full, and her waist tucked so that when she walked her bottom swayed. And when she let her chestnut mane down and brushed it before bed, it took all the will he had not to run his fingers through it. Sometimes, after Olivia was asleep, he would let her hair run through his fingers like a mountain stream. It was fluid and fresh and a dangerous thing to do, he'd found out more than once.

"If only," he said, and followed it with a sigh.

"Too soon or too late?" she asked.

"Hm?" He had lost the thread of the conversation, wishing again that he could allow himself to take her in his arms, enjoy the comforts of her body and damn the consequences. More and more lately, thoughts of what he was denying himself came unbidden into his mind.

"Did you want them to come sooner, or later?"

"Who? Oh, the children . . ." *Did he want them to come sooner or later?* Was she joking? "I don't suppose . . ." he started, but then stopped himself. He could do this one thing for her and make her happy. And what would it cost him? He didn't know these children, didn't love them. He would simply keep it that way. And maybe, just maybe, having them in the house would take his mind off other things, like the way her gold watch swayed across her bosom when she made a sudden movement, as she had now, reaching for his cup to refill it.

"Spencer? You aren't going to change your mind, are you?" she asked.

"They can come, Olivia. I said they could, didn't I? You ever known me to go back on my word? I'll even clean out my workroom for them. The girls can sleep in there. The boy can bunk in the barn."

Olivia's jaw dropped and her eyes widened until he was looking at two enormous black pot lids, just staring at him without any comprehension.

"You didn't think——" he began. "Not in Peter and Margaret's——The loft is——I couldn't——that is——" He stumbled to recover himself, taking a deep breath and then swallowing. "You know the loft belongs to Peter and Margaret, will always belong to Peter and Margaret. Your nieces and nephew are not to set foot into that room."

"But——" Olivia tried to argue.

Bile rose in his throat at the thought of dirty hands touching the dolls that Margaret had treasured. His head spun and his stomach lurched. Their clothes were in that room, the little dresses in which Margaret had looked so precious, the suit Peter had been so proud to have outgrown just a month or so before he died. All the little birds he and his son had carved together when he was teaching Peter to whittle perched on the top of the bookshelf there.

"Promise me, Olivia, that they'll never go into that loft. That, or I cannot let them come into my home. I cannot. Do you understand?"

Olivia understood all too well. She remembered clearly the time Spencer had caught her in the children's sleeping loft.

She had gone up to dust, nearly taking her life in her hands on the little steps he had built for the children. How he had managed to come up after her, being so much bigger than she, and not have made a sound, she would never know. But suddenly he had been standing there, his head bent, his shoulders stooped over, seething with rage.

He had grabbed her wrist forcefully and yanked open her hand. Then with exquisite gentleness he had taken the coarse little wooden bird and laid it tenderly on the shelf. After examining the room with his dark eyes, he had backed halfway down the steps and then directed her to follow him, carefully guiding her feet onto each step. When his feet had hit the kitchen floor, he'd simply reached up and carried her off the ladder and set her down.

Then, with his jaw muscle twitching furiously, he had told her never to go up there again. "There's no railing anymore, Olivia. It's not safe," he had added harshly, but she wasn't sure whether he had been warning her about the ladder or himself.

It was a perfectly good room and she bet a boy like Neil, not that she knew him, but any ten-year-old boy, would adore being in the loft. It was like a bird's nest, where a child could perch and watch the world and fly from someday when he was grown. "Peter must have loved it up there," she said, hoping to soften her husband's resolve.

"He did." His lips were a thin line across his face, and the hollows in his cheeks pulsed with emotion so strong that she knew it took every ounce of self-control he had not to explode. But then she'd never met a man with more self-control. He held everything in, kept all his feelings to himself.

He hadn't always been that way. He and her brother, Remy, had been friends forever, and she'd watched a younger, wilder man challenge life at every turn. She'd seen him chase a greased pig at Kermiss celebrations and win nearly each and every autumn. She'd seen him drink beer after beer and laugh until his sides ached from too much food and too much drink and too much joy.

She'd seen every emotion he'd ever had written on his face and etched on the muscles of his body. The way his leg shook when he was nervous, the way he couldn't sit still when he was happy.

She'd seen him full of life, once upon a time. She'd seen him laugh, seen him cry, seen him so proud the day Peter was born that she thought he'd burst apart.

But all of that was before the diphtheria epidemic. Before twelve people in Maple Stand had died, and four of them had belonged to her husband. It was before he'd lost Kirsten and the children and his mother, too. Livvy had had such hope when she'd married him. Oh, she knew he didn't love her the way she had always loved him. She knew Remy had pushed him into it and she was a poor second choice, not much more than a housekeeper with whom he could . . . well . . . be a husband.

She hadn't wanted much, not for herself. All she had wanted was to bring back the Spencer Williamson she knew. To make him whole again. And she knew only one way to do that. But it seemed that wasn't to be.

Still, she had one chance left, and she couldn't afford to let it slip away over sleeping arrangements that could always be discussed again once Spencer had met the children, once he'd seen them as promises of all their tomorrows instead of memories of all his yesterdays. And he was right about the railing, after all.

"I won't let them go into the loft," she agreed.

"Children are a lot of work, you know." He pulled his pipe down from the rack above the fireplace and busied himself cleaning it with a small knife and a fresh pipe cleaner.

"It's work I'm longing to do."

"You don't know beans about little ones, Olivia," he said, setting down the pipe and reaching blindly for the pouch of tobacco, his eyes on her. "You were the baby and now you want to take three stragglers in like they're a litter of lost mutts. Jeez."

"It's not as if I've never been around children. Ask the boys if I'm not a wonderful aunt. Ask Bess and Remy if I wasn't a help when I lived with them. And I'll thank you not to take the Lord's name in vain, if that's what that word's supposed to mean."

"Well then, since you're such an expert, do what you want. But don't expect any help from me," he said, his teeth gripping the pipe stem so that his words hissed from his open lips.

"You won't have to have anything to do with them," she promised, unable to keep the smile from her face.

Children. Oh, God in heaven, she was going to have children! A houseful of them. In the morning she would go back to the little shrine and give thanks. "I'll take care of everything," she said, wondering if she couldn't set the boy up in the kitchen instead of the cold barn.

Spencer stared at her for a long moment, long enough for her to feel self-conscious, and then shook his head and turned to open the highest cabinet in the kitchen. From it he pulled a bottle of that awful whiskey he kept bringing into the house. She'd thrown out several bottles in the early months of their marriage, but they were always replaced, and she'd had to shut her eyes to his weakness or they would never be able to save a penny.

She had no problem with his drinking beer and wine like everyone else in their community. She wasn't some kind of temperance woman, after all. But while the beer and wine were for gaiety, the whiskey was for sorrow. And what it did to him . . . that was another matter entirely.

"Guess this calls for a celebration," he said without any joy. Without bothering to offer her the opportunity to decline, he pulled the cork from the bottle and, tilting his head back, took a long slow swig of the stuff. He grimaced at the taste but took another swallow, nonetheless.

"Spencer, I don't think . . ." Olivia started.

He raised his eyes slowly up her body, from the hem of her well-worn navy wool skirt upward, taking in her waist, settling blatantly on the swell of her breasts for a moment, and then struggling to focus on her face. "Go to bed, Olivia," he said, raising the bottle once again to his lips.

"Bed? But we haven't even had supper yet. I've got fish stew from last night that I could . . ."

"Go to bed, Olivia. Now." His voice was ragged and his gaze returned once again to her breasts.

"Don't be ridiculous. The sun's hardly set. I've made us some genoise. I'll make us some dinner first, and if you'll just put away that bottle. . . ."

He took one last gulp and put the bottle down, then headed for the door and grabbed his jacket. He cast a long look in her direction and opened the door.

"Spencer?"

He shook his head. Without turning to look at her, he asked, "Are you going to go to bed?"

"No, Spencer, I . . ." she said cautiously, not liking the way he was threatening her.

"Then I've got to go out, Olivia. I need some air."

"Are you that angry with me?" she asked him, wondering if she hadn't pushed him further than he could willingly go.

He laughed. Not a drunken, sloppy laugh, but a tight, sad noise that came from deep in his chest. "No, Olivia. I'm not mad. Leastwise not at you." He stood in the doorway with his shoulders slumped, staring at her sadly. "Don't wait up for me, Livvy-love. I'll be very late."

It was cold when he opened the door, but even colder when it closed and she stood in the kitchen of their home, alone, his words ringing in her ears. Had he called her Livvy-love? He hadn't called her that since she was twelve years old and he had stolen a kiss behind the barn.

But that was before Kirsten had come into his life. And left it.

Damn him! Two little words and he'd managed to fan the fire of hope that kept burning in her chest no matter how hard she tried to put it out. For three years he'd poured cold water on her hopes and dreams and plans for the future. And just when she'd made peace with his coldness, his distance, he up and called her *Livvy-love*. And then walked out the door.

Don't even hope, Olivia, she warned herself.

But a smile found its way to the corners of her mouth.

He's gone out for hard drinking, of all things, she reminded herself.

But the smile remained there, just the same.

Chapter Two

The sun seared Spencer's eyes right through his lids. He squeezed them more tightly closed, but just moving his facial muscles hurt like hell. Inside his mouth a fire raged out of control, but his lips were sealed with the same glue that attached his tongue to the roof of his mouth. Whatever he had eaten the previous day was working its way up from his stomach through his chest, and he rolled over as slowly as he could and stuck his hand beneath the bed to find the chamber pot to puke in.

His hand smashed hard against the porch floor, sending a jarring pain up to his elbow. Of course. He wasn't in his bed. He had spent the night on the porch settee, afraid of what might happen if he crawled into the warm bed he shared with Olivia.

"You awake?"

He shielded his eyes from the rising sun that threatened to blind him and opened one gingerly. The shadow of a heavyset man leaned against his porch railing. "Remy? That you?"

He saw the shadow's head nod and searched the floor with his hands until he found his glasses.

"Something wrong?" he asked, blinking until Remy came into focus.

"Shouldn't I be asking you that?" Remy said. He looked to be leaning casually on the rail, but his voice was so tense that Spencer forced himself to sit up.

The excesses of the previous night moved along with him

and he gagged, then wiped his mouth with the back of his hand.

"You reek, you know," Remy said with more than a little disgust dripping from his voice.

"You come here just to tell me that?" Spencer asked. His head was swimming, but the rest of his body was going down for the third time.

"I came here because I heard you had quite a brick in your hat last night," Remy said. "Then I find you spent the night on the porch. Olivia finally throw you out?"

Spencer grimaced as he tried to right himself on the settee. Maple Stand was too damn small a town for a man like him. A man spent just one lousy night drinking whiskey instead of beer, corn juice instead of wine, and before he was up the next morning his neighbors knew all about it. Wasn't it bad enough he'd have to face Olivia? Did he have to take on her damn brother, too?

"Olivia must be cross as two sticks," Remy said, his voice betraying the shift from anger at Spencer's actions to pity for his condition. "Must have been quite a night."

"Yeah, I guess," Spencer said, sitting up and settling himself on the bench at last. It had been quite a night, indeed. He'd begun drinking to forget and when he was drunk enough not to feel the pain, he continued drinking to remember. Of course, remembering brought a new round of pain that needed to be forgotten. And so it went for longer than he cared to recall. He was grateful, in the end, that Curly George knew the way home without needing to be guided.

"I ought to broach your claret, you know. Right here and now. Loosen a few teeth and maybe jiggle those brains straight."

"Great, Remy. You do that." He leaned back against the newly sewn pillows on the settee and closed his eyes. "If I'm still alive when you're done, wake me up."

"This time she's not gonna forgive you, Williamson. You know that."

"Remy," Spencer said with contempt, "you knew when you suggested I marry her that she don't get mad. If Olivia's got a mean, unforgiving bone in her body, I sure haven't found it yet. And believe me, I've tried."

"So you gotta keep testing her? Keep pushing at her till she finally breaks?"

"Liv hasn't got a breaking point, or she would have reached it before now. I swear it, Remy." His stomach rumbled, but the thought of food nauseated him. "Can't say the same for me, though. So say your piece and get it over with. What are you doing here this early, anyway?"

"You really bear away the bell, don't you?" Remy asked, studying Spencer and making him uncomfortable. "Think you're the only one who ever lost someone they loved? Didn't the diphtheria take Charlie Zephin's wife? Didn't it take the little Delisse girl? Didn't it—"

Spencer interrupted him. "I didn't lose *someone*. I lost *everyone*. And I didn't lose Wilma Zephin. I lost Kirsten."

Remy let out a heavy sigh. They'd both been over this territory too many times. And still the pain was there, raw and putrid like some open wound.

Finally, after what seemed to Spencer like forever as memories danced in his head, his friend just shrugged and said, "I guess I was worried about you. And Livvy, too. I know things aren't working out so well and I just wanted to help if I could."

"Wouldn't you say you've helped enough?" Spencer asked. What a mistake this whole marriage had turned out to be. And while it was no day in the park for him, it had to be a slow burn in Hades for Olivia. He shut his eyes and tried to control the rising tide of emotion that just last night had overtaken him and left him crying like a baby on his own front porch. Oh, what he'd done to poor Olivia, who had always loved him.

"You complaining? 'Cause I'll be real happy to take my sister home anytime she wants to come. If I'd have known you'd become such a goddamn heel I'd never have let her marry you in the first place."

"Let her?" Spencer said, raising one eyebrow in question.

"We woulda been real happy if she'd stayed with us forever, but no, she wanted you and nobody but you, God help her. She loved you. Seems like she still does, though for the life of me I can't figure out why. I can't see that there's anything worth loving anymore."

Remy was right. Olivia did love him, loved him from way back when they were all just kids. Still loved him, despite how hard he tried to change her mind. Why couldn't she see, as he and Remy did, that there was very little, if anything, left to love? If only she could stop loving him, maybe he could stop hurting her.

He caught his upper lip between his teeth and bit down to regain control of himself. But the truth wouldn't go away, even if he could keep the tears at bay.

"Spence? You all right?"

He nodded, unable to speak. He should have refused to marry Olivia, insisted that she marry someone else, anyone else. If he wasn't going to give her what she hoped for, what she deserved, he should have stepped aside and left her to someone who would. And there were plenty that would. There wasn't a person in Maple Stand that didn't have a soft spot for his wife. Probably because there wasn't a person in Maple Stand she hadn't done something kind for. And this was the thanks she got. A drunk who wouldn't even see his duty through in her bed.

Yes, he should have let someone else have her. Someone who could love her. She deserved that, at the very least.

But the truth was that had he not married her, she never

would have married at all. When he'd chosen Kirsten over her, never having taken Olivia's affection seriously, she had solemnly vowed that she would never love anyone else. And she had proven true to her word, much to his disappointment. When he thought about it, and he rarely let himself think about it, he had to admit that he had been making Olivia unhappy for more years than he cared to count.

"Well, it's good that you slept out here," Remy said, looking off toward the horizon.

Spencer had no doubt of that. Olivia's warm, willing body had been waiting for him inside, that silky skin that smelled like lilacs and felt like rose petals. He might have forgotten himself, got carried away, on a night like last night. But the pleasure came with too high a price. A price he swore he'd never pay.

"You being drunk, and all," Remy continued when Spencer said nothing. "Everyone knows that if you're drunk when . . . well, the kid'll turn out addled, and that surely wouldn't make Olivia too happy, would it?"

Spencer wasn't sure. Olivia had become so desperate that maybe even an afflicted baby was better than no baby at all. Besides, the idea was ridiculous. "You don't believe that old wives' tale, do you?" he asked.

"It's no tale," Remy assured him. "I read it in a book. *Transmission of Life*. It's by a doctor. I'll bring it over for you. It could—"

"What are you doing with a book about that kind of stuff?" Spencer asked, studying his old friend and wondering, maybe for the first time, what went on between Remy and Bess.

Remy smiled wryly, as if he knew that Spencer had been so wrapped up in himself he hadn't even thought about anyone else in years. It seemed to please him that he had some kind of proof that Spencer was a selfish bastard. Hell, it had taken Remy long enough to realize it.

Remy just shrugged in answer. Like all the Sacottes, his wife included, Remy was private by nature. And Spencer was grateful. He had enough problems of his own. He didn't need Remy and Bess's, too.

"I'll bring it over," Remy said again. "It might help with your problem." He raised his eyebrows toward the house.

"I don't have a problem!" Spencer shouted, hurting his head and making himself dizzy.

"Want to make a wager on that?" Remy asked, his eyes on the door that had just opened and revealed a very angry-looking Olivia.

"I never bet anymore," Spencer said quietly as he rose unsteadily to his full height. Betting required luck, and Spencer didn't have any, that was for sure. "Morning, Olivia."

"Morning yourself, Mr. Williamson." She looked him up and down with disdain, but all she said was "Breakfast'll be ready in a few minutes. You might take the time to get cleaned up." She turned to her brother. "Remy, you staying for something to eat?"

"No, no," Remy said, raising his hand up and backing off the porch. "Just needed to discuss something with Spencer. Gotta get back to the farm. Got the boys helping out with the planting. I ought to be around, helping, overseeing, you know. Those boys of mine haven't got one farmer's bone in their bodies. If it didn't speak ill of Bessie, I'd swear they had someone else's blood running through their veins." His voice trailed off as he took the steps backward.

"What's the matter with you?" Olivia asked, surprised to see her brother babbling.

"You hear anything about the spur?" he asked, his tone hushed.

"Heard it's just a rumor. And speaking of rumors, I suppose his drinking's all over town?"

Remy shrugged and gave her a stupid grin as if he were the one with something to apologize for.

"Grand. I don't get enough pitying looks in church? Dammit, Spencer . . ." She looked up for him, but he was gone, no doubt at the pump trying to make himself presentable enough to come into her clean house.

As always, he was trying. Sometimes he succeeded at smoothing things over. Sometimes he didn't. But to her way of thinking, except for his very occasional excesses at drinking, Spencer Williamson wasn't nearly as bad a husband as he seemed to think. He was fair, considerate, and kind as ever a man could be. Even in their bed, he was patient and gentle, never hurting her, never getting so carried away that he forgot she was his wife and not some harlot there for the pleasure of it.

No, Spencer's fault lay not in what he did, but in what he couldn't do. He couldn't forget and he couldn't move on, and who was to blame for that but her? She hadn't been able to replace Kirsten in his heart and she hadn't been able to give him a child to replace the ones he had lost.

Not that he ever made her feel guilty about her inability to give him a child. In fact, he pretended to be relieved, half the time, as if he didn't even want her to bear him another son or daughter at all. But she'd seen him with Peter and Margaret, and no matter what he said, how he denied it, Spencer Williamson loved children more than any man on the face of this earth. More than Remy loved his children. More than Julian loved his. Just the thought of Julian's children lifted her spirits and made her forget her anger.

Julian's children! Spencer and she would take Julian's children into their home and into their hearts. She knew that was what would happen. She just knew it. Her heart sang at the very thought. So loudly, in fact, that she didn't even hear Spencer at first.

"Olivia? All right if I come in?" Spencer asked meekly through the screen door. "I'm clean, dripping and freezing my tail off. I could dress out here, though, if you like."

"Spencer Williamson!" Olivia said, fairly singing. "You come right in here this minute and get dry." She came toward him and opened the door wide enough for him to come through without getting her as wet as he was. "Go by the stove and I'll get you some fresh clothes."

Going through his drawers, Olivia hummed the first two stanzas of "Amazing Grace" and tried to remember the songs of her childhood. In just about a month or so she'd be singing lullabies, and wiping noses, and tying boots. And laughing. Houses with children should always be filled with laughter.

"Here you go," she said, handing Spencer a pile of clean clothing and lifting his jaw to close the mouth that stood gaping at her. "Quickly, now, or your eggs'll burn."

She rushed past him in a blur, anxious to save breakfast, but he reached out a hand and clasped her shoulder. "Slow down, Liv, or I'm likely to lose whatever's left in my stomach."

Teach you to go out drinking hard liquor, she thought, but even the knowledge that the whole town knew he needed to drown his sorrows couldn't put a damper on her spirits. With exaggerated slowness she made her way to the stove and dished rather brown eggs and decidedly crisp bacon onto the fancy china.

Out of the corner of her eye she watched Spencer lower his work pants and step out of them. His woolen drawers hung loosely around his waist, dipping well below his belly button and revealing damp curly hair that thickened the lower it went. It matched the hair on his chest and looked equally coarse. She'd never actually felt it, except through her nightgown. Was it soft, or . . . ?

She snapped her attention back to the plates in her hands, mortified by the road her mind had wandered down. Decent women, she was sure, didn't think about their husband's bodies. It was just that Spencer was filling out again, no longer the skeleton she had married three years ago. She took his form as silent praise of her cooking and noted that even his cheeks were fuller now. His heavy bottom lip no longer seemed to dominate his face and make him look so sad.

He stretched, and the hard-earned muscles that he complained about at the end of a day in the field rippled and drew her attention down his chest again, farther and farther until they seemed to disappear into well-worn drawers that hardly hid what made him a man. *Don't look,* she chided herself. *Think about something else.*

"I think I'll go over to Remy's today and see if he still has my mama's old tin plates," she said. She glued her eyes to the dishes in her hands while Spencer finished buttoning his pants before sitting down across from her and starting in on his eggs.

"Aren't you gonna eat anything?" Spencer asked her.

She looked down at her cold eggs and gave him a smile and a shrug. "I'm not too hungry," she said.

"Aren't you gonna yell at me, then?" he asked. "This Little Miss Sunshine, ain't-everything-grand act is getting on my nerves. Out with it now, Olivia. I downed enough whiskey to rot my insides and those of the men on either side of me. I came home well after the moon was heading down and the sun was thinking about coming up, and I passed out on the porch. This was no Sunday lift-a-few with the men after church. And by church tomorrow there won't be a soul in Maple Stand who hasn't heard about it. No doubt Father Martin will use me in his sermon against evil."

While he waited for her to say something, he ran his hands through the sandy hair that was nearly as gray as it was blond and tried to convince it to stay out of his eyes. The straight locks fell forward at the edges of his forehead, and he sheepishly pushed at them again and then adjusted the round glasses that he needed to wear all the time now.

"If it's any consolation, I feel worse than you do about it. I keep thinking I must have been set upon by some ruffians or attacked by a bear or something in my sleep to account for feeling this bad. But there isn't a bruise on me, so I must've done it all by myself, with a little help from the devil, of course.''

"I'm sorry you feel so bad," she said. "Would more coffee help?"

"Maybe it would've last night, but not now. The only thing that would make me feel better now is a shotgun blast between the temples." He knew that kind of talk bothered her, and she waited for the apology. "Sorry," he finally mumbled.

"You aren't going to go out drinking after the children come, are you, Spence?" she asked.

He looked surprised. "Liv," he said with more confidence than he'd shown all morning, "the day you have a kid, I won't touch another drop."

The words stung, and she blinked back a sudden onslaught of tears. Well, they both had their faults, didn't they? He drank too hard and she failed to make babies. But she had always made allowances for him, and he for her, unspoken though they were. She'd bitten her tongue and refused to make an issue of his need to find solace in a bottle. And until now, Spencer had never been cruel about her inability to bear him a child.

"Oh, God. I'm sorry, Olivia. There must still be some booze in my brain. I didn't mean that to sound like . . . It's not as if I drink *because* you haven't . . . I mean, I think if you did . . ." He looked at her so pitifully she wasn't sure whether she felt sorrier for herself or for him. "I'm just making it worse, aren't I?"

She nodded and rose to clear away the dirty dishes. On the mantel, the clock chimed seven times. An hour. Couldn't he have let her be happy for an hour? Was that so much to ask?

"Well, Miss Lily'll be bursting by now. I best go milk her for you." Spencer rose from the table and replaced his chair as silently as possible.

Olivia was by the sink, with her back to him, patting the soil around one of those little plants she tended with such care. Some kind of violet, he thought, but he couldn't remember the kind and didn't suppose it made any difference. It was destined to die whatever it was, so why bother learning to tell one from the other? Maybe once things began to bloom outside he could ask Livvy to get rid of the houseplants altogether. Now somehow didn't seem like the best of times to bring the subject up.

"Well, I'm going now," he said, but didn't leave. Miss Lily could wait a few more minutes. She wasn't producing like she did when she was younger, but then again, who was? "You okay?"

She nodded, her back still to him, and he could tell from the rise in her shoulders that she was sniffing back tears. The back of her hand was pressed to her lips and he was willing to bet that when she lowered it, there would be teeth marks there.

"Gonna do some work in your garden today?" he asked. "I don't want you breaking any new ground without me, Olivia. You just make your markings and I'll do the rest."

"Maybe when I get back from Remy's," she said, turning and trying, as she always did, to give him a bright face.

"Remy's? Why are you going to Remy's on a Saturday? Something wrong with the kids?" He tried to keep the panic out of his voice. There were a million reasons Olivia could be going to her brother's. The boys didn't have to be sick.

"I told you," she said. "I want to see if he still has Mama's old dishes."

He tried to remember her mentioning that, but couldn't. All he knew was that he hated it when she went over to her brother's when the boys were out of school. Seeing all those kids just made her wanting that much stronger, which in turn whipped up his guilt like so much cream until it hardened and they could both become stuck in it and drown.

Besides, he liked the dishes they had. They had been given to him and Kirsten on their wedding day by Kirsten's mother. He'd be damned if he'd get rid of yet another piece of Kirsten from his life. "What would you want her old dishes for? What's the matter with these?" He came up beside her and picked up one of the fancy dishes from the drying rack.

"Nothing's wrong with these," she said. "I just don't want to see them get broken when the children come."

"The children?" It began to come back to him. The discussion yesterday, the nieces, the nephew. Eggs and bacon raced each other up his throat.

"Marion's children, Spence. You said we could . . . Spence, you haven't changed your mind, have you?"

The plate in his hands clattered to the floor and shattered.

And then he pushed her aside and lost his breakfast in the sink.

The birthday cake she'd baked remained untouched, each day sinking a little further into itself until she'd been forced to throw it out and replace it with a small hazelnut torte, which Spencer chose to pass on, as well. He'd eat her meals eagerly enough, as if he understood the need for sustenance, but the desserts he refused until the torte, too, had to be discarded. Livvy baked a plum pie with fruit she'd canned last summer, and hoped.

But hoping never got the cows milked or the chickens fed, her mother always said, and it didn't seem to make the husband happy, either. Day after day one thing after another seemed to go wrong. Curly George picked up a stone in his shoe and couldn't plow for the better part of a week. When he was well, it rained so hard that Spencer had to spend the day tending to leaks in the barn.

Then, when the skies finally cleared and things appeared to be looking up, some sort of strap on the plow broke. It was the last straw and Spencer put away Curly George and came in early, chilled to the bone.

After a warm dinner that Olivia thought was truly one of her best but about which Spencer had no comment, he went into his little room and came out with his account books. He wore a grimmer than usual face and his sigh blew the dandruff off the last of the pussy willows that had gone to seed in the vase on the kitchen table.

Three groans and a crumpled sheet of paper later, she couldn't hold her tongue. "I could help you with that," she said as he swore again at the columns of numbers in front of him. It was after nine and he'd grunted and groaned as if every muscle in his body were trying to tell him it was time to pack it in and go to bed. All evening she'd bustled around him trying to make his work lighter, throwing a shoulder shawl around him, bringing the lantern closer to his book. She even made him some cocoa with a touch of vanilla in it, just the way he liked.

And she'd gotten a smile out of him, once or maybe twice, a genuine smile that went straight to her heart and made her so warm she had to loosen her dressing gown belt a little. "Really," she said, flipping out of her way the braid that had fallen over her shoulder. "Won't you let me help?"

"Seems to me one of the people in this room was always flunking arithmetic and having her little bottom tanned by her papa for not studying hard enough." There was just the bud of a smile around his lips. Could she coax it into blooming? "And that person's offering to help me with my numbers?"

"Well, I remember one time my big brother's friend tried to help me with my homework and I wound up with two whoppings——one for cheating and one for still getting all the answers wrong!"

"I don't remember it happening quite like that," he said, but the smile was blossoming, all the same.

"Don't you remember telling me it was a good thing I

had so much padding?'' She touched a hand to her bottom and watched the color come into his face.

"I shouldn't have said that," he said quietly, his mood shifting so quickly Olivia wasn't sure whether it was a genuine change or if he was going to tease her some more, tell her that the padding she had then was nothing compared to what she carried behind her now. But he said nothing. He just sat, pencil dangling from his fingers, and stared at her, his gaze roaming from her messy hair to the toes of her slippers.

"I really did learn my numbers, finally," she said when the silence became unbearable.

"Oh, did you? When was that?"

When I figured out how many days until I would lose you forever to Kirsten. And every month when I add by sevens until I count four weeks . . . "When you and Remy grew up and there wasn't anything for me to do but my lessons."

Spencer studied her with a faraway look on his face. Finally he put the pencil into his account book to hold his place and then closed the ledger. "You turned out real nice, Livvy. I ever tell you that?" he asked as he rose to his feet and stretched.

She swallowed hard. Those were some of the nicest words he had ever said to her. "No, Spence. You never did."

He picked up his empty cocoa mug and was headed for the stove when he stopped just inches from her. With just the pads of his callused fingers he gently stroked her cheek and shook his head sadly. "So damn soft," he muttered.

She reached up, hoping to capture his hand and stay it, but she wasn't fast enough. "I'll get you some more," she offered, following him to the stove and hovering as he helped himself. "There's still some pie left from the other day. Want some?"

"Pie?" he asked, as if he were trying to remember what that was. "I thought it was a cake of some sort."

"You mean my birthday genoise? With the coconut frosting? I couldn't even feed it to the chickens by the end of last week. So I made . . . well, it really doesn't matter. There's plum pie, from the fruit I canned from the new trees at the back of Bess's yard. You know, the ones that I planted when we got married.'' At least they were bearing fruit, she thought bitterly before wiping the thought away and continuing. ''Just another few weeks and we should be having rhubarb. I checked the plants today and they're looking good for so early in the season. Of course, I'll have to be careful about the weeding. Last year . . .''

''There's no call to be nervous,'' he said in response to her babbling. ''I've got no intention of making your life miserable over those children, Olivia.''

''Oh, Spencer! I just know we're doing the right thing. We're going to be so happy, the five of us. . . .''

Spencer put his finger to her lips to silence her and shook his head. ''I want you to be happy, Olivia. I really do. But like I told you last night, don't include me in this little happy family of yours. They can live under my roof, they can eat the food I put on the table, but they're not my flesh and blood and they never will be. They're coming here for you, not for me. Don't ever forget that. I'll tolerate them, Liv, for your sake. I owe you that.''

Oh, how she wished she could tell him that he didn't owe her anything. How she wanted to tell him he needn't do her any favors, that if he didn't want the children, well, then fine—the children needn't come. But she couldn't get her mouth to form the words because whether he owed her or not, whether it was what he wanted or not, she needed those children more than the crops needed the rain to grow, more than she needed the air to breathe. And she would endure whatever Spencer dished out to her, whatever guilt he placed on her plate, and she would consume it greedily and ask for more, if only he didn't change his mind.

''It's getting late, Spencer. Don't you want some pie?''

"If I wanted the damn pie, I'd take it." His voice was gruff and she had to blink back the tears that came unbidden into her eyes, turning quickly so that he wouldn't see them.

Gently he gave her a nudge in the direction of their bedroom. "Sorry," he said more softly. "You go ahead to bed. You must be tired, too."

"Spencer," she said very quietly, obviously embarrassed to bring up a delicate subject. "Tonight's a good night to—that is, Widow Grillot says that sometimes, right before a woman's time—well, I—I was just wondering when you were coming to bed."

"You and Widow Grillot have a good talk about what goes on in our marriage bed, did you?" Spencer asked her, returning to the table and opening up the account book as though he was asking her about the weather. "Discuss how long it takes or what goes where?" He raised his gaze without lifting his head and looked over his glasses at her, waiting for her to answer.

"Of course not. People, *women,* are just eager to help. They know I've got a problem and they just want to—"

"They just want to butt their, in the case of Widow Grillot, very long noses into our private business. Maybe we should invite them all over and they could give us pointers. What do you think? We could move the chairs into the bedroom and turn up the lamps and old Widow Grillot, who probably hasn't ever shown so much as an ankle never mind her nether regions—which probably shriveled up and disappeared from lack of use—could tell us what we're doing wrong." His voice was so steady and calm that she couldn't even yell at him in return.

"I'm not blaming *you,* Spencer. Peter and Margaret are proof that *you're* not the problem." She stood by the bedroom door, her body clothed but her soul bare. "Are you coming to bed, Spencer? Please."

He nodded, resigned. "You get ready for me. I'll be in after I finish. It should only take me another few minutes."

"Thank you," she said quietly.

"You don't have to thank me," he said, running his hands through his straight hair and looking as desperate as a man with wheat rotting in the field and a broken thresher in the barn. "A man enjoys making love to his wife. Didn't they tell you that when they were telling you how and when?"

"I had heard a rumor to that effect," she said with a smile that left her face the minute she turned her back on her husband and shut the door. ". . . But they couldn't prove it by you."

She sat heavily on the bed and yanked at her boot laces, snarling one and having to move her foot closer to the lamp to see what she had done. Hunched over for the light, she nearly lost her balance and wound up smashing her elbow against the headboard. As if Kirsten's fancy headboard hadn't caused her pain enough.

"Damn," she said aloud, startling herself. Next she'd be taking the Lord's name in vain.

She fought valiantly with the shoelace, her patience so close to breaking that she considered holding her foot over the lamp and just burning the uncooperative piece of round leather. When she finally freed her foot, she threw the boot across the room with enough force to rattle the window. Then she yanked the buttons on her shirtwaist and nearly ripped the waistband from her skirts.

Did he have to make her feel as if she were begging him? Was she so very undesirable that he couldn't stand the thought of coming to bed?

Selfish. Mean. A miser with his affection. That's what he was. Someday he would be sorry for making her feel like he was doing her such a big favor. She swore he would, as she backhanded the tear that rolled down her left cheek. Someday he'd realize she was the most desirable woman in all of Maple Stand. Maybe all of Wisconsin.

She looked at herself in the mirror. Her braid was half undone, her face streaked with tears. One side of her mouth was caught between her teeth. *All right. Maybe not in all of Wisconsin. Maybe not even in all of Door County, or even Maple Stand.* She tried to laugh and sniff at the same time and an awful noise that sounded like a lamb stuck in the barn door came out of her throat. *Well, she was the most desirable woman in Spencer Williamson's house, anyway. No one could take that away from her.*

Her smile didn't fool him. He'd made her miserable again. And this time without even trying. Lord, crying over some stupid pie. He decided against having any, just as he had forgone the cakes before it. It seemed to him that the house was crawling with pies and cakes these days, starting with that damn birthday genoise. He hadn't realized that she even made birthday cakes, but it didn't surprise him. If he so much as mentioned something that Kirsten did once, Olivia did it daily. And then she stood there and waited for him to love her because of it. At least that was how it made him feel.

Especially with those tears that seemed to perch continually on the rims of her big brown eyes. Who'd have thought Olivia to be such a crybaby? Kirsten had never cried at the things that brought Olivia to tears.

Of course, he'd never refused Kirsten anything that she asked for, nor anything that she gave.

But Livvy—Lord, there were times . . . He counted on his fingers the weeks he so carefully kept track of and smacked his forehead at his stupidity. Hadn't she just said as much? Her time was coming soon and so now she was shooting the rapids with her feelings once again. Dancing and singing one moment, crying and fighting with him the next. And later tonight, no doubt, her shoes would be outside their door, one facing in, one out, in a superstitious attempt to cut the pain that accompanied her time. If only something could soften the disappointment.

Yeah, his life stunk, but that came from what had happened to him, not what he was. Being a woman . . . well, at least he had that to be grateful for.

He returned to his books, and it took him longer than the few minutes he had promised Olivia to finish up. Long enough, he supposed, that she might even have fallen asleep. He got up and stretched out his aching muscles, then picked up the books and returned them to his study. Through the window he could make out the barn. Was the door ajar or was that just a trick of the moonlight?

Better to check, he thought, and stifled a yawn as he shuffled through the kitchen and took his coat from the hook. He closed the door behind him as silently as possible and made his way slowly to the barn, enjoying the brisk fresh air after spending the evening huddled over his ledgers. The door was closed up tight, but he opened it and listened to hear any unusual noises. Curly George whinnied softly and he answered with a nicker of his own. Everything was as it should be.

On the way back to the house he stopped at Olivia's birdbath and lifted the rock she always left near it to break any ice that coated the surface in the winter. The water was cold but not nearly frozen, and he dropped the rock back to the ground. Tilting his head back, he located Cygnus, the swan, the Big Dipper, and a few other constellations he'd learned as a boy. All still there.

In the house once again, he checked the stove, making sure that the fire was out, and shrugged out of his jacket. It would be a shame for Olivia to wake up to dirty cups, he figured, so he pumped a little water and rinsed out the mugs in which she had served him hot chocolate.

Finally, he slipped out of his work boots and headed for

the bedroom door, cracking it open soundlessly. He tiptoed into their room, the big oak headboard looming in the semi-darkness, each curlicue glowing in the soft light of the oil lamp on the bedside table. Olivia's hair, released from the braid it had been in, lay spread against the white pillow making an elaborate frame for her face. The top two buttons of her gown lay open, a very modest invitation to him. He wondered if that, too, had been Widow Grillot's suggestion.

Looking at her, he was struck once again by the contrast between her and Kirsten, whose blond hair had surrounded her head like a halo and who, in the early years of their marriage before the children were old enough to notice, had often waited for him clothed in nothing but her silken skin. Her thin, reedlike voice would beckon him even before her arms and legs reached out to him, drew him in, captured his body and his soul within those fragile limbs and held him. Still held him, even five years after her death.

"Spence? You get the numbers to match up?" Olivia asked, catching him by surprise with her dreamy, nearly asleep voice. She had a wonderful voice at night, husky and deep. A woman's voice. A voice that said *come to me* even when the words asked about his day or his night. In the daytime it was a matter-of-fact voice that was strong and said what it meant. But at night it sent other messages that only he could hear. Messages that every night got louder as he missed more and more the comforts her body could offer him. Comforts he couldn't dare to take.

"Mm," he answered, pulling the suspenders from his shoulders and unbuttoning his work pants. "No richer than last year at this time, but no poorer, either. I think most of your butter and egg money is safe for another month." He turned and slipped his pants down his legs and raised his shirt over his head.

At the edge of the bed he turned down the lamp and lifted the covers, sliding beneath them. He had hoped to find her asleep. So soundly asleep that if he touched an errant curl, or snuggled against her for a moment's warmth, she would never even know it.

But next to him, Olivia lay with her gown raised to her thighs, awaiting his visit. Through his woolen long johns he could feel her cold legs next to his. A pain went through him when he thought about how he was cheating her of so much more than just the child she wanted, and in the darkness he hated himself just a little bit more.

"Cold tonight," he said, and the shiver in his voice confirmed his words. "Guess old man winter just doesn't want to give up yet."

"No," she agreed.

She smelled wonderful, like lilacs and powder.

"What happened to your braid?" he asked, lifting a long strand and letting it slink through his fingers.

"I thought——" she began, then stopped herself. "I could do it now, if you want."

Another idea of old lady Grillot? he wondered. For an old battle-ax she knew her stuff. Livvy's hair was soft and silky and just the feel of it across his palm made drawing a deep breath harder.

"Leave it." His voice sounded gruff to his own ears. More softly he added, "You can tie it up later."

He turned to face her, knowing that sooner or later he had to get started, and his leg slipped between hers as if by its own accord. Before he could pull it back, her hand rested on his thigh. It was, perhaps, the boldest thing she had ever done.

She wet her lips. Nervousness, no doubt, and he found his breathing more irregular than he would have expected. Reaching out with just one finger, he traced the fullness of her lower lip, while she lay as motionless as a rabbit afraid that a coyote had seen her. Again she went to wet her lips, and this time the tip of her tongue came in contact with his finger.

"Uh, I," she stammered, shifting slightly and causing his

leg to sink deeper between her thighs until he could feel the warmth of her body against him. "Oh!"

He had meant to tell her he was too tired. He had thought to put her off until tomorrow or the next day, or a moment when for some reason he might feel stronger, more in control. But now he grew hard against the roundness of her hip, and the hand that he had been pressing to her lips had jumped away and rested on her breast. He was sure he hadn't put it there, but he could feel beneath it the hammering of her heart. He edged his way back up to her collar bone, exposed by her open buttons, and played with the small gold heart that rested in the hollow of her throat.

Had he ever seen it before? Had he ever seen her throat, for that matter? His hand moved to the tiny row of buttons and he tried to stop it from opening them, tried to concentrate on things he could control in the hope of stopping things he couldn't. *Sixteen rows of pear trees, each with ten trees to the row.* One after the other the buttons slipped through the tiny holes beneath his hand. *Twenty rows of cherry trees with eight trees to the row.* Her heart pulsed against his palm.

He counted rows in the fields, trees in the rows. He counted windows in the room, panes in the glass. He counted the breaths she took, and noted that each was faster than the last as he lowered his head to her chest. His mouth found her breast, his tongue teased her nipple.

All right. Just this, he promised himself. *What harm can just this do?* Like a drunk, he tried to convince himself that if he wanted to, *when* he wanted to, he could stop. And all the time he forced his brain to do what he couldn't make his body do— leave his bed and return to his fields.

Sixteen rows times ten trees is sixty. His hand pushed her nightdress out of his way, baring her body to his exploring fingers. Soft. Everywhere was soft. Softer. *Not sixty. One hundred sixty.*

Twenty times eight. One sixty again.

And then he heard her gasp and found that his fingers had reached her femininity and were inching lower still until he was nearly inside her. Beneath him she squirmed, whether out of fear or pleasure, he wasn't sure. He pulled his hand away and lifted his head to look at the expression on her face, hoping she would want him to stop, hoping he could, wishing it didn't matter to him whether she was trying to escape his touch or respond to it. He found her eyes closed and her head tipped back. Blood rushed through him. Warmth curled low in his abdomen.

He leaned back and looked at the length of her, glistening in the moonlight. Spreading her gown, he watched the rise and fall of her breasts quicken under his gaze. "So beautiful. So strong and beautiful," he murmured, while in his head a familiar voice shouted at him to stop before it was too late. *Keep counting,* it said. *How many days since your children died?* "I only want to kiss them," he murmured, as much to the voice as to the woman trembling against his side. "Don't be afraid."

He eased her back down beneath him and ran his tongue over the tip of one breast while he fondled the other. Her nipple hardened against his tongue and another sharp intake of breath encouraged him, drowning out the warnings in his head.

She pulled at her nightgown, raising it higher still, and spread her legs for him, anxious no doubt to fulfill their purpose, achieve their goal. He ignored the invitation, burying his head between her breasts, kneading them, suckling on one, switching to the other. The smell of lilacs was intoxicating. It surrounded him and he breathed in greedily.

"I'm ready, Spencer," she said, trying to angle herself beneath him. He raised the knee between her legs and let his thigh tease her femininity.

"I want you to be happy, Livvy," he said, his words muffled against her smooth skin. "I want it so much." One hand stole its way down her midriff and spanned her belly before dipping farther still to the soft curls between her legs.

She tried to say something, but his mouth covered hers, silencing her while his hand rubbed her rhythmically until she began to move in time to it and then began to increase the pace on her own. At least this time he knew it wouldn't hurt her as he felt the increasing slickness against his fingers.

He moved himself into position above her and freed himself from the confines of his cotton drawers. Beneath him she was breathing hard, squirming slightly as if there were something she wanted, something she needed that only he could give her.

"Now you're ready, Olivia," he said and guided himself into the narrow passageway that lay between her legs, looking only to stoke the fire a little more but not set himself ablaze.

A few strokes then, and he would stop himself. It had become so routine it was beginning to seem normal to him. Half a dozen thrusts and he would stop. He could do that. Of course he could. He could. He could. He could. His lungs were bursting, and still he gulped for air. He could. He could.

He plunged into her, again, and again, deeper and deeper, as if he could bury his memories within her and lose them. Beneath him, her soft body rose and fell with his, setting off the warning bells in his head, ringing them louder and louder until he knew he had better not ignore them any longer.

Just three more thrusts, he promised himself. *Two. Just one.* He withdrew quickly and fell on top of her with a groan.

In the quiet, it came to him.

He hadn't wanted to stop.

Dear God, this time he really hadn't wanted to stop. His heart was pounding in his chest and he fought to control his breathing. He forced himself to think of Peter and Margaret and tried to be proud that he had managed to contain himself. He made himself imagine Kirsten standing beside the bed, watching him kiss another woman's breasts, sweat between another woman's legs, and tried to be ashamed that he had nearly enjoyed himself.

It was only his body that wanted her, he told himself. A man's body seeking out the comforts of a woman.

She shifted beneath him, his weight no doubt making it hard for her to breathe. He rolled off her and bent his legs to hide the evidence of his treason.

"I didn't hurt you, did I?"

He felt her shake her head, but she said nothing, just pulled the blankets to her chin and from the jabs of her elbow against his side he knew she was refastening her gown.

"Are you all right?"

"Spencer?" There was a quiver in her voice. "You won't tell anyone, will you?"

He turned and looked at her, not understanding. "Tell them what?"

"I liked it, a little." She pulled the pillow from beneath her head and hugged it to her body. He had an urge to replace the pillow with himself, but fought it. "More than just a little. Much more. Like you feel, probably. Not like a woman. Do you think I'm very wicked?"

"You're not wicked," he assured her, pulling the pillow out of her grasp and putting it back where it belonged, then laying her head gently onto it. He almost laughed out loud at the irony. "Not even a little bit. Now go to sleep."

"Did *she* like it? Kirsten?" Her voice was small, and yet it filled the room as if she had shouted out in the darkness.

"Yes," he said honestly. He supposed he owed her that much. "She did."

She reached out for him, but somehow he eluded her grasp and sat up on the side of the bed feeling around the floor unsuccessfully for his slippers. "I'll just go have a cigar," he said, pushing himself up with his hands.

"Do you have to go?" Her hand trailed down his arm as he rose.

"I'll be back soon," he said without turning to face her. "You go ahead and get some sleep."

"It was special this time, wasn't it? So, maybe this time . . ." she said softly, the words slurred by her exhaustion. He looked over his shoulder and saw her eyes close. There was a smile on her face as she drifted toward sleep. Her full lips looked lush, inviting. Her rounded cheeks begged to be stroked.

It was dangerous ground he was treading on. Too dangerous. He'd been down this road before, and he wasn't about to walk this path again. No, sir. He was not going to fall in love with Olivia. And they were not going to bring a new life into this world. Not even if it meant never touching the woman again. Monks did it all the time. Priests, too. Of course, they didn't lie down every night next to a woman who smelled like lilacs and whose hair . . . A shiver ran up his body from the cold wooden floor.

Maybe it was a good thing she'd sent for Marion's children. Three children in the house might be just the distraction they both needed. The pressure eased in his loins and his breath steadied.

A good thing she'd sent for Julian's brats?

Now he knew for sure he was losing his mind.

Chapter Three

Oh, how lovely the other night had been. It had left Olivia in the most wonderful of moods. Wonderful enough to ignore Spencer's door slamming and furniture kicking. He'd called her beautiful, and though he hadn't touched her since, had hardly even looked at her, she couldn't help but be elated. Her husband, the man she had always loved, thought she was beautiful.

And every time she thought about that night, Spencer's hands touching her so intimately, her face flushed and her belly warmed. Why, if she was sitting, she'd find herself squirming in her chair, and if she was standing she'd have to hug herself to keep from melting right away.

Their lovemaking certainly hadn't had the same effect on Spencer. While she was all dreamy and slow, he had never worked harder in his life. Olivia guessed they had enough wood on the pile for the next two years—four if they had mild winters. And when he finally came in from the fields, and he didn't do that before dark, he was nervous as a turkey the week before Thanksgiving.

The door slammed again, signaling her husband's readiness for supper, she supposed. She turned from the stove where she was putting the finishing touches on the chicken booyah and gave him her brightest smile.

"You seem pretty damn chipper," he said accusingly, as if it were a crime to be happy in the same house he occupied.

She shrugged and from the corner of her eye she caught

him watching her, his gaze following each of her trips to and from the stove, all the while chewing at the inside of his cheek.

She didn't know what was bothering him, but she couldn't remember the last time she'd felt better or more hopeful. Almost as if something wonderful was just about to happen.

"You ever see a prettier day than today?" she asked. "It felt just like July out there. Must have been nearly seventy-five degrees."

He grunted at her, still watching her every move.

"I must have turned enough soil to plant a garden for a family of a dozen today. I don't know where I got the energy." She sighed and stretched out the muscles in her back which were beginning to tighten. "Lord, I am tired now."

"Course you're tired, you little nit. Probably nothing more than all that hard work. Didn't I tell you not to work the garden yourself?"

What in the world was he so angry about now? And they said that women were moody. She rubbed her lower back and then sat down heavily in the rickety chair by the table. Spencer was picking at the food on his plate, pushing the peas around with his fork, drawing lines with the gravy in his mashed potatoes.

"Chicken's a little crisp," she apologized. "Guess I wasn't thinking about the time."

He poked at the bird with his fork. "Expect it to just walk out of the oven itself?"

"Spencer, if you're angry with me, you best just get it off your chest. You've been scowling at me for two days and I'm tired of it. Like Shakespeare says, *what's done is done,* and you best learn to live with it."

The fork dropped from his hand. It clattered on the plate and came to rest in his mountain of potatoes. "You're sure?"

he asked, the muscles in his jaw working like crazy while he waited for her answer.

"I think it was Shakespeare," she answered, trying to remember Mr. Larsen's books and deciding it really wasn't important. "You plan on making me miserable for the rest of my life over this, Spencer? Well, you're gonna have to work pretty hard, because I've got no intention of being unhappy on your account. If I can't have your kids, then I'll just have to be glad to have my sister's, and you can just—"

"Then you're not?" he asked hoarsely. He reached over the table and grabbed her arm roughly. "You on the rag or not, Olivia?"

"Spencer!" She pulled free of his grasp and stared at him, her breathing heavy. "And at the dinner table!"

Clearly he had spoken his mind without thinking. His question still hung in the air and it was plain he was waiting for her answer, propriety be damned. Since the first month of their marriage he had waited and watched and clocked her monthly cycles almost as closely as she had, despite his words to the contrary. He had noted the shoes by the bedroom door. He had watched the bushes behind the barn for drying rags. Oh, he said he didn't want a child, but if that was so, why was he standing before her now, shaking her and demanding to know if she was finally expecting?

"Oh, Spencer," she said, and a small sigh escaped her lips. "I'm sorry. So sorry."

"Are you, Livvy, or aren't you? I lost the thread of this somewhere. One minute you're singing and the next you're crying." He sat her down gently in her chair and wiped away a tear from her cheek. "You carrying, Liv, or not?"

She shook her head, unable to utter the words and break her husband's heart. She hadn't been surprised earlier in the day to find she wasn't pregnant. She'd faced the disappointment so many times before that she would probably have been more shocked to find herself expecting than not.

The surprise was how little it bothered her. The sun still shone and there was gardening to do. Her butter and egg money was safe and there was cloth to buy and clothing and bedding to be made for the children. Bess was sending over some things that Neil might be able to make use of, and promised to look for the high chair for little Josephina. The spare room Spencer used for his record keeping would need to be cleaned out.

No, she hadn't had the time this month to mourn what might have been, not when such glorious things were soon to be. But as Spencer dragged her to him and held her tight against his chest she felt the loss for him and tears flooded her eyes and fell on his shoulder.

He mumbled something against her hair.

"What?"

"I don't deserve you, Livvy. I really don't. You should have married someone else. Anyone else."

She pulled away from him and sniffed back her tears. He'd told her that a hundred times. But this time he had said something else before he started in on that old saw. "Did you say *thank God?*" That was what it had sounded like to her.

"Why would I say that?" he asked, turning her chair back to the table and guiding her into it, then returning to his own. "Let's finish up and go to bed. You look real tired."

"Remy's coming over," she said, trying to recapture her happy mood. *Thank God?* She must have heard him wrong. "Bess went through some of Mama's boxes, and also some of the boys' things that they outgrew. And there was something about a book."

"Sounds like that's them now," Spencer said, cocking his head toward the door.

"I didn't expect he'd bring the boys with him," she said when she heard all the footsteps on the porch. "I've only half a pie left."

The knock on the door was tentative, no doubt one of the

kids. It was followed by a bolder knock to which Spencer and Olivia both responded, "Come in."

The door creaked open slowly. In the light of the opening stood three children Olivia had never seen before. Behind them was a familiar, if somewhat older, face, lined where it had once been smooth, framed by hair that was just as tidily combed but now had more than a little gray in it.

"Julian?" She hadn't expected him for weeks. In fact she hadn't expected *him* at all. Only the children. And not for another few weeks, at least. She glanced at Spencer. He glowered over his shoulder at the group standing in his doorway. Julian took off his hat and bowed toward Olivia.

"A sight for sore eyes," he said. "As lovely as the last time I saw you."

Neil Bouche looked at the flustered woman standing in the middle of an enormous room in the house that they had fled to so quickly it seemed their tails were on fire. True, their father had been ready and waiting for years. Still, to leave the very day after the letter came, well . . . all Neil could make of it was that his father thought that his aunt and uncle might change their minds if they were given a moment to think about what they'd agreed to.

He couldn't blame his father for worrying. Why should complete strangers, even if they were related by blood, take him and his sisters in? But they'd said they would, and here his aunt stood, her smile welcoming, her eyes misting over at the sight of them. She looked so much like the mother on some advertisement for hot cocoa that he had to rub his eyes. Even then he wasn't sure whether he had simply fallen asleep in the wagon and this was just another one of his dreams. He was having them all the time now, even when he was awake. Just thinking about what his life would be like once he got to his aunt's and uncle's farm would set him imagining the most wonderful of things.

Not that he was prone to dreaming. Since his mother had died he hadn't even let himself wish that things would ever be good again. Now and then he'd allow himself a prayer, but praying, his mama had taught him, was different, as long as he didn't pray for himself. And so he prayed that his sisters would find what they were looking for at his aunt and uncle's house, and if it happened that he, too, was happy, well . . .

And now, as if his prayers had been answered, here he was in his aunt's kitchen, some wonderful smell filling his nostrils, and the softest woman he had ever seen smiling at him.

"You're here," she said, and even her voice was warm. The women his father brought home never sounded like maple syrup ran in their veins. "I . . . We didn't expect you quite this soon." It seemed to Neil she kind of choked on the words before turning to the man who sat with his back to the door. From the sound of silverware against a plate, it was clear he was still eating his supper and nothing was going to disturb him. He wondered if this man was his uncle. He hoped not, since the man with the stiff back and the broad shoulders did not seem pleased that they were there. Maybe his father had known that they weren't really wanted, and that accounted for probably the quickest trip anyone had ever managed between Chicago and Wisconsin.

"Well," the woman with the warm smile said, rushing toward the door and trying to coax them in. "Come in, come in. I'm your Aunt Olivia." She pointed toward the table. "This is your Uncle Spencer."

Neil looked to his father, who motioned with his chin as if to say *go ahead in*. Being well mannered, and not particularly anxious to venture in, he stepped back and allowed his older sister, Louisa, with Josie in her arms, to step through the doorway first. Neil, following his father's lead, removed his hat respectfully and came in behind his sisters.

"Here, let me take her," his Aunt Olivia said, reaching out for Josie. He saw Louisa's jaw clench as she threw a panicked glance at their father. Usually his father paid close attention to Louisa, but now he seemed to have eyes only for Aunt Olivia, and he ignored Louisa entirely, giving his aunt the same smile he used for the women he sometimes brought home with him.

Louisa held Josie tightly to her body, and Neil waited for their father to stop their aunt from trying to separate Josie from Louisa's arms.

But he didn't, so Aunt Olivia just reached out and put her hands under Josie's armpits, then cradled her like an infant against her chest. Josie's familiar howl pierced the quiet of the house, scaring his poor aunt half to death.

"I'd better take her back. Josie doesn't like strangers," Louisa shouted over the baby's cries and reached for her little sister.

"No, no," Aunt Olivia said, patting the child's back and trying to get loose the fistful of hair his stupid sister had grabbed. "You take off your coat and I'll just—"

"Let her cry," his father said, the same as always, ignoring what his baby sister was doing to his poor aunt's hair. "Good for her lungs. Good for her circulation. Tires her out when nothing else does." Would his aunt know that what his father meant was that he let Josie cry herself out every night until she finally fell asleep?

The man Aunt Olivia had said was his uncle rose from his seat at the table. Even though they didn't look alike, the man reminded him of his father. It must have been that look that said *don't mess with me, don't get in my way.*

Neil backed up as the man passed him.

"Jeez." The man moaned, disgusted, and reached slowly for the cookie jar above the sink as if Josie weren't screaming like a banshee and trying to pull out every strand of long dark hair on Aunt Olivia's head. He turned and shook his head at all of them, not seeming to like Aunt Olivia any more than he liked Neil or the baby. And Josie kept on screaming, only now it looked like she was trying to do that Belgian Dust Dance in her aunt's arms, thrashing wildly with her arms and legs.

The man came over and lifted Josie from Aunt Olivia's arms, told her to hush since she was scaring years off her aunt's life, and then resettled her comfortably on the woman's hip with a cookie for each hand. Josie quieted the minute she had those cookies, hiccuped twice, then tasted first one and then the other. Neil thought about crying himself and seeing if he, too, could get something to eat. It had been a long time since dinner and his stomach was rumbling loud enough to drown out Josie's sobs.

Josie, surprising even Neil, stopped crying and put one hand around Aunt Olivia's neck to steady herself. Neil turned to look at his uncle, amazed at the miracle the man had performed, but saw only his rigid back as he silently left the house without a word to anyone.

"Well, this is going to be fine. Just fine," his aunt said brightly.

Josie was studying Aunt Olivia's face closely, narrowing her eyes the way she did just before she decided she didn't like something. Knowing what was coming, Neil leaped toward his little sister, but before he had a chance to stop her, Josie reached back and swung her fist smack against Aunt Olivia's nose.

"Oh my God!" Louisa screamed, while all he seemed able to do was stand, his mouth open, and watch as blood spurted from his beautiful aunt's nose. Rivers of red ran furiously down her face and splattered her dress. She gasped, and he felt himself wince at her pain. She seemed even more surprised than hurt, if that was possible. And all he could think was that now that he had finally found the mother he'd been dreaming of, she was going to die. Just like his own mother.

"Take the baby," his father ordered, but Neil couldn't make his feet move. He just stood there staring, grateful that Louisa was able to grab Josie out of their aunt's arms.

Josie, though she didn't want to stay in Aunt Olivia's arms, still held on tightly to her hair, taking two handfuls with her, plucked by the roots, and then kicked her soundly for good measure.

"Get some water," his father barked at him.

Somehow he got to the sink, but there were no faucets, and he had no idea what to do with the long metal handle that jutted out from the counter. Even if he had known what to do with it, he couldn't reach it without standing on a chair.

"You've got to pump it, fool," his father shouted, embarrassing him. Then he told his aunt, "He's a city boy," as if that meant he was a fool. Leading his aunt to the sofa, keeping her head tipped back, and pinching the bridge of her nose despite all the swiping she seemed to be doing at his hand, his father eased her down. More gently than he'd ever treated Neil, the man lifted his aunt's feet up and placed them on the couch.

Neil handed his father a wet cloth that he'd found on the edge of the sink and his father tenderly touched it to her face.

"Spence?" she asked, squinting up at his father and then at him, blinking and trying to focus.

"It's me, Olivia. Julian. Are you all right?" His father's face was inches from hers and he was wiping her nose and pushing her hair back toward the bun Josie had managed to destroy. Her hair, too, Neil noticed, looked soft.

"Is she still bleeding?" Louisa asked, hovering over the group, the hint of a smile on her lips. "Is she going to die?"

"I'm fine," she said weakly, trying to sit up. His father's firm hand on her shoulder held her down.

"Spunky as ever," his father said with a laugh, as if Josie hadn't just smashed in the nose of one of the loveliest women he had ever seen.

Neil turned and ran, seeing a ladder and taking it, trying to get as far from the sight of his aunt's last moments as he could.

"Is she all right?" he asked when he turned at the top of the ladder and looked over his shoulder.

Aunt Olivia tried to sit up again, fighting his father's hands determinedly.

"Lie down," he ordered as the blood began to spurt once more.

"Make him come down," she said in a pitifully weak voice. Neil supposed she was talking about him. "Quickly before Spencer sees."

The door slammed open and hit the wall behind it. "What in the hell is all the screaming about?" No one answered his uncle. "Where's Olivia?"

"She's there," Neil said, looking down on his uncle and noticing that the man was beginning to lose his hair.

"Get down from there," his uncle yelled, coming up the ladder toward him so that it was impossible, unless he wanted Neil to jump the eight or so feet, for him to obey the command. "Olivia!" Uncle Spencer shouted over his shoulder as he climbed higher and higher. Neil backed farther and farther away from the ladder. "Where is she? I told her you were not to—Ow! Let go, little one!"

Neil couldn't see, but from the look on his uncle's face he could guess what Josie was doing. And when his uncle bent down and threw her over one shoulder like a sack of flour, all the while continuing to come up the ladder after him, Neil was sure that Josie had tried to bite their uncle's ankle.

"Come down, right now," his uncle said sternly.

Neil stood at the edge trying to show that he was ready to come down as soon as his uncle was out of the way, but that wasn't enough for the man, and Uncle Spencer grabbed his foot and placed it on the top rung of the ladder.

"Spencuh, he thithn't know," Aunt Olivia started. With

the cloth pressed against her nose she sounded as if she were talking through a long tube.

"Olivia," his uncle said, turning to her with his finger raised. "I thought we had an understanding. I thought I made it clear——" He stopped suddenly and just stared for a moment. "Livvy? What are you doing on the couch? Is that blood?"

She nodded meekly and let his father lower her head gently to the pillow. In what seemed like two steps, his Uncle Spencer was down from the ladder and pushing aside his father from Aunt Olivia's side.

Neil meekly came down from the loft in time to hear a new voice come through the still open doorway. "You want to help me with these crates, Spence? Hey, whose wagon is this? You got company?"

"Is that Remy?" his father asked.

Another uncle. This one, his mother's brother.

"Papa, you can't expect us to live in this barn of a house," Louisa was saying, trying to be heard over Josie, who was still crying.

"Spence? You gonna give me a hand?" the man yelled from outside.

Aunt Olivia's face was soaking wet, but Neil didn't know if it was from tears or the wet cloth. All he knew was that there were streaks of her blood running across her cheeks and down toward her mouth and that she was still the prettiest thing he had ever seen.

Uncle Spencer blotted at her cheeks with his sleeve and leaned down close to her.

"Well," he asked, shaking his head at her. "Are we all happy now?"

Chapter Four

"You," Spencer shouted over his shoulder at one of the children as he leaned over Olivia, his enormous eyes the only thing Livvy could see over his handkerchief which was pressed to her nose. "Get some ice. The top layer of the birdbath might be frozen. Use the rock that's right near it. Break up a couple of pieces and bring them here."

"Birdbath?" It was the boy, Neil, who answered.

"It's in line with the kitchen window. Your aunt likes to watch the . . . Oh, never mind. The light from the house'll guide you. Don't just stand there. Your aunt's bleeding here."

Despite his surly tone, he was gentle in his ministrations, not pressing the cloth as hard as Julian had been, tipping her head softly back by placing his hand beneath her neck.

"You all right?" he asked. She tried to nod. "Don't shake your head, you ninny. You'll just bleed harder."

"How'd you know about the rock?" she asked, the words muffled by the hankie which fluttered as she spoke.

He ignored her, but still she had her answer. He had been watching her, all those times she'd thought she felt his eyes on her. He had been watching as she broke up the water for her birds during the winter, watching when she scattered the crumbs of bread beneath the bath, too, no doubt. And clearly he was rattled, since there was no chance that the water could possibly be frozen this late in the year.

"You. Girl. You want to tell me what happened here?"

"Louisa," Olivia prompted. "Her name's Louisa."

Spencer's gaze had been locked on her face. Now he raised it to the ceiling in annoyance. "Five minutes I'm out of the house, and what happens? My wife is bleeding to death on the couch, children are running amok—"

"Bleeding to death!" Remy shouted, and came forward to peer over Spencer's shoulder. "What in blue blazes happened?"

"Girl?" Spencer asked.

"Louisa," Olivia reminded him.

Julian cleared his throat and started. "It was all an unavoidable misunderstanding. You see, Josephina has come to look upon Louisa as her mother, in the absence of dear Marion . . ."

"Your name Louisa?" Spencer asked evenly. " 'Cause I sure remember asking Louisa to tell me just what the he— what happened."

"Actually," Louisa said, "you asked *girl*. I'm not used to being called that, as I have a lovely name given to me by my mother. It's Louisa."

"Well, Louisa!" Remy, said and bowed slightly. "I'm your Uncle Remy. It's a pleasure to meet you."

"A civilized person in the wilderness," she said in response, and extended her hand. "It's a pleasure to meet you, as well."

"And this little one must be Josephina," Remy said before Spencer exploded, jumping up from the sofa like a madman.

"Will someone please tell me what the hell happened to my wife?" he shouted, jumping to his feet so quickly that the couch rocked like a small boat on the lake.

Except for Josephina's sniffling, the room was eerily silent. Olivia struggled to raise herself on her elbows, but the soft cushions fought her every step of the way.

"Well?" Spencer demanded, his hands on his hips. "And

not you," he said, spinning around and pointing a finger at Julian. "I'm interested in the truth."

Neil came in, his eyes on the floor in front of him, droplets falling from his cupped hands. "Not much ice." He shrugged, offering up some slivers to his very angry uncle. "It's not particularly cold out."

"Oh, it's not *particularly* cold?" Spencer bellowed. "Well, this here isn't *particularly* ice, and your aunt's sure *particularly* bleeding."

The boy's left shoulder went up and he winced, as if preparing himself for a blow that he had no way of knowing would never come.

"Don't let your Uncle Spencer frighten you," Olivia said in as soothing a voice as she could find under the circumstances. "He's been known to carry ladybugs outside rather than swat at them. I don't think he's likely to change his ways for a small boy who's trying to help."

Spencer glowered at her and shoved his hands in his pockets.

"Are you, Spencer?" she demanded.

"He's a bigger target," Spencer mumbled, one corner of his mouth twitching as if he couldn't help enjoying the role he was playing.

"I'll go down to the cellar," Remy offered. Then to Neil he said, "Maybe you could come along and help me. I'll need someone to hold the lamp while I hack off a piece of ice."

"It's stopped," Olivia said, lowering the hanky and touching the back of her hand gingerly to her throbbing nose.

"Take the porch lantern," Spencer said. "And watch the steps."

"But it's stopped," she said again.

Remy reached out for Neil, but the boy was busy wiping his hands on his pant legs while he followed his uncle out the door.

"Now, Miss Louisa, who doesn't like being called *girl*,

you gonna tell me how your aunt came to be dripping blood down the front of my favorite dress?"

Olivia looked down. Her pale-blue calico wrapper was splattered with deep red drops. The dress was so plain otherwise that the stains seemed to decorate it merrily, like holly berries looking for leaves. *His favorite dress?* Why, he never noticed what she wore. Never once gave her a compliment until the other night.

"Livvy, lie back, for God's sake," he said when he noticed she was sitting up. He looked around the room, assessing who was where. "Bouche, your little one's about to discover the hard way that mousetraps aren't toys. And you, Miss Louisa, I'm still waiting."

"Josie didn't exactly take to your wife," Louisa said. Her chin was stuck out, and her eyes met Spencer's fearlessly, which wasn't easy the way he was strutting and booming and making demands. "But your wife insisted on holding her, and since Josie couldn't get free, she objected in the only way available to her."

"Are you saying, in your fancy city way, that the little peanut over there bashed in her aunt's nose? And all because she wanted to get down?" Julian had whisked up the child and smacked her soundly on both hands, but left the mousetrap where it was. The baby stared at him but didn't utter a sound.

Olivia ran her fingers cautiously over her nose, wishing there was a mirror in the room. It was painful and swollen, but it didn't feel broken. *Bashed in? Please let him be exaggerating,* she thought.

"Nice manners you taught your kids, Bouche," he said with all the hostility he harbored for his brother-in-law showing. "Leastwise they talk well. Guess they take after you, don't they?"

"Spencer!"

"Olivia, will you lay down! You lose any more blood you're likely to faint." He shook his head slowly. "Jeez."

The fact that she had stopped bleeding didn't seem to matter to him, so she put her head down and closed her eyes, listening to the sounds of the baby sniffing and Louisa trying to comfort her. How many times had she imagined the arrival of her nieces and nephew, Livvy wondered, and how perfect it was going to be? She would be there when the stage let them off, would have gifts for each of them waiting, and was going to welcome them with open arms into which they would all run, no doubt knocking her off her feet. Then she had planned to pile them into the wagon, and by the time they would have arrived home even Spencer was going to have been singing along with them.

Instead, she had scared the baby, and Spencer had seen to scaring everyone else.

"Ice," Remy announced when he and Neil came back through the doorway.

Julian stepped forward and took it from him, coming with it to sit next to Olivia and wrapping the ice in a cloth before raising it to her nose. It stung and she let out a sharp little cry, then apologized. "It's a little sore," she said meekly.

"I know," Julian said with utmost tenderness, as if she were a child. He brushed the hair away from her face and moved the ice slightly so that it made opening and closing her right eye difficult. She closed both eyes and concentrated on not whimpering like a dog that had been kicked in the ribs. "It'll feel better soon. You'll see."

Spencer hovered over them, snorting like a bull. "She could probably do with some tea," he said. "I don't suppose Miss Louisa knows how to boil water?"

"I have been preparing tea since I was six, Mr. Williamson. On finer stoves than this one, you can be sure."

"I can make the tea," Olivia said, struggling to get out from under Julian's heavy hand that held the ice to her now unbearably throbbing nose.

"Just like your sister," Julian said with a laugh in his

voice. "Never liked anyone to fuss over her. Of course, after several years of marriage she got used to my considerations and even relished the niceties that at first distressed her so. She came to cherish what she called the 'good life,' you know."

"If you mean she enjoyed putting on airs," Spencer said, "it didn't take marrying you to get that going. You just seemed to raise it to . . . what do they call it? An art form. A regular art form."

"Spencer Williamson! That's my sister you're talking about, and the mother of these children." It didn't make what he said any less true, but Olivia would never admit that.

"And she loved you, too," Julian said as he rested his hand against the ice on her face. "Always wishing you would come to Chicago and visit us, but you'd just never leave Maple Stand. She thought that after Spencer married Kirsten you'd want to get away, but . . ."

"I don't belong in a fancy place like Chicago, Julian. Never did. But I did love to hear all about it from Marion."

"You're a lot like her," Julian said, fingering her hair before pushing it off her face. "The hair, the bones, the voice. You look quite a bit like her, you know."

"She doesn't," Louisa said as she slammed the kettle onto the stove with a resounding clang, "look one bit like Mama. My mother was beautiful, just beautiful."

Livvy didn't expect Spencer to jump to her defense. After all, who knew better than she that she wasn't pretty? It was Marion who was the pretty one, while Remy had been the industrious one. That left Olivia to be the good one. Besides, she'd like to know, when had big blue eyes ever gotten a cow milked or blond hair ever gotten a garden weeded? All looks were good for was getting a husband, and she'd gotten the one she wanted. Maybe not in the best possible way, but she'd gotten him, nevertheless.

"You will apologize to your aunt at once, young lady, for your rudeness as well as your incorrectness. It may be difficult to tell at the present moment"—Julian took the ice pack off Livvy's face and scrunched up his own sympathetically—"but I think perhaps your aunt is even more lovely than your mother was."

Spencer loomed over Julian suddenly and forcefully assisted his departure from the couch. If she hadn't known him so well, she'd have thought Spencer was jealous, and not just angry with Julian. Sitting down next to her, he examined her swollen face, no doubt full of red patches from the ice, and touched it with just the tip of his finger. "You don't have to apologize to your aunt," he said over his shoulder. "You've got every right to think your mama was prettier. In fact, you ought to do just that. You lose something you love, you realize what a treasure it really was."

He helped Livvy sit up and handed the wet rag to Neil, indicating that he should put it in the sink.

"You know," he said to Louisa as if they were the only two people in the room, "your Aunt Liv was your mama's sister. She worshipped her just about how that little one over there looks up to you. She didn't think your mama could do anything wrong. I don't think she'd mind much if you thought your mama was the most beautiful woman on the earth. In fact, she'd probably agree with you, wouldn't you, Liv?

"In fact, your mama was the most elegant woman I have ever known, children. Seemed like a mistake that she was born in Maple Stand, Wisconsin. But your daddy fixed that when he married her and whisked her off to Chicago."

"And where do you belong, Olivia?" Julian asked. "It's a big country. And opportunity doesn't stop at its borders."

"She belongs right here," Remy said before she had a chance to respond. "Where she's got a husband and a farm and plenty of family."

"And you, Spencer? Are you where you belong?" Julian asked, grinning openly at his hostile brother-in-law.

"I belong in bed," Spencer answered, pushing off on his

knees and rising. "We didn't expect you so soon, Bouche, so we aren't prepared."

"There's two beds up in that little room above the kitchen," Neil said before Olivia could stop him.

"You aren't to go up there, boy," Spencer said in that same menacing tone he'd used with Olivia the time he'd caught her in the loft. "That room belonged to my son and my daughter and they never did like anyone touching their things."

"Where are they?" Josie asked. It was the first time the little girl had spoken, and Spencer seemed as surprised as Olivia.

"They're gone," he said bluntly.

"They'll come home," she said as if she were reassuring him. "You'll see."

Louisa pulled the little girl onto her lap and wrapped her arms protectively around her. "No, Josie, they won't. They're angels, like Mama."

"Maybe Mama's taking care of them while you're taking care of us," Neil said, trying to put everything into place in his mind.

"They got a mama of their own," Spencer said.

"Well, these children don't," Olivia reminded him.

"That's not my fault," Spencer said, glowering at Julian before disappearing into the bedroom.

"I'm sorry," Olivia said after he was gone. "I so wanted your first evening to be special."

"The water must be ready," Louisa said, rising with her sister in her arms and heading for the stove.

"I can take care of that." Olivia raced to beat her niece to the kitchen.

"I don't need any help," the girl insisted, measuring out the tea leaves into the pot.

"But you must be exhausted," Olivia said gently, not

wanting to offend the child. "It was such a long trip. There'll be plenty of time to show me how grown up you are."

Louisa glared at her, the anger so palpable that Olivia found herself leaning away from her to avoid it.

"You think you're all grown up and I'm not? All you are is old. I've been raising two children since my mama died. All you know how to do is make them cry."

Well, Livvy thought, good start. Both of the girls hated her, and Neil hated Spencer.

Spencer, meanwhile, was making his way out of the bedroom carrying several blankets and pillows, which he threw down onto the couch. "You'll have to make do for tonight," he said. He turned on his heel and apparently noticed Remy. "What are you still doing here?" he asked.

"I got the crate Livvy wanted," Remy said defensively. Then in a whisper he added, "And the book."

"What book?" He opened the door and gestured for Remy to precede him outside.

"You know," Remy said. "The one by that doctor fellow. To help you. You know."

"Jeez," Spencer said loud enough for everyone in the house to hear him even though he and Remy were halfway to the wagon. "Does it look to you like I need any more children in that house? Let's just get the damn crate in so I can get to bed."

"Who wants some tea?" Livvy asked in as cheerful a voice as she could muster. "And I've some plum pie." Finally, she thought, someone to eat the desserts she kept making as if they could make her life sweet.

"What do you say?" Julian said, slapping the top of Neil's head when the boy stood sullen and silent. His eyes shined brighter, but he didn't cry.

"No thank you, ma'am," he said quietly.

"You can call me Aunt Liv." She tried to cup his chin, but he backed away just enough to avoid her contact.

"And what should we call him?" the boy asked, gesturing toward the door. "Uncle Die?"

Spencer stood in the doorway, staring at the boy. There was something in his hand, a stone perhaps, and the child ran his thumb back and forth over it like a whittler smoothing a piece of wood. He stood defiantly staring at Spencer, who noticed that the buttons on his jacket pulled and the sleeves were a good two inches too short for his arms. He could just hear Kirsten saying how Peter seemed to outgrow things on the way home from Zephin's Mercantile.

Without bothering to answer the boy, who obviously hadn't meant to be overheard anyway, Spencer headed for the high cabinet in the kitchen, feeling Livvy's eyes on him the whole way. She couldn't really expect him to get through this without a drink, could she?

"Spencer?"

She could.

His fingers were looped around the little metal door handle.

"Spence?"

He let his hand drop to his side and turned to face his wife. She looked more in need of a drink than he felt. Her face was covered with blotches of red skin where the ice had been pressed against her, there was dried blood like a mustache above her lip, and her bodice was splattered with deep red dots.

"Come by the sink, Liv. I'll warm a little water and clean you up."

She raised a hand to cover her face, scurrying to the sink and reaching for a cloth to see to the mess herself.

He grabbed the wet rag from her hand and tilted her face toward the lantern. "I said I'll do it," he said through gritted teeth as he examined her bruised nose. He looked over at

Neil, noticed the thumb still rubbing away at the stone, and tried to catch his eye. The boy just looked at the floor, so Spencer spoke, more gruffly somehow, than he intended. "Bring a chair over here, boy. Make yourself useful."

The boy was quick to obey, lifting the chair with difficulty and placing it just behind his aunt so that all Spencer had to do was ease her down and tilt her head back. The boy continued to stand behind the chair as if waiting for further instructions.

"The kettle's still hot. Maybe you could put a little hot water on a clean towel and then add some cold till it's not too hot for your Aunt Liv's face."

The boy jumped to obey.

"He's a good boy," Julian said, reminding Spencer he was there. "Not much appreciation for the finer things in life, but he'll learn."

"Jeez," Spencer said. "The finer things, huh? Well, you always appreciated the *finer things,* didn't you, Bouche? And you always wanted them now." He grabbed the cloth from Neil's hands and waved it once in the air to cool it down a little more. "Perfect. Now just be patient with me, Livvy. It's been a while since I washed a dirty face other than my own."

He cupped her chin, tilting her head back, and gently patted her nose, easing up when he saw the pain in her face.

"Sorry."

She smiled up at him, her wet face glistening in the lamplight and he quickly looked away. What had happened to his resolve not to touch her any more? God, her skin was soft.

"Where's that little one?" he barked, looking for the child who had tried to put his wife's nose right through her bun. With a deftness that seemed borne of habit, Louisa slipped the little child behind her skirts.

"If you were thinking of hitting her," Louisa began, sounding at least twice her twelve or so years, "you can——"

"What I was thinking, Miss Louisa, was that she ought to

take a good close look at what she did to her aunt here, and maybe she'll be a little slower to raise her fist again. Maybe a good closeup look at her aunt's pain is all she needs to show her the error of her ways."

Louisa's mouth dropped open slightly, making a small O. Her little brows knit together and then she pulled the child from behind her back with a firm hand. "Go see what you did, Josie. And mind, he's cleaned her up. She looked even more awful before."

Josie made her way to Livvy, one finger in her mouth. Her chin was stuck out as if she didn't care what she'd done, or what she was about to see, but her squinted eyes gave her away.

After one look, Spencer was convinced that Josephina Bouche had learned her lesson about hitting people in the nose. He wondered where she would strike next.

"Well, it's getting late," Julian said, looking around the room. "And as you said, you're not quite prepared for overnight guests."

"We weren't expecting you so soon," Livvy said, trying to smile without moving any part of her face but her lips. Spencer reached for the handle of the high cupboard, this time ignoring the narrowed eyes with which Livvy was watching him. Instead of the whiskey, he pulled down a bottle of Port and poured her a small wineglass.

Handing it to her, he said, "It'll ease the pain some."

She raised one of those fine dark eyebrows at him in doubt, and he knew she was reading more into his words than he intended, but he let it go. His drinking habits were no concern of Julian Bouche's and his children.

"Well," Louisa said, tapping her chin with her forefinger as she assessed the room. "Papa and I can sleep on the couch and the children can sleep on the floor."

The sofa was small. In fact, it was really a tête-à-tête, but Kirsten had been so taken with the picture in the Sears' catalog that they'd ignored the fine print. The backs of each piece of furniture in the parlor suite had reminded her of hearts and so he'd ordered it in the crushed plush for what had seemed like a bargain price of $25.50. When it had arrived there seemed to be barely room for the two of them on it, but Kirsten was small enough to fit next to him, and if they had to squeeze, so much the better. He couldn't recall ever sitting on it with Livvy.

The thought of Julian Bouche and his daughter cuddled on the couch turned Spencer's stomach. He exchanged a look with Livvy and then watched as Louisa expertly covered the small sofa with a quilt and placed a pillow at one end.

"You'll sleep with the baby on the couch," he announced when he could finally find his voice. "Josie on the inside so she doesn't fall off. Bouche, you and the boy'll sleep in the barn."

Neil picked up a blanket from the pile Spencer had carried out from the bedroom and headed for the door. "You got cows in there? Or sheep or anything good like that?"

Bouche eyed the couch and studied his daughter's face. Spencer thought he saw the man shake his head at Louisa, but he wasn't sure.

"Maybe you wanna help the girls get outta their traveling clothes, Liv," he said, giving her a hand to help her up from the chair.

"Papa can help us," Louisa said. "He gets my buttons and I undress the baby."

Bouche cleared his throat. "One makes do, Louisa, with what one has at hand. Now that Aunt Olivia is available, she can assist you."

Spencer picked up a blanket, the thinnest one on the pile, and thrust it at his brother-in-law.

"It hasn't been easy since Marion died," Julian said to Livvy as he took the woolen cloth from Spencer and headed for the door. "But we've managed."

They stood and watched the door close behind Julian

Bouche, each with thoughts of his own. For Spencer's part, he had a lot of questions, and he had a strong feeling in his gut that he didn't want to know the answers. He searched Livvy's face, wondering if her mind had gone down the same depraved path his was wandering.

"Can I help you two get ready for bed?" she asked as she cautiously neared the little hellion who had bashed her pretty face.

"I'll see to Josie," Louisa said sharply, grabbing Josie's arm and shepherding her toward the couch.

"Well then," Olivia said, trying as always to hide her hurt. "How about you? Can I get those buttons for you?"

"It's not necessary," Louisa said with the same high-handed tone with which she said everything else. Spencer balled his fists and shoved them in his pockets to keep himself from smacking her across the face for the way she was treating her aunt. Didn't she realize Olivia was only trying to help?

"Good night, then," Olivia said, her voice a little weak. "If you need anything . . ."

Louisa opened her mouth, but Spencer didn't need to hear her say the words to know her response was "We won't."

"Come, Aunt Olivia," he said solicitously, trying to set an example for how the children ought to treat a woman of Olivia's good mind and heart. "We best get you settled for the night. It's been quite a day."

He put his arm under her elbow and guided her into their room.

"They hate us," she said after he shut the door. Undoubtedly she was right.

"Of course they don't hate us," he said anyway. "They're children. They've lost their mama and they've been dragged from their home. And all the security they've got is that poor excuse for a father that's bedding down with the pigs where he belongs."

She had slipped behind the screen where pieces of her wardrobe were gathering over the top. She stuck her head out and shook it at him. "Spencer, that's my sister's husband you're talking about, the children's father . . ."

"Yeah, well, he'd do well to remember both those facts. Seems to me he's the one that needs reminding." He sat down on the edge of the bed and began unlacing his boots. He could sense his wife's movements behind the screen and couldn't suppress a smile when he saw her frilly white chemise come up over the top, slide down, and get tossed back up a second and then a third time.

"What do you mean by that?" she asked finally, peering around the screen to look at him in complete innocence. He could see one bare shoulder and found himself leaning so far over to see what else she was hiding that he nearly fell off the bed.

"Well," he said as calmly as he could under the circumstances, "didn't it strike you as odd when the girl suggested she and Bouche sleep together on the tête-à-tête?"

"You mean because it's so small?" she asked, and the nightdress that hung on the edge of the screen vanished behind it.

She'd just been smacked in the face and had lain bleeding for a good quarter of an hour. He'd already sworn that he was never going to touch her again. And yet he was quite literally holding his foot in both hands to prevent it from touching the floor and carrying him over to the screen to get a good look at the charms his wife was right now hiding from him.

He had a dirty mind. No question about it.

"Spencer?" She stepped out from behind the screen, her dark hair loosely falling on her white cotton–clad shoulders. Even without a corset she had an hourglass figure.

He closed his eyes, but the sight of her didn't go away.

"Spencer? Why do you hate Julian so much?"

He thought about Julian Bouche and what he knew as well

as what he simply suspected. It was on the tip of his tongue to tell her, and he supposed he would have if he'd kept his eyes closed and never seen that innocent face.

That trusting face.

But he'd be damned if he'd rob her of that, too.

Chapter Five

When trouble broke out three days later, it didn't surprise Olivia at all. But she'd expected it to be between Spencer, who paced around the house like a caged bear with only an occasional pause in his tracks to growl, and Julian, who spent his days bent over maps that Spencer kept pushing him to follow. Instead the yelling came from outside the house, and Olivia looked up just in time to see her birdbath come tumbling down with Neil on top of it and Philip, Remy's middle boy, on top of him.

By the time she got to the door, Remy's youngest had joined in, too, and she ran out after them, Spencer and Julian on her heels.

"It ain't your farm, neither," Philip was yelling, while his little brother Thomas tried to climb on Neil's back and hold him for his big brother.

"Stop it, all of you! Thom-Tom! Philip! I said stop it!" Olivia reached out to separate the boys, then screamed when Philip backed up and accidentally came down hard on her instep with his heavy work boots.

"For Christ's sake, boy," Julian shouted at his son. "To the eye! The nose! Not his chest if you want to hurt him!"

Before Olivia could turn her shocked face in her brother-in-law's direction, she heard Spencer's even voice.

"Want my shotgun?" he drawled.

The boys stopped fighting and stared at him. Philip swallowed and found his voice first. "Your shotgun? I don't wanna kill 'im, Uncle Spence."

"Oh. Just hurt him, huh?" He crossed his arms and tapped one booted toe as if he were carefully considering the boy's position. "How much?" he asked finally.

All three boys shrugged in unison.

"Well, a whole lot? Like broken bones and bloody lips?" Spencer asked, suddenly finding the palm of his hand very interesting and examining it closely.

Philip shook his head. Thom-Tom made a face as if the whole idea gave him the willies. Only Neil remained unrepentant.

"Well, seems to me if you're not gonna do it right, it's just not worth doing. Maybe it's something you ought to talk about with words instead of fists." He seemed wholly disinterested.

"He says our farm is really his," Thom-Tom said.

"That so?" Spencer looked first at Neil and then at Julian. "Wonder where he got that idea."

"My pa told me so," Neil said, and Olivia could see when he spoke that there was blood in his mouth.

"Go rinse your mouth, boy," Spencer said. "And you," he added, glaring at Philip. "You proud of yourself? You got nearly two years and a good twenty pounds on him and you probably managed to loosen a tooth or two. Jeez."

"Well, he said——" Philip began.

"Yeah, yeah, I know what he said. I'll get to that in a minute. But first I wanna be sure you understand things here. The boy with the bleeding mouth? He's your cousin. The blood he's losing flows through your own veins, Philip. Now I understand that you haven't had cousins around before, but you do now, and I won't understand should there come a next time. You get me?"

Philip nodded his head.

"You?" he asked Thom-Tom.

Thom-Tom nodded his head, as well, and wiped at his nose with his sleeve.

Livvy stood there in amazement. Where did a man learn to father like that? Surely not from Spencer's father. Max Williamson was just an average man, who lived a very mediocre life and died a mediocre death. And the way Spencer was handling these boys was nothing short of miraculous.

"Livvy?" Spencer asked breaking into her reverie. "Louisa in the house with the little one?"

Oh, some mother she was making. While Spencer was winning Father of the Year contests, she would be brought before a magistrate for neglecting the very same children. She hadn't given a moment's thought to the baby. Lucky thing Louisa was around. "Of course," she said, trying to imply that Spencer was foolish for asking.

"Oh, you needn't worry about Josephina," Julian said. "Louisa is quite the little mother to her. She won't let anything happen to her."

"She's not the girl's mama, Liv. Maybe you best go inside and see to her."

Livvy nodded reluctantly. In the past couple of days she'd watched her two nieces and come to the conclusion that there was no room for her in their relationship, and no need for her, either. "You'll explain to the boys about the farm, then?"

"Your pa on his way over?" Spencer asked the boys. "I'd like him here to make things clear as crystal to everyone."

"He's staying with Ma," Thom-Tom said. "She's not feeling too good this morning."

The sky was bright and clear, the weather warm. It was the kind of day Bess was at her best. "Your mama's hip bothering her today?"

"No, ma'am," Philip said, his eyes on the ground. "But she's not feeling so good, all the same."

"Maybe I'll take her a little supper," Olivia said, trying

to draw out from Philip what could be wrong with Bess. "For her and your pa and Henry."

"Henry's over to Jenny's, like always," Thom-Tom said. "He's always there and Philip is always down at Zephin's. Spends every spare minute there workin' for old man Zephin for stuff the man don't want anymore. And I gotta do all the real work."

Spencer did a pretty poor job of trying to hide his smirk, and Livvy kicked his foot gently to remind him not to embarrass the boy, who already felt like the runt of the family and of very little use.

"Mr. Zephin doesn't pay him?" Julian asked, examining Neil's mouth and shaking his head in annoyance.

"Oh, Philip says the stuff he gets is better than the few pennies old miser Zephin'd give him, don't you, Philip? Last week he got some old balls with the bounce gone out of them."

"Old balls?" Livvy said, wondering how her nephew could have made such a bad deal.

Philip picked up the story. "And I took them to the Widow Grillot, who said they were just the right size for darning socks and she gave me her old Gem pan for them. Then I took the old Gem pan to that new bakery on the corner of Main and Aspen and got two day-old loaves of bread for it." He looked very satisfied with himself for someone who had put in a lot of work for two day-old loaves of bread.

"What did you want with two old loaves of bread?" Neil asked. "You couldn't eat that much."

"No, but Mrs. Cote's birds sure could, and she gave me the old wheels from her son's carriage, now that he's grown and all."

"And what did you do with the wheels?" Spencer asked, obviously fighting to keep a straight face and losing.

"Made a wagon," Philip said.

"And for a penny a ride he's takin' the little ones all over town," Thom-Tom said.

"And deliverin' the papers for Mr. Seaton for a nickel a day, too," Philip said, by now rocking proudly on his heels.

He was a born salesman, Livvy thought, buying and selling from the time he was old enough to trade a rattle for a ball. If only he liked farming half as much as wheeling and dealing he could be a real help to his ma and pa.

"You leave your mama in bed?" Olivia asked Philip as they all headed into the house, where Louisa stood watching with Josie on her hip.

"She was on the sofa when she shooed us out," Thom-Tom said. "Looked to be crying, to me."

"I think I'll just head over there," Olivia said, reaching for her coat.

"Take the baby with you," Spencer said. "So Louisa can get to know her cousins."

Olivia hesitated, knowing that Josie wouldn't like leaving her sister any more than Louisa would like letting her go.

"I don't think that's a real good idea," Philip said, looking at the floor and playing with the corner of the rag rug with his toe. "I wouldn't bring a baby over there today."

"But your mama loves babies," Olivia said, confused by Philip's sudden shyness.

"Tell her what Henry said," Thom-Tom prompted his brother, but Philip shook his head.

"That's not for us to say."

Well, she could take Josie and head on over to Bess's, but for some reason that didn't seem to be a very good idea. In truth, she was relieved that the boys had advised against bringing the baby, since she wasn't sure she could stand another bloody nose. The one she'd already gotten was just healing and still smarted when she washed her face.

She stood, her hat hanging from her hand, not sure what she should do. What a difference three days and as many children made in a person's life. She'd have been out the door and halfway to Bess and Remy's by now if it was still just her and Spencer.

"Go," Spencer finally said. "Bouche'll watch his daughter while Philip and Thom-Tom show Louisa around."

"All right," Olivia agreed, anxious to see what was wrong with Bess. "Be sure to show her where the school is, boys. I'll be signing the children up come Monday."

"The children?" Louisa asked. "You mean Neil, don't you?"

She looked positively indignant, as if Olivia had suggested she suck on a nipple and sleep in a cradle.

"She means *you,* Miss Louisa," Spencer said, reassuring Olivia that she was right to expect Louisa to attend school. "All children go to school, no matter how fancy they talk."

"Yes," Louisa agreed, "but I'm no child. I'm too old for school. I've got responsibilities. I've got to watch Josie. I've got—"

"You, Miss Louisa Bouche," Spencer said in a voice that brooked no argument, "are most certainly a child. You *are* one, you're gonna be *treated* like one, and you're gonna learn to *act* like one while you're living here under my roof. How old are you, anyways?"

"She's eleven and a half," Neil said, his eyes following the exchange between his sister and his uncle.

"Eleven and a half? Jeez. You ought to have a doll baby instead of a real one," Spencer said. He turned to Julian and opened his mouth, then thought better of it.

"I'm almost old enough to have a real baby," Louisa said, blushing despite her attempt to appear nonchalant. "And I have to take care of Josie." She hugged the child tightly to her chest.

"That's why you're here," Spencer said, shooing Livvy out the door. "So you don't have to take care of Josie. So you don't even have to take care of you. Go on now, Aunt Liv.

You go see to Aunt Bess. Oh, and Liv? Say good-bye to Bouche. He'll be gone by the time you get back.''

Before she got a chance to open her mouth, he'd shut the door. If she had to guess, she'd suppose he was leaning against it, too.

His house, his sanctuary, was overrun with his wife's relatives. Before him stood two nieces and three nephews, all belonging to her sister or her brother. Behind them, at the table, sat her late sister's husband.

To his knowledge, with the exception of distant relations, there wasn't a soul in Wisconsin with blood ties to him. The thought might have cut him to the quick a week ago. Today he simply wished the same might be said of his wife.

Not that he didn't love Remy and Bess and the boys. He did. He just loved his privacy, too. Since Bouche and his brood had shown up there had been nothing but chaos reigning in his house. It didn't even feel like it was *his* house anymore.

"Now," he said, and pulled a chair away from the table, swung it around, and straddled it backward, "as to the matter of the Sacotte Farm."

"The *Remy* Sacotte Farm," Philip corrected. If he'd been younger, Spencer would have expected the boy to stick his tongue out at his cousin.

"The *Henri* Sacotte Farm," Julian said, invoking the name of his father-in-law.

"The *Xavier* Sacotte Farm," Spencer said, going back a generation further.

"Who?" the boys asked.

"Xavier Sacotte was your great-grandfather. All of yours'. He came over here from Belgium with his three sons: Henri, Constant, and Wolfgang."

"Wolfgang!" The boys laughed, making howling noises and jabbing each other in the ribs. Neil moved a little closer to

Thom-Tom, who seemed to make room for him without moving away.

"That'd be your pa's Uncle Wolfgang, boys," he said, pointing to Philip and Thomas. He gestured at Neil. "And your ma's. Well, the boys were young at the time, maybe just about in their teens."

"Like Philip's age," Thom-Tom said.

Spencer nodded. "Well, the way old Henri—that was your grandpa—told it, Xavier came to Wisconsin to buy some land, along with a whole shipload of Belgians. But the Dutch who they met on the way over from the old country already had relatives here who'd saved all the best land for them. So Xavier and the rest of the Belgians moved on until they came to Door County, where Xavier found just the piece of land he wanted and settled right in. Everything was going just fine until Wolfgang—he was the oldest—decided he was ready to marry."

"Like Henry and Jenny Watchell are gonna do," Philip said, and Thom-Tom roared with laughter.

"Henry thinks Jenny's got wings, but she don't want anything to do with a farmer boy," Thom-Tom explained to Neil, then added, "but don't tell him I told you so."

"The truth of the matter is," Julian interrupted, keeping his eyes fixed on the cigar he was lighting, "that Henri Sacotte left the farm in equal parts to his three children and that as the surviving husband of one of those children, that farm, if it were worth anything, is one-third mine."

"Livvy don't like cigars in the house," Spencer said. "Mind smoking that on the porch?"

Julian shrugged and headed for the door, opened it and remained in the doorway, waiting for Spencer to dispute his claim.

"See? Your farm is one-third mine," Neil said. "I want the part with the animals."

"Heck, no," Thom-Tom said, and raised his hand once again.

"Thomas," Spencer said quietly. "You don't weigh as much as a cock's sickle feathers, and Aunt Liv's not here to see to the scars. You sure you wanna put that fist anywheres beside your pocket?"

"But he's gonna take Blackie and Whitey and Spotty and . . ."

"He ain't taking nothing," Philip said, his tone quite menacing for a twelve-year-old.

"No, he's not," Spencer agreed. "See, even if he wanted to, and I don't believe for one minute that Bouche here has an ounce of farmer's blood in his veins, that's not the way the will reads."

Julian puffed a cloud of cigar smoke toward the sky and said, "The land is mine, Williamson. Says it right in the will *'in equal shares to my children and their heirs.'* "

"And it also says, and this is because your grandpa Henri didn't want the fight over *his* land that had split him from his brothers when *his* pa passed on, that the land is left in trust to his son—that'd be Remy—and to his son's heirs, unless and until it passed out of the family. Long as Remy wants it, it's his free and clear. And he can keep it or give it to any Sacotte he wants."

"But if he sells it," Julian said, pointing his cigar at his son, "one-third of the money is yours."

"My pa would never sell Sacotte Farm," Philip said.

"Never," Thom-Tom echoed.

"No," Spencer agreed, mustering an innocent smile at his brother-in-law. "Never."

Julian flicked an ash off the end of his cigar and smiled back like he was a friend of the devil himself. "Never's a long time."

"Especially if you're around," Spencer said, signaling with a jerk of his head for the boys to leave the house.

"I could be out of here in ten minutes," Julian said, eyeing the horizon to the west. "They've discovered gold in the Klondike, you know."

"The what?" He'd heard about another gold rush, but he'd paid it no mind. Any gold he expected to find had better be on his own farm for all the traveling he planned to do in his life.

"The Klondike. Alaska. There are steamers out of San Francisco Bay nearly every day, and every one of them is loaded with men looking to find themselves a gold mine."

"So?"

"So there are fortunes to be made. Why shouldn't I be the one to make them?" Bouche looked at him earnestly. He'd had a hunger from the day Spencer had met him that had never been sated. Because what Bouche had always wanted was more. More, and sooner. Two commodities some people could never get enough of.

Still, as badly as Julian might want wealth, Spencer just couldn't see him dirtying his hands to get it. "Mining? In Alaska? Somehow Bouche, I just can't see you in overalls and boots to your hips panning in some frozen—"

Bouche threw back his head and laughed. "You've never quite gotten the concept, have you, Williamson? There are worker bees and queens—or in this case, kings. A man with money in Alaska's gonna need a place to spend it. Someone's gotta sell them booze, provide them with a little warmth on those cold winter nights, sell them a heavy coat. Why not me? It would only take a small stake. I repeat, so why not me?"

"Because you got three kids, Bouche. And my guess is not a dime in your pocket."

Julian Bouche shrugged. "You could fix that, and I'd be outta here before that sun finishes setting." He gestured in the general direction of some dark clouds.

"Yeah, and I'd be stuck with your children for the rest of my life."

Bouche shrugged a second time, then stretched and yawned. "Wonder what Livvy's making for dinner."

Try as he might, Spencer couldn't keep his fists from balling. "You won't be here to eat it," he said. "So sorry, but you'd best be on your way before it gets dark."

"I'll only be back," Julian said, grinding out his cigar on Olivia's freshly swept porch and heading on into the house.

"Damn right," Spencer called out after him. "Don't go thinking this is a permanent thing."

Livvy knocked on the door of the house in which she'd been born and raised and had lived until the day she'd married Spencer Williamson, and waited for her sister-in-law to answer it. After a moment of silence, she knocked again.

"Bess? Remy? You home?" she called out.

"It's Livvy," she heard Remy say despite the closed door. "Just a second, Livvy."

Her hand had been on the latch, but now she waited. Never, not in all of the eighteen years of their marriage, had Bess and Remy ever asked her to wait before entering their house. In fact, she couldn't remember them ever asking anyone to wait.

Remy opened the door a crack, looked back over his shoulder at Bess, and then opened it fully to allow Livvy entrance. The house was dim, the shades closed, the lamps unlit.

On the couch, Bess sat like a giant discarded rag doll, her shoulders slumped, her apron lifted to her nose. Clearly she had been crying, and even in the dim light, Olivia could tell she had been at it all morning.

"What on earth . . . ?" she asked, rushing to sit next to her best friend in the world and putting an arm around her. "What is it? What's wrong?"

Bess waved Remy away with her right hand and held her

apron to her nose with her left. She blew hard and then wiped at her face, which was red and raw.

"Should I make you ladies some tea?" Remy asked, looking decidedly lost in his own parlor. "Or something cold?"

"Go check the pigs," Bess said, a hiccup escaping her lips. "Or the chickens."

"The stock's all fine, Bessie," he assured her. "It's you I'm worried about."

Olivia felt sick with fear, her heart thudding in her throat, her palms sweating so much that she had to wipe them on her skirt. "Bess? You want to tell me what's wrong?"

"Remy," Bess said firmly. "Go check the fields. Check the sun. Check something."

Remy nodded, his face revealing that he understood his wife wanted to be alone with his sister. "I, uh, I think I'll just check on Blackie's hoof. You know I put some new medicine on it yesterday, and . . ." His voice trailed off as he backed his way toward the door.

"You do that," Bess said gently. "And take your time. I'm fine here with Livvy."

"It's not such a big deal, Bessie. I swear it's not," he said, and Livvy could hear the tears in his throat.

"Maybe it's not to you," Bessie said. "But Livvy'll understand. Go on. Check the horse."

He left quietly, shutting the door without a sound. Bess's breathing was heavy and labored and filled the room.

"Saw Doc LeMense," Bess said finally. "Old coot. You think he knows what he's talkin' about?"

The saliva pooled in her mouth, but Olivia couldn't swallow. She pursed her lips, moved her tongue, but still she couldn't make her throat cooperate. *Dear God, don't let anything be wrong with Bess.*

"Livvy?" Bess asked, her head tipped so that she could look her full in the face. "You look worse than me."

"Tell me what's wrong," Livvy said when she could finally get her tongue and lips under control. "Are you sick? What did Dr. LeMense say?"

Bess let out a heavy sigh and dropped both hands in her lap.

"Besides that I gotta lose fifty pounds, at least?"

"He always says that. It never upset you so before."

"There's more. Says my weight's so bad that my heart doesn't sound good."

"What does that mean?" Livvy demanded. "I mean, you can lose the weight and then you'll be all right, yes?"

"He says I can't . . . that if I . . . oh, Liv!" Bess turned and took Livvy in her arms, her bulk nearly suffocating her sister-in-law. "I can't have any more babies. The strain on my heart'd be too much. Leastwise, that's what he says."

"But if you didn't have any more?" Livvy said, extricating herself from the embrace and backing up enough to read her sister-in-law's face. "Then you'd be all right?"

"Well, I have to lose some weight. Says that's why my joints hurt so bad, from all the extra weight, but that's not the point. Livvy, I can't have any more children."

Livvy tried to keep the anger from her voice but was sure it was written all over her face. Bess was looking to her for sympathy. Well, she surely had the wrong sow by the ear if she thought that Olivia would feel sorry for her, what with her three children and her loving husband. No *more* children? Bess had felt the flutter of life inside her, the strains of childbirth, the tug of an infant at her breast, and she was expecting Livvy to hurt for her because after three—not one, not two, but three children—she couldn't have that pleasure again?

"That's it?" Livvy asked tight-lipped, when she thought she had herself under control. "Just no more children and lose some weight?"

Bess rose with great effort and walked stiffly to the window. She drew back the shade and searched the fields, no doubt looking for Remy. "I should have known you wouldn't understand."

"Yes," Livvy agreed. "You should have."

"I suppose it was kind of thoughtless of me," Bess said after a few moments. "To you I must seem kind of greedy."

"Well," Livvy said. "Kind of."

"It's not just the babies," Bess said, still with her back to Olivia. "But Remy. A woman has a duty to her husband and, well, Remy's always enjoyed trying, if you know what I mean."

Olivia was silent. Did Bess really mean only Remy? How she wished she had talked to Bess before she'd married Spencer. But Bess had assumed she'd known the facts of life by twenty-five, and both her mother and Marion were already gone. How could she ask her now, after she'd been married for three years, whether a woman should find any pleasure with her husband? How could she ask Bess if she enjoyed it?

It had never been a question in her mind until that night before the children came when she had wished that instead of getting it over with, Spencer had never stopped. Even thinking about it now, in Bess's parlor, her blood rushed and her insides warmed.

"I don't even know how to try not making babies," Bess said. "I just know that the possibility made it all the more worth trying."

Olivia bit the side of her lip. "I wouldn't know," she said quietly.

"It's getting late," Bess said, despite the brilliant sunshine that was streaming through the window where she held the shade away. It couldn't be much past three. "Guess you wanna be getting back home."

She was being asked to leave. "I'm sorry you're so sad," she said honestly. "I do wish you could have everything you want."

Bess patted her own hip and laughed. "Think that's what got me in this fix, Livvy."

"You really are going to have to stop eating those pies, Bess."

Bess nodded.

"And those cakes."

Bess nodded again.

"And the cookies, the puddings, the breads. I love you too much, Bess Sacotte, to watch you eat yourself into an early grave."

"Now, Livvy, I'm not gonna kill myself with sweets any more." She smiled. "But it would be a nice way to go, wouldn't it?" Bess dabbed at her eyes with the edge of her apron and gave Livvy a genuine smile.

"You feeling better?" Livvy asked.

Bess nodded. "Now, you wanna tell me what's troubling you?"

"I was only worried about you," Livvy answered. *At least that was before I came.* "You were the only thing on my mind."

Chapter Six

Well, if there was a stupider stallion in all of Wisconsin than Curly George, Spencer Williamson didn't even want to imagine him. A mare in heat in the near field and Curly George couldn't find her with a damn treasure map. Even with Remy's help the two men could hardly get the stallion to cover Peaches, who couldn't lift her tail fast enough, and nearly trampled George in her haste to back up toward him. With a female that eager, that ready, he'd have thought Curly George would have been nipping the back of her neck before the sun was even up.

But no, he and Remy had nearly had to do the act for the horse, coaxing him up over Peaches's rump and reminding him what went where.

It was the goddamn longest morning of Spencer's life, trying to convince the horse to do what he damn well ought to know he'd enjoy, and he burst through the door for the mid-day meal with a grunt that went ignored by his wife and the little girl who sat naked in the kitchen sink.

"Because a little girl who doesn't wash starts to smell a lot like a little pig." Livvy stood with her back to him, apparently bathing a reluctant Josie. The water splashed up and his wife shook her head like a dog coming in from the rain and then wiped her eyes against her sleeve. "Keep it up, honey bunch, but you're still not getting out of that sink until that hair is soaped and rinsed. Then we're going to buy you the prettiest white dress anyone's ever worn to La Chapelle and you're going to throw the prettiest flowers."

Livvy's own hair appeared to be getting a washing, too, quite incidentally. Several strands had escaped from that damnable bun and were corkscrewing down her back nearly as far as her waist.

"That's a good girl," she cooed at the child encouragingly. After just two weeks with the children in the house, it appeared that Livvy was getting the hang of mothering a lot faster than he'd expected. "I'll just get a towel."

She turned and reached for the towel, a broad smile of accomplishment on her pretty face.

"Oh, Spencer," she said, turning further still to face him, all the while keeping one hand on the little girl in the sink. "I didn't realize you'd come in. I'll get your dinner in just a minute."

Her bodice was soaked, the front of it plastered to her like she'd been whitewashed. Two dusky nipples stood out erect and taut from the cold. She said something else, but he wasn't sure what. He wasn't sure of anything except that he might burst from the sight of her. He gulped for air like a drowning man, his eyes riveted on the two spheres that rose and fell around the locket that hung between them, his senses fully aware of the pressure in his loins.

"You're wet," he said when he found his voice. "That is, your dress is wet."

"Well, we were having a bath, weren't we, Josie?" she said, gesturing with her arm and causing her breasts to quiver. "We're getting ready for the Blessed Sacrament at La Chapelle. Imagine, Spencer! I've finally got a little girl to bring to the celebration. What thanks I've got to give!" Her eyes sparkled, but it was the glistening buttons on her blouse that captured his attention. The buttons, and the wet blouse, and what was no longer concealed from him.

She was killing him, as sure as if she had a knife and was twisting it in his gut.

"I can come back in when you're done," he offered, though he wasn't sure he could move from the spot where he stood.

"We're done," she said, spinning on her heel and lifting the baby from the sink, setting her on the floor, then drying her briskly with the towel. "Run and get your clothes, now, and I'll help you get into them."

She wiped her hands on the towel and brushed at her blouse with the cloth.

"Cold," she said, lifting her shoulders and squeezing her arms together so that her breasts were pushed against each other like one of those cloverleaf buns.

"Jeez," he said, gawking like he was fourteen and had never seen a woman's breasts before.

"Where's Remy?" she asked, running her hands up and down her arms and making her chest do some kind of dance in front of his eyes.

"Who?"

"Remy. You know, my brother, the man who was helping you with Curly George . . . Spencer?"

Remy. Spencer seemed to remember him taking off as soon as Curly George had finally begun to thrust in earnest. He didn't know about Remy, but the damn horse was getting more satisfaction than he was, that was for sure.

"Went home." God, she was beautiful like that, her hair half a mess, her face flushed and moist, her attributes showing like some kind of wanton hussy. And she didn't even know what it was she was doing to him, standing there like that, smiling that smile, swaying just a little from the cold, her breasts rising and falling and rising again.

"I'd better go dress Josie," she said softly, as if she was loath to break some spell. "Can you wait?"

Not one more minute. "Wait for what?"

"Dinner, of course. I'll just be a moment. I want to make sure Josie doesn't catch cold."

"Or you," he said, pointing at her wet blouse in a vague, I'm-not-staring-at-your-nipples kind of way.

"Oh, this'll dry," she said, as if she wasn't revealing anything that might be torturing the life out of him just by standing there.

She reached down to dry the floor by her feet and he could see her breasts fall forward, grow beneath his eyes to proportions he'd only dreamed about.

"I'm not hungry," he lied, rushing for the door without risking a look back.

"All right," she said, raising her voice so that he could hear her even after he closed the farm house door. "But it's always here if you want it."

The afternoon was a haze of feelings that Olivia revelled in. There was no mistaking the way Spencer had stared at her when he'd found her giving Josie her bath. Enough men had looked at her with lust in their eyes when she was younger for her to recognize it even in a man who didn't want to let it show. And when she'd crossed her arms, well, she thought the poor man's eyes were going to pop out of his head.

He wanted her. Wanted her as much as she wanted him, and the minute he'd bedded down the animals and she'd settled the kids she was going to let him know she was ready to let him have his way with her. Ever since that night before the children had come, she'd wished that Spencer might visit her again, suckle at her breast, touch her in her secret place.

And each time she thought about it she felt her heart race and her cheeks color, and worst, worst of all, her private parts grow moist.

Supper probably didn't take more than ten minutes start to finish. It felt, of course, longer than a carriage ride to

Duluth. In the rain. With no padding on the seat. And nothing to eat.

Neil had seconds. Good for a growing boy, Spencer said. Spencer had thirds. Louisa barely touched what was on her plate, claiming the fish stew was too salty, the potatoes too soft. Naturally, Josie followed her sister in this as in everything else.

"Well," Spencer said after he'd eaten enough fish to leave Lake Michigan lifeless, "I've got some work to do in the barn."

"Work?" she asked, trying to hide her dissappointment. Of course, he was right. They could hardly go to bed so early with a houseful of children.

"The harnesses need dressing," he said. "And I want to throw a blanket over Peaches."

Neil offered to help and Olivia held her breath hoping Spencer wouldn't snap at the boy. Instead he simply nodded. It wasn't a riproaring welcome, but acceptance came first. She hadn't expected two weeks to produce a bond meant to last a lifetime. She'd settle for a mere halt to the feud that had begun the day the children first showed up.

Louisa and Josie took off for their room, rejecting Olivia's offer to help get Josie ready for bed and read her a story. In a few more days, when Josie was more used to her new surroundings and didn't need the comfort that repetition brought a child, Olivia intended to pull out some of the books she had saved from her own childhood and read them to the little girl whether she liked it or not. Sometimes a body just needed a push in the right direction, and no one had had more practice in the gentle art of pushing than Olivia Williamson.

But for now, Livvy had the first few minutes of utter peace she had known in over a week. And she knew precisely what she wanted to do with them.

She headed for the bedroom and shut the door behind her, turning the lamp up to reading level. Checking over her shoulder twice even though the door was closed, she went straight to Spencer's bottom drawer and dug through his winter underwear until she felt the book in her hands.

Spencer had no idea that she knew where he'd put it, or that he was even reading it. He had presumed she was asleep when he'd thrown back the covers and tiptoed to the dresser, coming back to their bed with Dr. Napheys's book. From all his humphs and grunts, the book seemed a source of great displeasure, but still he had gone back to it just last night and read a few more pages before slamming it shut and thrusting it back in the drawer with enough noise that she couldn't even pretend to sleep through it.

"Something wrong?" she'd asked him, sitting up and blinking in their bed.

"Everything, Olivia. Just everything. And there doesn't seem to be a damn thing I can do about it."

"Come to bed, Spence," she'd said, reaching out her arms to him in the hopes that he would seek comfort there.

"That's the last thing you can do to help, Livvy-love." He'd snorted.

Well, as the cover of the book promised in gold letters on brown leather, *Knowledge Is Safety,* and she wanted to be as safe as she could be. She flipped rapidly through the pages, unsure how long Spencer would be in the barn, and ignored the chapters on adolescence and puberty, as well as the shocking one on the *social evil* and diseases resulting therefrom, and finally found what she was looking for.

Page 171. Husbands and Wives.

Well, according to the book, their bedchamber was the right size and they were both clean. Dr. Napheys would be satisfied so far.

Page 173. Of Marital Relations. Livvy closed the book, her finger keeping the page. She listened for sounds in the house but heard none. She promised herself she would read only a paragraph; surely a woman need not know more than that.

Passion in women leaped out from the page, written in a scriptlike manner. She took a deep breath and read on.

> *A vulgar opinion prevails that they are creatures of like passions with ourselves; that they experience desires as ardent, and often as ungovernable, as those which lead to so much evil in our sex. Vicious writers, brutal and ignorant men, and some shameless women combine to favor and extend this opinion.*
>
> *Nothing is more utterly untrue. Only in very rare instances do women experience one tithe of the sexual feeling which is familiar to most men. Many of them are entirely frigid, and not even in marriage do they ever perceive any real desire.*

Well, she thought, slamming the book closed and making noises that reminded her of Spencer, she must be a shameless hussy. A wanton woman. She yanked open Spencer's drawer with so much force it nearly toppled out of the dresser, and then shoved the book back under his clothes in exactly the same place that he had left it. If only she could ask Bess whether she was the only decent woman who wished her husband's hands would explore her secret places again.

"Liv?"

She jumped away from the dresser at the sound of Spencer's voice with such speed that she upset the furniture, then hurried to right it and nearly knocked over the lamp.

"You all right?" Spencer asked, rushing to steady the lamp and studying her face. "You look all flushed."

Her hands flew to her cheeks, covered her mouth, hid her eyes.

"What's the matter? The girls upset you again?" He had his hand on her arm and she felt the heat of it through her sleeve. She looked down at it and he pulled it away as if he was the one being burned by their contact instead of her.

She bent to close the drawer then straightened, smoothing

her skirts as if that would somehow restore her dignity. It did not.

He was studying her, waiting for an answer. She had trouble remembering the question with him standing so near. "Louisa shut you out of bedtime again? That what's got you so rattled?"

"Yes. That is . . . no. You just startled me, is all." She studied the screen behind which she changed, the window, with its curtain hiding the moon. Anything but the bottom drawer of the dresser that contained Remy's book, or her husband's eyes, which were still fixed on her.

"You're sure you're okay?"

She had been reading a book about, well, the S word. Worse than that, she'd been thinking about, well, *that*.

"I'm fine," she insisted.

"What were you doing in here by yourself?" He looked around the room like some Pinkerton looking for evidence. His eyes studied the dresser. "Liv?"

"Laundry," she said, probably too quickly. "Putting away some laundry."

"At this time of night? I didn't see anything on the line today."

"Darning. Did I say laundry? I meant darning," she said. *Or simply darn.* "Neil settled down for the night?"

Now it was Spencer's turn to look uncomfortable. "Boy's sleeping on the sofa, if it's all right with you."

All right? He knew she wanted all the children under her roof where she could rest easier knowing they were safe. He'd been the one who had insisted Neil stay in the barn.

"Dumb cow ate something that disagreed with her. Whole barn smells like . . . well, smells like a dumb cow ate something that disagreed with her!"

Livvy nodded but didn't say a word. Clearly Spencer, his fathering ability shining like the Eagle Bluff Lighthouse beacon to lost children, was making more progress with Neil than she was with the girls, despite the fact that she was trying so hard and Spencer was fighting any relationship with all his might.

"And could you take him in to Zephin's tomorrow and order him a pair of kip boots? Boy can't be much help with his feet stuck in the mire every other step."

"No, I suppose he can't," she said, trying to keep the smile from her face. She liked Neil, liked the way he looked at Spencer as if the man had the sun and the moon on the end of a harness.

"He doesn't know a cock from a hen, but I gotta say he's trying."

She positioned herself in front of the mirror where she could unfasten her hair and still watch Spencer's face at the same time. "No one's got your head under the oxen's hoof, Spence. You don't have to say anything nice about the boy."

"You gonna get ready for bed now?" he asked her, shifting his weight to get a clearer view of her face. At least she thought it was her face, but his eyes could surely be roving lower than that.

"Thought I'd just put on my nightclothes before I checked on the children one last time." She took a brush to her hair and watched his eyes follow it hungrily as it smoothed her curls.

"Who was it decided that women ought to put their hair up in those tight little buns?" he asked.

"You want to brush it?" she asked, extending the brush toward Spencer. He backed away as if she were the serpent and her hairbrush the apple of knowledge. He was nearly against the door before he spoke.

"I think I'll check on the children, Olivia. You go on and get into bed."

So he was anxious, too. Relief flooded her.

"Don't expect much from Louisa. Just make sure the lamps are out and Josie has enough blankets. She kicks them off if you don't tuck them in."

"All right," he said, still watching her bedtime preparations, the hair over her shoulder, which she decided at that moment to leave unbraided.

"And take my pillow and give it to Neil. I don't expect that couch is all that comfortable after all these years." Her hair was fully brushed and untangled, but while she had her husband mesmerized, she wouldn't stop.

"I'll be a while," he said finally, turning away from her and putting a hand on the latch. "Don't wait up."

"I'm not that tired," she said. "If you want to . . . talk."

His head came slowly over his shoulder as if he didn't really want to take another look at her but couldn't help himself. She opened the shirt button at her neck and then the one just under it.

"I'm real tired, Liv," he said. She opened a third button and he groaned. "Tireder than you know."

Since the night she had admitted enjoying their time together he had avoided her like a thornbush in bloom, but tonight he was losing the battle with whatever it was that was keeping him away. She slipped behind the screen and eased one arm out of her sleeve. She put the naked arm on the edge of the screen for balance, then dipped her head around the blind to look at her husband.

His suspenders were hanging limply at his hips. The collar to his workshirt lay open, the top two buttons undone. Maybe if he wasn't so swooning handsome, she thought. Maybe if the curls of hair on his chest didn't catch the light and glisten. Maybe if there wasn't a sadness that clouded his face and begged for her to kiss it away. Maybe then her chest wouldn't tighten at the very sight of him and she wouldn't want to lay beneath him again.

And maybe pigs were growing wings and flying south for the winter, Livvy girl.

She licked her lips and tried to think of just the right

words to say, words that would let him know that she wanted him just the way he wanted her. Words that would convince him that he should hurry back to her arms.

His hand was on the latch, but his eyes were on her naked shoulder. "Go to sleep, Liv," he said with a heavy sigh as he reached for a pillow from their bed. "I want to talk to Louisa anyway."

He was flat out telling her he wasn't interested. Blinking back tears, she slid behind the screen, ashamed and embarrassed for flaunting herself in front of him.

"Good night, then," he said huskily, clearing his throat after pushing out the words.

"Mm," she agreed, finding the same trouble forcing any words past the lump in her throat.

He shut the door behind him and leaned against it, his heart beating so strongly he was afraid she would hear it knocking right through the wood. Even with his eyes closed he could see her bare shoulder, chestnut hair teasing it, the lamp-light dancing on it, and he ached to run a finger against its softness. But one finger would never be enough, and her shoulder would only be the beginning of things he had sworn would never happen again.

"Aunt Liv asleep?" the boy asked from his makeshift bed on the sofa, startling Spencer and yanking him back from a precipice that threatened to send him to his ruin.

"Yeah, boy, she's going to bed. Didn't I work you hard enough for you to be driving your pigs to market?"

"Yes, sir," he said, obviously unsure what the expression meant, but willing to oblige with the answer he thought Spencer wanted to hear.

"Snoring, boy," Spencer explained. "What's the matter? Can't sleep?" He didn't know about the boy, but he knew that despite the hard day in the field it would be a long time before he himself found any rest. He wasn't even in the same room as Livvy, couldn't even see her silky hair or smell her lilac scent, and his blood was simmering and on the way to a quick boil. He looked around for something to do. "It's hot in here. You want me to open a window?"

The boy shook his head. "I was just wondering," he said softly, picking at his blanket, "how'd you know that it was gonna rain this morning? I mean, last night when you made me get the windows all shut and take the lid off the rain barrel . . . how'd you know by this morning it would be raining pitchforks?"

"You notice the sunset last night?"

Neil shook his head.

"Me neither, so it wasn't too remarkable then, was it? You notice any stars last night?"

Neil shook his head again. The boy's hair was getting long. It moved softly about his face, making him look younger than he was. Making him look maybe seven or eight.

"How about the moon? You notice a ring around it? All kind of hazy?"

Neil scratched at his head and shrugged. "Maybe," he allowed.

"Farmers have to notice these things. They're all telling signs. It's like Mother Nature has her own way of writing things, and a farmer has to learn how to read the messages she leaves on the sky and the water and the wind." Of course, it hadn't hurt that stupid old Curly George was swatting at imaginary flies and twitching his skin like it itched something awful, a sure sign of a storm.

"Is there anything you don't know about farming?" Neil asked, his eyes full of so much admiration it made Spencer uncomfortable.

"Don't know how a boy your size manages to do all his work and still have energy at the end of the day to badger me with questions. You sure you did all I told you, boy?"

"Yes, sir," Neil said, his voice quivering slightly. "I didn't mean to bother you."

"You and Ju . . . your pa—you get along all right?" he asked.

"Same as most, I guess."

"And the girls? They get along okay with your pa?"

Once again Neil was picking at the comforter that surrounded him. He shrugged. "Guess I'm tireder than I thought," he said, making a big show of yawning and covering his mouth. "Each day feels like two since I got here. One for school and one for farming."

"It's not an easy life," Spencer agreed. "But no life is these days."

"No, sir," Neil agreed, sliding down under the covers and laying his head on the pillow.

"You ever disagree with anything, boy?"

"Not anymore," he said, his big eyes staring into Spencer's.

"I see," Spencer said. So that was how it was. "Maybe someday you'll tell me what he hit you with."

The boy's eyes snapped shut and his breathing became heavy.

"Oh," Spencer said, playing along. "Well, I see you've fallen asleep." He walked over and stood above the couch looking down at the boy whose cheeks still held the pudginess of childhood, whose hair still curled around his face like a halo, and reached his hand out to smooth away the worries that drew his brows together. Inches before he came in contact with the soft skin that marked the boy's youth, he stopped.

In a few minutes, sleep would take the boy and release his cares. His head would sweat and his body would emit that warm, faintly sweet smell that Peter's always had.

Best if tomorrow Neil went back to sleeping in the barn. Jeez. His wife in their bedroom, this boy on their couch—how much was he going to be asked to bear on top of what he had already borne?

Dread slowing his steps, he dragged himself to the girls' bedroom to turn off the lamp that still glowed from under their door. He knocked softly.

"Good night, Olivia." The words were crisp, dismissive.

"It's not your *Aunt* Olivia," Spencer said. "It's Spencer, and I'm coming in."

Chapter Seven

Josie was asleep, looking uncharacteristically angelic with her long eyelashes brushing her round cheeks and a chubby fist just inches from her bow mouth. One leg was thrown over the covers, and Spencer fought the memories that assailed him as he gently eased the little girl's bare limb under the quilt and bent to tuck the blanket tightly between the mattress and the bed frame.

She shifted in her sleep, acclimating to the new position, and made little sucking noises with her mouth that drained his heart dry until she found her thumb and quieted.

"Now," he said as he stretched to his full height and faced Louisa. "You."

Louisa clutched the neckline of her nightdress tightly together, the wide dark eyes she shared with her mother and her aunt watching his every move, and shivered.

"You cold?"

She shook her head silently.

"You could use a little more meat on your bones," he said, assessing how lost she looked amid the covers. "You might try eating your aunt's cooking, setting a good example for your sister there."

"I don't like her cooking," Louisa said, raising her chin defiantly.

"Well, I've tasted better," Spencer agreed. "But I've tasted worse, too. Your mama's venison was about the worst thing I ever ate with a fork."

Louisa looked skeptical. "You ate my mama's cooking?"

"Not enough to kill me, but darn close," he answered with a quiet laugh. Marion had tested more than one recipe on him and Remy. They both felt lucky they'd lived to tell about it.

"My mother was an excellent cook."

Spencer raised his eyebrows dubiously. They'd both eaten Marion's food. Did Louisa really think it was more than a step above palatable? "Guess you think your mama was near perfect," he said, dropping the subject of Marion's cooking.

"I don't just think it," Louisa said.

"She sew good, too? 'Cause I noticed a pile of calico in the corner of our bedroom that wasn't there a couple weeks ago. Figured it's earmarked for you and your sister."

"She wants to dress me like a little farm girl."

"She? Oh, you mean your Aunt Livvy. Well, you gotta admit that your dresses are a little fancy for feeding the chickens and raking the coop."

He sat down at the edge of his niece's bed. He was too damn tired to beat around the bush with the child, but her frightened eyes and the jerking of her legs away from his body caught him off guard.

"Hey, I'm not gonna bite you. I've been on my feet all day and I'm tired."

"Then go back to your room," Louisa said, more a plea than a suggestion.

He nodded. There was nothing he'd rather do, but some things just needed saying, and he was the one elected to say them.

"You're giving your aunt a real hard time of it, Miss Louisa. An uncalled-for hard time. I've never seen a woman work so hard to please someone with so little in return. Cooking, sewing, offering to help you with your homework, and you turning her down every chance you get."

"I don't need a woman to take care of me. I can take care

of myself and of Josie and Neil, too. I have since Mama died and I can keep doing it now.''

"So you think she's mothering you too much? Is that it?''

"She always there, being so nice, trying to make us like her, cooking special pies for us, kissing us good night, buying us things, trying to pretend she's our mama . . .''

"So she's too nice. Is that it?''

The girl traced the little log-cabin patterns on the patchwork quilt with her finger, silent, as if she were deciding how much to confide. "Neil likes her," she finally said. "He probably wishes she was our real mama.''

"And you think it's not right, him liking her while your mama's dead and buried, huh?''

"It's like he doesn't even remember Mama.'' She looked over at her baby sister, sleeping peacefully a few feet away. "And she doesn't remember her. She never even knew her. There's only me.''

"And your pa.''

She snorted and he decided to leave Julian out of it.

"So I guess if you were to like Olivia, even just a little, it would take something away from your mama's memory, the way you see it. Is that so?''

She kept her eyes on the quilt and continued to run her fingers over all the cozy little houses, following the smoke lines out of the chimneys without answering him.

"And you think that somehow you'd be being disloyal to your mama if you enjoyed someone else's cooking, or let someone give you a kiss on the forehead before you went off to dreamland, huh?''

"I loved my mama. For me, anyway, everything was perfect until she died.'' She sniffed and he pulled out his hanky and handed it to her. "And I'll never love anyone else like I loved her.''

"Of course not,'' he said. "But I don't see how letting Livvy love you is going to take away one ounce of the feeling you have for your mama." He pointed toward her chest. "You only got room enough in there to love one person?"

"In that way," she said, finally raising her eyes to her uncle's.

"Then find another way," he said, tiredness getting the best of his patience. "Find some damn other way to love her. Love her 'cause she's strong and kind, and she doesn't give up. Love her 'cause you're not going to find too many other people in the world who care so much about your being happy."

"I thought you'd understand," Louisa said. "But you're just like any grown-up. You think that it's all right for *you* to want to keep your precious memories, but I can't have mine. You won't even let us go up that loft, never mind sleep in those stupid beds, so that my brother has to sleep on the sofa or in the barn when there's a perfectly good—"

"I thought it was a *stupid* bed," he corrected.

"It is. And everything else in this house is, too. And you just think it's so great because your children lived here." She narrowed her eyes and added sharply, pointing toward his chest, "You only have room to love those children in there?"

At first he didn't answer. He simply rose and walked to the door on legs hobbled from being on his niece's low bed. Once there he looked over his shoulder and stared at the face that was crumbling on the pillow and dissolving into tears. "That's what's the matter with children," he told her. "They think they know stuff they don't have any idea about. Your situation and mine don't have anything in common. But I'll tell you this—I thank the Lord that Olivia came into my life, and when Sunday comes I'll expect you to do the same."

With that he lifted the children's lamp and took it with him out of their room. He had been right to oppose these children coming to live with him. He stood in the parlor and heard Neil's soft breathing. They were everywhere.

And if three small children weren't enough, from beneath his bedroom door a soft light still glowed. *Damn,* he thought, and grabbed his jacket before heading out onto the porch to wait for Olivia to fall asleep.

She heard the front door open and close and paused in the letter she was composing to Julian. Well, he'd told her not to wait up, hadn't he? But if he was so all-fired tired, what was he doing going out at this hour?

She put down the pen and tried to see out the window. A light from the porch cast shadows on the ground. She reached for a shawl and eased her feet into her slippers, determined, at least, to speak to her husband before she went to bed.

She passed Neil's sleeping form on the couch and opened the door as quietly as she could. On the porch sat her husband, his head in his hands, his shoulders rising and falling unevenly. Sobs rode the wind back to her and she realized with a start that he was crying. Crying openly on their porch on a cool spring evening as if he were all alone in the world without a soul whose heart would gladly halve his sorrow— no, would take all that sorrow to see a genuine smile on his face again.

She sank back through the doorway into the house and closed the door soundlessly. One thing her marriage to Spencer had taught her, and taught her well. Things could be shared only when they were given, not taken. She couldn't take his sorrows, but should he want to share them, she was still there, still willing. She supposed she'd always be.

Back in the bedroom, her letter to Julian in San Francisco waited. What did a father want to hear about his children? Surely not that they were miserable, or that they were doing their best to make her as unhappy as they were. She started with Neil, knowing that it would be easiest to praise him for his helpful ways if not his real usefulness, which was doubtful.

Neil has learned so much about farming in the short time he has been helping Spencer that I fear before we know it he'll be running the farm himself. He shows an interest in all the machinery and a special fondness for the various livestock. In just the past week he has helped plow and ready the earth, cleaned the barn and slopped the pigs.

There wasn't one of those jobs that Spencer hadn't had to redo after Neil had done them, but a father ought to be able to take pride in a son, and Olivia had seen sorry little evidence of pride when Julian had been with them.

Josephina and I are beginning to warm to each other after the rocky start we got off to. She shows an avid interest in everything and fills my days with the wonderment of children.

The avid interest in everything was surely not an over-statement. Josie had emptied every drawer in the kitchen, spilled out every canister of staples, burned two fingers on the stove . . .

She learns very quickly and retains the knowledge well.

But, Livvy wanted to add, she tries first and asks questions later, when her tears have subsided. Three times she fell off the ladder to the loft over the kitchen, but each time she had managed to get one rung farther up the steps.

She is persistent, too.

And Spencer had better fix the railing that he kicked out all those years ago or remove the ladder before Josie got herself to the top.

Louisa, Olivia continued,

> *is quite the little mother, as I believe you once called her. She takes such good care of Josie that I almost hate to push her out the door for school in the mornings.*

Of course, Louisa hated it far more than Olivia, but was that something Julian really needed to know?

> *Though it would be hard to imagine her even more help-ful, I am thinking of letting Louisa try her hand in the kitchen.*

Maybe then she'll eat something. Lord knows I can't get her to eat what I cook, and if she gets any skinnier we won't see her sideways.

> *There's talk of a railroad spur possibly coming to Maple Stand, though I can't see why anyone has an interest in coming to a town whose only new industry in the last ten years has been a cider press. But the railroad runs both ways, and I suppose it'll aid the young folks in hightailing it to the big city the way you and Marion did.*
>
> *Well, seeing as I've got my hands full with children I guess I'd better close this letter and get back to work. It surely is a busy household now.*

She lifted her pen. The house was so quiet she could hear the coal shifting and sinking in the stove in the parlor. Was it never going to warm up?

Spencer coughed somewhere, reassuring her that at least he hadn't up and gone drinking or out on the town.

> *Don't worry about your children. Spencer and I are look-ing after them as if they were our own.*

And since it was hardly likely that they'd ever have any children of their own, Olivia was determined to enjoy every moment she had with Neil, Josie, and even Louisa.

    Love, Olivia.

She folded the pretty paper, a gift from Bess, and slipped it into the envelope, then left it on the nightstand to remember to take with her to Zephin's. She turned the light way down, then decided that Spencer could find his way in the dark, if indeed he ever decided to come in, and put out the lamp. In the darkness she listened to the sound of her own breathing and wished Spencer was lying beside her, his heavy breathing drowning out her own, just as his sorrows overpowered hers and his life eclipsed the one she had chosen for herself.

He must have come to bed at some point, because when Olivia awoke in the morning he was lying next to her, his head propped up on his hand, watching her sleep.

"You didn't braid your hair" were the first words out of his mouth, and she saw that he was holding a lock of it in his free hand.

She didn't know how to answer him. He had seemed so fascinated by her hair that she had left it loose in the hopes that he would touch it, lose himself in it, and then touch her. That wasn't exactly something she could tell her husband. "Do you mind it loose?" she asked, sweeping it back from her face.

"Mm," he said, dropping the lock and rolling onto his back, his hands locked behind his head. "It gets all over in the night."

"I'm sorry," she said. "I'll remember to braid it from now on."

"That'd be good," he said without enthusiasm.

"I'm taking Neil into town today," she said as she sat up and stretched.

"I'll need the boy," he said, springing from the bed and going to the window to check the day. "I've been waitin' all week for a full day in the field with him. Remy's bringing over his boys and we're gonna try the new hayloader, then we're all going over to Sacotte Farm."

"Can he make do with the shoes he's got?" she asked, hoping not to ruin all of the plans for the day, being the closest thing to a family outing Spencer had experienced in five years, and the first time she'd seen him excited in all that time.

"Julian was a damn fool, bringing him to work on a farm with city-slicker banker shoes. What did he think the boy was going to do here? Play hopscotch on cement? Roll a hoop on concrete?"

"Maybe if we stuffed the toes of my boots?" Livvy offered.

"He's a damn sight smaller than you, Liv. He's a puny runt for a boy his age. Hardly much bigger than Peter was for all the extra years he's had."

Livvy tried to hide her surprise at the reference to Spencer's son. The name, like the loft, was forbidden.

"Can you take him to Zephin's now, first thing?" he asked quickly, as if he were afraid that Livvy might suggest that perhaps Neil could wear Peter's shoes. Did he think she'd really suggest that? After all this time?

"What about the girls? And breakfast? And my chores?" she asked, slipping behind the screen and hurrying to get dressed, her bladder nearly bursting.

"Louisa can make breakfast and take care of Josie. Lord knows she keeps saying she can. Let her prove it. And I'll get the milking done and have Louisa do the rest. That hayloader could cut our work time in half and get Henry off the farm if he's a mind to try his luck elsewhere."

Livvy came out from behind the screen, still working

on the buttons of her shirtwaist. "For heaven's sake, Spence, Henry's just a boy. And the girl is eleven years old. She can't . . ."

Spencer was watching her fingers as they nestled between her breasts trying to get the little pearl buttons through the holes. Why couldn't he look at her like that at night? Why now, with a house full of children, two fields of hay waiting to be raked and loaded, and all her nephews on their way over, along with her brother?

"Livvy, I—"

There was a knock at the door. Spencer padded over in his bare feet and opened the door a crack while Olivia turned away and finished fastening her buttons.

"I'm ready," Neil said. "And I got my arrowheads to trade Philip, too." He proudly held up two arrowheads he had found while helping to turn Livvy's garden.

"Aunt Liv's gonna take you to town and get you some boots, boy. Slap some jam on a slab of bread and you can eat it on the way."

"Yes, sir," Neil said, scooting from the door.

"And don't let Philip take advantage of you none. You be sure you get something worthwhile for those arrowheads," Spencer shouted at the boy's back.

"Yes, sir," Neil said again.

"I'll hook up Curly George," Spencer said, slipping his workpants over his longjohns. "It'll save you the time of walking."

"Are you going to put him and Peaches together in the corral again today?" she asked.

" 'Less you have some objection. George is getting on and it sure would be a shame for him to go out of this world without leaving something of himself in it."

Like it would be for Spencer, Olivia thought sadly. In a world of *if onlys,* that was her most cherished one. If only she could give Spencer a child of his own.

"You don't want me to?" he asked, not knowing what it was that troubled her.

"It's just that Louisa's home today, and never living on a farm, I don't think she'd be too accustomed to seeing spring in the barnyard."

"Well," Spencer said over his shoulder as he hurried for the door. "Glad to see that those kids aren't gonna be any trouble. I gotta hook up George, you gotta run to town and spend good money on shoes that the boy'll outgrow before we've got the field planted, and now *Miss* Louisa's sensibilities are gonna be offended if I let the damn horses behave like horses." He yanked open the front door and shouted back, "And that little one's crying again, Liv. But don't worry because I don't even know they're here, just like you said."

Then the door slammed with enough force to rattle the dishes in the kitchen and set Josie off on a howl that Spencer could no doubt hear all the way in the barn.

And with all the chaos, and all Spencer's yelling and Louisa burning something at the stove, how come, she wondered, all she could think of was Spencer staring at her when she woke up, her hair in his hand?

Chapter Eight

"Boys' boots, Miss Zephin," Livvy said as soon as she and Neil crossed the threshold to Zephin's Mercantile. "As fast as you can find them and fit them. This young man has a field to plant and his city shoes aren't going to do the trick."

"Yes, ma'am," Emma said, her voice unusually chipper. "And what size would that be?"

Livvy stared down at Neil, who seemed younger in the midst of a store full of adults instead of a house full of children, and put a gentle hand on his head, sliding the cap he wore backward until he realized that etiquette demanded he remove it. She leaned down and quietly asked if he knew his shoe size.

"Size two last time we got any," he said, his eyes studying Emma Zephin. "Ma'am," he added, respectfully.

"What a nice young man you have there, Mrs. Williamson," Emma said, bending forward to examine him nearly nose to nose. "Very well mannered."

"He's too young for you, Emma," Charlie Zephin said from behind the counter where he had been kneeling out of sight. "By the time he's ripe for marrying, you'll have one foot in the grave."

"Papa!" Emma said, straightening and making sure her shirtwaist was well tucked into her waistband. She stuck her nose in the air and glared at her father. "Make all the jokes you want, Mr. Zephin. One day soon I'll be leaving here and you'll be in a fine mess without me, you know you will."

"Leaving?" Livvy asked, but Emma just raised her eyebrows at her father and then muttered something about boots starting at size three before disappearing into the back room.

"Leaving?" Livvy repeated to Charlie Zephin. "Is Emma going somewhere?"

"Oh," Charlie said with a heavy sigh and moved closer to Olivia and Neil. "She's got it in her head that Waylon Makeridge fellow is gonna come sweep her off her feet and take her for his wife." He shook his head with a look that at once pronounced the notion foolish and pathetic.

"Someone's gonna marry *her*?" Neil said incredulously, then covered his mouth as if he hadn't meant for the words to be said aloud.

"Not likely son, is it?" Charlie said, ruffling the boy's hair. "Too bad she don't look like your aunt here, or she'd a given me a grandchild or two by now."

"Not necessarily," Olivia said, trying to keep the hurt out of her voice. "And who's this Mr. Makeridge? I don't think I've ever heard that name before."

"Waylon Makeridge is the railroad surveyor," Emma said, emerging from the curtain that separated the storeroom from the main room of the mercantile. She was carrying two boxes and a pair of loose boots, as well, and the smile had most definitely returned to her face at the mention of Mr. Makeridge's name.

"I like trains," Neil said, sitting on a bench and working at the laces to his banker's shoes. "We came on a train from Chicago most of the ways here. Papa mostly played cards and stayed with some dandy, but me and Josie and Louisa went up and down the cars, and there was a man selling muffins and another with drinks. And a whole car that was set up just like a restaurant with fancy linens and all."

"Well, boy, if these here women can conjur up some magic, we just might have a train stop right here in Maple Stand, we might. Now what would you think of that?" Charlie crossed his arms over his stock apron and looked very pleased with himself.

"I thought, Charlie Zephin, that all this railroad talk was just so much stuff and nonsense." Olivia shook her head at him. "You aren't trying to tell me—" she started.

"Well, Mr. Makeridge is coming to Maple Stand to do some surveying," Emma said, then blushed furiously. "I've been having a correspondence with him . . . in that regard, of course."

She had put the boxes of shoes next to Neil and had been untying the laces so that he would be able to try them on. Now one boot hung limply from her hand as she stared off into space.

"Papa will have to fetch him from Milwaukee."

"Milwaukee?" Livvy's ears picked up even as she took the boot from Emma and helped Neil push his foot into it. "You're going all the way to Milwaukee, Mr. Zephin?"

"It's kinda big," Neil said, clomping around the store, one foot still clad in his old shoe and coming down softly, the other smacking and slurping against the wooden floor. "You got anything smaller?"

"Boy's gonna grow," Charlie said, rifling through some boxes behind the counter and coming up with a pair of thick woolen socks. "Try these on and see if, with 'em laced up good, they'll do. Don't want you outgrowing 'em before lunch."

Livvy looked at the big clock on the wall. Lord, this had taken longer than she'd figured already, and she hadn't even started trying to get Mr. Zephin to lower the price any. Spencer would be fuming in the fields by now.

Spencer. His rejection still burned her eyes and closed her throat.

"Boy, she's ugly," Neil whispered when Emma went into the back to see if there were any smaller boots.

Olivia shot him a look that said she wouldn't tolerate such

talk, but she couldn't help wondering if Neil thought the same of her. Was she ugly? Is that why Spencer didn't want her? *So beautiful,* he had said that night. *So beautiful.* And while she knew she certainly wasn't beautiful, not Kirsten-beautiful, or Marion-beautiful, she didn't really believe she was Emma-ugly, either.

"And Waylon, that is, Mr. Makeridge, will be staying here with us when he comes," Emma said as she handed a box to Olivia that contained shoes that looked very small. "And he's looking forward to my cherry pie, he says."

"That's real nice," Olivia said, showing the shoes to Neil and watching him shake his head at even trying them on.

He had put the heavy woolen socks over his own and was trying on the second pair of boots, ones that looked a lot like the type Spencer wore, while keeping one eye on the grown-ups.

"Would you be willing to take a couple of passengers with you to Milwaukee, Mr. Zephin?" she asked. "Maybe Mrs. Sacotte and I could go along, if Mr. Williamson and Remy don't mind. Bess hasn't been all that well and I'd sure like her to see a good doctor. That is, if you're planning on only staying one night. It's not easy for either of us to get away for too long."

"Why, Mrs. Williamson, I'd be happy for the company. Even considered closing down the store and letting Emma come with me, but this is so much better." He bowed slightly at the waist. "I'd be delighted if you'd do me the honor. And looks like he found the boots he wants."

Neil stood in the heavy boots like a proud peacock, his chin raised, his hands on his hips. "These are the ones, Aunt Liv. They fit me great."

"You're sure?" she asked, never having bought shoes for a child and having no way of knowing whether they were half a dozen sizes too small or too large, only knowing that Neil wanted them because they looked just like Spencer's.

"They'll be fine," Charlie said, bending over and feeling through the shoe for Neil's toe. "Enough room to grow but not so much that he'll leave 'em in a pile of muck. And they're a bargain, too. Only a dollar and eighty cents. Less than the catalog, like always."

"A dollar eighty," Olivia said, checking the clock again. She wished Philip were here to close a deal for her, as she wasn't very good at bargaining even when she had all the time in the world. She was too honest to make a good haggler, so she said what was on her mind. "Mr. Williamson's gonna ask if I paid your first price, Mr. Zephin, and you know how I feel about lying."

Mr. Zephin laughed. "I suppose I could take off another nickel and make it one seventy-five."

"Olivia, your pie won that blue ribbon last year didn't it?" Emma asked, absentmindedly packing up the shoes that Neil had tried and rejected. "The cherry one, didn't it?"

"Well, it was a good year for cherries at Sacotte Farm," Livvy said. "The fruit really should have gotten the ribbon."

"Aunt Liv is a real good cook," Neil said. "Even Uncle Spencer says so."

"About the recipe for that pie, Olivia," she said, looking plaintively at Livvy.

"About the price of the shoes, Mr. Zephin," Livvy said in turn.

"About the ride to Milwaukee, Mrs. Williamson," Charlie said and the three all waited for a moment while no one threw another favor into the pot.

"Can't go lower," Charlie finally said. "But I could throw in an extra set of laces and some polish."

"I'll copy down that recipe tonight," Livvy said to Emma. "And I hope it beats the Dutch out of Mr. Makeridge."

"She'll need real good cherries," Charlie said, sensing an

opportunity. "You could bring 'em when you come for your ride to Milwaukee."

Livvy laughed and nodded her agreement. "If it turns out that we can go, then with pleasure, Mr. Zephin."

"Pleasure's all mine, Mrs. Williamson."

"Could I wear them home?" Neil asked.

"I don't know," Livvy said, looking skeptically at the enormous boots on her spindly nephew's feet and then throwing one last glance at the clock. "Can you run in them?"

"Course I can," Neil said, his chest puffed out like a peacock before he tripped on the way out the door.

"Well," Livvy said with a shrug. "At least we've got Curly George to carry us the rest of the way!"

Spencer and his nephews had tried out the hayloader and had a row and a half of corn turned and planted by the time he saw Olivia and Neil in the wagon coming down the dirt path from town. He didn't know what he'd been thinking, sending his wife to get the boy shoes. Lord knew what he'd wound up with, for Livvy was so soft-hearted she'd get the child whatever he asked for. And Neil, while he was quick to catch on, came as natural to farming as a chicken came to puckering up and whistling.

She steered the wagon to within a few yards of the barn and then stopped, said something to Neil, and fixed the brake. The boy jumped down and headed for Spencer, kicking dirt on the way with what looked to be good sturdy work boots.

"Aunt Liv wants to know where you want Curly George," he said when he was within shouting distance of his uncle.

"Hey, Neil," Henry said at his cousin's approach. "You owe us four rows of work."

"It'll go faster now that I'm here," Neil said, and Spencer stifled a laugh. If there was a way for Neil to foul up the work and make it take twice as long, quite unintentionally, the boy would find it.

"I'll just go unhitch George," Spencer said to the boys and sauntered toward the wagon.

Olivia was making her way down from the buckboard, one foot searching for the hub of the wheel, her fanny sticking out roundly behind her. He stood behind her, paralyzed. He didn't dare reach for her waist, knowing he couldn't help but skim her bottom on his way toward that slim waist that he thought his hands could probably span. How was it he still didn't know that after they'd been married so long?

Because he'd kept his damn hands to himself, and that was surely what he ought to be doing right now, instead of lifting her skirt enough to find her ankle and guide it onto the wheel hub. Because the little voice in his head warned him that taking her into his arms was just one step away from taking her into his heart.

"Oh!" she said, nearly losing her balance when she felt his hand on her ankle. Her foot missed the hub and continued down, her leg running through his hand until it tightened just under her knee. How could a leg be so soft, so smooth? If he let go now, she'd fall. If he held on much longer, he'd never let go. With his free hand he scooped her up and deposited her firmly beside the wagon.

Recovering her balance and catching her hat as it tumbled from her head, she stared at him as if he'd lost his mind. Much more of this and he was sure he would. Kids everywhere, his wife in wet shirtwaists, her cheeks always flushed . . .

George stomped and snorted, rattling his harness as if he were in a hurry to either go somewhere or be unhitched. Unhitched. He and Curly George had too damn many desires in common.

"I didn't know if you wanted the horse in the barn or the corral," Olivia said, squinting at him in the sunshine and looking like she'd been set aglow.

"The horse is here to work," he said. "Put on this earth to work, just like me." What on earth was he talking about? Couldn't he simply say *I need him in the field?* All this chaos had rendered him incapable of talking sense.

"Oh, of course," she said, appearing slightly embarrassed. "You're using Peaches for plowing, anyway. I don't know what I was thinking."

If she'd been a man he'd have guessed she was thinking about the horses mating. She'd have been thinking about Spring and a young man's fancy or whatever it was that poet had said. She'd have been thinking about the smell of a woman and what it did to a man's brain even in the middle of a sunny morning in May when there was planting and plowing to be done and a field full of children waiting on him.

"I guess I'd better check on the girls," she said, so shyly he could swear she had been reading his thoughts. For a minute he wished he could read hers, but then he knew he did every time he looked into her face. And it was a book he didn't want to read again. Never again.

Neil wished there was a mirror where he could watch his aunt as she cut his hair. It wasn't that he was stuck up or anything, but she seemed so distracted that he was afraid he might wind up bald for the Petition to the Blessed Virgin. And he could see that her eyes weren't on his hair but on the white dress she had bought for Josie at Zephin's.

"Watch what you're doing," his uncle said, sitting on the sofa and reading a newspaper as if there weren't a houseful of chaos around him.

"Oh, Spencer," his aunt said, her voice all dreamy. "Did you see the little veil for her? Won't she look just like an angel?"

His uncle made some kind of noise that was more a choke than a laugh and took off his glasses to wipe his eyes. "She won't fool the Lord," he said. "Under all that white stuff will be the same black-hearted little beggar who nearly broke your nose and keeps sharpening her teeth on my ankles."

"He doesn't mean that," Aunt Olivia said under her breath so that only Neil could hear. He wasn't so sure. Neither of his sisters was doing anything to endear themselves to their relatives.

For his part, Neil was doing everything he could. He worked in the fields until he was ready to drop, ate whatever was put on his plate, remembered to remove his hat indoors, and went to bed whenever he was told.

"Done," Aunt Olivia said, stepping back to look at him. "And a handsomer boy there won't be in the procession. Now go put on that little suit I pressed for you and tell Josie I'm ready for her."

"I doubt that," Uncle Spencer said.

Aunt Olivia laughed, a girlish laugh that surprised and pleased Neil, and bent to clean up the hair clippings on the floor.

"Are you going to cut Uncle Spencer's hair, too?" he asked. Uncle Spencer looked like he was ready to put in a good day in the fields instead of attending the most important religious festivities of the year. He'd skipped services on Sunday, same as he had each Sunday they'd been there, but his aunt had made it clear that while missing Sunday service might be acceptable, the Procession was something else entirely.

Aunt Liv looked at Uncle Spencer over her shoulder and tilted her head. "You could use a trim, Spence. We should have thought of it last week so you could have had it cut in town. You want me to just neaten it up some?"

Uncle Spencer shook his head. It got really quiet in the room, and Neil had the sense that something was going on between his aunt and uncle although neither one was saying anything.

Finally his aunt broke the silence. It seemed to Neil that

she was always the one to give in. "Spencer, a farmer of all people has to petition the Virgin for a blessing of abundant crops. A farmer has to give thanks. He has to——"

"Not this farmer, Livvy. This farmer's got fields waiting for him. I gave the Lord Sunday by not working. I'll be damned if I'll give him Monday, too."

"Isn't it more likely you'll be damned if you don't?" she asked him, and her lip twitched as if she might cry, right there in front of him.

His uncle snorted, something Neil was learning he did quite often. It meant that he found something funny that no one else did.

Most especially not his aunt, who went over to the couch where Uncle Spencer was sitting and knelt beside the stuffed and rounded arm. "Please, Spence. I've waited my whole life for this day. I remember so clearly the first time my mother dressed me all in white and placed that veil on my head and those flowers in my hand. . . . I remember Father Martin smiling at me in his special robes with the monstrance held up high. . . . Please, Spence. Don't do this."

Had she asked Neil to raise a barn in that voice, he'd have found a way to do it. But his uncle seemed unmoved and just shook his head at her like a disappointed teacher whose pupil still didn't understand something he had explained a thousand times.

"I'm not stopping you," he said, and for a moment Neil thought his uncle was going to cup his aunt's chin just the way a mother did to a child, but then the hand stopped in midair and the gesture turned into a shrug. "You take them, Livvy. I can manage without the boy for the day. He'd be in school, anyway, if it wasn't for the Rogation."

"Yes, but . . ." she began, almost like she was begging his uncle. Neil wished she would stand up, but she didn't. She just stayed there on her knees and touched Uncle Spencer lightly on the arm. "I wanted it to be all of us, a family, Spencer. You know how I've wanted that."

This time his uncle did cup his aunt's chin, and Neil could see the regret on his uncle's face. "I know," he said, then repeated himself. "I know. But I can't go. You're not the only one with memories. My family's gone, Liv. No one knows that better than you. That you could even ask me . . . Margaret's dress is still up in that little cupboard, all white and ready. I . . ."

His aunt rose and nodded. Her bottom lip, which Neil liked because it was so full and soft-looking, not a hard thin line like his father's, was quivering.

"You've got to get dressed, honey," she said when she looked his way and saw that he hadn't made a move toward his freshly pressed Sunday suit. Another lady would probably have been mad at him for standing there and watching her, but it didn't surprise Neil that she wasn't angry with him. She never got angry. She wasn't even mad at his uncle for ruining her day.

"I'm going to stay with Uncle Spencer," he said with more conviction than he felt. Maybe if he said he wouldn't go unless his uncle did, then his uncle might give in and go, as well. "You just take the girls."

"Get dressed, boy," his uncle said in that voice he used that brooked no argument.

"But you're not going," Neil tried. "I'll go if you do." He was thinking maybe his aunt would ask his uncle to set a good example. After all, if his uncle wasn't going, why should he?

"You don't want to make your aunt late. She's been waiting for this day for a long time."

"Will you go?"

His uncle didn't even bother answering him.

Now Neil really didn't even want to go himself. His aunt would think he was just going because he was being forced to, instead of because he wanted so much to see the smile return to her pretty face. She'd have to be annoyed with him, and all because of his uncle.

"I don't want to go if you don't," Neil argued. "Why can't I just stay here with you?"

His uncle rose to his full height, so that Neil came only to his chest. Muscles from hard work strained his shirt. Even leaning back, Neil couldn't make out the expression on his uncle's face. "Because you'll disappoint your aunt," he said simply. "You don't want to do that, do you?"

Aunt Livvy stood by the kitchen table, a brush in her hand, trying to convince Josie's curls to accept the veil she was attaching to her hair. But her eyes were on Uncle Spencer and Neil.

"What about you?" Neil asked. "Aren't you disappointing her?"

His uncle nodded and scratched at his chin as if he thought he needed a shave. "I do it all the time," he said quietly. He crossed the room, only the sound of his heavy boots echoing around them. "Don't I?" he asked, but opened the door and left before Aunt Livvy could answer him.

Chapter Nine

He'd had two weeks to get used to the idea, and now Spencer thought that maybe Olivia's plan to go to Milwaukee wasn't all that crazy, after all. Sure, it would mean some extra work for him and Remy, but two grown men ought to be able to take care of two farms for one night, especially with the help of Louisa, who would be only too happy to prove herself an adult. Really, what was it Livvy did besides cook, which she promised to do in advance, clean, which she said could wait, milk the cows and feed the livestock, which Neil offered to take care of, and look after the children, who insisted they could look after themselves and each other?

So fine. Let her go. He could use a little break from her constant chatter and fussing over him. He could use some time to stretch out to full size in his own bed without risking bumping into her. It would be a relief to go to sleep without that expectant face staring at him, a pleasure to wake up without that damn smile greeting him and wishing him a good morning. Hey, she could go a lot farther than Milwaukee and it would be just fine with him.

He had to admit, though, that he was relieved that she wouldn't be there alone. Not that she needed Bess to look after her, but she wasn't exactly wise to city ways and some unscrupulous man, taken with her fresh farm looks, might have ideas she didn't even understand. Who knew the trouble she could get into in a city the size of Milwaukee, a girl as pretty as she was?

Not that he found her pretty, but surely there were those that would. After all, she did have a very womanly figure without an extra ounce on her. Standing next to Bess, as she would be, she'd look even more attractive. And that hair. Of course, when it was bunned there was no telling how long or how silky it really was.

Not that it mattered, anyway. Let her have her fun. He'd even give her a little spending money in case she saw something extra special that couldn't be had in Maple Stand. That shouldn't be too hard.

"Spencer? You almost done?" Livvy shouted from the porch. A dog barked and he wondered if he owned one of those now, too.

"No, I'm not done," he shouted back. *I'm not done 'cause I've been standing here thinking when I should have been digging.* "Ground's harder than I expected," he lied.

"Really?" she said, sashaying toward him with a furrowed brow. "But it's been raining for three days, on and off. I was hoping to get those berries in before I left for Milwaukee."

"You're not going for long, Olivia. A day or two won't make a difference."

"No," she said, and sighed as if he had said something profound. "I suppose it won't make any difference at all."

"Got another hour or so's work," he said, pushing the pitchfork into the soft earth and turning it with greater effort than it required.

"You want me to bring you out something to drink?" she offered. Josie came wandering up behind her and she lifted the child to her hip and ruffled her hair. "You done feeding the chickens?" she asked the child, who sat happily enough playing with the locks of hair that had escaped his wife's bun and were teasing her neck.

When had that happened? He thought Josie hated Liv, but there they stood, blowing at each other's hair and laughing.

"I suppose there'll be seed all over the barn," he said, picturing the mess one three-year-old could make.

Josie shook her head solemnly. "One at a time," she said with great seriousness.

"Huh?"

"I gave her a little cupful and told her to give them just one seed at a time to make it last longer. Is that what you did?" she asked the child, who nodded and wiggled to get down.

"You don't think she really gave them one at a time, do you?" he asked, amazed she hadn't learned anything from having the tireless little girl around.

"Spencer," she said, "it wouldn't be the first time there was seed in the barn. If those chicks haven't finished off whatever she spilled, I'll clean it myself. One seed at a time."

"Humph!" seemed to be the only appropriate response, and so that was what he said to her retreating back as she went after Josie, the skip in her step making her look a lot younger than her twenty-eight years.

"Oh," she shouted over her shoulder as she picked up her pace to catch up to the running little girl. "Remy's coming over before the meeting. Said he needs to talk to you."

"What meeting?" he shouted back, but she was already inside the barn, and if she heard him she didn't stick her head back out to answer.

"Jeez," he muttered to himself, and buried the pitchfork several inches into the muddy soil. He had better things to do than turn the soil in a garden patch. He stalked out to the field to check on the damage from all the rain.

Neil always wanted to please his Aunt Liv. Let him get the soil turned.

Giggles pealed from the barn and floated on the wind up to where he knelt by the seedlings. From the look of things, Josie was pretending to be a chicken and Olivia was a fox trying to catch her. He watched his wife, a woman whose dignity was unassailable, crawl after the little girl on all fours, her apron tied around her soft fanny so that it acted as a tail.

Josie squealed when she was caught and scooped up in his wife's arms. For a moment his breath caught as the little girl's hand flew out, but instead of smacking Livvy's nose, she wound the arm around Livvy's neck and appeared to kiss her.

Spencer stretched to his full height, but the two disappeared behind the barn door. It was hard to believe that his wife had nothing better to do than fritter away the day playing children's games. He certainly had better things to do than watch them, anyway.

The ground was wet, not merely damp, and without some good strong sunshine, mildew would get his whole crop. When was he going to give in and plant cherry and apple trees like at Sacotte Farm? He didn't know how many times he had considered the idea and then discarded it, knowing he didn't have the time to wait for trees to come to maturity before producing crops big enough to support his mortgage.

Fool that he was, he'd borrowed the money to furnish the house just the way Kirsten had wanted it. And he was still paying for chairs she'd never sit in again. All the things she'd wanted just so, and she'd hardly had the chance to enjoy them. Was Livvy enjoying them? he wondered. He wasn't sure she even noticed them at all.

Peaches whinnied, that peculiar whinny she always made as she came out into the fresh air, and, surprised that she was out of the barn, Spencer looked up. Livvy had the mare lead on her and upon her bare back sat Josie, her hands buried in the horse's mane, shrieking at Peaches to "go."

He swallowed hard, but the lump in his throat refused to go away. Josie looked nothing like Margaret, whose blond curly cap had glowed nearly white in the sunshine and who'd sat frozen with fear on Curly George's big rump. This little one was full of life and guts and if anyone was terrorized, it was Peaches, who tried to keep the child balanced on her back as if she were well aware of her precious cargo.

So if she looked nothing like his daughter, why was it that Margaret falling from Curly George's rump was all that he could see as he came tearing down from the rise at the three-some making its way slowly around the corral. Memories. The bane of his existence.

Without a word, for he knew if he stopped gritting his teeth out would come things that should never be said, he yanked the child off the horse and thrust her at Olivia. Then he smacked Peaches's rump so hard the horse galloped to the far end of the confines of the pen and turned to stare at him.

That made three sets of wide eyes that all seemed stunned by his actions, as if a man had never taken a child off a horse before.

"She's in heat, dammit," he said as if that explained everything.

"Are you, too?" Olivia asked him pointedly.

Now who was crazy? he wondered, taken aback by Olivia's sudden sassiness.

"You're acting very oddly," she said as if that somehow explained her remark. "Even for you."

His niece clung to his wife's leg, more afraid of him than she was of the horse. He took two steps backward, trying to ease the little girl's fear and at the same time move out of the path of the warm breeze that carried Livvy's lilac scent past his nostrils and into a brain that no longer seemed able to function within his head.

They stood staring at him as if they were waiting for him to do something, and he supposed they would have continued to watch him for signs of dementia for the rest of the hot and dusty afternoon if the clomping of horses' hooves and the accompanying rattling of tackle hadn't announced the arrival of his brother-in-law.

"There's Remy," he said. "We've got more important things to talk about."

He stalked off toward the oncoming wagon with more purpose than he felt. He couldn't even remember why it was she said Remy was coming over. Lately it was hard to remember anything except how good Olivia smelled and how silky her skin was when he made the mistake of touching it.

"Remy," he said in greeting. "Bess. Good to see you two."

Remy nodded and put the brake on the buckboard. "You just wait up here, honeybunch. I'll only be a minute. No reason for you to get down just to get back up."

Bess looked annoyed, but he planted a big wet kiss on her cheek and coaxed a smile out of her before jumping down from the wagon. By then Livvy was standing beside the wagon with the baby on her hip.

"She's too big to be carried all over the place," Spencer said to her. "You shouldn't carry her so much."

Olivia put Josie down reluctantly, obviously not happy to give up the closeness they were just developing.

"Are you coming to the meeting?" Bess asked Livvy as Remy tugged at Spencer's sleeve and motioned for him to come up on the porch.

"The railroad assembly? With Emma Zephin telling us more about her beau?" Livvy's laughter tinkled like pieces of glass hitting each other in the wind, and she said she thought she just might, or something like that. It was hard for Spencer to hear her as they moved farther from the women.

"I need the book back," Remy said in a whisper. "The one I loaned you."

Spencer laughed. "Forget how it's done?"

Remy shook his head. "It's not a laughing matter. Doc says Bess can't have any more children or it might kill her. And I'm so randy, if I have to stay away from her much longer I don't know what I'll do." His voice cracked. "Spencer, you

don't know what it's like. I'm going crazy. This morning I
gave Thom-Tom the back of my hand for spilling his milk.
Imagine me doing something like that.

"If I don't touch her, I'm hurting her feelings. If I do, I'm
not sure I'll be able to stop. I'm going out of my mind. We're
hoping that doctor in Milwaukee'll have some answers."

Spencer had all the answers Remy needed. And he knew
firsthand that none of them really worked. He didn't know
what good Remy expected Dr. Napheys's book to do, but he
agreed to get it. The book certainly hadn't done him any
good, with its suggestion of abstinence. It was an easy thing
for Dr. Napheys to suggest. His wife probably resembled his
horse. But let the good doctor spend a few nights in the same
bed as Olivia, let her hair trail across *his* chest or her scent
invade *his* nostrils, and then let him see how easy abstinence
was.

Spencer opened the bottom drawer and dug beneath his
winter underwear. He took out his Balbriggan undershorts.
He threw his merino drawers on the floor and lifted out the
whole stack of undershirts. The book wasn't there.

He'd read it just two nights ago, hoping against hope he'd
missed some secret to end his agony. He tried the other bottom drawer, figuring that in his disappointment perhaps he had
been careless. With some embarrassment he rifled through
Olivia's underthings, all frilly whites with lace and ribbons and
bows and while he found a corset he didn't even know she
owned, he didn't find the book.

Livvy! She must have found it and been shocked. Dr.
Napheys was a very candid man. He called the water wet and
the sand scratchy, and was no less accurate about anatomy.
And now Spencer was going to have to ask her what she'd
done with it. Well, if she was scandalized, it was her own
fault. No one asked her to read the book, though Lord knew
she might have made a better wife from their wedding night if

she had. . . . Still, she'd sought out the book, which had been well hidden, and read it of her own accord.

The idea both angered and frightened him. Dr. Napheys's book was graphic enough for even Livvy to grasp what had and hadn't occurred between them.

"Jeez," he muttered, stuffing back their underthings into the drawers. He didn't know whether to be outraged or to run for the hills.

And yet she hadn't changed her attitude toward him. She was still treating him the way she always had. A woman like Livvy, had she known what he'd been doing, wouldn't just smile and offer him a drink in the garden. A woman like Livvy would . . . he cringed just thinking about it.

So maybe she had taken the book, but she hadn't read it yet. He lit from the room as if at that very moment she had it in her hands and if he just hurried he could stop her from getting to the part that concerned their marriage.

"Olivia," he yelled from the doorway and waved, motioning her to come in. "I need to see you."

She said something to Bess and Remy, who had joined his wife in the wagon, and then walked slowly toward him, her eyebrows drawn in question.

"Is something wrong?" she asked when she reached him and got a good look at his face.

"I—I," he stammered. "There was a book," he tried again. "Remy's book. And he wants it back."

Olivia turned red as a beet. The apples in Bess's orchard weren't as bright as Livvy's cheeks.

He felt his own warm and he wondered if he was painted as guilty as she. "Then you have it?"

"Have it?" She couldn't even look him in the eye.

"Livvy, I can see by the color of your face you've been in it, so there's no use playing coy. We can talk about you reading such a book later, but right now Remy wants it back."

She folded her hands modestly over her chest and looked at the floor, shrugging. "So give it back."

"Where is it?" he asked quietly, softening his voice when he saw how very embarrassed she was. Married three years and it was still like talking to an innocent.

She went into the bedroom and bent over to pull at the bottom drawer. Much as he like the view of her upturned derriere, he didn't see much point in the charade.

"It's not in there, Liv. Where'd you hide it?" He supposed that she hadn't read it after all, but perhaps she'd tried to stop him from reading it. "It's all right. All I want to do is give it back. There's nothing to be afraid of."

She was still bending over the drawer, feeling through his underwear with her hands in earnest. "Spencer," she said, turning to him with her eyes wide and her eyebrows raised. "It's not here. And I don't have it, and you don't have it."

"Well, then who . . . ?" Spencer asked.

"You don't think . . ." Livvy began, her hand rushing to cover her mouth. "Oh, he wouldn't . . ."

"Boys are curious, Liv. That's all. Though he seems a little young."

"It's not just the book, Spencer. What was he doing in our underthings?" She shivered and he ran one hand up and down her arm, then grasped her elbow and helped her up. Even shaken she was graceful, even with worry creasing her brow she was still . . . well . . . The only word that came to his mind was pretty, and that wasn't what he meant. Not at all.

"I'll talk to him," Spencer said. "But boys are just naturally curious about such things." He didn't like the idea of the children rifling through their personal garments any more than she did, but he remembered being a young man with lots of questions and not enough guts to ask them.

"Maybe I should . . ." she began.

"No," he said, cutting her off. "A boy needs to talk to a man."

"I'm sorry, Spencer," she said, looking guiltily at him. "I could ask Remy to talk to Neil, if you don't want to."

"I said I would," he snapped at her, more sharply than he intended. "I'm just surprised it came up so soon. But then, being Bouche's boy, he probably was raised on *Aristotle's Masterpiece.*"

She looked at him blankly and he fought to keep a straight face as he remembered leafing through a copy of the book with Remy behind his father's barn. The woodcuts might have been primitive, but to a couple of thirteen-year-old boys hungry for information, it had been a feast for the eyes and enough to provide the boys with more than one good boner. But Neil was only what, ten? What could he know of such things?

"Do you suppose it's in the barn?" she asked about the book. "Should I go look?"

Spencer shook his head. He'd rather the boy returned it on his own than go and take it. Remy could wait a few days. After all, Bess would be away in Milwaukee and Spencer could talk to Neil while the women were away. His nephews had probably had a peek at Napheys's tome themselves. Remy'd understand.

"We'd better get on to the meeting," Spencer said. "You taking that little one with us?"

"Mm-hm," she said, a little pride showing in her smile. Having the children around sure did seem to agree with her, even if it was setting his nerves on edge. "Louisa's off somewheres and Neil said he was going home with Thom-Tom and Philip after school to do their chores, then they were coming over here."

Ah, Spencer thought—the book. *History repeats itself.* "Chores," he said, trying not to sound too dubious. "Yes, well, Thom-Tom and Philip sure seem to have taken to their cousin."

"Yes," she agreed, too pleased for him to tell her the obvious truth. "Isn't it wonderful?"

"And where'd you say Miss Louisa is?" The girl worried him, such an odd mixture of woman and child, at once trying to be all grown up and failing miserably, and then trying to hide the breasts that were budding on her chest and the hips that were beginning to spread.

"I don't honestly know," she admitted with a slight shrug. "But, like boys, girls have got certain things that they've got to get through at eleven or twelve that aren't easy. I think she's off thinking somewheres."

Spencer had been around for Olivia's growing up, just old enough to know what she was about, but not old enough to have any sympathy for the tag-along sister of a friend who would sit and stare at nothing for hours and then proclaim Maple Stand the dullest place on earth.

"You might want to have a talk with her when you get back," Spencer suggested, but Olivia just gave a jerk of her head as if to remind Spencer that Louisa wanted nothing to do with her. He supposed she was right. Any attempt by Livvy to help Louisa understand what was happening to her could be mistaken for an attempt to replace the girl's mother. "Well, there's time," he said, escorting her from the room as Remy yelled out that it was getting late.

From the way Charlie Zephin and his daughter had been talking, Olivia had just assumed it was all settled. She'd written for appointments, one for herself and one for Bess, with the lady doctor she'd read about in the *Badger State Banner*. She'd counted out the pennies from her butter and egg money and raided the sugar bowl where she kept anything she had left over from the spending money Spencer gave her to run the household.

Now here were her friends and neighbors arguing over

whether the railroad surveyor should be invited at all. He had to be. How else could she manage to go to Milwaukee to see Dr. Sarah Roberts? And if she didn't see Dr. Roberts, how would she know if there was even a glimmer of hope for her to give Spencer a child?

". . . because a train means noise and smoke and no-accounts and everyone knows that it costs a barrel of apples to ship a barrel of apples, that's why," she heard her husband say.

"It'll bring in business and you can't fight progress, Mr. Williamson. It's nearly the twentieth century and you're living in the eighteenth." Charlie Zephin's usually smiling face was grim.

"I read where there was an accident in Gilmour, Montana, just last month and four people were hurt. Why, it seems to me that nearly every week there's the report of another one—"

"They were tramps," someone said. "They don't count."

"Didn't you hear about the collision in Hudson? Six killed and two hurt not two hundred miles from here, and it was only last week."

"It's the way of the future and Maple Stand can't afford to be left behind."

"Well, I vote no," Spencer said, rising to his feet.

"I can't see that having Mr. Makeridge come and take a look could cause any harm," Olivia said, coming to a stand next to her husband.

The room quieted.

"Sit down," Spencer said. "You can't vote for the railroad, so just look after that little one you were so anxious to get hold of."

"Are you telling me that I don't have a say in this?" Livvy asked, checking on Josie and seeing that the child was just fine and happy eating the cookies she had brought for her. With her hands on her hips, she was joined by several other women who stood and turned to face her husband, the same expectant looks on their faces that she supposed was on her own. "Because more than a few of these ladies own along with their husbands the land that the railroad just might be interested in buying. Some, like Mrs. Trencher there, own it whole. So if the ladies aren't going to be allowed to vote along with the men, same as—"

"I didn't say *they* can't vote," Spencer said and then lowered his voice to a loud whisper. "I said *you* can't vote. Unless you want to vote against the railroad along with me. Otherwise we just cancel each other out and there's not a damn reason for us to be here."

"Well, there may not be a reason for you to be here," she said, leaving out the profanity that came so easily to her husband's lips, "but there is for me. I've got an interest in two pieces of land here, and I suspect that while Mr. Makeridge isn't gonna be interested in either one, I've got as much right as the next man, maybe more, to hear what he has to say."

"Makeridge?" Spencer said. "Who the . . ." Olivia glared at him and he watched his words. "Who is this Makeridge? And how do you know him?"

"Mr. Makeridge," Emma Zephin said, taking the podium and clearing her voice, "is the surveyor for the Ahnapee and Western Railroad. Actually, his title is civil engineer."

A buzz went around the room, especially amongst the ladies when they noticed Emma's new hairdo, a sort of puffed-out bun like the ones that artist C. D. Gibson was drawing. At least, Livvy suspected that was the look Emma was trying for. She wondered how her own hair would look done that way. Better than Emma's, she hoped.

"What ya got on your head there, Miss Zephin?" someone asked, and a few men, Spencer included, guffawed.

Livvy came down hard on his instep. "She's not deaf," Livvy whispered at him.

"No," he agreed. "Just ugly."

Emma ignored the question about her hair. "Mr. Maker-idge," she continued, "is a fine upstanding gentlemen of excellent breeding. He has brown hair with a wave above one eyebrow and eyes the color of the sky in June."

"Regardless," Olivia said loudly, trying to prevent Emma from embarrassing herself further, "there's no stopping the man if he wants to come, and perhaps we can turn his visit to our advantage."

She hoped someone else in favor of the railroad would take up the gauntlet, since she had no idea what to say next. *I have to go to Milwaukee because I want a baby of my own* didn't seem a useful follow up.

"And maybe if we don't invite him, don't make cheese of him, then he'll go someplace else that will, and we'll be rid of the whole problem before it even starts," Spencer said. He was speaking to the whole crowd, but when he finished he glared at Livvy.

"That's my point," Mr. Zephin said. "If we don't court him, someone else will. . . ."

"Looks like Miss Emma's the one looking to court him," somebody said.

"We have corresponded," Emma said proudly, her nose in the air.

"Corresponded," Spencer said softly so that only the few people around him could hear. "That explains it. Man's buying a pig in a poke. Seems to me it's our duty to protect him."

"I'd like to see that railroad engineer come and buy Sacotte Farm right out from under my Bess's weary legs," Remy said, taking Olivia by surprise. "Sell him the whole thing from Dan to Beersheba to get Bess off that farm and into some cushy little house in town with no steps and no chores but to sit and churn the butter for her heavenly biscuits."

"And would you like to give a third of that money to

Bouche so he can never be heard from again? And another third to your sister who'd probably give it to the first needy child who crossed her path?" Spencer asked.

"It's my opinion that Waylon, that is, Mr. Makeridge, could be persuaded to route the spur right through Maple Stand," Emma said.

"Sounds like he's willin' to run his railroad right through your"—a raucous voice said before having the air knocked out of him—"town, ma'am. Run that railroad right through our town."

There were a lot of snickers and hoots, and Olivia figured that whoever it was that made the comment had some thoughts not fit for mixed company.

"I call for a vote," Charlie Zephin said, pushing his daughter away from the podium and pounding on it for order. "All those in favor of letting Mr. Makeridge come to Maple Stand and have a look-see; stand over here on my left. Those that don't even wanna see what the man might be offering, who want to see Maple Stand passed by and left to dry up and turn to dust and blow away, stand to my right."

In the end, he looked like a preacher ready for the benediction, his hands raised right and left like he was offering a blessing. Spencer wrapped his fingers around Livvy's arm, but she shook him off, carrying Josie with her and moving along with the group that was embracing the future and all its potential.

She stood looking at her husband defiantly as he glared back at her. Not that her one vote would have mattered, since had the election been conducted on a boat it would surely have capsized. Less than a handful of people stood with Spencer, clinging to the past and to keeping things the way they were.

Livvy wished that some of those people standing by her side now could come home with her and face Spencer later. She didn't relish doing it alone.

Chapter Ten

Well, she was gussied up, all right. All ready to go to the big city. Studying her, he wondered if he'd ever seen the suit she was wearing before. It was a pearl gray and hugged her waist tightly, spreading wider and wider to accommodate her bosom and hips. He hardly knew the woman who stood with the feathered hat by their bedroom door. But the expectant look in her eye was familiar enough. She looked so hopeful anyone would have thought she was the one with the doctor's appointment instead of Bess. But that was Livvy, caring more about others than herself.

"You got a lotta faith in this Dr. Roberts, don't you?" he asked. "Think she'll be able to help Bess?"

She looked startled at his words, then gave him a small shrug, the feathers on her hat shaking even after her head had stopped. "We have to try, at least," she said. "I mean, if there is some way, I surely wouldn't want to have missed it because we live in Maple Stand and not Milwaukee."

"No," he agreed, not sure what it was she was talking about. "But don't you think if Bess could just lose some of that extra weight, she'd be all right? Maybe this trip isn't really necessary, Liv."

"Supper is in the icebox. Louisa knows how to heat it up. She's staying home from school to watch after Josie, but I told Neil he's to go." She pulled on her gloves. They matched her traveling outfit perfectly.

"I don't see what one doctor's gonna tell her that another

can't. Doc LeMense has been practicing since I was a boy. Don't you think he knows what's what?" She smoothed her skirt and the light shone off it like sunshine off a frozen field. He looked away. "I'm not so sure you have to go, at all."

"Neil will take care of the stock and there'll be enough left over from supper to take care of tomorrow's dinner. There are two loaves in the oven that'll be ready in about twenty minutes or so." She raised her voice and yelled, "Louisa, you won't forget about that bread now, will you?"

A grunt came from the direction of Louisa's room. They both took it as an affirmation.

"You sure this trip is good for Bess? Maybe it's not a good idea for her to be making such a long trip. Have you thought of that?"

Her eyes widened and she focused her attention on him instead of her traveling clothes, which to his mind were already perfect and didn't require any of the fussing she was doing.

"Why, Spencer, I'd swear you didn't want me to go."

Nothing was further from the truth. He couldn't wait for her to go. In fact, he wished she'd gone last night. Preferably before the damn meeting. "Livvy, you'd never swear," he said, avoiding answering her. "You got the extra money I gave you?" He took the satchel she had left by the bedroom and placed it by the door.

"For the third time," she said, "yes. Don't worry so. I was on my own a long time before I married you, remember? I've been to Milwaukee before, and it's not so big and fearsome."

"A town where the only street without a beer garden is filled with women who . . ." He didn't know how to put what the women did into words that were suitable for Livvy's ears, and he didn't like it when she seemed amused by his discomfort.

"I've been around beer all my life, Spencer. And I hardly

think the women will be any threat to me. Why ever are you so worried?''

"I'm not worried," he said. He noticed a hangnail on his thumb and began to pick at it.

"Good," she said, a note of finality in her voice.

"Yeah," he agreed. He bit at the skin by his nail and felt it rip away from his finger painfully.

"And you can talk to Neil while I'm gone," she whispered and added, "about *you know*."

As if he didn't know what she meant. He was dreading it already. Talking about the birds and the bees to a boy Neil's age gave him the willies.

"Spencer?" She was looking at him expectantly.

"I will, Olivia. I said I would, didn't I?" This was going to be a great couple of days. Now instead of just thinking about having his ashes hauled, he could talk about it—to a ten-year-old. Instead of the torture of sleeping next to his lilac scented wife, he would be sleeping alone. And the girls. They hadn't taken to him all that well. Louisa acted like he had an unpleasant odor, keeping six feet away from him whenever she could, and Josie still seemed to think parts of him were designed for teething, especially when he tried to take her down from wherever she managed to climb.

"Poor Spencer," Olivia said sympathetically. "I know none of this is what you had planned."

Before he could even reflect on the truth of her statement, she threw open the door and waved.

"They're here," she announced. "Louisa, Josie? Come let me say good-bye before I leave."

Neil came running from the barn, trying not to spill the milk he had coaxed from Miss Lily as he hurried. Olivia ruffled his hair and gave him a kiss on his cheek and told him to be good to his Uncle Spencer. Then she turned and looked for the girls who were emerging from the bedroom.

Louisa came slowly forward, a piece of her lip caught between her teeth and the baby in her arms.

"Don't look so worried," Olivia said, cupping the girl's chin. "Your uncle isn't so hard to please. You'll do fine."

The lip quivered, but Louisa gave her a slight nod and clung more tightly to her sister.

"And you," Olivia said, poking Josie in her belly and making her laugh. "No tricks while I'm gone. You mind your sister and Uncle Spencer and stay out of trouble, you hear me?"

The little hellion was all big innocent eyes as she kissed her Aunt Livvy good-bye.

And then it was his turn. She stood awkwardly in front of him, waiting for him to tell her to have a good trip and that he would miss her. He knew that. The children were watching him expectantly. He knew that, too. Lord, the last time he'd had a private moment was beyond his remembering. He removed his glasses and cleaned them with his handkerchief, making sure that every last speck was gone.

Then he picked up her suitcase and carried it to Zephin's ridiculously fancy surrey. "You better go."

She hurried after him, reminding the children of this and that on her way, as if she were a real mother, and then allowing him to help her into the carriage. He exchanged quick pleasantries with Bess, wishing her a successful trip, and shook Charlie Zephin's hand.

"Don't you worry none," Charlie reassured him. "I'll take good care of your missus."

Inside his chest, his heart was hammering against his ribs as he watched his wife settle herself. Words fought to leave his lips, but he held them back by biting down on his tongue. It wasn't as if he really wanted to tell her he would miss her. It was just that it was expected of him. And he'd be damned if he'd be forced into saying what he didn't mean just to make her and the children happy.

"Well, bye, Spencer," Bess said cheerily.

And he wasn't about to say it for Bess, either.

"That it then?" Charlie said, as if it were required of a husband to say such things to a wife.

Well, hanged if he would. "Yup, that's it."

Everyone stared at him, waiting.

"Spencer?" Livvy asked quietly. "Was there something else?"

"No," he bit out, annoyed by all the prompting. "You can go any time now."

"Not unless you let go of that harness." Charlie laughed, pointing at the leather strap clutched in Spencer's hand.

Spencer let go of it as if it were suddenly burning him and slapped the horse on the rump.

It wasn't until the wagon was nearly out of sight that he finally uttered the words aloud.

"Have a safe trip, Livvy-love."

"She can't hear you now," Neil said softly.

When he turned to hurry the boy for school, all three of the children were gone.

The day was one revelation after another, none of them welcome. Senses he hadn't used since Kirsten and the children had lived in his house suddenly came back to haunt him like their ghosts. For example, he learned that he could still tell someone was gone from the house without even being in it. He could simply feel Livvy wasn't there even from the most distant of their fields.

Then he found that he could be sure two children were in the house, only to find when he returned for his dinner that they weren't there at all. On the kitchen table had been a note assuring him they would be back.

He'd returned to the fields, not having any idea where to begin looking for the girls, and spent the better part of an hour trying to convince himself there was nothing to worry about.

Wrong again.

When they'd finally turned up, Louisa's face had been streaked with tears and her eyes rimmed with red. And it was clear that he was the last person she wanted to discuss her problems with.

Which had only served to remind him that he had a matter to discuss with Neil.

The boy came dawdling up the lane after school humming a tune and watching the clouds as if the mysteries of the universe were written in the sky. He dropped his books on the front porch and bustled out to the field without even stopping in the house for a glass of cold milk.

"Aren't you hungry, boy?" he asked the scrawny child. "You don't start eating more, a good summer storm'll just blow you clear to Michigan."

"I could wait," the child said, pointing to the darkening sky that Spencer had somehow failed to notice. "Looks like rain, doesn't it?" he asked.

"Better get the horses in," Spencer agreed.

"Yessir," the runt said, and raced ahead to open the barn door before Spencer and Curly George arrived.

Spencer showed him how to unharness the horse and handed him the tin of Colgate's Black Harness Soap. Without wasting words, he dipped in a rag and showed him the proper way to apply the paste and rub it in.

When he was sure that Neil wouldn't wreck the leather beyond repair, he made a tentative stab at talking to the boy.

"School okay?" he asked.

"I guess," the boy answered.

There was a minute or two of silence.

"Any nice girls in your class?"

"Girls?"

"Yeah," Spencer said. "You know, those pretty things with the hair bows and petticoats."

"Ugh," Neil replied. "The ones who don't want to carry their own books and who you can't hit, but they can sock you fine if they want to?"

Spencer couldn't help laughing. "Those are the ones. Any pretty ones in your class?"

"Never thought about it," Neil said, obviously considering it now.

"Anybody special?"

"Nah," he said after considerable thought.

"Oh." They worked on the leads and bridles, and fell into a rhythm, Neil working the soap well into the leather and Spencer doing the polishing.

"Boy," Spencer said as they sat side by side. "It's not easy for a kid to be away from his father while he's growing up."

"I suppose," the child said, a slight quiver in his voice.

"You miss your pa?"

The boy shook his head solemnly. Spencer wasn't sure whether he was so sad because he did miss Bouche and felt he'd be offending his uncle by admitting it, or just the thought of his father had turned him suddenly serious. Either way, Spencer thought it best to stay off the subject of Bouche.

"Well, I just wanted you to know that I'm pretty good at answering a boy's questions, having been one myself and all."

"Okay," the child said, working the devil out of the leather in his hands.

"So if you've got any questions," he prompted, "go on and ask 'em."

"Well," Neil began. "There is something."

Spencer steeled himself.

"That harrow machine? How do you suppose they knew how far apart to put those teeth? I mean, they're just the right distance for the planting, aren't they? How'd they—"

"They're what you call adjustable," Spencer answered. "Now what I really meant about being able to ask me questions, was, well . . . You might want to know some more personal, just between boy type things, and the girls are nowhere around, Aunt Liv's all the way in Milwaukee . . . You want to ask me something that only boys might talk about?"

Neil thought for a while. Spencer knew he was thinking because he was chewing hard on the inside of his cheek. Finally, he said, "Well, I didn't think girls had much of an interest in farming."

"No, I suppose they don't," he agreed.

"So, could I ask you another question about farming?"

Spencer couldn't help sighing. At this rate their discussion would take all night and they'd never get to the book.

"I'd kinda like to confine this discussion to stuff boys wanna talk about when girls aren't around."

Neil looked at him as if he were some kind of degenerate. He was beginning to feel like one.

"I mean since Aunt Liv's away, and all."

"I guess you don't get to talk to boys much," Neil said. He seemed to be considering whether to continue the discussion. "Okay," he said reluctantly. "I guess we could talk about that kind of stuff. If you want to."

"I want to," Spencer said.

There was silence again. It lasted until a clap of thunder roared over the barn and the first drops of rain began to fall hard on the roof.

He kept thinking of the girls in the house in the storm and his impatience got the better of him. "Ask me your damn questions, boy," he said, then wanted to bite his own tongue. "I mean, there must be things you want to know. About boys and girls, I mean."

Neil had stopped working and was staring at him. "What about boys and girls?"

"Okay," he tried again. "What about where babies come from. You want to know about that?"

Neil looked horrified. "No!" he said, putting up his hands. "I know all about that."

"You do?"

Neil nodded, the sickened look still covering his face. "Mama swallowed a watermelon seed and it grew in her belly until it was so big that it hurt to get it out and she screamed and screamed and when she finally, you know, got it out"— he pointed to his behind with his eyes shut and his nose squinched up—"she traded it for Josie."

Spencer covered his mouth with his hand. Finally he managed to say "I see. And is that all you want to know about it?"

"Do I have to know more?" the child asked with so much fear that Spencer found himself putting his arm around the boy's back and hugging him gently before rising and stretching.

"No, boy, I don't think you do."

He didn't suppose that Neil had taken the book, after all.

They ran into the house together, running between the raindrops and then shaking themselves like wet dogs in the middle of the parlor.

Josie laughed at their antics, as Spencer had expected she would. Louisa grimaced. That, too, was no surprise. She was a surly child, no two ways about it. But the smell that was coming from whatever it was she had on the stove was worth all the scowls she wanted to throw his way.

"Supper almost ready?" he asked.

"Aunt Liv said I should serve it at five-thirty," she said, checking the clock on the mantel.

"The woman's not even here and she's running my life," he said. "Well, I don't suppose anybody's gonna tell her if we break a rule or two while she's gone, do you?"

He let the fragrance from the stove lure him closer and then lifted the cover from the pot.

"I think it's done," he said, and reached above the sink for the dishes that still sat in the draining rack where Livvy had left them.

"It isn't five-thirty," Louisa snapped at him, and tried to get her arm between him and the pot in order to replace the lid. At least he supposed that was what she was trying to do. Instead, she gasped and leaped away from the stove clutching her arm.

"Oh, Jeez. Let me see it," he said, reaching for her arm, which she held tightly against her body.

"It's all right," she said, tears flooding those dark-brown eyes of hers that looked so much like Livvy's he could imagine that she was Liv's own daughter. "I'm sure it's not really burned."

"Neil, get some lard from the cabinet." He picked the girl up, surprised that she weighed so little for a child who threw her weight around so much, and plopped her on the counter. "Let me see it," he said again, this time making it clear she was not free to refuse.

She untied the ribbon that gathered her sleeve and pushed it up. Big tears fell first onto her skirt, then on her shoulder as she averted her head, each drop making a dark circle on the pale blue calico.

"It's all right," he crooned as softly as he could, all the while thinking that Livvy was going to kill him for letting this happen. If he didn't kill himself first. Letting a girl Louisa's age take care of supper . . . what was he thinking?

He sucked in his breath at the red mark on her forearm. It didn't look too bad and surely would never leave a scar, but it must have stung, nonetheless. "Hurt much?"

She shook her head and refused to meet his gaze.

"Looks all right," he said, spreading a bit of lard on the inflamed area and returning the small limb gently to her side. "No permanent damage."

He pulled her against his chest and rubbed her back

gently, feeling her sobs as if they were within him. The fabric was soft and through it he could feel her tiny backbones, like some sort of delicate bird. She hadn't much more meat on her than her brother or sister. She just seemed to carry herself more proudly. He supposed that was because Marion had had more time with her.

"Pretty dress," he said, wondering if Livvy had made it. The sprigs of embroidered flowers made him think she had. The sobs stopped and she was quiet in his arms. He stepped back, one hand steadying her on the counter, and studied her face, trying to decide how badly she'd been hurt. She looked past him, biting furiously at her lip.

There was something, he couldn't say what, some feeling that made him want to take a step back from her. Some silent voice begging him not to touch her, yet she didn't pull away. Quickly he helped her down and then purposely ignored the silent plea and swatted her gently on the behind, steering her toward her room. "You go pull yourself together," he said. "I'll see to dinner."

She went silently into her bedroom, twice peeking over her shoulder at him and looking quickly away when her eyes met his.

He tried to lighten the mood at supper, but even Josie was subdued, and he longed for the chatter his wife always seemed to so easily provide.

"Wonder how your Aunt Liv is doing in Milwaukee," he said cheerily, only to produce even more sullen faces, if that were possible. He was sorry he'd brought up her name when Josie's lip began to quiver and her eyes filled with tears.

They agreed to make it an early night. Louisa took Josie off for bed while he and Neil saw to the dishes.

"You need to talk about anything else?" Neil asked Spencer as he dried the plates. "You know, boy talk?"

Spencer couldn't help smiling at the child. He had a hundred questions he wanted to ask, all of them about Julian

Bouche and what he'd done to these children that made Neil so eager to please, Josie so wild to escape, and Louisa so afraid to be touched. "You ever seen a baseball game?" he asked instead.

"I saw a practice once, in Chicago," Neil answered, his face glowing.

"Maybe one day we'll go see a game," Spencer said, surprising both of them. Now whatever, he wondered, had made him say that?

By eight o'clock the house was quite. Neil was asleep on the couch, where he had been sleeping every night since Miss Lily's fart that rocked the world, and there was no noise coming from the girls' room.

Spencer got out of his clothes and stretched out on his bed with his pipe and a new story about that clever detective with the deerstalker hat, enjoying the luxury of having the whole bed to himself. After a few minutes he decided to see if Livvy's side was any softer.

It wasn't.

He rolled back to his own, now cold, side. He fluffed his pillow, folded it, and put it against the headboard. He took Livvy's pillow and tucked it closely to his side. He lay on his left side, but the lamplight wasn't bright enough to read so he turned to his right, where the light shone in his eyes.

Guilt. That's what it was. His impatience had gotten the better of him and a little girl's arm was burned as a result. Maybe it wouldn't scar her skin, but he had a feeling it would scar his conscience. As if that didn't have scars enough.

After rising from his bed, he paced his room for a minute or two wondering what Livvy would do if she were there, then picked up the lamp and soundlessly made his way to the girls' room to take another look at Louisa's arm.

The room was dark, the girls both asleep. He looked first at Josie, noting that her thumb was stuck in her mouth and that even as she slept she sucked on it. Then he turned to Louisa.

The covers were around her neck, and he peeled them back gently, hoping not to rouse her. He found her arm and unbuttoned the cuff of her nightdress with a dexterity he was surprised he possessed. Moving the lamp so that he could see her arm, he then raised the sleeve of the gown to reveal the shiny patch of skin that was still coated in lard.

He touched it gently to check its warmth, and Louisa stirred and pulled away from him.

"Oh," she said, her voice so quiet he could hardly hear her. "Please, Papa, no."

At least that was what he thought she said. But when he held the lamp up so that he could see her face, her eyes were closed and he wasn't sure she had even awakened.

He rolled down the sleeve of her nightgown and tucked her arm back under the quilt. "Louisa?" he whispered. She nestled deeper into the covers, her features taut, not those of someone who was truly lost in sleep.

He put a soothing hand on her brow and then stood, his knees cracking as he rose. "It's just me, Miss Louisa. Just Uncle Spence. Go back to sleep now," he said softly. Then silently, with another look at each of the girls, he left the room, shutting the door behind him.

It turned out to be a long, long night.

The night had been interminable for Livvy. She'd tossed and turned for hours on the small cot at the YWCA where Charlie had left her and Bess. She'd played *what if* in her head until she thought it would explode. *What if the doctor said she could never have children? What if she needed some sort of operation? What would she tell Spencer?*

She'd made eight trips to the bathroom, each one commented upon by the two other women occupying their warm, windowless room. They'd whispered about her and speculated on what she was doing there, guessing one outlandish reason after another. That she was pregnant and seeking to get rid of the child was her favorite. She nearly laughed out loud.

But the night and all her imaginings weren't half as bad as the cold hard truth of sitting across from the gray-haired, steely-eyed Dr. Roberts, whose glasses sat perched at the end of a pinched nose as she studied the piece of paper that reduced Olivia's life to one unfulfilled wish.

"Only married three years?" the doctor asked her suspiciously. "What took you so long?"

Livvy shrugged when no ready answer came to mind.

"I only ask," the doctor continued, "because I wondered what you might have done before your marriage that may have resulted in this condition. No pregnancies before this marriage?"

Livvy shook her head. "Of course not. I've never had any children."

The doctor removed the glasses from her nose and rubbed her forehead. "Honey," she said rather dispassionately. "You wouldn't be the first woman to have made a mistake and tried to rectify it only to have to pay for it in the end. You'll save us a lot of time if that's the case and you just say so."

"Oh!" Livvy gasped when she realized what the doctor meant. "I never . . . oh! No . . . I . . . ."

The doctor shook her head and waved away Livvy's words with her hand. "Okay. We can rule that out then. Your husband—he has erections regularly, maintains them, ejaculates appropriately?"

Livvy felt her cheeks burn. She bit at her lip and balled a fistful of her skirt within her gloved hand.

"Oh, for heaven's sake," the doctor said, leaning back on her chair and studying Livvy. "You guess so. Is that it?"

She gave a quick little nod at the doctor. "He had two children with his first wife. It's not him that's the problem."

The doctor came close to smiling. "Good. We're making progress now. Pain?"

"What?"

Dr. Roberts sighed. "Pain. Discomfort. During intercourse? When you menstruate? Backaches? Constipation? Tenderness in the abdomen?"

Livvy shook her head but the doctor was peeling an apple deftly with a thin silver knife, the apple's skin falling in a long curl into the wastebasket beside her desk. "No," Livvy said aloud.

"Sorry," Dr. Roberts apologized, gesturing with the apple. "No time for lunch. Your time comes regular? No heavy bleeding? No gushes with fibrous matter?" She cut a slice of the apple, pierced it with the scalpel, and held it out to Livvy.

"No," Livvy said, both to the fruit and the questions.

"You try any of the cures?" There was resignation in her voice, and Livvy didn't know if it was because that was all the hope she had to offer or because there wasn't any hope at all.

"Viavi," she said, her voice barely above a whisper. Even the memory of inserting those pills inside her most private place made her press her legs together more tightly. "The cream and the . . ."

"Yeah," the doctor said. "I know the rest. Anything else?"

"Lydia Pinkham's."

"And?"

"Imperial Granum."

Dr. Roberts groaned. "And?"

Livvy closed her eyes. If only the doctor would reach over and put a hand on her shoulder. If only she would nod once instead of shaking her head.

"The rest of it, Mrs. Williamson. Just how far did you go in your quest for an infant?"

"Wilson's Electric Belt."

The doctor tsked and threw the core to her apple in the

garbage. "Well, you must be damn healthy to have survived all those cures. Anything else?"

Livvy shook her head, then raised her eyes to the doctor's. "No, that's not true. Prayer. I've made a hundred promises to the Blessed Virgin and I've followed every suggestion every woman has made no matter how strange it sounded. I've pushed empty carriages, and ones with other people's children in them. I've slapped myself when I've been with women who are expecting. I've put everything under my pillow from a teething ring to a piece of dead fish, and I've lied to my husband and pretended I was only accompanying my sister-in-law when I came here."

From behind her desk, the doctor rose, smaller and stouter than she had seemed. A smile cracked the stern face as she said, "I never heard the one about the fish," and laid a gentle hand on Livvy's shoulder. "You go in there and remove your skirts," she said, pointing to a door with the number "2" on it. "Wrap a sheet around you if you like. I'll be in shortly."

Livvy laughed nervously. The little woman couldn't come any other way.

Her humor died a quick death when she opened the examination room door. The sparsely furnished room was dominated by a wooden table that wasn't nearly as long as she was tall. At one end was a step, above which, on some kind of swivels, were two wooden planks that rose from the table and had notches cut out of them. Standing next to that end of the table was a lamp on a flexible neck that aimed the light right at the space between the two planks.

Against her throat her blood throbbed, nearly choking her.

"Doctor says to remove your corset and loosen your shirtwaist, ma'am," a female voice said through the door. "Will you be needing help?"

No sound came out when she tried to talk. *Baby,* she told herself. *You want a baby.*

"Ma'am?" There was a light knock, and then a young woman's face appeared, tipped slightly so that the small white hat on her head was in danger of falling off as she peered around the door. "Having trouble?"

Livvy could only shake her head. With her fingers trembling uncontrollably, she managed to unbutton two buttons. That seemed to satisfy the girl, who smiled and assured her that the doctor would be in soon, then bustled the rest of the way in and set down a tray with gleaming silver objects Livvy had never seen before.

"Don't touch anything, please." The nurse—Livvy supposed that she was one from the white outfit and hat—smiled in her direction and then left the room.

It took forever, or so it seemed to Livvy, alone and covered only by a sheet from the waist down, in the little airless room that reeked from carbolic acid. Footsteps came and went, and with each set her heart sped up until she thought she would choke.

How she managed to get the buttons of her shirtwaist undone seemed a mystery to her. Clutching it closed she waited for the doctor, alternately praying that she could go through with the examination and wishing she would just expire, then and there, and be saved the embarrassment she knew awaited her.

"Okay," the doctor said, coming into the room and heading for a basin of water that stood in the corner, a sign above it announcing *for the doctor's use only.* "Any questions before we start?"

"Will you be able to tell what's wrong with me?" Livvy asked, then corrected herself. "I mean, right away? Just from . . ." She gestured toward the table. This was worse than her wedding night, and that hadn't been any too good.

"Frankly, Mrs. Williamson, I already have my suspicions. How 'bout we get you up on the table and have a look-see?"

She wanted to. Lord, she really did, but her feet refused to move. The nurse held out her hand. Dr. Roberts crossed her arms over her chest. The clock on the wall ticked so loudly she could hardly hear the tapping of the doctor's impatient foot.

"Up or out, Mrs. Williamson? I've an office full of patients waiting for me."

Livvy nodded and reached for the nurse's hand. As she got up onto the table, she saw the doctor roll her eyes and grimace.

"You've been married three years?" she asked Livvy, as if she weren't sure she'd gotten it right.

"Yes."

"Scoot down here more," the doctor instructed. "Knees over the wood. More. Lord," she said with a heavy sigh. "Let's get this straight. I'm going to reach up inside you with my hand and make sure your husband hasn't moved anything God put somewhere else. Won't feel all that different. You just tell me if it hurts."

The doctor flicked on the lamp and Livvy felt its heat on her shins. The doctor's fingers jabbed at her thighs as if digging for buried treasure.

"What a surprise," she said with a groan. "I'm going to need some soap, Miss McKenzie. She's dry as a bone."

One of the doctor's hands rested on Livvy's stomach, easing her against the table. The other began to insinuate itself between her legs. She smacked them closed, locking the doctor's hand between them.

"Oh, you must be just what your husband dreamed about when he was still taking care of his own business. Miss McKenzie, I'm going to need a little help here."

Cold hands pried her knees apart. Something slipped inside her. A finger. Two. The hand on her belly pressed down.

"Okay," the doctor said when Livvy was sufficiently humiliated and the sound of her sniffling filled the room. "Now. This is going to feel cold and a bit uncomfortable."

Something larger and harder than Spencer entered her. Olivia grasped the edges of the table and bit down on the inside of her cheek until the warm taste of blood filled her mouth.

"It lets me see right up inside you," Dr. Roberts said. "Now scoot down just a little more so I can get my finger into your——"

Something metallic fell to the floor with a clang as Livvy tried to jump up and away from the doctor's probing hands. One leg was still locked over the wooden support, caught in the sheet that covered part of her thigh but left her other parts shamefully exposed.

"Don't," she said, choking on her words. "I can't. I . . ."

The doctor backed away and spoke to her very softly, as if she were a mad dog with foam running from her mouth. "We're done. It's all over. Just sit a minute and catch your breath and we'll talk."

Talk? She couldn't swallow. She couldn't breathe. She certainly couldn't talk. And what would she say, anyway? She dropped her head into her hands and cried. Cried for the baby she wasn't going to have and the hope she would have to let go of.

"There's nothing wrong with you," the doctor said, leaning against the door with her feet and her arms crossed casually. "Everything's where it should be, from what I can see. Except your sexuality."

Livvy had no idea what she was talking about. "My . . . ?"

The doctor shook her head and scratched at her ear, inserting her pinky and shaking it. "You, my dear, are a victim of your time. Repressed, afraid, hysterically shy. You are the reason there are more whores on River Street than breweries. Before you are going to become a mother, madam, you are going to have to become a woman.''

Livvy covered herself with the sheet and stared at the doctor, trying to understand what the old woman had said. "I can have babies?" she asked, finally finding her voice.

"That's what I said," the doctor answered, rolling down her sleeves and turning to leave.

"Then why haven't I?"

The doctor looked her up and down as if she were wearing one of those sandwich boards and parading her condition about Milwaukee. "Nerves," she said, and opened the door. "Same as I see nearly every day of the week, nearly every week of the month. Like more patients than I can count, it would be my guess that until you learn to enjoy what God made miraculous, you aren't likely to produce any miracles. But maybe then . . .

"There is no pill, no cure, no operation. You are your own worst enemy, Mrs. Williamson, in my opinion. Your husband knows what to do. Let him do it.''

And with that, she shooed the nurse out in front of her and shut the door.

Chapter Eleven

Bess hadn't wanted to talk about the doctor any more than Olivia. She'd clutched her purse to her chest all the way back to their room and muttered to herself under her breath. She seemed so beside herself that Livvy temporarily forgot her own troubles and demanded to know what Dr. Roberts had told her.

"Nothing." Bess held the handbag so tightly Livvy was afraid it would break in two.

"What did she give you?"

"Give me? Nothing. Nothing I'd ever use, anyways."

Now she had Livvy's curiosity piqued. "Because?"

"Because I'm a good Catholic and I know what marriage and the marriage bed are for!" She blushed to her graying roots.

Livvy hadn't noticed how old Bess was getting, but now she could see the little lines by her eyes and the silver in her fading reddish hair. Time was running out for Bess, and Livvy knew she wasn't far behind. She put out her hand, palm up, and waited for Bess to open her purse and place her secret into it.

"I can't," Bess said, shaking her head. "I just can't."

"Bess Sacotte! What in the world has gotten into you? Is it some sort of medicine? A tonic?" She knew how much alcohol, or even opium, some of the medicines on the market contained, and she was as leery of them as the next woman, but it was nothing for Bess to be ashamed of. Not with her, of all people.

"It's a"—Bess lowered her voice so that no one rushing by on the street could overhear them—"fremph lope."

At least that was what it sounded like to Livvy.

"A what?"

"A French envelope," Bess said, a little louder as she was frustrated and fed up and Livvy thought she might even be near tears.

Livvy put her hand around her sister-in-law and patted her gently on the back. "Well, that's not so bad, is it?" she asked. "Are there special instructions inside?"

Bess looked at her as if she were daft. "Instructions? I figure that Remy'll surely know where to put the thing, don't you?"

"Put what?"

Bess's eyes widened. "You don't know what I'm talking about, do you?"

Livvy had assumed that the French had figured out some special system to aid Bess in her problem, but from the look on Bess's face, she was obviously missing some vital piece of information.

"It goes on his . . . That is, it catches the . . . So that a woman doesn't . . . Oh, Livvy! I can't talk about this!" She hid her chubby reddened face in her hands.

"It's a thing? From France?"

"No, it's just called that because a man puts . . . and it holds . . ."

Livvy had no idea what her sister-in-law was getting at.

"Oh, Lord," Bess said with a sob. "It catches his . . . and the Lord says that loving is for the making of babies, and with this there won't be any making of babies because . . . Well, you know. You're a married woman, for goodness sake!"

Livvy just patted Bess's back some more and nodded. Dr.

Roberts was right. Before she became a mother, she was going to have to learn a lot about being a woman. Bess had just confirmed what the doctor had told her. She was repressed. She was hysterically shy. Her own worst enemy. The doctor had laid all the blame on Livvy's nerves. But, and it was a glorious, wonderful *but*, if it was only nerves and fear, she could give Spencer a baby of his own.

In a silence that was one shade shy of companionable, the two women sat on a bench in front of the YWCA and waited for Charlie Zephin to pick them up and return them to where they belonged. Milwaukee was full of conventioneers and wild women and beer gardens and doctors who expected women to know more than they should.

They both seemed relieved when Mr. Zephin's carriage finally pulled up, his friendly face breaking into a smile at the sight of them.

Well, Livvy thought, *at least I'm not repulsive. Charlie Zephin's happy to see me.* Lord, now she didn't know whether she wanted to believe the doctor or not. It would take an awful lot on her part to live up to the doctor's recommendations. But the rewards were so great!

"Just gotta make a quick stop," Charlie said when the women were settled in the carriage. "You women have a nice morning?"

Livvy and Bess exchanged looks, Bess hugging that purse of hers even more tightly to her bosom. Livvy searched for something to say in answer, but before she could come up with anything, Charlie pointed toward a dapper gentleman standing by the corner and pulled the carriage up beside him.

"Makeridge?" he asked, and the man nodded. He was pleasant-enough looking, though from this distance it was hard to tell how accurate Emma's description of his blue eyes and wavy brown hair had been. He carried a leather satchel and several packages and next to him there stood a valise.

Charlie got down from the carriage and grabbed Mr.

Makeridge's suitcase, then ushered the man toward them, all the while talking animatedly no doubt about the merits of placing a railroad line through Maple Stand. Livvy didn't care very much one way or the other. Maybe Dr. Roberts was right. Maybe if she just relaxed, it would happen.

"Mr. Makeridge, allow me to introduce Mrs. Williamson and Mrs. Sacotte, only two of the lovely women that hail from Maple Stand. Ladies, Mr. Makeridge."

The man came close enough for Livvy to get a good look at him, and Emma hadn't been exaggerating by much. If his eyes weren't as blue as a June sky, they were certainly late May. And that rakish curl that dipped over his left eye, well, there was a time a man like that could have probably made her swoon. But now she valued a strong back over a full head of hair, a careworn face over a slick smile.

Still, she couldn't help but notice his fine manners and the way he complimented her on her traveling dress and hat. He took notice, too, of the fancy needlework on Bess's gloves and then asked the ladies' preference regarding seating for the ride. Stunned at being given the choice, she stuttered for a moment and let Bess answer for them.

"Back of this wagon rides like a plow over a rocky field, Mr. Makeridge. If you don't mind awfully, I'd sure prefer to ride up front with Mr. Zephin."

Makeridge smile widely at Olivia, as if he could think of nothing more pleasant that spending an entire day next to the wife of some stranger, then extended his hand to Bess and assisted her in getting down from the wagon and then up again into the front seat.

Climbing in next to her, Mr. Makeridge asked Olivia if she would mind holding his packages for a moment, took his satchel from Charlie, and settled himself.

"Chocolates," he said by way of explanation when he took the parcels back from Olivia and settled them on his own lap. "Love them, don't you? Ambrosia from the gods."

Olivia smiled and nodded. She'd had chocolates only a
few times in her life, and remembered the occasions well. The
last time had been when Spencer proposed marriage. He'd
brought a box of chocolates and a bouquet of pussy willows, it
being too early in the season for anything else to be in bloom.
He'd explained that he couldn't manage the farm himself and
that he thought they could get on well enough.

There had been no mention of love, no flowery words
exchanged. But that once, at least, there had been the chocolates and the pussy willows.

"You know there is no chocolate that compares to that
which one can find in Milwaukee," he said. "Perhaps later I
can interest you in sampling some."

"I'm sure you can," she agreed, perhaps a little too
readily for good manners. "Later. It's a long ride."

And indeed it was. The afternoon sun lost its brilliance
and the day turned cooler the farther they traveled from Milwaukee until the sun began to set somewhere around the halfway point of their journey.

Bess had fallen asleep long ago, her head alternately
tipped back with her mouth ajar or leaned down deep against
her chest. Charlie shouted back to his passengers every now
and then, but it was difficult to hear him and Olivia felt most
of the time as if she and Makeridge were all alone in the
world, vast fields laid out on either side of them and no one
passing for miles at a time.

"I enjoy my work immensely," he said after one of the
many periods of silence between them. "There's a wonderful
opportunity to travel, to meet new people, to influence the
future on a grand scale as well as on a personal level."

"There are a great many people opposed to the railroad,
Mr. Makeridge. How do you deal with them?" she asked,
wondering if Spencer would still be angry at her when she
returned home. Why had she disagreed with him about the

railroad? How could she have opposed him publicly the way she had? No wonder he hadn't even said good-bye.

"Throughout time there have been people who have refused the opportunity the future was willing to hand them. People who want to stay mired in the past because they are comfortable in it, or simply because they are afraid of the unknown. I view these people with pity, Mrs. Williamson, or sometimes even with contempt, for they don't want merely to stay in the past themselves but hold to everyone back with them."

"About an hour or two more to go," Charlie said over his shoulder. "Wish we'd stopped for supper back in Green Bay."

Olivia was sorry, too, but the doctor had cost her all the money she'd saved. And she'd had to lend Bess the little bit Spencer had given her for a book by Dr. Alice Stockham that had a diet Bess was to follow. Since the two women hadn't enough money for a meal in Green Bay, they had suggested pressing on. Livvy's stomach rumbled, as it had been doing for the last half hour, and she hoped Mr. Makeridge didn't hear it.

"You know," the man next to her said, lifting one of his parcels onto his lap and peeling the brown paper off it, "I could surely go for a chocolate about now. I adore the chocolates you can get in Milwaukee. The French cream roses are beyond compare. But the very best that this city—or any other that I've been in, and I have been around"—he placed a hand on hers and patted it knowingly, giving her a wink—"has to offer are the imported chocolate-covered cherry cordials."

He ripped what remained of brown paper from the box, revealing a fancy satin cover imprinted with writing that Olivia thought she recognized as French, but wasn't sure. *French envelopes* popped into her head. She wished it was too dark for Mr. Makeridge to see her embarrassed blush, but doubted it. She guessed she fairly glowed.

"Won't you try one?" he said, lifting the cover and letting the moon's light reveal perfect rows of sweet dark chocolate mounds with a swirl atop each one. "I assure you they will take you to heaven."

"Perhaps just one," Olivia agreed, the juices in her mouth pooling at the smell that was rising from the box.

He leaned forward and extended the box toward Charlie and Bess. "Chocolates?" he offered.

Bess's chubby hand reached for one and then pulled back. Livvy had thought she was still asleep. "I think I'll wait awhile," she said. It seemed she was looking for an alternative to the doctor's solution.

"Love chocolate," Charlie said, reaching in and grabbing several. "Little enough sweetness in life. Take what you can get."

"Yes," Mr. Makeridge agreed and placed the box in Olivia's lap. "Never look a gift horse in the mouth. That's what I always say, Mrs. Williamson. Or may I call you Olivia?"

Livvy lifted a soft chocolate from the box, its melted edges clinging to her fingers, and took a bite, letting the lush center stream into her mouth. She tipped her head back quickly but still some of the cream dribbled onto her chin. She felt Makeridge's finger catch the drop before it fell to her bodice, and he traced its path upward toward her lip, then placed the finger in his own mouth and sucked it clean.

Between the moist sweetness that swirled in her mouth and the sight of the handsome man next to her licking his finger and watching her clean her lips with her tongue, she felt a dizziness like nothing she had ever felt before.

She popped the rest of the bonbon into her mouth and chased the cherry with her tongue, coaxing it out of its candied shell. At his insistence she had three more before he shifted in his seat and eased her against him ever so gently. "You must be getting tired," he said solicitously. "If you'd like to rest, I would be honored to act as your pillow."

Livvy let herself sink against him slightly. It had been a long ride and there was still awhile to go. Her corset cut into her stomach and her breasts, and she marveled that city women wore them every day. She could feel more than see the gooey mess on her hand, and seeing no alternative, she licked her fingers as daintily as she could.

"You may let yourself go," he said, easing an arm around her shoulder and encouraging her to sink closer into his chest. "I hardly feel you against me, you're so very delicate."

Livvy had been called many things, but never delicate. She was good, sturdy stock, meant for a life of hard work. She had strong muscles and tough bones. Still, in the quiet carriage, the moon shining down on her, her belly full of chocolate cordials and her back resting against a very handsome man, she felt almost delicate. And maybe a trifle wicked, as well. If only Dr. Roberts could see her now.

"Have another chocolate," he said near her ear, rustling the box in her lap until she agreed. She had an astoundingly hard time finding a bonbon with her fingers, then an equally hard time finding her own mouth. It wasn't all that surprising when a piece of the chocolate shell, perhaps because she wasn't sitting quite upright, fell onto her bodice. Before she could react, Mr. Makeridge's quick hand whisked it away and popped it into her mouth.

His fingers were salty in her mouth, and firm. They slid on the cream that was already there and then disappeared through her pursed lips. "Mr. Makeridge!" she managed to get out, after swallowing the cherry whole and nearly choking on it. She tried to right herself, but it seemed too great an effort. And he was whispering so quietly that if she moved, she'd never be able to hear him.

"Waylon," he said smoothly, as if she hadn't tried to yell at him. "And we couldn't have such a pretty suit ruined, now could we? And you surely wouldn't want to waste this chocolate."

He handed her another, touching it to her lips before she took it with her own hands. "These are really good," she told him, struggling once again to sit up but feeling somewhat off balance. "Really good." Not only did they taste good, but they seemed to make her feel good, too. The air felt warmer, the breeze stronger, and the carriage wheels seemed to be rolling on air.

After some time and a few more cordials, Charlie pulled the team to a stop near the side of the road. "Been watching for bushes for quite some time and I'm afraid that those trees are gonna have to do before I burst. If you women need a little privacy . . ." He jumped down from the wagon and hurried off to the copse of trees without finishing his thought.

"I would like to stretch a bit," Olivia said, looking over the side of the carriage. "My, but we're up high, aren't we?"

"Just wait for me to help you," Mr. Makeridge said, leaping from the wagon and rushing around in time to catch her as she tried to get down from the wagon herself.

"Oh," she said as her ankle turned beneath her and she tumbled to the ground despite Mr. Makeridge's attempts to keep her on her feet.

He kneeled down next to her and looked at her closely. "Are you quite all right?" he asked, his brows eased down and forming a big V across his forehead.

He looked so silly, she thought as she swayed slightly and found herself being righted by his hand on her arm. "I think I hurt my ankle," she admitted. "Do we have any more chocolates?"

"I think you've had enough," Bess said, peering down from the coach at Olivia as if she heartily disapproved of Olivia sitting on the ground with the civil engineer from the Ahnapee and Western Railroad. Well, what did Bess know? Hadn't Dr. Roberts told her she needed to become a woman? And accused her of being afraid?

"Ha! And I thought you were apeep," she said. The word

didn't sound right, and her voice sounded like it was dancing around in her head, making her wish she could get up and dance to the tune of this new woman in her body.

"Mr. Makeridge," Bess said in what sounded to Olivia to be a very accusatory voice, "might those chocolate candies have some liquor in them?"

"Don't be ridiculous," Olivia said, trying to get to her feet but finding her ankle would not cooperate. "They are delicious. You should try some. In fact, I'd like another. Waylon?"

"Whatever you'd like," he said, and rose to bring her down the box. "I don't think your friend approves," he said in a stage whisper.

"Bess isn't my friend. She's my sister-in-law. She can't have any fun." She thought for a minute. "Unless that thing in her purse is a . . . what do they call those? Something French. A French . . . What is it, Bess?"

"Olivia Williamson! I'd swear you were drunk," Bess said.

In the distance they could hear Charlie Zephin singing. As he came closer the words became clear. ". . . She pulled down her drawers to a lot of guffaws, and proved she wasn't a she cat at all." He doffed his hat and looked down at Olivia, still sprawled on the ground with Mr. Makeridge standing beside her. "Evening, Miss Olivia. Enjoying the view?"

"You been eating those chocolates, too?" Bess asked. "They got liquor in them, Charlie Zephin?"

Charlie gave a broad wink at Waylon Makeridge and then shook his head. "I don't believe so, Mrs. Sacotte. A fine lady such as Mrs. Williamson would never partake of liquor, now would she?"

"Certainly not," Livvy agreed. "Wasn't the moon over your left shoulder before, Mr. Makeridge?"

Waylon smiled at her and asked if she needed help to the bushes.

"No, I'll just shit here," she said, leaning against the carriage wheel.

"Olivia!"

"What?" she said at Bess's sharp tone. "What did I say? I just want to sit here for a minute. Then I'll get back in the wagon, if Mr. Makeridge can help me up."

"Of course," he said solicitously. "And just call me Waylon, please. You just lean on me, Olivia. That's it."

The man had a lot of hands. One brushed a breast, one was against her bottom. One was supporting her around her waist, and one was slipping behind both knees and lifting her into the carriage. He leaned her like a rag doll against the corner of the seat and then lifted her foot onto his lap.

"We'd better get this boot off before your foot swells," he said, and struggled to undo her pearl gray vici kid button shoe. "There now," he said as he slid her foot out and checked her ankle and calf.

"Mm," she said, righting herself and returning her foot to the floorboards. "That feels much better."

"Anybody up there want another cherry cordial?" Waylon asked, holding the box out to Bess and Charlie, who each took a piece. He poised the box in front of Livvy. "Olivia?"

"I think I've had enough," she said, but her hand plucked another from the box and shoved it in her mouth despite her words.

"So tell me," Mr. Makeridge said quietly, "about growing up on Sacotte Farm."

Spencer heard the trio singing off key from all the way down by the main road. The children had all been asleep for hours, with thankfully fewer mishaps than the previous day, though he had suffered a bite from Josie when he'd removed her from halfway up the steps to the loft, and Neil had managed to spill not one but both buckets of milk that morning by tripping over them, which meant not only the loss of the milk but wet messy trousers that would reek by the time Olivia got back. Louisa had been quiet and leery all day, and he'd curbed his tongue in her honor.

One of those voices was Olivia's, as surely as if she were singing at church, but the song was one he'd never heard her, or any other lady, sing. He opened the door and peered out in time to see the carriage come weaving up his path with Charlie Zephin in the front and what looked to be two passengers in the rear seat. He came out onto the porch and watched in utter amazement as Livvy stood and then fell back down onto her seat.

"Whoops," she said, and then broke into giggles.

"Whoops," Charlie repeated, and guffawed so loudly Spencer was sure he would wake the children. Maybe even the dead.

"This is where I get off," Livvy said, and stood again. This time when she lost her balance she fell smack into some man's lap. Spencer covered the distance to the wagon in two strides and yanked her up and out of the carriage in one quick motion.

"Olivia?" he said, trying to make heads or tails out of her behavior. "Do you want to explain . . ." Before he could finish, the man in the backseat handed him a gray boot.

"Oh!" she said, reaching for the boot and holding on to Spencer to keep from falling over. "That's where it went. Ground's cold," she said, raising her skirt.

"You're drunk," he said, realizing what in the world was wrong with his demure wife. "You're falling-down-lying-in-the-gutter-step-over-me-while-I-puke drunk!" He took a step away from her and she wobbled, smiling sweetly at him.

"That's ridipolous," she said, covering her mouth and

looking ashamed. "I am a temperate woman. I am a pillar of the church. A beacon of righteousness. I am hot." She began unbuttoning her jacket.

"Olivia," he said as calmly as he could manage. "Get into the house. And keep quiet. The children are asleep."

"Oh," she crooned. "My little ones. Were they good to their Uncle Spencer?"

"Go inside," he repeated as she worked at getting herself out of her jacket.

"Are you coming? Doctor says we can make all the babies we want. You want to make a baby?"

"You know," the man in the carriage said, "I must have been wrong about those chocolates. I'm beginning to feel a bit of a buzz myself."

"Who the hell are you?" Spencer demanded, standing beside the wagon and pulling on the front of the man's suit until he was kneeling in the carriage face to face with him. "I want to know what to put on your headstone."

"Williamson's jealous?" Charlie said with surprise. "I'd a never believed it."

"I asked your name," Spencer repeated, aware from the shadows that were being cast on the curtain that Livvy was now in their bedroom. All three men watched as she peeled the jacket from her body and started on the buttons of her blouse. Sure. When it was just him, she was always hiding behind that damn screen. Now, with an audience, she was doing a regular bump and grind.

The curtains parted and Livvy raised the window. In a loud whisper she bade good-bye to Charlie and Waylon.

"Waylon?" Spencer asked. "You that railroad man?"

"Shit. I'd better get him home to Emma before he can see straight." Charlie laughed and flicked the reins. The railroad man fell over on the floor of the wagon as Charlie turned the horses around and left Spencer standing stunned in their wake.

She was humming when he entered the bedroom, rolling

a fine white-tipped lisle stocking down her leg like a two-bit tart. Her hair had escaped her bun and was tumbling over her shoulders and down her back. Her blouse lay on the floor, along with her skirt. Both looked like she had aimed for the back of the chair and missed.

"Oh, Spencer," she said, her color high and her smile seductive. "Look. It doesn't even need me." She was pointing to her corset, which stood on the floor in a circle by itself, supporting nothing but air.

"Mm," he said, not knowing how he was supposed to respond.

"And I don't need it," she said proudly, standing and thrusting her breasts out before falling back on the bed. She stretched and Spencer was sure he had never seen anything so provocative in his life. "Did you miss me?"

"Get under the covers, Olivia. It's very late." *And I have very little self-control. Roll over again and I'm done for.*

She flipped onto her stomach, the slit in her underthings revealing a soft round bottom cheek. He groaned. "Isn't it hot in here, Spence?" she asked him, her words even more slurred than before.

"Yes, Olivia. It's damn hot in here," he agreed, searching for a sheet to throw over her nearly naked body.

"Damn hot," she agreed, and he turned around to stare at the mouth that had uttered his favorite profanity.

It was half open, and out of it came a very faint sigh.

"For my next birthday, Spence," she said dreamily. "If we don't get any more children, can I have some of those chocolates?"

"Chocolates?" he asked, and then remembered the comment that railroad slick had made in the carriage. "Is that how you got like this, Liv? Eating cordials?"

"Do you think I'm pretty, Spence?" she asked.

Her dark hair was everywhere, surrounding her face and

crawling across her naked shoulders. She lay now on her side, and her breasts were pushed together and escaping out the top of her camisole, one dusky nipple almost totally exposed. Her hip flared out from a wasplike waist, making him wonder why she had even donned the corset that now stood on the floor, and her voice was soft and slurred and a little husky.

"Do you?" she asked again with lips that looked swollen with passion and want. "Do you think I'm a woman and want to make a miracle with me?"

"I think you're drunk," he said, laying the sheet over her and tucking it under her chin.

"I can't bear it that you don't want me," she said, followed first by a hiccup and then by a sob.

Want her, he thought, *want her.* He wanted her more than he could remember ever wanting anything, wanted to do things to her that he'd only read about, and not in Dr. Naphey's book, either. He wanted to kiss every inch of her, touch her everywhere and make her pant for more, for him. He wanted to plunge his tongue in the sweetness of her mouth and taste the chocolate that had left her lying on the bed waiting for him to ravish her.

"What kind of man would I be if I took advantage of a drunken wife?" he asked her gently, smoothing the hair from her face and torturing himself just a little more.

"A weak one?" she asked, sniffing and rubbing her nose with the back of her hand.

"Try to go to sleep, Livvy. You're gonna have one helluva headache come morning." He turned down the lamp.

"You don't love me, do you?" she asked.

"Sex has nothing to do with love, Olivia," he answered evasively. "Go to sleep."

"I bet Waylon wouldn't turn down an opportunity like this." Her eyes were shut tight, but tears fell from them, anyway.

"He'd have to be an idiot or a gentleman," Spencer agreed. He doubted the man was either.

"You're just lucky I love you," she said in that voice that signaled she'd be asleep any moment.

He had no answer for her, so he just lay down next to her in his clothes, every inch stiff as a rod, and waited for her to fall asleep.

Chapter Twelve

Spencer was well aware that the first hangover was always the worst. With sympathy he vaguely remembered his own through the haze that softens the pains of growing up. No doubt Livvy had probably seen him in the throes of it. He'd never paid attention to when she was and wasn't underfoot, never noticed when she was around.

But before her feet even hit the floor he knew how poorly she was feeling by the groan she let escape her lips and the way she was clutching the bedsheets as if she were afraid of falling overboard and drowning in her own misery on the bedroom floor.

"It'll get better after you're up awhile," he said to her back.

She began to nod, than caught herself and stopped.

"You okay?" he asked as she eased herself up from the bed, keeping her body as stiff as possible, as if any sudden movement might be her last.

"Yes," she said, no doubt through gritted teeth. Clomping unevenly across the floor, one boot still on her foot from the previous night, she managed to gather her clothing and take it behind the screen without letting him see her face.

"Well, you sure were full as a tick last night," he said, trying appear more understanding than he felt. "You sure were in bed with your boots on . . . that is, your boot."

She didn't answer him.

"There's nothing to be ashamed of, Liv." At least he hoped there wasn't.

Still she said nothing and moved about so quietly he wasn't even sure she was dressing.

"You have a good time in the city?"

When she still didn't answer, he rose and began getting out of his dirty underwear and into fresh clothes for the day.

"Hey," he yelled at the screen. "I didn't get you drunk, you know. There's no call to be mad at me."

He shoved his legs into his summer balbriggans and pulled his blue jeans on over them.

"If anybody ought to be mad, it's me. I find you lying all over some man in the back of Charlie Zephin's wagon, drunk as a skunk and smelling as bad, your dress is full of mud, You've got one shoe off . . . I think I was pretty tolerant there."

He grabbed the same white shirt he had worn the day before and thrust one arm and then the other through the sleeves. He thought that steaming about his wife's behavior all night long had gotten it out of his system, but apparently it hadn't. Not that he was jealous, dammit, he was sure of that. If he was, that would mean he loved Olivia, another thing he was sure he'd avoided. But even if he didn't love her, and he didn't, she was his wife, and that alone was reason enough for the anger he felt still welling within him.

"I should have taken you over my knee and whipped you good."

He buttoned the shirt. The tails came out wrong and he ripped open the buttons and started again.

"In fact, I should have demanded an explanation before I let you pass out like that. And I probably should have beaten you senseless over that fop in the wagon."

He got the shirttails right and sat down on the edge of the bed to put on his socks and boots.

". . . After I broke the guy's pretty nose."

She was taking forever back there. He could have gotten dressed three times and plowed two fields in the time it was taking her to get into her shirtwaist.

"Come out of there now, or I'm coming after you," he shouted. "We got kids to ready for church and a cow that hasn't been milked proper in two days."

Nothing.

"Fine," he said. "Remember, you asked for this." He pushed the screen so hard it fell over like a house of cards, crumbling from the weight of the clothing hanging over its top. Behind it, sitting on a chair and fighting with the lace to her boot, was his wife, her vision so blurred by her tears he wasn't sure she could even tell where her boot ended and her leg began.

It was hard to hold on to his anger in the face of so pathetic a scene. He grabbed at her ankle and undid the lace for her, eased the shoe off her foot, and thrust it at her.

"Another man would've beat his wife within an inch of her life," he said, standing there looking at the miserable woman holding her boot as if she had no idea what to do with it. "You know that?"

She nodded. With her face streaked with silent tears she looked up at him. "Why didn't you?" she asked as if what he'd done hadn't been kind, hadn't been decent and adult and understanding. As if it hadn't taken all the strength he had left not to assert the rights that the law gave him and his own heart had given away.

"Do you know how lucky you are that I didn't? That I feel the way I do? That I've never laid a hand on you?"

Two dark eyes, glistening with tears, stared up at him. She sure didn't seem to realize her good fortune in having married a man with so mild a temper. A man who didn't have a possessive bone in his body where she was concerned. A man who, as he stood there staring at the soft swell of his wife's bosom, was quickly losing that mild temper.

"Jeez," he said, fed up with trying to understand women. "Next time I just might give you what-for."

She looked up at him with doubt in her eyes, doubt and disappointment.

"Try it again, Livvy, and see if I don't."

His hands itched to touch her. But he wasn't at all certain that it would be in anger.

He wasn't even jealous. She'd made a perfect fool of herself—not that she'd planned to, but it had turned out that way—and he wasn't even jealous. She'd come home lying in another man's arms, for heaven's sake. What more did she have to do?

What more *could* she do, but give in and give up?

Her head hurt so much in church that she wished she could just die and get it over with. Her ankle felt like it was caught in the oven door every time she stepped down onto it as she hobbled down the aisle to their pew with the children, and it got worse as she made her way back home.

But nothing hurt as much as her heart, which was surely broken so completely it could never be mended.

Of course, he hadn't bothered to turn the soil in her garden, which was just fine with her. She hardly felt like getting down on her hands and knees and planting strawberries for his pies. She had been foolish enough to believe that those pies could make him love her, just as she believed each supper she made, each shirt she washed and ironed, each kindness she performed would somehow build, like little flakes of snow until the weight of them together would break through the roof he had built over his heart and smother his pain.

She was an idiot.

An idiot with a pounding head and a throbbing foot. And bread to be baked and beds to be stripped and linens to be washed, along with children to be fed and cared for.

Thank goodness for the children. Josie stuck to her like a shadow, clearly relieved she had returned. By the time Louisa and Neil were due home from Bess and Remy's, she and Josie had fed the chickens, milked Miss Lily, made two loaves of quick bread, fixed a dinner for Spencer that he had taken back with him to the fields, and gotten the linens done.

All of that and she had come to terms with her life, too.

She had three children who filled her days with joy and exhausted her enough to see her through her nights. Why, Emma Zephin would trade places with her in a heartbeat.

But Olivia, fool that she was, had wanted three children, a beautiful home, a husband who provided well for her, and love on top of all that. And she'd thought that she could earn it, or steal it, or trick it out of Spencer. Well, she'd cast beyond the moon and come out not too badly. Maybe she didn't have love, but she had Josie and Neil and Louisa, and that would have to be enough.

Just as she was hanging up the last of the sheets, with little Josie holding up the pins for her, the older children came walking up the path. Neil was waving his arms and talking a mile a minute. Louisa was taking giant strides, but she kept her eyes on the dirt before her and her expression was grim.

"Didn't you sleep well?" Livvy asked her when she got close enough to see the dark smudges under her eyes. "You look awfully tired."

"I slept," the girl said, hurrying past her and on into the house.

Livvy went to follow but felt a hand, warm even through her cotton sleeve, staying her. "Let them all go on in," Spencer said in a whisper. His soft voice twisted her insides. He was sweaty from the fields and smelled of wet soil and hard work. Despite her resolutions she still inhaled deeply as if she could capture a piece of him that way.

"Something you wanted, Spencer?" Her voice was formal, foreign, as if they were two acquaintances who were exchanging pleasantries on the street.

"Still mad about me not going to church?" he asked as if the old hurts could do as much damage as the new ones.

"I've got work to do," she said, trying to shrug her arm from his grasp.

"Wait. It's about Louisa," he said, his hand still on her as though nothing between them had changed. But then, for him, nothing had. He hadn't loved her yesterday and he still didn't love her today. Only now she knew it, knew it for a fact. Believed it.

"I think it's her that's got the book," he said, finally letting go of Livvy's arm. Grimacing, he shook his head and pointed to her arm. "I got you dirty."

"Louisa's got the book?" The girl had to be a lot braver than Livvy, who'd never have had the nerve actually to take it.

"I think so," he said, still frowning at her arm. "Will that come out in the wash?" He rubbed his hands on his pants and then brushed at her sleeve.

She wished he'd forget about her dress. His nearness confused her. It was hard to concentrate on their conversation with him fingering her sleeve. "Did you ask her?"

"I didn't think she'd admit it, and I sure didn't want to embarrass her. That little one shames easier than . . ." He stopped abruptly as Louisa came out of the house in the calico dress Livvy had made for her to do her chores in.

"I'm going for a walk," she said.

Spencer gave Livvy a wink, sending spirals of warmth up her spine to do battle with the chills running down her back, then said, "Oh, yeah, Liv. Remy said he wanted that book back. Remind me to get it out of my drawer after dinner and bring it over to him."

The stiffening of Louisa's back told them what they wanted to know, but Spencer said nothing to the girl. Instead he apologized to Livvy again about her dress and made small talk until Louisa was well down the path.

"I think I'll just follow our little miss a ways," he said. "I sure would like to know where it is she keeps going."

Just the mention of Dr. Napheys's book led Livvy's thoughts down a path she couldn't control. A path that put her once again in Spencer's strong arms, beneath his warm body, at the mercy of his desires and of her own. "You think she's reading that book?" she asked. She could feel the heat in her cheeks.

"Well, you know," he said with a smirk before leaving her, "women have been known to take a peek between those covers."

Livvy hands flew to her cheeks hoping to cover them before he could see her furious blush.

He was laughing quietly as he walked away, his shoulders shaking as he set out after Louisa. Olivia squinted her eyes against the bright sun and wished she'd never sampled those cherries. Mr. Makeridge might just as well have offered her an apple, for the fruit had surely brought the ruination of what she'd hoped would be Eden.

Inside the house, Neil was enjoying a tall glass of milk and teasing Josie by holding a cookie out of her reach. The little girl was trying to climb his leg.

"No wonder she's always trying to get higher and higher," Livvy said, and scooped the little girl up so that she could grab the cookie from her brother. Frustration was surely something Olivia understood and not something she was likely to put up with.

Neil had stopped at the door to slip on his work boots, the ones that reminded her so much of Spencer's, when she remembered that there was something she wanted to ask him.

"I'm writing a letter to your papa today," she said. Neil seemed to flinch and his shoulders went up defensively. "Is there anything you want me to tell him for you?"

"Why are you writing to him?"

"Well," she answered, "he's your papa, for one thing. I'm sure he wants to know how you and your sisters are getting on. It must be hard for him, all alone out in San Francisco, and when he gets a letter about you three it must make him feel closer to home." And she wanted to assure him that the children were fine where they were and that he needn't give a moment's thought to sending for them. Ever. He could go off to the Klondike, or wherever it was he was wishing to go, and she'd watch over his children and love them like her own. Forever.

"You don't have to tell him about me, Aunt Liv. He doesn't miss me. That's for sure." He was squatting, tying up his boots, his face more intent on the job than was necessary.

"Of course he misses you," she said, afraid that it was no doubt true. "A father belongs with his children. It can't be easy for him, leaving you in someone else's care. I bet he worries about whether you're eating proper, and getting enough rest and working too hard."

"What are you going to tell him?" He ripped the laces open and started again, his fingers tangled in the long black strings.

She knelt beside him and took over tying his shoe as if he were still a small boy. The throbbing in her head was getting better as the day wore on. If only the same could be said for her heart.

"I'm going to tell him about the railroad," she said, trying to reassure him that there was nothing for him to worry about, though she wasn't sure what it was that had him, as well as his laces, tied in knots. "That man I met in Milwaukee, Mr. Makeridge? Well, he thinks that Maple Stand surely is a good place for a train stop on the way up from Sturgeon Bay. How would you like to wake up to the sound of a train whistle?"

"You aren't gonna tell him to come get us, are you?

Josie's being much better, don't you think? She hardly ever bites anymore. And anyone can see that Uncle Spence needs me. He can't do that whole job alone. He needs a boy to unharness Curly George and rub him down and . . ."

She finished tying the laces despite the tears that blurred her vision. The boy was happy here, on the farm, with her and Spencer. The one letter she had received from Julian made no mention of the children joining him any time soon. In fact, it had been a request for money, claiming that Spencer was getting Neil's services for free and so he ought to be able to lend Julian a few dollars for a short time.

Spencer had thrown the letter out, but Livvy had retrieved the envelope with its return address.

"No, I'm not gonna tell him to come get you." Not now, not ever. She hugged the boy and then straightened his hat. "Go on now. Uncle Spence needs a hand, like you said."

For a day that had started out so badly, it was amazing how much worse it could get. Her mind was unable to escape the thoughts that Neil had unwittingly placed there. Someday the letter from Julian asking for his children would arrive. Someday she would have to pack up their things, kiss them on their foreheads, and send them away, maybe on the very train that Waylon Makeridge was planning for. As lonely as the house had been before the children came, she knew how much worse it would be after they were gone.

Josie helped her with her afternoon chores. They weeded in the garden, the child pulling out as many seedlings as weeds, with Livvy following behind her and replanting the tiny stems as they went. They cleaned out the coop and then had to clean Josie, who, by the time they had finished, smelled worse than the coop. When Louisa finally came down the path with her hands behind her back, supper was cooking on the stove and Spencer was back in the fields.

So he'd been right about the book, Livvy supposed. Taking Josie by the hand, she hurriedly limped off toward the barn, leaving the house empty so that Louisa could return Dr. Napheys to his proper place.

Lord, the woman was glum. Her mood cast a pallor over the whole house. Funny how one woman could make a whole house frown. Well, it was quiet, anyway. That was something he had to be grateful for. Except for the uneven footsteps as his wife moved back and forth between the stove and the table, still favoring that ankle of hers, all Spencer heard was the clinking of silverware against plates.

"Guess I'll take that book over to Remy and Bess's after supper," he said, breaking the silence.

"Can I come?" Neil asked. "I've got three blood aggies and a ballot marble I wanna trade with Philip."

"For what?" Josie asked. No one else seemed at all interested.

"Well, the way we work it is, I give them to Philip and he kind of shops them around and gets my best deal."

"You mean you don't know what you're getting?" Louisa asked, obviously disapproving the plan.

"A Sacotte wouldn't cheat a Williamson," Neil said, defending his cousin. "He'll get me a good deal. You see if he doesn't."

"You're not a Williamson," Louisa said. "You are a Bouche."

Neil's gaze flew to Spencer, as if there were anything he could say that would change the way things were. "Well," he said, supposing it wouldn't do any harm. "For the time being, I guess you could think of yourselves as Williamsons. You're living in my house, eating my food . . . I guess for now, *just for now,* you could be considered Williamsons."

Before he'd spit it out, he was sorry he'd said it. The boy had that same damn look Livvy got so often. As if they thought everything was going to work out fine. Worse—as if they thought that he could make it all work out just fine.

"You want to come, Liv?"

She shook her head. Had she said a word all through dinner? Beyond "eat your pea soup" to Josie and "use your napkin" to Neil? She couldn't still be mad from the morning. She'd had no right to the anger even then. For heaven's sake, was she going to be mad forever?

"I want to take a look at that ankle before I go," he said. "I don't like the way you're limping on it."

"It's all right," she said, starting to rise.

"Sit down," he told her, figuring all the walking she was doing surely wasn't helping her leg heal. "You want something? One of the kids'll get it."

"I was just gonna clear the table," she said, still in her chair.

He directed the bigger children to see to the dishes and told Josie to get into her bedclothes. Then he stood, stretched, and put his hand out to help his wife from the chair. Putting weight on her foot suddenly after sitting through the meal was a bad idea, and she winced, her eyes widening with pain.

"Damn," he said, and whisked her off her feet, carrying her to the couch, then thinking better of it and continuing on to the bedroom. "You're pretty light for your size," he told her, surprised at how easily he was able to lift her, how well she seemed to fit in his arms. Oh, he'd helped her in and out of buggies and wagons, but he couldn't remember ever carrying her around. It felt surprisingly good.

He lowered her on to the bed and knelt to unlace her boot. Her leg was swollen above the top of her shoe and the leather had left an impression on her stocking.

"Lean back," he said, and reached up beneath her dress for the top of her stocking. She let him trace the cotton hose over her knee and peel it from her warm thigh with no resistance. Her skin was beyond soft as his fingers traced down her leg, cupping her calf, then easing the sock from her foot.

Angry marks crisscrossed her ankle like a work of art defiled.

"Does it hurt much?" he asked, touching it gently, wiggling her foot to make sure it wasn't, in fact, broken. It would be just like her, with her dedication to taking care of someone else's children, seeing to all her responsibilities, to limp around on a broken leg.

She jumped back at his touch, and he felt for her bones more gently. Even swollen, it was a delicate ankle. He'd never realized how small her feet were before. Surely he'd noticed that her boots were smaller than his, but her whole foot fit within his hand. And while that hand held her foot, the other began traveling higher and higher until it was examining her knee, and then above her knee, and then it was at the lacy edge of her drawers.

"You're right about not going to Remy's," he said, his hand kneading softly the muscles of her calf. "I think it's best if you stay off this leg tonight."

"But the children," she said, trying to sit up and move toward the edge of the bed.

"Louisa is quite capable of getting herself and Josie to bed," he said, standing and twisting her body around on the bed so that her head was on the pillow as it should be. "She did just fine while you were gone."

"She doesn't seem fine to me," Livvy grumbled, as if she were annoyed with him. As if he could be held accountable for the mood of the females in his household. "And I like to read to Josie at night." She pushed against his hand to sit up and it slipped from her shoulder to her breast.

Stunned, they both stared at his suntanned hand cupping the pale-yellow fabric covering her bosom as if it were a spider crawling down her dress. He had no thought to move it, no feeling that it was connected to him in any way that involved his ability to move. It didn't squeeze, or rub, or fondle her. It just held her, transmitting the beating of her heart to something deep inside him that warmed him in places he was sure were dead.

And then, still without his approval, without his instigation, the hand moved, slid up his wife's chest, and his fingers felt her pulse racing as they skimmed her long slim neck until they cradled it from behind and pulled her face toward his. A slight pressure with two fingers, and her head was tipped just enough for his lips to seek out hers and taste the sweetness of her kiss.

He lowered her head softly to the pillow, his hand still holding her head to his, his lips still working against hers, and climbed up onto the bed beside her. There were twelve buttons that ran down the front of her dress. He had counted them a hundred times when he had tried to keep his mind on other things than what lay beneath those twelve tiny buttons and a bit of white cotton. Now he opened the top one and laid a kiss against her neck.

The smell of hot lilacs rose from the hollow of her neck and he dipped his tongue, wondering if the taste would be as sweet.

"Aunt Liv?" It was Neil, his voice tentative as if he knew he might have interrupted something, but didn't seem to know what. Spencer wasn't so sure himself.

Spencer jumped away from Olivia, up off the bed and to the other side of the room, as if he had been caught by Livvy's parents seducing their daughter. Away from her, his head cleared and he wondered what in the hell he had been doing. He knew better than that. It was just as his father had warned him when he was a boy. Kissing led to touching, touching to more serious things, and before you knew it some girl with a pretty face was pregnant and you were stuck in a marriage you sure hadn't been thinking of when you'd stolen that first kiss.

Livvy looked sleepy, dreamy, confused, as if she were

having trouble returning to the here and the now. He'd have liked to kick himself for what he was doing to her. Not to mention what he was doing to himself.

"What is it, boy?" he asked, shoving his hands in his pockets to hide what would have been obvious to someone just a little older than his nephew.

"Josie wants to know if Aunt Liv'll read to her even if her leg hurts."

Livvy was watching Spencer, looking for signs of what he wanted from her. "Yeah," he said on her behalf. "Tell Josie to come in here when she's all ready for bed. And tell Louisa she's to get her aunt whatever she needs while we're gone."

He reached down into his dresser drawer and pulled out *Transmissions of Life,* happy to be getting it out of his home. He held it up to Livvy as if to prove to her that he was right, but her eyes were closed, the very tip of her tongue escaping her mouth and pressed tightly between her lips.

"Don't get out of this bed for anything. I'll be back later," he said, and headed for the door without looking back. He knew he'd be seeing the hollow of her neck the whole way to his brother-in-law's house, feeling the smoothness of her leg, tasting the warmth of her lips. That would be torture enough.

Long as the trip was to Sacotte Farm, the way back seemed twice as long. And the visit with Remy and Bess, brief though he had made it, had done nothing to calm his frayed nerves. The two of them seemed as frustrated as he was, jumping at casual touches, snapping at innocent words.

Now, his home just down the road, all Spencer could think about was spending another night in the same bed as the lilac princess. He couldn't do it. Not and keep the promises he'd made himself.

"Tell Aunt Liv I had to go in to town," he said as he pulled the wagon up in front of the house and Neil jumped down.

"You want me to come with you?" Neil offered, that eager face smiling up at him. For Spencer it was simply the last straw.

They all wanted a piece of him, and he had none to give. Any part of him that could belong to someone else was dead and buried at the Maple Stand Belgian Cemetery. And the sooner they all got used to that fact, the better.

"No, I don't want you coming with me," he said to the boy. "I don't want anything more than to be left alone. Get inside now."

The boy, dejected, walked slowly up the porch steps and turned to wave. Spencer gave him a slight nod, more than he intended, but less than would satisfy the boy, and yelled at Curly George to get a move on.

Lord, he thought, the back end of George swaying in front of him, why didn't they understand what it was he needed from them? It seemed simple enough to him. If they would just all leave him alone and let him be miserable, he'd be happy.

It wasn't until he got to the Lucky Clover Saloon that he realized where he was headed, nor what it was he had in mind for his evening's pleasure. Jumping down from the wagon, he sighed heavily and headed for the hottest place in Maple Stand.

That wasn't, he had to admit, saying much. Maple Stand was a small town, even by Door County standards. A lumber mill, a mercantile, a tavern, a post office, and a bank. That was about it, except for the church and the Lucky Clover, tacked on to the back of Grace Linden's house on the edge of town. Anything went at Grace's—gambling, drinking, and, if Grace was in the mood and you had enough cash, even she was available.

The women of Maple Stand all knew it, but typical of the women he knew, they pretended the place didn't exist. The men, on the other hand, pretended they did things there that

Spencer didn't quite believe they did. After all, Grace was still alive, wasn't she?

There was, to Spencer's mind, only one thing wrong with the Lucky Clover, and it wasn't Grace or the gambling, or the liquor, which put to shame the beer and wine served at the tavern. No, it was the fact that it was too damn crowded, most nights, to get drunk in peace. There was always someone wanting to tell Spencer his troubles and interfering with Spencer drowning his own. Not like the tavern, which was spacious and fine for a social drink, the Lucky Clover was a tiny hole in the wall meant for hard drinkers bent on getting drunk.

This night was no exception. Among the crowd, which was two deep at the bar, was Charlie Zephin and that fop who had been in the wagon with Livvy. Makebreath, or whatever the hell his name was. If there'd been another place to get a real drink, Spencer would have turned around and left the Lucky Clover in a second. But Sturgeon Bay was a hell of a long distance going, and as drunk as he wanted to get, too far coming back home.

"Scotch, Gracie," he said when he caught her eye. He motioned with his thumb and his forefinger, indicating a good-size glass.

Gracie nodded and then under her breath said something to Charlie, who turned around and looked at Spencer with glassed-over eyes. Spencer gave him a tight nod and studied the handsome man with him, wondering how attractive Livvy must have found him. Spencer had no illusions about himself. He was getting too heavy, his hair was too long, too gray, and he was too used up. But this man was fresh and lively and he had a twinkle in his eye that had gone out of Spencer's years ago.

He watched as Charlie pointed him out, nodding and no doubt telling whatever his name was that he was Olivia Williamson's husband.

The scotch beat Makebreath to him by half a minute and

Spencer had already downed it before the man even got a chance to extend his hand.

"Waylon Makeridge at your service," the man said, bowing slightly.

It seemed to Spencer that more than a few eyes were on the pair. In fact, the men on either side of him had backed up slightly, as if to give them room. That should have been a warning to Makeridge, but some people missed the subtleties of life. They needed to be hit over the head, so to speak.

Spencer ignored Makeridge's hand and put the glass down on the bar, signaling with his fingers for another shot.

"I had the pleasure of meeting your wife the other day," Makeridge continued.

"Shouldn't you be over at the mercantile?" Spencer asked without looking up from his glass. "I thought Miss Emma was expecting you."

Makeridge must have pruned his face, for several patrons laughed, and one claimed that he wasn't drunk enough yet to stand Emma Zephin's face.

"But Livvy Williamson, now that's another pair of shoes altogether," Frank Saugus, a farmer from the other side of town, said with a laugh.

"That is, when she's got her shoes on," Charlie Zephin said to a round of laughter.

"According to Makeridge here, she's even prettier with those shoes off!"

Spencer threw back his head and gulped down the second whiskey. It burned his throat and his lungs and set his stomach ablaze.

"She's one mighty fine-looking woman," Makeridge said admiringly. "You're a lucky man, Mr. Williamson."

"The way you tell it, Makeridge, sounded like you got lucky yourself," a voice boomed from somewhere behind Spencer.

The liquor was doing its work, but not as quickly as

Spencer would have hoped. He downed another double and tried to focus on Makeridge's smiling face.

"She's got a fine pair of"—Makeridge's grin widened and he threw back his shoulders and extended his chest—"boots!" he shouted, and it felt to Spencer as if the whole Lucky Clover saloon were rocking back and forth in time to the laughter around him.

Makeridge was right. Livvy did have a fine pair of breasts. Spencer had spent enough time staring at them, mooning over them, guessing at how they would feel resting in the palms of his hands. She had a fine pair of legs, too, and often enough he had imagined them encircling his waist and drawing him into her.

Then, too, she had a fine pair of feet, small, dainty, and always cold. How often he longed to take them between his thighs and warm them for her. And eyes. She had a fine pair of eyes, dark and soft and searching. And her hands, delicate boned but strong; they could make his heart beat double when she touched him.

"I tell you," Makeridge drawled, studying Spencer like he was some new garden slug the man had never seen before. "If I could be between the sheets with Olivia Williamson, I sure as hell wouldn't be here drinking myself silly. But your brother-in-law warned me you didn't have a lick of sense."

Odd that Remy should have had anything to do with the man, but then Spencer was well aware of how much Remy wanted Makeridge to buy Sacotte Farm. Carefully, deliberately, Spencer put the glass down and turned toward Makeridge. He smiled slowly, indulgently. Some men never knew just how far was too far. Some men needed a lesson. And Spencer was surely in the mood for teaching tonight. He stood, kicking the stool back and guessing someone must have caught it, since it never made a sound in the suddenly quiet room. He unbuttoned the cuff of his right sleeve. If he popped the button he might have to explain to Livvy how he'd lost it.

Besides, he didn't want any of Makeridge's blood on his nice white shirt, which, like everything else his wife washed for him, smelled of lemon.

"Now, Spence," Charlie said, one hand up to quiet his anger.

Spencer ignored him and raised his eyebrows at Makeridge as if to say *You ready?*

Makeridge jutted out his jaw and smirked as if he thought Spencer either wouldn't dare, or simply wouldn't do damage.

Spence's arm worked as well as it always had, whether it was punching a hole in a wall or relocating a man's jaw. And as always, it felt damn good. Rarely, though, did it feel as good as this.

"I guess Sacotte forgot to tell you about my right cross," he said simply. Makeridge stared up at him uncomprehendingly. Spencer rolled his sleeve back down and stepped over the civil engineer on his way out of the bar.

He turned at the door. "Anyone got anything else they want to say about my wife?" He swore he could hear the ice melting in the glasses on the bar. "Fine, then. I guess that's all."

In the wagon he flexed his fist, making sure nothing was broken. He supposed that by now they'd have revived Makeridge and he was testing his jaw about the same way. If his jaw felt half as bad as Spencer's fist, it was worth it.

Of course, in the morning when the effects of the liquor had worn off, he wasn't sure he'd feel quite the same. He was going to have to remember he was getting older. Pains ran deeper, lasted longer, left more scars.

The house was quiet when he and Curly George arrived. He took his time settling the horse for the night, still trying to get his breathing anywhere near normal enough to lay down next to his wife without scaring the hell out of her. He sounded like an asthmatic bear with a hive of bees chasing him.

He tried to tell himself *he'd* embarrassed *her* often

enough, drinking, brawling, making a general ass of himself. Wasn't she entitled to one slip in three years of marriage? Hell, one slip in a whole lifetime? It wasn't as if she'd really done anything with Makebreath. . . .

Clearly, he wasn't drunk enough. The railroad dandy's words still mattered, the niggling thought that maybe there could be something to them still mattered, and the fact that she was lying, soft and warm and available in his bed, still mattered.

He ought to make up his damn mind. If he didn't want her, then what difference did it make if Makeridge did?

He slammed the barn door hard enough to wake the ghosts of Curly George's ancestors and stormed toward the house. A house that teemed with children. He made a detour to the privy and then stopped at the pump to wash up. The night was hot and muggy. Or maybe it was the whiskey.

He washed up and studied his house from the outside. Only one light glowed. Was she still awake? Well, let her say one word about his drinking, just one, and he'd tell her a thing or two about hearing his wife's name and her attributes bandied about the Lucky Clover. His hand was getting stiff. He flexed it and winced. It could have been worse. Makeridge could have hit him back.

He took off his boots on the porch. If there was a chance that Livvy was asleep, he wasn't going to risk waking her and having to look her disappointment in the eyes yet again. He ought to consider carving a sign to hang over the front door: *Hangover House*. But not tonight. Tonight he was too tired to do anything but crawl into bed and sleep off his anger.

On the couch a lump shifted at the close of the front door. The boy was no farmer yet, but he had a good shot at being a watchdog, should all else fail.

"Go back to sleep," Spencer said in a whisper, and watched the covers smooth down without a word.

The door to his bedroom was open, the soft light calling to him, and like a moth, he followed it.

She was asleep on the bed. He could tell from the rise and fall of her back, so even, the seams of her dress straining with each intake of breath. She was still fully clothed, from the tight bun of her hair to the tips of her still-stockinged toes. And she wasn't alone.

Josie lay in the curve of her body, the book Livvy had been reading to her covering a portion of her cheek. He lifted it quietly, closed it, and put it on the nightstand. With the knowledge that comes with years of fatherhood, he slipped his arms beneath the sleeping little girl and lifted her from the bed without rousing her.

The warm baby in his arms squirmed closer to him, her ragged sigh hot against his freshly washed chest, her lips searching for her thumb. On the bed beneath his gaze, Livvy stirred but settled once again. Watching her, but carrying the child, he smashed his shin on the corner of the bed.

"Spence?" It was that raspy whispery night voice, and it crawled up his arms and burrowed in his neck. "I'm glad you're home."

Four words and his anger was gone. Four words and his jaw slacked and his shoulders eased. "Get out of your dress, Liv. You fell asleep. I'll put Josie in her bed."

She nodded, her head not rising from the pillow, and fumbled with her top button.

He didn't stay to see the rest, but carried Josie into the room she shared with Louisa and settled her into her bed.

There was no sound coming from Louisa, and he figured she was pretending to be asleep. She was stiller than a corpse.

"Night, Miss Louisa," he said softly, tweaking her toes through the covers on his way out. She jerked her foot away, and he chuckled almost soundlessly. At least he could be sure she wasn't dead. Damn disagreeable girl, though.

He'd given Livvy too little time and too much credit, if he

thought that she'd be undressed and under the covers by the time he got back to their room. She was just where he'd left her, three buttons undone and snoring softly.

"Come on, Liv," he said, sitting on the edge of the bed and shaking her gently. "You don't want to sleep in your clothes, do you?"

She shook her head, tried to lift it off the pillow, failed, and turned onto her side, away from him. He fumbled in her hair for the pins that held her bun, his fingers tangling in the curls. So much hair, and all of it so soft.

Warmth spread inside him like another glass of whiskey, suffusing his face, burning his belly, moving lower still.

Damn! He should have had a couple drinks less or several more. Now he had both the desire and the capacity. And a distinct lack of will to control either.

Easing the pins out of her hair, pulling it to its full length to free them, he found the smell of lilacs dizzying. He bent his head and burrowed his face in the chestnut locks. The smell, the feel . . . He rolled her onto her back and worked the buttons on her shirtwaist easily.

"Oh, Liv," he whispered as he spread her blouse and lifted her slightly from the mattress to ease it off her shoulders and down her arms, where it was stopped by tightly buttoned cuffs.

"Help me, Liv," he begged as he fumbled with the buttons at her waist, then stood and eased her skirt down over her hips and passed the ruffled edge of her drawers until he could free her feet and toss the skirt toward her screen.

She fought him in her sleep, anxious to get comfortable once again, and her stretch revealed not only a swell of breast but the very slight darkening at the edge of her nipple.

That would have been enough. More than enough. But he lay her back down and she turned quickly onto her side, revealing the slit in her drawers and most of what should have remained hidden from his eyes.

And then there was that hair of hers. Long silky hair everywhere. Hair, and skin, and the scent of lilacs and lemon, and the sound of deep breathing, and only the faint glow of the oil lamp to make him see clearly what he already knew.

Olivia Williamson was irresistible.

"Dammit!" He kicked the bed and spun blindly toward the door, fumbling for the handle. It swung back on its hinges and hit the wall with a thud. But he no longer cared if he woke up everyone in Maple Stand. For sure, he'd never sleep tonight. . . .

How long had he been on the porch? A minute? Two? Was a little privacy too much to ask for at two o'clock in the morning on a hot night in June?

"Spencer? Are you all right?"

There was only the moonlight on her white cotton nightdress, clutched tightly at the neck to prevent him from seeing what had already done its damage.

"Go to bed," he said, turning away from her and moving to the far end of the porch.

"What's the matter?" She crept up behind him despite how clear he was making it that he didn't want her anywhere near him. Not on the same porch, not in the same bedroom, not even in the same house. Heck, the same state might be too close for him to keep the promises he'd made.

"The matter? The matter is I married you, Olivia, and now I'm stuck with you."

"Yes," she agreed, her voice surprisingly steady. "I suppose you are. Can't you make the best of it? I know I'm not Kirsten, but I'm not Emma Zephin, either."

"I'd have been a lot smarter to marry her," he said. "I bet she'd know to stay out of a man's way."

There was only silence and he fought the urge to turn around and see what she was doing, if she was even there. At least she wasn't sobbing.

He ached, his blue jeans cutting his privates in two, his

hand throbbing with only a fraction of the intensity of his manhood.

"Go inside, dammit," he swore at her. "And let me regret marrying you in peace. Why can't you just go away and leave me alone?"

They could probably hear the sharp intake of her breath in Sturgeon Bay, or even in Milwaukee, but only he could hear the faint creak of the door as she opened it to go into the house. And with his heart he knew she was biting on the back of her hand, holding back her tears.

He smashed his wounded hand against the side of the house. As always, he thought, they were both in pain.

Chapter Thirteen

By five in the morning Olivia had cried the last of her tears and had accepted the fact that Spencer did not love her and nothing she did or would ever do was ever going to change that. Nor did she even want to anymore. *Couldn't she go away and leave him alone?*

Oh, yes, she could.

She threw off the covers, wrinkled and balled from her sleepless night, and reached under the bed for the suitcase she had taken to Milwaukee. *Go away?* She opened her underwear drawer and pulled out her two best pairs of drawers and her favorite chemise.

Leave him alone? She shoved them in the suitcase and reached for her cotton stockings, which she rolled into two balls and jammed into the corners of the leather bag.

She'd have to find some way to pay back Bess and Remy for taking her in. She could take over the cooking and cleaning and give Bess the rest she needed. She could make cherry pies and preserves and sell them at Zephin's. Neil could help in the field.

She ran a brush through her hair and pulled it back, watching herself in the mirror as if the determined woman she saw there was someone she'd never seen before. Maybe she'd try a new hairstyle, like the one the women in Milwaukee were wearing. Maybe she'd even move to Milwaukee when the children were older.

She pushed her hair forward some, making it softer

around her face, and tried to give herself a smile at the results. If only her eyes weren't red, her cheeks weren't splotchy, and her lips weren't puffy, she might almost be attractive.

She put two pins in her bun and then threw the brush into the suitcase to join the other things. Maybe he should have married Emma Zephin. At least someone would be happy, then.

That was his problem. He didn't want to be happy. And he didn't want anyone around him to be happy. Lord, one only had to look at the way he treated those poor children. Working Neil to death in the fields, teasing Louisa unmercifully, threatening to hit Josie at every turn . . . Of course, in all fairness, Neil did seem to love the work, coming in all red-cheeked and excited about a new discovery every day. And Louisa surely needed to get off that uppity high horse of hers, and if someone didn't take Josie in hand . . .

She could hear Josie now out in the main room babbling something about chicken lips. As soon as Livvy was finished getting herself together, she'd go out there and get the kids organized. Neil wasn't going to like moving to Sacotte Farm, despite how close he'd grown to his cousins. Although he'd been given very little encouragement from Spencer, as far as she could see, Neil truly loved his uncle.

Louisa wasn't likely to hate living at Sacotte Farm any more or less than she hated living with Spencer. Oh, but the two of them were alike. Two miserable souls committed to making sure no one was any happier than they were.

"Get down, Jo," Neil said, so loudly that it stood out from all the other childish banter that was going on beyond her bedroom door. "You're not supposed to go up there."

Livvy let out a big breath and the hair around her face flew out in several directions. No wonder she usually kept it more tightly bunned.

"Josephina," Louisa said sharply. "Don't move!"

Livvy, slipperless, still in her nightdress, put down the

toiletries she was about to pack and opened the door to her room to see what new disaster was about to strike.

Louisa and Neil were both staring up into the loft at the little girl who stood too precariously close to the edge.

"Oh, Lord," Livvy said, putting up her hands to keep everyone calm as she closed in on the rickety ladder. She had to keep Josie away from the edge. "Josie, honey, I want you to go see if there's a doll on the far bed."

The little girl turned and looked toward the back wall, which was as far as Livvy could send her from the open rim of the loft. "Yes, honey, that one."

Louisa already had one foot on the ladder when Livvy got there.

"No," Livvy said. "I'll get her. Just hold the ladder steady, will you?"

"I can get her," Louisa argued, but Livvy made it clear she was having none of it.

"*I* will get her, young lady," she repeated, this time through gritted teeth. Louisa backed away, her head cocked at Olivia's unusual tone, and Livvy lifted her nightgown and climbed up several steps until her eyes were above the level of the loft's floor and she could see Josie rising from the bed and coming toward her.

"No!" she shouted at her. "You just wait there. I'll come and get you."

She put one hand on the loft floor and lifted her foot in search of the next rung. Instead, she found only nightgown.

"Watch it, Aunt Liv!" Neil shouted as she fought desperately to free her foot from the yards of fabric in which it was tangled.

Someone yelled, "No!" before her hand slipped across the wooden floor of the loft and the end of the ladder smacked her cheek.

There was another scream as her upper body swung back while her feet still fought to stay where they were.

There was a shout of warning, but it was no use. Her left foot rested on air.

She tried to yell to Josie to stay where she was, but she wasn't sure if anyone heard her before she hit the floor.

"How long has it been now?" Bess asked, her palms pressed to her knees and her body rocking in the worn gent's easy chair.

"Forty-eight minutes," Remy said, checking his pocket watch which sat on the coffee table in front of him. Neil sat beside him rubbing his hands up and down his worn brown workpants, sniffing back tears.

Spencer stood and ran his hands through his hair. Only forty-eight minutes? It seemed like a lifetime since he'd heard the screams and run in from the porch, sleep still clouding his eyes, and found her. The sight of her lying motionless on the kitchen floor, her white gown spread around her like she was already some sort of angel, was branded on the back of his eyelids, perhaps forever.

"Sit, Spence," Bess said as if he were a small boy with no patience. "The doctor said he'd tell us if there was any change."

Spencer had sent Neil to Remy's with instructions to fetch a doctor and carried Livvy to their bed, only to find her suitcase there. Despite having pushed her and pushed her, he'd still been surprised at the sight of that leather bag.

But the thought that she was leaving him paled in light of her accident, and now, nearly an hour later, he knew he couldn't just sit out in his parlor while she lay unconscious on his bed.

From the doorway to their room he watched the doctor run his hands up and down Livvy's body searching for broken bones.

"Nothing?" he asked when the doctor lifted her eyelids and let them fall of their own accord.

He looked up at Spencer as he sat down, his head shaking sadly. "Nothing I can do for her," he said with a heavy sigh. "Sometimes these things just have to run their course."

He'd heard those words before, and they didn't sound any better now, despite everything he had done to make sure that this time they wouldn't matter, that she wouldn't matter, that losing her wouldn't matter.

It was hard to swallow, and he struggled around the tears in his throat. He had done a lot of foolish things in his life, most of them in the last three years, but none had been as damn stupid as thinking that he could share a life with a woman like Olivia and manage to resist loving her.

"You want a chair?" Doc LeMense asked him, rising from his seat and offering it to Spencer. "I could use a little stretch."

Spencer pulled the chair closer to the bed and lowered himself into it, taking Livvy's hand as he sat. He waited for the doctor to leave the room and then, eyes closed, he said quietly, "So you finally gave up on me, huh, Liv? I saw the bag. I guess I shouldn't be surprised. The truth is, I'm probably not worth your getting well."

Something pressed against his leg and he opened his eyes to find Josie leaning against him, the doll from Margaret's bed clutched in her hand. He lifted her onto his lap and held her close, burying his face in the mass of curls that covered her head.

"That's Winnie," Spencer said as he fingered the doll's limp arms. "Haven't seen her in a long time. Bet she needed a hug almost as badly as you, huh?"

"Will Aunt Liv be okay?" Josie asked, rolling herself into a ball on her uncle's lap.

"There you are," Louisa said when she tipped her head into the bedroom, obviously looking for Josie. "Come out of there now." She extended her hand, but Josie ignored it and shook her head, burrowing deeper into his chest and belly, a foot digging beneath his thigh, an arm hanging around his neck.

"Let her be," he said, a wetness seeping through his shirt and soaking his chest.

Louisa ignored his words. "Josie," she said. "Come out of there."

Reluctantly the child crawled down from his lap and looked at him sadly. He ruffled her hair and fought the urge to grab her up against him and hold on to her forever. With a look that made him think she was wishing he would do just that, she leaned forward and placed a kiss on his knee, the closest thing to her little bow mouth. Then Louisa reached in and grabbed her hand to lead her from the room.

He wasn't going to love Livvy and he wasn't going to love these kids. That was the plan, wasn't it? So why had his heart stopped beating when he saw Livvy on the floor, and why was he so sure that until she opened those dark eyes and smiled at him, it would never beat again?

And this little one. If he lost Livvy, would the children be the next to go? His useless heart lodged in his throat. Still worse, he had very carefully seen to it that if Livvy didn't open those eyes, if she didn't fully recover, there would be nothing left of her to go on in this world. Not one child with her sweet disposition, or her beautiful long hair, or that ready smile on those full lips. And he had seen to it, all by himself. There was no one else, on earth or in heaven, for him to blame.

"Livvy," he said, leaning over her and rubbing her arms as if to warm her, "Livvy-love? You had enough rest now? It's time to wake up and see to your family."

There was only the rise and fall of her chest to indicate she was alive at all, and that seemed to him to get shallower and shallower with every breath she took. What if she just slipped away from him? What if she just simply stopped taking those tiny breaths and left him all alone?

"Dammit, Livvy," he said, shaking her madly as if she were just sleeping and he could rouse her. "Don't do this, Liv. Not now when I finally know what I'm losing."

Dr. LeMense pulled Livvy from his hands. Spencer hadn't even been aware of the old man's return. The doctor fussed over her, settling her back against the pillows, crossing her hands on her chest.

"Don't do that," Spencer said, rearranging her arms to lay at her sides, then moving them again to a more natural position, one hand on her hip, one raised near her face. "She's not dead."

"Mr. Williamson, she's not just asleep. You have to understand that. It's likely your wife has suffered skull fissures. There could be extensive bleeding within the skull. There could be a fracture of the skull itself. . . ."

"You understand this, Doc. I'm not losing Livvy. I can't. I haven't made her happy yet."

Neil wished Uncle Spencer would come back out of his room. Uncle Remy, who sat with his arm around Neil's shoulder, smelled like fear. It was a smell he had been trying to forget for three years, ever since his mother had left them and gone to heaven. Sometimes, in Chicago, in the dark of night when he and Louisa would wait for their father to return, wondering if he would, and when he did, how drunk he would be, he would smell that foul air and gag on his fear.

He had already lost one mother and that had been enough. Not that he'd ever forget his mama, but he was getting pretty used to Aunt Liv and had come to count on that smile every morning and that kiss on the forehead at night when she thought he was asleep.

"You want something to eat?" Aunt Bess asked him. She

was always offering food to him, slipping him little treats, giving him whatever she gave her own boys. But he wasn't one of hers, and the look she gave to Thom-Tom or Philip just wasn't the look she gave to him. But Aunt Liv . . . she gave him that look. Him, and Josie, and when Louisa wasn't looking, she even gave it to her.

"No," he said quietly. He wasn't hungry. Not for anything that could be served on a plate or in a glass. "Do you think Aunt Liv will . . ." He couldn't make the words come out of his mouth no matter how hard he tried.

"Aunt Liv'll be fine," Uncle Remy said, and patted Neil's knee. "Don't you worry." When he returned his hand to his lap, it had left sweat marks on Neil's trousers.

"I'm gonna go check," he said, unable to just sit still while his wishes dried up and blew away like a stalk of wheat in a parched field.

"If she was better—or worse, I suppose—the doctor would tell us," Aunt Bess said, holding on to his arm to stop him from leaving.

"I'm not checking on Aunt Liv," he said, though he supposed in part he was. "I'm checking on Uncle Spence."

"Let the boy go," Uncle Remy said, and she released his sleeve.

"Quietly," Aunt Bess warned, stroking his arm as he went past her. As if his noise would wake up his aunt. And besides, wasn't that what they were all hoping for, anyway?

His uncle's eyes were red, and he was wiping at his nose with his sleeve, just the way Aunt Liv always told Neil not to. It didn't seem right, him doing that, even if Aunt Liv couldn't see him.

"You can come on in," his uncle told him, but his eyes never left his aunt's face. Neil wasn't sure Uncle Spence even knew which one of them was in the doorway until he asked if Neil's sisters were all right.

"Yes, sir," Neil answered, inching his way closer to the

bed. There had been blood in his mother's room, another smell that had stayed with him, but there was none here.

"Look, Liv," Uncle Spencer said just as if she could hear him. "It's Neil. Did I tell you how he figured out that Miss Lily always licks her lips before it rains? I never noticed that, did you?"

Neil cleared his throat. "I don't think she can hear you," he said. "Can she?"

His uncle shrugged and shook his head. "Maybe not, son."

The word caught him unawares. *Son*. His uncle had never called him that before. He was sure. Something like that he'd remember. It made him want to give his uncle something in return. He couldn't call him *Pa*, and he already called him Uncle Spence. His mind raced for something that might make his uncle happy.

"Could I talk to her?" He knew she'd never hear him, but Uncle Spence would, and the man's eager nod made him think that maybe he'd done the right thing. "Aunt Liv? I don't want you to die. Nobody does. We'd miss your pies, and your bedtime stories, and . . ."

"And your smile," Uncle Spencer continued when he'd run out of things to say. "And your voice . . ."

Uncle Spencer's own voice broke then, and a chicken wing could have knocked either of them over when they heard Louisa's words come through the open door.

"And the way you ask us if we need anything, and never get angry . . ."

She was just lying there, Aunt Livvy, as if there weren't anyone else in the room with her and she were just napping in the middle of a real hard day. But then, Aunt Liv never napped. As far as he could tell, she never slept at all. She was up before he was in the morning, making breakfast, seeing to the animals, humming softly to herself and anyone around her, and she was still awake when he fell asleep at night.

He looked at her more closely. He didn't know why Uncle Spencer kept saying she wasn't as pretty as his ma.

"We're all here, Liv," Uncle Spencer said, putting his hands out and gathering all of the children to him. "You gonna trust me with them?"

He didn't know about Aunt Liv, but the idea sure scared Neil. He knew what happened to a pa after a mama died. He'd seen his dad, and while he'd never been a prize at the county fair before his mama had passed on, he was a pretty poor excuse for a dad afterward. Just the thought that he was coming home soon would get Louisa crying, and Josie's bottom . . . Well, things were just better with Aunt Liv and Uncle Spence, that was all.

"Think I'll let 'em have pie for dinner, Liv, and let 'em stay up as late as they want. And I guess I'll just go out drinkin' and . . ."

"There's stew in the icebox." Aunt Liv's voice sounded like it was coming from the bottom of the well. And she looked like she'd just been pulled up from there, too. She was squinting at them all like she'd just come outside on a sunny day and found the world too bright.

"Doc!" Uncle Spence yelled. "She's coming around. Dear God in heaven, she's coming around!"

Aunt Liv was struggling to sit up and she looked at him like he'd lost his mind, but he pushed her back down until she was flat on the bed again, and kissed her smack on the lips, and then on each eyelid, and he didn't seem to want to stop until Dr. LeMense finally pulled him off like they were two kids fighting instead of two grown-ups smooching.

"Spencer," Aunt Liv said in that I-am-shocked-at-you voice. "What in the world?"

"Well, I see you remember Mr. Williamson," the doctor said, as if his aunt were likely to forget her own husband. "You remember what happened to you?"

Josie was studying Neil, and he was studying Uncle Spencer, who was studying Aunt Liv, who was looking at the doctor as if he were the one who'd taken a fall and maybe lost his mind. Neil took Josie's hand and squeezed it as if to tell her not to worry. It was what he would have liked Uncle Spencer to do for him.

"What happened to me?" Aunt Liv said. She looked down at herself, realized she was still in her nightdress, and turned pinker than Josie's favorite ribbons.

"What's the last thing you remember?" the doctor asked, shining a light in her eyes and looking for who knew what.

Aunt Liv looked from face to face as if she were hoping someone would help her answer the doctor's question. Neil had a sinking feeling that Aunt Liv might not even remember them.

"You've had a fall," the doctor explained to her. "And you've been unconscious for a while. There may be some things you don't remember just yet. You remember how you fell?"

Aunt Liv shook her head real sadly.

"You remember anything about this morning?" the doctor continued.

She looked like she was going to cry, Neil thought.

"Last night?"

Her eyes searched Uncle Spencer's face, then his, Louisa's, and finally Josie's. There they paused and she bit her lip and raised her eyebrows a little. "We were reading?" she asked. "Josie and I? Is that right?"

"*Black Beauty,*" Josie said, squeezing her way through to stand by the edge of the bed. "And you fell asleep." She pointed her finger at Aunt Liv accusingly.

"And then what happened?" Aunt Liv asked.

"Then I got home, put Josie to bed, and this morning it seems she finally made her way all the way up that stupid ladder," Uncle Spencer said.

Neil thought Uncle Spencer was leaving out a few important details. He had heard Uncle Spencer come home. He'd heard him yell at Aunt Liv on the porch, say mean things and make her cry, and he knew that Uncle Spencer had remained on the porch all night.

"Oh, Josie!" Aunt Liv said, reaching out for his sister. "You didn't get hurt, did you?"

Uncle Spencer threw back his head and laughed. He laughed so hard he had to sit down in his chair and pull off his glasses to wipe his eyes. "Livvy, Livvy, Livvy," he said when he could catch his breath and wipe the tears from his eyes. "Isn't it just like you to be worried about someone else?"

Aunt Livvy looked down at her nightgown again and then up at Dr. LeMense. Neil could almost see the wheels going around in her head, taking her from being all muddled up to suddenly understanding. "I fell?"

Uncle Spencer leaned forward and looked at her like there wasn't another soul in the room. Maybe not on the whole planet. And then he said the strangest thing Neil had ever heard.

"Not half so hard as I did, Livvy-love. Not half so hard as me."

Chapter Fourteen

Nobody had wanted to leave, not the doctor, not Remy or Bess, not the children. It was as if none of them trusted Spencer to take good enough care of his own wife. And he couldn't really blame them. He'd done a pretty poor job of it so far, hadn't he? He'd made her miserable enough to want to leave him.

He watched over her while she slept, pushing the hair away from her face as she napped. She had no recollection of the morning's events, even accusing him of hiding her hairbrush to keep her in bed. Doc LeMense told him not to worry, her memory was likely to return, but Spencer prayed it wouldn't, prayed she would never remember the hurtful things he'd shouted at her on the porch the night before.

Miss Lily needed milking. The chickens had no doubt pecked every seed Josie had ever spilled and were searching for more. The sun was probably burning his crops. And all that mattered was that Livvy was sleeping in his bed, turning this way and that, scratching her nose when he brushed it with the end of her braid to assure himself she was just resting and not unconscious again.

It was torture to let her sleep when he had so much to tell her, so much to apologize for, so much to celebrate. She stretched and opened the dark eyes that he had come to know so well. Confusion clouded them.

"Spencer? What time is it?" She sat up and he let her, filled with awe at the magic of her movements and her voice.

"It's midafternoon," he told her, reaching for the pitcher of water he'd kept by her bed and pouring her a glass. "Are you thirsty?"

"Midafternoon!" She gasped, pushing back the covers and throwing her legs over the side of the bed. She closed her eyes and grimaced.

"Slow," he warned her. "The doc says you might be dizzy and have a bit of a headache for a while, but it'll all pass if you take it easy."

She rose from the bed and straightened her nightgown, searching with her feet for her slippers as if he hadn't spoken at all.

The sunlight glowed through her nightdress, revealing every curve of her body. Enjoying the view, he grabbed a handful of the soft white cotton in his fist and held on tight. "Going somewhere?" he asked.

"Spencer, the children. They have to have lunch and . . . where's Josie?" She swatted at his hand trying to break free, but he held the garment firm.

"The children are with Bess. She figured she was in better shape than you were, and I'm sure Louisa's happy for the chance to show off how grown up she is." He twisted his hand in the fabric, pulling her closer to him. "You smell so good, Livvy-love. Just like lilacs."

"I smell like I always smell," she said, looking down at him very suspiciously. "Did something happen this morning I ought to know about?"

She bit at the edge of her lip, and he reached up and ran one finger against the fullness of her bottom lip. "You are so soft," he said, unable to keep the huskiness out of his voice.

"You didn't answer me," she said, fidgeting with her hair like a nervous bride. "Is there something I ought to know?"

"Oh, Liv," he said, looking up at her frightened face. There was so much she ought to know, but he'd be damned if he'd tell her all of it. The past was behind them and the future was everything he knew she wished it would be. "Something did happen. Something that's going to change our lives."

"They're leaving?" she asked, tears gathering in her eyes, shoulders shaking, lips drawn and lost between her teeth. "He's come for them, then?"

"No," he said, using her fear to coax her into his arms, down onto his lap, tight against his chest. "The children are just gone for the night, or until I go over there and pick them up. What's changed, Liv, is between you and me."

He'd been rubbing her back, but in gathering her closer, his arm had found its way to her breast. She stiffened and he stilled his movements, but left his hand exactly where it was.

"When I saw you on that floor . . ." He swallowed hard, the memory closing his throat and making it hard to continue. He took a deep breath. "When I saw you on that floor, I thought I'd lost you. And the thought nearly killed me. I love you, Livvy. You can't even guess at how much."

His fingers traced the outline of her breast, skimming the fullness over and over until he had to shift her slightly on his lap to accommodate what was happening to him.

"You *what?*" she asked, looking at him with eyes that were wide with disbelief.

"I love you. I do. We'll talk more about it when you're feeling better. In the meantime, just know I love you. And I swear that I will make up these years to you, Liv," he said, kissing the top of her head and inhaling deeply. "And I'll enjoy every minute of it, too."

"Am I dreaming?" she asked quietly, searching his eyes for the truth.

"No, Livvy-love. All your dreams have finally come true. And I'm so lucky they have."

He made her rest the remainder of the day, which wasn't easy for either of them. She wanted to get up and see to the farm, see to the children, see where it was she stood in a life that was missing an important chunk that connected today to the day before. He, on the other hand, wanted to forget the farm, forget the children, and fill her void by taking her, again and again, until what she'd forgotten didn't matter half as much as what she'd have to remember.

Bess sent over supper with the boys, who were instructed to ask Livvy how she was, if she needed anything, and what seemed to Spencer like a hundred other inane questions that kept the children in the house far longer than they were welcome as far as he was concerned.

He saw her to the privy twice, amused by her embarrassment each time.

"I really feel quite fine," she insisted the second time.

"Good," he said, but he refused to remove his hand from around her waist until they stood at the door, Livvy so shy she couldn't lift her gaze to him.

When she was done he offered her help with a bath, as much because the idea appealed to him as because he wanted to watch her blush yet another time.

"You could get dizzy and wind up drowning," he warned her. "I really think—"

"I'm not about to drown in a basin of water. A birdbath will do me for tonight."

He thought about touching every wet, soapy inch of her and knew that tonight was not the night. She wasn't up to giving in, and he wasn't up to holding back. And so he brought a wash basin of warm water to their bedroom and sat in the parlor insisting that she sing or talk to him so that he would know she was all right.

"I remember something else," she said, interrupting herself just before the line about hopes vanishing in *After the Ball*.

He held his breath.

"Didn't you go to Remy's to return that book?"

"The water still warm enough?" he asked.

"And then . . ." Her voice got kind of dreamy. "You dropped off Neil, right?"

"You about done? I think you must be clean enough by now and you ought to get some rest." He rose to his feet but hesitated to walk in on her.

"I must have fallen asleep before you got home."

"Better be done now," he warned. "I'm coming in."

He caught her with the towel only half wrapped around her, and though she turned away too rapidly to give him a good look, it was enough to raise the temperature in the room by ten degrees.

"I'll get your gown," he said, measuring her legs with his eyes and noting they were longer than he'd thought, and well turned.

As he went around her she twisted so that he could still only see her back. It would have been a better plan if the towel had been large enough to cover the whole of her full round bottom. He'd have thought that three years of restraint would have prepared him well for just one more night.

Lord, they didn't come any dumber than him.

"You dry?" he asked, looking out the window at the rising moon. He held the gown at arm's length and felt her take it from him.

When he turned around, she was under the sheet, damp curls corkscrewing around her face.

"Guess you're tired, huh?" he asked.

"How could I be tired?" she said with a nervous laugh. "All I've done all day is rest."

"You dizzy, then?" He undid the buttons on his shirt and slipped out of it without looking directly at her.

"No, Spence. I'm fine."

Well, good, one of them was. He, on the other hand, was as unsure of himself as a fledgling robin taking his first solo flight. When was the last time he'd satisfied a woman? This was worse than a wedding night, since neither of them were innocents.

The thought of his wedding night sent him crashing all the

faster toward the hard dry earth. What if he couldn't make himself wait until tomorrow and somehow, after tonight, she figured out what he had done, what he'd let her believe, let the whole of Maple Stand believe?

He undid the waist of his pants and eased them over his hips with difficulty. "You're a good cook, Liv," he said. "Guess I've put on a pound or two."

"I'll let your seams out," she said. "With cherry pie season coming, you'll need some extra room."

He slid under the covers next to her and wondered why he felt so damn awkward. This was his wife. He loved her. He moved over until their hips touched. She didn't jump away, and he took that as a good sign.

"How are you feeling?" he asked.

"Mostly just grateful," she said. "You made me feel real special today, Spencer. Thank you."

Oh, but she was special. "It was nothing. That's what husbands do for wives whenever they fall out of lofts."

He turned on his side and trailed his hand up and down her arm.

"If I'd known that, I think I'd have fallen out of that loft years ago." She seemed to hold her breath, waiting for his response.

"There's other things, Liv, that husbands can do to make wives feel special. . . ."

He wasn't sure she was still breathing. "Liv?"

"Mm?" He didn't know that such a short sound could crack in two.

"Liv, I could show you one of those things, if you like."

He figured she'd say no if she didn't want him to, so he took her silence as agreement and bent his head over hers and kissed her.

And while he was kissing her, he ran his tongue along the seam of her lips, nudging her to open them until she did, and he slipped his tongue inside the warm cavern of her mouth and groaned.

Slowly, almost torturously, her hands climbed his arms and wound their way about his neck. He wanted to bind them there somehow and never be free of her grasp.

Easy, he warned himself, knowing he should wait, knowing he wouldn't. Still, this was a night for leisure. A night for patience. A night for both of them to know the rewards of love.

He brushed her breast lightly through her gown, finding the nipple and then barely grazing it until it hardened and seemed to reach out toward him. With just his pointer he made lazy circles around the tip until he realized that she was no longer kissing him back but breathing heavily against his lips.

He fumbled with her buttons like a schoolboy who had never undressed a woman even with his eyes, and finally he had to ask for help. Even she seemed to have trouble with the tiny buttons, and it took mountains of self-restraint not to simply rip the gown from her body.

But he didn't have mountains of self-restraint left, and when, after what felt like hours, she still hadn't managed to free herself, he followed his instincts and pulled the nightgown apart, breaking tiny little bits of button and freeing her glorious breasts to glisten in the moonlight. He bent his head to them and teased a nipple with his tongue. She arched against him and he teased her some more while his hand followed the hourglass curve of her waist to the spread of her hips. His thumb made tiny circles against her hipbone, imitating his tongue against her breast.

His hand inched its way to her womanhood and his fingers became lost in the curls. Wedging his knee between her legs, he spread them gently so that he could reach the very spot that would bring her the happiness he had promised.

She was moist. He took that to mean that so far she had

enjoyed what he was doing. Lord, he felt like an idiot, married to the woman for three years and he didn't even know what she liked. He felt worse than stupid, for he hadn't even cared.

"I'll make it all up to you," he said, his breath raising goose flesh on her wet breast. "Whatever it takes, I will."

He worked his magic, gauging his speed by her sighs, measuring his success by her gasps, and when he thought she was ready, he positioned himself above her and eased himself into the velvet glove that was meant for his hardness alone, and let it envelop him.

No dreams haunted him, no memories assailed him. There was no one in the carved oak bed but this man and this woman, husband and wife, and he reveled in it.

He rolled them to their sides, still locked together, and took her face in his hands. "Tell me it's all right, Livvy," he begged. Her leg was caught beneath his body and she tried to free it before she spoke. He lifted his weight and slipped from her body's hold on him.

"Oh," she cried, her disappointment as obvious as her surprise.

"Is it too late, Livvy-love?" he asked her, his hands everywhere as he searched for a way to fill her once again with his love. He rolled to his back and pulled her against him, encouraging her with his hands to bend her knees and straddle him.

As wonderful as it felt to slide within her silken nest, it was not nearly so magical as watching the joy that lit her face as she took him inside her and arched against him.

She was naked above him, her breasts full and erect, her treasures there for him to gape at, and all he could see were those eyes, those dark brown, surprised eyes, filled with the wonder of what he was making happen inside her.

He watched the slackening of her jaw, felt the clutching of her fists, heard the sudden intake of breath, and knew that he had finally begun paying the debt he would owe forever. It was a debt he would look forward eagerly to making nightly payments on. And should there be a bonus. . . .

And then it happened inside of him, an explosion that rocked him heart and soul and body, for that was how she had him, for now and forever.

For a moment they lay still in each other's arms, then she lifted her head and started searching for something with one hand.

"What are you doing?" he asked, wondering if he might have fallen asleep for a second or two.

"My gown," she said, holding the sheet up over her breasts and feeling around with her other hand. "I can't lie here like this."

"Excuse me, Mrs. Williamson," he said, trying not to laugh at his prim wife in light of her performance atop him just moments ago. "But I've just run my barge up your canal. You can lie anyway you damn please."

"Spencer!" she said, blushing furiously. "What a thing to say!"

"I am sorry," he said. "You are a lady of refinement and taste. Now, come here and let me run my train through your tunnel again."

He rolled over and pulled her beneath him, covering her face with kisses as she laughed. What a wonderful laugh she had, deep and sexy. He couldn't remember having heard it before, but he planned to hear it over and over for the rest of his life.

"I could plant my hoe in your furrow," he teased. He felt himself grow hard against her leg, and was sure she could feel it too. "Why, here's an ear of corn now. Wherever is your shucker?"

His hands were on her waist, her hips, her buttocks, tickling her thighs and she was squirming and laughing like a young girl.

"Touch me back," he begged. "I dare you."

"Spencer!" He really was going to have to get the proper lady out of her. He searched for where she had it hidden, checking in one particular spot until surely he had managed to rid her of it, for no proper lady would ever do what she was doing to him with her left hand.

"Oh, Liv!" he shouted, grateful the children were off with their cousins. "It feels so good. Loving you feels so good. What kind of fool would fight this? Oh, God!"

He was getting to know her body quickly. Lush and ripe and soft everywhere, she liked teasing here and stroking there. Fondling her whole breast frustrated her, barely touching the tip drove her wild. In the journal he was keeping in his head, he made entry after entry so that he could please her again and again.

Again he climaxed with her, at least he was pretty sure she had found her piece of heaven, too, and collapsed half on, half off her.

At first he thought she was just breathing hard, but through a haze it came to him that she was crying.

"What? What is it? Did I hurt you?"

She shook her head against him and sniffed. "Have I died?"

"What?"

"Nothing we ever did felt like that. Did I die?"

He laughed and resettled them both against the pillows, dragging her up into the crook of his arm. "No, you ninny. Though we did go to heaven, didn't we?"

She was silent, her hands busy beneath the blankets.

"Liv? Didn't we? Didn't you like it?"

She sat up, pulling the sheets with her to keep those tempting mounds covered. "Turn around, okay?" she said nervously.

He didn't understand.

"Face the door, Spence. Please."

"Livvy, I've already seen everything you've got, and if

you've got any more, I couldn't do anything about it now anyway.'' He was lucky his mouth still worked. But his other parts . . . there wasn't a chance without a good rest.

''Please,'' she asked again. He didn't like the sound of her voice, but he complied with her request.

''Liv? Something wrong?''

''I don't know,'' she admitted. ''Maybe. Spencer, we've made love before, but it's never . . . I've never . . . I'm . . . there's something . . .''

''What? What is it?'' He turned around, her privacy be damned, and saw her staring at her hand, which glistened, damp in the moonlight.

''Spencer?'' There was fear in her voice where there should have been anger.

He didn't even consider lying. ''I'm sorry'' was all he said.

Sorry? Whatever did he have to be sorry about? It was her mess, wasn't it? At first she'd thought she was bleeding, but it wasn't her time and there was no color to the stickiness on her thigh.

Sorry?

Was this . . . ? But they had made love before. He had planted his seed so many times and it had been her garden that had refused to allow it to grow.

Sorry?

Dear Lord, could it be? Was this what Bess had meant? She thought back to the other times, but a new memory assailed her. *Why can't you just go away and leave me alone?* Was she remembering right?

''Did we have a fight last night?'' The wetness continued to seep from her body, and she leaped from the bed, hoping every ounce of him would leave her.

''Yes,'' he admitted, pulling on the sheets she had

wrapped around her, trying to coax her back to his bed, back to his arms. "And the truth of it is you were packing this morning. But that was before, Liv. All of that was before."

She stood stock still by the edge of the mattress and asked, "Before I fell?"

"Yes, that, too, but I meant before I realized that no matter how hard I tried, I couldn't stop myself from loving you. Damn, Liv, I didn't want to hurt you, I just couldn't risk it. After Kirsten, I couldn't stand the thought of losing another woman I loved, and I thought if I could just stop myself from loving you . . ."

She backed away from him, the bedding slipping from his fingers until she was free of his grasp. The stickiness between her thighs took on its full meaning, and she had no doubt what Bess's French envelope was for. "And children? What was your plan about children?"

"I want a hundred of them. And I want them all to be just like you, not stubborn and stupid like me. And I want—"

"We were talking about before," she said, trying to keep her voice even, fighting the hysteria she was afraid would overwhelm her. "When you didn't love me."

"Then," he admitted, not denying that he hadn't loved her, not even trying to deny it, though it wouldn't have done him any good, "I didn't want more children."

She couldn't resist touching the moisture on her legs. Her stomach turned over at the contact.

"You have to understand," Spencer was saying. "I had lost everyone I loved. I thought if I protected myself, that I *had to* protect myself . . . Of course, I was an idiot. I'm always an idiot. I live in a state of perpetual idiocy. But that's all from before."

Again he reached out to pull her toward him, grabbing the edge of the comforter that shielded her nakedness from his eyes.

"Livvy," he pleaded. "I'm sorry. I said I was a fool. I'm

going to make it up to you. We'll have a child. Lots of children. We might have made a baby tonight.''

"But not before tonight," she said, just trying to be absolutely sure that she understood what a sham the past three years had been. "Is that right?"

"It was unlikely," he admitted. "But now . . . Your family is full of children. My family . . . well, I . . . now, Livvy, we can have all the children you want.''

"That would be very difficult," she whispered, slipping behind the screen and searching in the dark for her underthings. Very difficult indeed, since she fully intended never to let Spencer use her again.

Chapter Fifteen

"You're being ridiculous, Liv," he said as he trudged alongside her in the dark.

This from the man who lived with her for three years pretending to love her or, if not that, pretending to . . . just the thought shamed and embarrassed her. A grown, married woman and she didn't know what was happening in her own bed. She bet that doctor in Milwaukee had enjoyed a good laugh after she and Bess left.

"If you still feel this way in the morning, I'll hitch up George and drive you over myself." He tripped over something in the dark and swore.

She was sorry he didn't break his neck.

"I don't blame you for being mad," he said, his voice conciliatory. "You certainly have a right. But I love you, Livvy. You can have everything you always wanted. Me, kids . . ."

She snorted. It was obviously the only proper response.

"Are you going to be mad at me forever? You know you're not. When I'm on my deathbed twenty years down the road, and you come to say your good-byes, you know you won't still be mad. And ten years? You couldn't stay mad at a fellow as handsome as me for ten years, now could you?"

Ten years? She could be mad at him for ten lifetimes.

"So we're down to five years. A lot can happen in five years. Louisa'll probably be getting married. And you'll expect me to pay for the wedding. And I will, and then how will you be mad at me then? So we're down to what, two years? Heck, Henry'll probably be getting married, and if Remy has his way, Sacotte Farm will be sold to the railroad and we'll have to have the wedding at our place, since the mercantile'll be too small for all those relatives of yours.''

It sure was dark out. And the owls weren't making the night sound any friendlier.

"So what? A year? Could you still be mad in a year? With me bringing you gifts and taking Neil under my wing? Could you give up what we just did in our bed for a year, Livvy-love?''

Did he think he was so wonderful in that bed that she would roll on her back for him whenever he asked? Did he think he was the only man in Maple Stand with a rolling pin between his legs?

"So a few months, tops. Now, Liv, is it worth it, for just a few months, to be upsetting the children, imposing on Bess and Remy, and her so sickly, just to punish me? Believe me, I was punished enough. Do you think I enjoyed one minute of keeping my distance from you? Tonight wasn't the first time I ever enjoyed myself, Olivia. *I* knew what *I* was missing.''

She stopped dead in her tracks. It was dark, but not so dark that she couldn't see her husband's face. And not so dark that she couldn't give him the slap he deserved.

The crack that reverberated in the still night surrounded Livvy, and for a moment she wasn't sure whether it was the sound of her hand coming into contact with Spencer's face, or perhaps the sound of her heart breaking in two.

"You're the reason I didn't know," she said, the heel of her hand stinging so badly she wanted to put it in her mouth, but she wouldn't give Spencer the satisfaction. "And reminding me about the grand time you and Kirsten had in my bed is not likely to make me take pity on you, Mr. William-son.''

"See," he said, touching his cheek gently as if he could

take the pain away with his hand, "I'm an idiot. I say the wrong things. I do the wrong things. But it's because I can't think around you."

"Well, that won't be a problem for you anymore."

"Livvy, I was happy. For the first time since they died, I was happy today. Are you going to take that away?"

"There was a time, Spencer, that I would have given my right arm to hear you say that."

"I'm saying it, Livvy." Sacotte Farm was just over the next rise. Having walked the distance a thousand times, neither Spencer nor Olivia had to see it to know it was there.

"It's too late."

"I could pick you up and carry you home." He put a hand on her arm.

"And are you going to chain me to the bed, or the stove?" she asked.

He let her go and kept pace next to her. "It's not too late," he said just as they were feet from the door. "You'll see, Liv. You loved me when I was at my worst. If you could do that, loving me at my best is gonna be as easy as rolling off a log."

"People who roll off logs drown," she said, one step on the porch where long ago she had spent her days mooning over the man who was now begging for forgiveness.

"I'd save you, Livvy," he said, cupping her chin and letting her see the tears in his eyes. "After all, I owe you one."

He owed her a lot more than one. If tonight was any indication of the sparks two people in love could produce, he owed her three years and as many children. She didn't see any way he'd be able to repay that debt. No way at all.

But even if she saw it clear as day even in the dark of night, that didn't mean he was ready to give up.

"You can't just turn off that love, Liv," he said when she stepped up onto the porch.

"Ssh," she warned him, pointing toward the screen door. "Someone will hear you."

"I don't care," he said, maybe even a little louder. "You love me, Olivia Williamson. You can't tell me you can just stop that feeling that you've had all your life."

"Well," she said, taking hold of the railing to steady herself. "For three years I've watched a master. I'm sure I've picked up a few tricks."

"That's not fair," Spencer said his voice a plaintive whine. "I lost everything. What have you lost that compares?"

"I thought I wasn't a woman, Spencer," she said, embarrassed by the admission. "Do you know what it feels like to think you can't bear a child? That you have no purpose on earth? That you're being punished?"

"I'm sorry, Livvy." He touched her gently on the shoulder and let his hand run down her arm. "I do know what it feels like to believe you're being punished, and I know what it feels like to lose a child, and given the choice of not bearing one or losing one, I know what I chose, and I would choose it again."

"I'm so tired of *your* pain, Spencer. *Your* loss. *Your* choice. Did you ask me? Did you tell me? Did you care that they all believed I was barren? That *I* believed I was barren?"

What was the point? It wasn't as if he would ever understand the pain he had caused her. He was too busy nursing his own to make sure it never died. She opened the door and let herself in.

"I'll come by in the morning to see if you've changed your mind," he shouted through the screen door into the darkened room.

"I won't," she said quietly, seeing Neil's form on the sofa and praying the boy had slept through yet another of his aunt and uncle's arguments.

"Then I'll come again the next day," Spencer said as she was closing the wooden door behind her. He raised his voice.

"And the day after that. For as long as it takes, Olivia. I won't give you up."

She leaned against the door with her back for a moment, then, feeling the tears welling up, she hurried to the kitchen, wanting to spare her nephew the sight of his aunt breaking down and crying for all the dreams that had died stillborn in Kristen's bed just an hour before.

Pressing the back of her hand to her mouth to silence her cries, she leaned against the kitchen sink and let the tears roll down her cheeks.

Neil had heard his uncle yelling the night before, and it had taken him a long time to fall back to sleep again. It seemed he had just managed to close his eyes when the sound of Uncle Spencer's voice roused him again.

"Somebody open this goddamn door!"

Aunt Bess's hand flew to her mouth, and Uncle Remy grimaced and shook his head.

"She doesn't want to see you," Uncle Remy yelled toward the closed door. "She's getting the children ready for school. All six of them."

Neil thought about correcting Uncle Remy. After all, Josie wasn't going to school, but he thought his uncle was just trying to sound put out, and he sure was doing a good job of it.

"I could help," Uncle Spencer said. Neil nearly fell off the sofa. Uncle Spencer was about as helpful around the kitchen as Thom-Tom was in the field. Aunt Liv must have felt the same way, judging from the sound of the spoon clattering to the floor.

But she must have said no, because Aunt Bess, stationed at the doorway to the kitchen, looked into the kitchen and then shook her head at Uncle Remy, who told Uncle Spencer that Aunt Liv still didn't want to see him. It reminded him of when

Thom-Tom and Philip had had a fight and they kept talking through Henry, asking him to tell the other one this or that. Uncle Remy had boxed Philip's ears and threatened to do the same to Thom-Tom if they kept on with it.

He wondered if Uncle Remy felt like boxing Aunt Liv's ears. From the looks of things, he sure would have liked to box Uncle Spence's.

"I'll just wait for the children, then," Uncle Spence said. "I could walk 'em all to school. Maybe even give Josie a ride in that wagon of Philip's."

"Philip traded the wagon for a beat-up bicycle," Uncle Remy said. "And the kids know where the school is by now. Go home, Spencer, you've done enough damage for one day."

"Remy, for crying out loud, open the damn door."

"You watch your language, Spencer Williamson. I got children living in this house," Bess yelled.

"You ain't heard language yet, Bess Sacotte. Now open this door or I'll give you a sample of gutter talk that'll have you repainting the porch before noon."

"And I'll take soap to your tongue sure as I would one of my boys. You hear me?"

The door might have been closed, but they could surely hear Aunt Bess in Sturgeon Bay.

"You can't keep my wife in there," Uncle Spencer yelled back. "Not now."

Aunt Bess and Uncle Remy exchanged questioning looks.

"Jeez, Remy, I love her," Uncle Spencer yelled from the porch. "She's got to know I'm sorry. I've promised . . . oh, never mind!"

Aunt Bess opened the door and stepped outside, following after Uncle Spencer's retreating back. Neil couldn't hear the words they exchanged, but he did see his aunt pat his uncle on the shoulder and look toward the house.

And he did have the distinct feeling that after he and his

cousins were out of the house, there was going to be a lot of talk he would be happy to miss.

"He wants to *what?*" Livvy asked incredulously once all the children but Josie were gone to school.

"He wants to take the children on a picnic," Bess said as if Spencer Williamson already had been nominated twice for father of the year.

"I won't go on a picnic or anywhere else with that man," Livvy said, seeing right through his little ploy. She put three spoons on the floor for Josie to play with and raised her voice so that she could be heard over the girl's banging. "Ever."

"You aren't invited." Bess was washing up from breakfast and didn't even turn to look at her sister-in-law.

"Oh? And when is this little outing? It probably didn't even occur to him that the children are in school all day." She took the spoons away from Josie and put her booted foot in front of the child. "Try to open the lace," she told the baby.

"Well, he's got this idea that's kinda nice," Bess said. It seemed to Livvy that Bess was purposely avoiding looking at her. Although with six children and three adults there were a lot of dishes to be washed. And Bess had set Livvy to the mending pile, claiming she had younger eyes. "He's planning a supper under the trees. It gets dark so late now that they can have dinner and play about before the moon even starts to rise."

It sounded beautiful, except that Spencer would be part of it. Livvy wished she'd thought of it first. An evening outside with the children was just the thing she felt she needed.

"He says he can show Neil how to tell the weather from the haze around the moon, and maybe point out the North Star, though he admits he isn't too good with the constellations. Kind of get them ready for that eclipse that's coming."

"What eclipse?" Her father had always pored over the

almanac and told her about what to expect from the heavens. The idea of Spencer doing the same thing . . . well, she just wasn't even going to think about it.

"Don't know," Bess admitted. "He was going on and on about at least being able to recognize Cygnus and the dipper, and sort of apologizing for not knowing more. And then he started in on that picnic thing."

Livvy knew the heavens as well as she knew the back of her hand. On summer nights she would lie on the grass with her father and brother and study the sky and wish on stars. Her fondest wish, of course, always had been that someday she and Spencer would lie out in a field teaching the heavens to children of their own.

"That's ridiculous," she said, putting down a repaired shirt. "It's a school night. They need their sleep."

"You're rather snippy this morning, Olivia. It might help you to get some of that anger out. You want to tell me about what you're doing here?"

"I'm growing up, Bess. No more fooling myself, no more being fooled. I know it's an imposition. I plan to earn our keep and pay our way. You can be sure of that."

Bess dried her hands on the dishrag and turned around to study Livvy as if she had grown another head. "You thinking that this is a permanent thing?"

Livvy didn't need to consider. "Yes."

"Livvy," Bess said softly, coming to the table and settling in a chair close enough to take her sister-in-law's hand. "Honey, this is a problem. I can barely manage with my own three, and they're big boys." Josie went after Bess's lace. "Don't, honey, I can hardly reach 'em once a day as it is."

"I'll take over your chores, Bess. In fact, things'll be even easier for you with us here. And I figure I can bake and sell my stuff to Charlie Zephin to earn enough to pay you back for our food until I can think of something else."

"You've loved that man all your life, Olivia Williamson. I wouldn't be making such long-range plans if I was you."

Livvy picked up Josie. It was time to get on with her day, time to get on with her life. "No," she said as she stood, felt the looseness of her boot, and sat again. "I was in love with somebody else. At every stage of loving him, I was in love with someone else."

She retied her laces and looked around the kitchen.

"Can I use those cherries?" she asked, pointing to the bowl at the edge of the counter. "I want to make a sample for Charlie."

Bess patted her on the back and pinched Josie's cheek. "If you'll make two," she answered.

"You, my dear, are on a diet. I'll make you something that isn't pure lard and sugar."

"But I like lard and sugar," Bess whined. "And your cherry pie."

"Think of my cherry pies as quarters," Livvy said, imagining herself getting rich on her baking skills.

"You can't eat quarters," Bess said glumly, making a sad face at Josie. "Can you, cutie?"

But Livvy had more to worry about than Bess's appetite. After rolling up her sleeves, she reached for the cherries and brought the bowl to the table. "You want to help me?" she asked Josie, who nodded exuberantly.

"All right, then," she said, pushing all thoughts of Spencer Williamson to the back of her mind. She would make the best darn pies Charlie Zephin had ever tasted. She would sell a million of them, this summer alone. She could make little ones for the fairgrounds and pies for two for picnics. . . .

"You want to have supper with Uncle Spencer in the field tonight?" she asked Josie. She supposed she could make an extra pie. She wouldn't want to cheat the children. And it wouldn't hurt to remind him what he'd lost.

* * *

It wasn't a matter of conceit, but of honesty, that set the smile on Olivia's face as she headed off to town with the best cherry pie ever produced in Door County snugly resting in the basket that swung from her arm. She'd won the blue ribbon at the county fair nearly every year since she was eleven, and women had even offered to pay for her secret to such a shiny and delicious glaze.

She knew better than to tell them. Not only would that let everyone make pies as good as hers, but the fact that she used sour milk, and that she'd discovered the trick by accident, didn't make her pies sound half as appealing as they looked.

It hadn't occurred to her that Mr. Makeridge might be at the mercantile. She hadn't seen him since they had all come back in Mr. Zephin's wagon together. But there he was, a dark bruise painting his chin, sitting on a stool by the edge of the counter, intently writing what appeared to be a letter. Seeing him with pen in hand reminded her that she would have to write to Julian and let him know that she and the children were now residing at Sacotte Farm. Maybe there was a chance he could send along a little money for the children's upkeep, not that she would ever suggest such a thing.

It pained her even to consider it, but she had to think of Remy and Bess's needs. And there was no reason that Spencer ought to be made to pay. They weren't his children, after all. And they weren't really Remy's problem. After all, he hadn't agreed to care for them. No, the children were her responsibility alone. And when she thought about it, that was exactly the way she wanted it.

"Mrs. Williamson!" Mr. Makeridge said when he looked up and discovered her standing in the doorway. He looked down at the letter he was writing. "Like speaking of the devil!

Not, of course, that you are anything but an angel. And even lovelier than when I saw you last."

"Olivia," Emma Zephin said, coming out from the back room with a stack of boxes. "I didn't hear you come in. Oh, and here's that darling little one. What's her name again?"

"That one must be Josie," Mr. Makeridge answered before Olivia could get the words out. She was struck speechless by Emma's appearance. Unless she was mistaken, Emma was wearing rouge! And her hair was done up in some puffed-out style that looked like she got her head stuck in a paper wasps' nest.

"Yes," she said, not remembering telling Mr. Makeridge about the children on their trip, but convinced she must have. The truth was, she didn't remember much about the trip beyond chocolate-covered cherries and a head that felt like a woodpecker had tried to make a home in it. "Josephina, this is Miss Zephin and Mr. Makeridge."

Emma leaned down toward Josie, who backed away in terror. Despite her getting comfortable with Livvy, she still was easily frightened by strangers. Even Bess, who was the most natural of mothers, set Josie on edge. Emma sent her into fits of hysteria.

"Children usually like me," Emma assured Mr. Makeridge. To Josie she held out a string of rock candy. "Here. This should sweeten your disposition. That's what my mother always said to me. Not," she said turning to Mr. Makeridge again, "that it ever needed sweetening. I am a very cheerful person. I always have been."

"Just so," he agreed.

"Not as cheerful as you've been the last two days," Charlie Zephin said, appearing from the far corner of the store where he must have been rearranging older goods. The front of his apron was covered with dust and he swiped at it, giving his daughter a dissatisfied look.

"Mr. Zephin," Olivia said, glad that Josie had quieted

and was now sucking happily on Emma's gift. "I've come to discuss a proposition with you."

Mr. Zephin smiled and exchanged a look with Mr. Makeridge that made Livvy decidedly uncomfortable. "Are you propositioning me, Mrs. Williamson?" he asked, apparently having difficulty keeping a straight face.

"You know that I have the best cherries in all of Door County . . ." she began, but Charlie and Mr. Makeridge's laughter stopped her. She looked questioningly at each man, and they sobered quickly. "Well, I suppose Bess has the best cherries, but I . . ."

They were having trouble maintaining any dignity at all, obviously enjoying the privacy of their little joke. Ordinarily she would ask Spencer when she got home what in the world she had said that was so funny, but those days were gone. Perhaps she could ask Remy. Emma stood looking from one man to the other, apparently as baffled as she.

"I'm sorry," Mr. Zephin said, wiping his eyes. "Something we were talking about before just came over me. You were telling me about how good your cherries are?"

This time he struggled to keep a straight face and had to bite on his lip to manage it.

"I'm offering you my cherries," she said, putting the basket on the counter and lifting the corners of the napkin in which the pie was wrapped. Mr. Makeridge virtually fell off his stool and, holding his sides, passed through the curtain into the back room. Charlie had turned his back on her and was fighting unsuccessfully to get hold of himself.

"Do you want a sample or not?" she demanded. Two grown men and they were guffawing like six-year-olds who had just discovered a new word they weren't supposed to know.

"I do" came the choked response from behind the curtain where Mr. Makeridge was obviously having a good laugh at her expense.

"I don't know what it is I've said that has you men so amused," Livvy said, doing her best imitation of a disappointed schoolmarm, "but I am offering you the chance of a lifetime."

Mr. Zephin couldn't make his lips stop quivering. "I don't doubt that you are," he agreed.

"My cherry goods are the best in town, probably in the whole county, and I'm offering to sell them to you so that you can offer them to the public. You know that if people know they're mine, there isn't a person in Maple Stand who won't want them."

That seemed to be the last straw. Charlie smashed up against the shelves, sending canned goods flying in every direction. From the back room it was clear that Mr. Makeridge was having the same fits as Mr. Zephin.

"Let me get this clear," Emma said, pointedly ignoring her father. "You want us to sell your pies for you here in the store?"

"And my preserves," Livvy added, grateful to find a rational voice amid the hysteria.

"And this pie is a sample?" Emma fingered the edges of the pie on the counter. The flaky crust broke off in her hand.

"Yes," Livvy said.

"How does Mr. Williamson feel about this, Olivia?" Charlie asked, finally gaining control over his tongue. "Last time I asked you to bake some of these for the store, that husband of yours said he hadn't married you so that you could feed half of Maple Stand and they could go get themselves wives if they wanted cherries of their own."

A howl came from the behind the curtain. Livvy was getting a pretty good idea about what the secret word was and what it meant.

"Mr. Williamson is no longer a concern," she said quite seriously. Then she added, with all the brazenness she could summon, "My cherries are no longer his problem."

There was a moment of stunned silence in the mercantile, punctuated only by Josie's sucking sounds, and then a somber Mr. Makeridge came out from the storeroom. "Well," he said looking at Livvy as though she were as appetizing as her pies, "I'd like to sample some."

Emma looked at Mr. Makeridge and then at Livvy before agreeing to get some plates. "I've an idea," she said. "Why don't Waylon and I go on upstairs and have some of your pie with our lunch. Papa can tend the store and have a piece down here. Then, if we like it, we'll let you know."

"You'll like it," Livvy said. No one had ever eaten her pie and been disappointed.

"I'm sure I will," Mr. Makeridge said. "But only a fraction as much as the baker."

"Doesn't he have a way with words?" Emma asked, picking up the pie and directing Mr. Makeridge to follow her.

"Won't you join us, Mrs. Williamson?" he asked. Emma turned and shook her head, signaling to Olivia that she should say no.

Accordingly, Livvy said, "I've got to get this little one home," and lifted Josie to her hip.

"I could come out to the farm and let you know about the pies," Charlie said. "That way I could be sure that Mr. Williamson is in agreement. Last thing I want is your husband hopping mad at me."

"I'm back at Sacotte Farm, Mr. Zephin," she said, raising her chin slightly. "You can come out there to pick up the pies if you like. I'll be baking them all day, as I know you are going to want them."

"Olivia?" Emma asked. "Back at Bess and Remy's? Why?"

She opened her mouth, but instead of hearing her own voice, she was grateful to hear Waylon Makeridge's. "I'm sure that's no one's business but her own," he said gently, as if his words were meant to be a soft pat on her back.

Emma looked at her sympathetically. "Then you've given up?" Emma said, and blushed furiously at having uttered her thoughts aloud.

"Yes," Livvy said. "I suppose I have."

Chapter Sixteen

In the five years since Kirsten and the children had died, Spencer had been to the cemetery only when he had to attend the funerals of others. He had exercised great care to avoid the graves of his wife and children, sometimes stepping over the short fence that surrounded the cemetery in his haste to escape.

But this day he walked purposefully toward the high metal archway that signified Maple Stand's only burial ground, going over once again in his head the words he wanted to utter to his precious family. The words had been a long time in coming. In fact, Spencer had never expected to tell Kirsten that he was returning to the world of the living, where he belonged, and locking her and the children within a sacred place in his heart where he would always keep them safe but separate from the life that now beckoned him.

Kirsten had always liked Olivia. And, too, she had liked laughter and love and everything that Olivia had tried to offer him for the last three years. He wasn't seeking Kirsten's approval, though he had no doubt that he would have received it.

He was coming to say good-bye.

While he hadn't seen the graves since the burial, even refusing to attend the placement of the headstones out of some ridiculous fear that once the stones were set, his family would be even more permanently dead then they already were, still he knew where they lay. And so, seeing a small figure, only slightly large than Peter's size, kneeling by their plots startled him so badly that he stopped in his tracks and closed his eyes, trying to blot out the sight.

". . . lucky. I mean, I know that you're dead, and all, and it must seem real dumb to you, but I'd trade places with you in a minute if I could have a papa like yours for a little while."

The boy was pulling out handfuls of grass as he spoke, but Spencer's legs had turned to granite and he could do nothing but listen and watch.

"I saw the birds you carved. They're still up there in your room. It's a nifty room, if you can call it that. I sure do like that bed you used to sleep in."

Spencer watched Neil turn slightly and begin work on Margaret's grave, pulling not clumps of grass, as he had thought, but weeds, piling them carefully between the two small plots.

"It's me again," the boy said quietly. "Your cousin. I thought you'd want to know that Josie, that's your little cousin, remember? Well, she borrowed the doll from your bed, but I put it back. It didn't get dirty or anything and she was real scared about Aunt Liv. So was your pa. Not that he doesn't still love your ma and all, but he loves Aunt Liv, too, and she gave us all a fright.

"Now we're staying at Uncle Remy's. That's your uncle and mine, too. I'm sleeping on the sofa there, just like at your place. The last time I had a bed of my own was before my mama died. There's nothing I mind as much as being privy to all you see sleeping in the parlor. I think maybe you and Peter were lucky to go along with your ma, so that she could still be taking care of you, and all. But I bet you miss your pa. . . ."

He stopped and began to gather the weeds in his arms. It was clear that he had done Kirsten's grave first, and he was finished with his work but not his thoughts.

"Your own bed in your own house. To a kid like you it probably doesn't sound like much, but—"

The weeds fell from the boy's hands as he looked up, and he cringed when he saw Spencer standing close enough to have heard his every word. Spencer licked his lips, searching for the right words to say, and tasted a salty tear.

"Thank you," he said from deep within a heart filled with regret. "I guess I should have seen to the weeds myself."

Neil lowered his shoulders cautiously. "I don't mind."

"Have you done it before?" Spencer asked and saw the defensive stance and the fear in his nephew's eyes. "Maybe I owe you more thanks than just for today."

The boy stood silently, throwing an eye toward Peter's grave as if he expected the dead boy to take his part.

"Often? I don't see too many weeds. I'd guess you probably have to come about once a week to keep them looking so nice."

"About," the boy admitted, his voice barely above a whisper.

"If you'll give me a minute alone with them," Spencer said, gesturing with his head toward the cluster of headstones, "I'll give you a ride back when I'm done."

"I could put the weeds over in the pile," Neil said. "And wait for you there." He looked questioningly at his uncle.

"That'd be real good," Spencer said, running his hand over the boy's tousled head. "I won't be long."

"Take your time," the boy said. "I'll wait." He huddled the dirty clumps against his body and, dropping and picking up bunches at regular intervals, made his way to the far corner of the cemetery.

"The boy had it a little backward," he said quietly to the ground beneath which his little family lay. "He does that a lot. But the fact of the matter is I was the lucky one, not you. I got to know a love so fine that I thought I could never know its like again.

"I think it'll make you all happy to know that I was wrong. Just like when you were here, I had my head in the sand and didn't know how lucky I truly was. But I've got a second chance now. So I've come to say good-bye. All three of you will be in my heart forever. In all I do and all I am, you will be a part. But Livvy taught me something I thought I'd never know.

"I've got room in my heart for more than just the three of you. I've got room for Livvy, and Neil, who you seem to be getting to know, and that little hellion Josie, and even Miss Louisa. And I'll have room for whoever else comes along.

"I love you all."

He stood by the graves another minute, reading the markers for the first time. His name was etched in granite above each of their heads. *Margaret, beloved daughter of Spencer and Kirsten. Peter, beloved son of Spencer and Kirsten. Kirsten Williamson, beloved wife of Spencer, beloved mother of Peter and Margaret.*

Beloved they were. Beloved they would always be. They and Livvy and the little boy who stood waiting next to a pile of weeds and wishing for a bed of his own.

"You on your way home?" Spencer asked Neil as he brushed the dirt off the boy's shirt and pulled out a hankie to clean his face.

"I was headed for Uncle Remy's," the boy said sadly.

"You in a rush?"

"No, sir," Neil answered, and looked expectantly at his uncle.

"I got some errands to run and I could use a little advice, if you can keep a secret."

"I'm not overly fond of secrets," Neil admitted, kicking the grass with his work boots. Spencer was surprised he wore the heavy shoes to school, but said nothing about them.

"Wouldn't that depend on the surprise?" he asked.

"I suppose it would."

"So you'll come? I'll drive you out to Sacotte Farm when we're done, okay?"

At the lumberyard, Spencer ordered the finest pine that Mr. Ostend carried. He would have liked to use a better wood, but the paint would hide the knots and his carvings hopefully would make beautiful what otherwise might be ordinary. He kept his plan from Neil for the moment, but it bubbled inside him like a geyser ready to blow.

"What are you building, Uncle Spence?" the boy asked as they made their way from the lumberyard to the mercantile.

"Secret," he answered, the smile on his face so wide it hurt.

At that the boy looked somewhat sullen, so Spencer amended his words. "A good secret. A secret you're bound to like."

Neil looked at him suspiciously.

"I'll give you a hint. I'm building four of them, and one is much bigger than the other three."

He could see Neil trying to come up with the answer, but one wasn't presenting itself.

"Okay. One of them would hold twice as many people as the other three."

He knew the minute the possibility occurred to Neil. It was written all over his hopeful face, but the child squelched the thought as quickly as it had come.

"Okay, okay," Spencer said, eager to put the stars back in the child's eyes. "Guess what I'm buying in the mercantile, then."

Neil shrugged. "Nails?"

Spencer nodded vehemently. "And?"

"Sandpaper?"

Again he nodded. "And?"

"Varnish?"

"Well, I thought I might use paint. With paint I could put in some details that would take me an awful long time to carve. Now, here's the part where you come in. You remember I said I needed your advice?"

"Uh-huh."

"But before I ask, you have to promise me that Aunt Liv will not hear a word of this. Not a word."

"Why?"

"Why?" It was a good question. And the truth was that she'd try to stop him. But once he had them done, once he showed her them and she understood what she and the children all meant to him, and what it was she was throwing away, heck, it would only take a second for her to cave in. And then he'd surely want all of them done and waiting. "Because Aunt Livvy likes surprises, even if you don't."

"It didn't sound like she liked 'em much last night," the boy mumbled, picking at a wood splinter that rose from the railing.

"I'm sorry you heard," Spencer said, and truly meant the words. "But, like I told your aunt, I'm gonna fix everything. Now, can you or can't you keep a secret?"

His curiosity got the better of him. "I can," he said with conviction.

"And if I tell a fib in Zephin's, you won't call me on it?"

"But why would you tell a fib?"

The boy had more questions than corn had kernels. "'Cause Aunt Liv is in and out of this store pretty regular with her eggs and butter, and somebody might let the cat out of the bag."

It satisfied him, and Spencer held the door open and let the boy walk under his arm and into the mercantile.

"Mr. Williamson," Charlie Zephin said with a quiver in his voice. "Something I can do for you?"

"Here for some nails," Spencer said, looking around and finding that fop who had complimented his wife's anatomy sitting on a stool near the counter. His jaw sported a deep-purple bruise, Spencer noted with satisfaction, and he was toying with some pie that sat on a dish on the counter.

Spencer ignored him and told Zephin what he needed in terms of hardware. Then he leaned close to Neil and asked for his advice on paint colors.

"Something appropriate for a little girl and another for a big girl. I was thinking maybe red? And I could carve a heart or two out in the center. What do you think?"

"Red's good," Neil agreed, but Spencer noticed that in his excitement Neil's feet were rising and falling within the confines of boots that Spencer had guessed all along were too big for him.

"And for a boy? About your age, say . . . What do you think a boy like that would like?"

"Blue," Neil said without a moment's hesitation. "Deep, deep blue, like Lake Michigan. And a sailboat carved out in the middle, and maybe some waves." He looked hopefully at his uncle.

"And I'll need a gallon of red paint, another gallon of blue, and two gallons of pure white, if you please, Mr. Zephin."

"Yea!" Neil said somewhat loudly, and then looked sheepishly at Spencer.

"It's all right, boy. Shout it from the rafters when you're happy. What does your Aunt Bess always say? Make a joyful noise?"

"I think she means in praise of the Lord," Neil said seriously.

"Heck." Spencer laughed. "I don't think the Lord's all that picky."

"That'll be four dollars and eighteen cents," Charlie said, figuring at the counter with his pencil.

Spencer came forward and got a good look at what still remained in the pan on the counter. If that wasn't one of

Livvy's pies that Makeridge had his finger in, Spencer would be a sow's underbelly.

Makeridge pushed his finger around in the gooey filling until he found a cherry. Then, red juice dripping from his fingers, he brought the cherry up toward his mouth, smirking at Spencer as he did.

"Hold it, Makebreath," he said, grabbing him by the wrist. "Isn't that an ant there?" He twisted the man's hand back until Makeridge howled, then he flicked the cherry off the man's finger. "I sure do think that was an ant."

He looked down at what was left of the pie. That brilliant red glaze, those flecks of flaky crust; there was no doubt his wife had made that pie. And the thought that she had made it for Makeridge didn't sit well with him, didn't sit well at all.

"Put it on my tab," Spencer said to Charlie Zephin. He picked up the tin with the remains of his wife's pie and added, "This, too."

Makeridge looked at the mess on his hands and pruned his pretty face. Spencer shot him his most innocent, most irritating smile. In answer, Makeridge stuck the length of his finger into his mouth and slowly withdrew it, sucking the cherry filling from it with relish.

"Gotten yourself into a bit of a mess," Spencer said. "If I were you, I'd wash my hands of the whole thing."

"There'll be more of it tomorrow," Zephin said pointing at the nearly empty pie tin in Spencer's hand as Makeridge left the room holding his hand away from his clean serge suit.

"Good," Spencer said to Zephin through gritted teeth. "I'll take that one, too."

"Oh, I'd expect there'll be more than one," Charlie said rocking on his heels.

"Even better." Then to Neil as well as Charlie he said, "And not a word of this to Olivia."

There were worse things than living on Olivia's cherry pie. After Kirsten had died he'd been left to fend for himself, and even with the occasional meal he shared with Bess and Remy, he knew for a certainty, there were a lot worse things than living on Livvy's pie.

Livvy spent the entire afternoon baking pies, listening to the sounds of a busy household, and pretending that she was happy. She was better at making pies than at pretending, and it was a good thing, too. If she had to live by her ability to lie, she and the children would starve to death.

Not so with Spencer. He had certainly fooled her. She had believed in her heart that he was in pain, but never, not for one moment, did she think that he had wanted her to be in the same kind of pain he was suffering. Now she knew better and she would never forgive his trickery.

As the day wore on, her anger grew, as did her shame. Her life with Spencer had been a sham, and it was over. Every time she had let him use her, had lain beneath him while he raised her gown, had been a lie.

And the thought of what it could have been like all those times haunted her as she moved about the kitchen of her childhood, which, it seemed, would become the kitchen of her old age.

Worse still, it was the memory of that last time he had made love to her and the knowledge that it was just that, *the last time,* that hurt more than anything else. He had known the joy he could have brought her, and he had given her a taste of it as his parting gift. Something she could never forget as she lay alone in her bed for the rest of her life. What might have been, if only he had been willing to love her.

She heard the familiar wagon pulling up the rutted path to Sacotte Farm, heard the screen door banging as Thom-Tom ran out to welcome Spencer, heard his greeting ring out in return, and felt the knot in her stomach twist yet another turn at the sound of his voice.

The two pies in the oven were nearly done; three more were cooling on racks in the hot kitchen. Sweat trickled down between her breasts and her heart lodged in her throat. If she ran now, the pies would burn. If she ran now, Spencer would know she was running from him.

Oh, but if she stayed!

The knock startled her. "Liv? Can I come in?" he called from beyond the screen door.

She couldn't find her voice.

"Liv?" he called again. "You still mad?"

She wiped her cherry-stained hands on the already dirty dishrag and marched purposefully from the kitchen until she stood five feet or so from the front door. The late-afternoon sun was low enough in the sky to turn Spencer Williamson into a black silhouette against the brightness.

"The children are ready," she said dully, finding it hard to push the words up through a throat already clogged with tears.

"I brought you something," he said softly, reaching for the door handle as he spoke.

"I don't want anything from you."

He let the door go, remaining where he was, outside of her home, outside of her life. "Guess I got my answer. I'll just leave it here on the porch," he said. Then more loudly, more sociably, he added, "Sure smells good around here. Those your cherry pies I smell baking?"

Livvy sniffed. "They're my pies you smell burning," she said, racing toward the kitchen. There were fifty cents' worth of pies and a lifetime of self-esteem in that oven, and Livvy wasn't about to watch either go up in smoke.

She flung open the oven door and a puff of smoke rose to sting her eyes. She reached for the pie on the left, but before she could get her hands on it she was yanked away from behind, her arms pressed to her sides.

"You want to burn those precious hands, you ninny?" Spencer asked.

She looked down at her unprotected hands and unwelcome tears flooded her vision. She hadn't burned herself on a stove since she was a little girl. That one time had been enough. After that her sensible side had always reigned in the kitchen. Until now.

Now, when her back was pressed up hard against Spencer's chest and his breath was ruffling her hair, her common sense seemed to have taken a walk behind the same old barn where a young boy had stolen a kiss from a young girl so many years ago.

"I'll get them," he offered, releasing her and grabbing a towel. Before she could object, the two pies sat on the counter and several children stood in the doorway attracted by the smoke and the commotion. "Not too bad, I don't think," Spencer said. "They don't look ruined, do they?"

Livvy looked at the blackened tops of her precious pies, pies known for their shine, their eye appeal as much as for their taste. All she could see on the counter was wasted flour, wasted sugar, and wasted cherries. "They're ruined, all right," she said.

"I don't think so," he argued, as if he had the slightest knowledge about pies beyond stuffing them in his mouth with never so much as a *This is good, Liv,* or a *thank you.* "I think they could be saved."

"You would," she said, unable to keep the bitterness out of her voice. "But when a pie is ruined, it's ruined. When something's over, Spencer, it's over."

He looked from her to the pie and back again. He'd taken her meaning all right, and she was glad. She might not be able to speak her mind in front of the children, but his reading it was good enough for her.

"I can't sell a pie like this," she said, then wished she could rip the tongue from her mouth. It was a natural response. After all, he'd forbidden her from selling her cooking. But that was when he had some say over what she did. It was no longer his concern if she was selling these pies or burying them in the yard. She raised her chin and looked at him defiantly, daring him to tell her what to do.

"Maybe if you sprinkled some of that sugar that looks like flour over it," he suggested, surprising her. Besides his attempt to be helpful, it was a good idea. "Be a shame to waste something that could be wonderful with a little bit of effort."

As well as he could read her mind, she could read his. She knew he wasn't just thinking about her pies, and she had no intention of agreeing. "No," she said, looking at the pies as if they revolted her. "You might as well take one with you on this little party of yours. Kids don't have real high standards when it comes to quality anyway."

He looked wounded, but he didn't argue. Just thanked her for the pie and called out to the children, even inviting Remy's boys to come along.

Tossing Josie up onto his shoulder and then warning her to duck through the doorway, he headed out of the house with Neil opening doors and Louisa reluctantly following a few feet behind. Thom-Tom came running from somewhere, having gotten permission from Bess to join them, and Spencer looked a bit like the Pied Piper of Hamlin as he waltzed out of the front door with her family following him.

"Better not leave this out in the heat too long," he yelled from the porch before stepping down to put Josie into the back of the wagon and waiting for all the children to climb in. "I left your present on the porch," he called out before settling himself on the seat, with Neil climbing up into the seat next to him. Livvy wondered whether Spencer was aware she was watching him through the window, but when he ruffled Neil's hair and then handed him the reins to Curly George, she decided he surely was. He'd never let the boy handle the horse before, and it was unlikely that once they got beyond her vision he was likely to do it now.

She went back to the kitchen. Bess had taken advantage of the fact that Olivia was there and had gone to town to visit her sister. She was glad her sister-in-law was gone, but it meant searching through Bess's cupboards until she could locate the confectioner's sugar. As she waited for the pie to cool she cleaned the kitchen with a vengeance. The floor showed evidence of how hard it was for Bess to get down on her hands and knees, and months of dirt were embedded in the grooves between the wooden slats.

Remy came into the kitchen and nearly tripped over her, shouting and letting out a small curse as he caught himself before tumbling down on top of her.

"What in the hell are you doing?" he asked. "Penance?"

Her hands ached and the knuckles were raw. Slowly she got to her feet and arched the kinks out of her back. "I'm helping," she said, maybe a trifle pitifully. "The best I can."

He looked at her and balled his fists at his sides. "I wish I could kill him," he admitted quietly. "Or that he'd died along with the rest of his precious family."

"Remy!" The slap rang out in the quiet of the kitchen and his hand went quickly to his cheek. "Oh, I'm so sorry," Olivia said when she realized what she had done. Hitting two men in as many days, and one her own brother! What depths had that husband of hers brought her to?

He waved off her apology and as he did the look in his eyes became one of undisguised pity. "It's that way, is it? Still hopelessly in love?"

"Just because I don't wish dead a man that we've known all our lives doesn't mean that I hold him in any higher regard than any other human being."

"And the back of your hand to me, Livvy? If I'd wished Emma or Charlie Zephin dead, would you have slapped me?"

She ignored him and put fresh water in her bucket, then

got back down to her knees. "I said I was sorry," she mumbled as she started in again on the floor.

"What you are, Olivia, is a fool. I'm going to town to get Bess. You wanna come?" He stood above her, looking down, extending one hand to help her rise.

Shaking her head, she scrubbed harder at the dirt she imagined must still lay between the cracks. The light was too poor to find it, but she scoured all the harder since she couldn't see any result. When she heard Remy pull away, she stopped. All the scrubbing in the world couldn't seem to erase the memory of Spencer's face when she'd come to after her fall. It couldn't rub out the night she had spent in his arms, laughing, aching, loving. It couldn't wipe out that moment when she'd realized that he had withheld from her the very thing she had wanted most in the world from him. What she had wanted, God help her, even more than his love.

She rose, washed up, and was just sprinkling powdered sugar on her burned pie and admiring the results when she heard the sound of a stranger's wagon coming up the path. Funny how she had come to recognize the sound of the wheels and rigging on Spencer's cart and the clomp of Curly George's gait.

As she glanced out the kitchen window, she caught a glimpse of Charlie Zephin's fancy rig. She supposed that Charlie had bought the Columbus A Grade Canopy Top Park Wagon Surrey with the hope that those must-have-the-latest-and-best-types would crush each other in the rush to the mercantile to order one of their very own. Only thing Charlie hadn't figured on was that there were no latest-and-best types in Maple Stand. And even if there were, they couldn't afford to throw their money away on something as frivolous as a Columbus canopy surrey when a plain old wagon would get them where they were going. He was lucky when a customer came in with cold hard cash rather than eggs or butter or something else to barter.

It was too bad, too, for Charlie Zephin. Liv had the feeling Charlie wished he could just sell the place and retire out to his daughter Celia's place in Green Bay, but he had Emma to worry about. Zephin's Mercantile was Emma's dowry, so to speak, and while it wasn't a bustling moneymaker, it would always keep a roof over a family's head and food in their bellies.

She was already at the front door, holding it open for Charlie, when he stopped the carriage by her front door. Speaking of dowries, she thought, alongside Charlie sat that Waylon Makeridge Emma so had her heart set on.

"Evening, Mrs. Williamson," Charlie said, tipping his hat.

"You come for my pies, Charlie Zephin?" she asked, unable to keep the smile from her face. "I knew you would."

"Mrs. Williamson, I'll take 'em as fast as you can bake 'em," he said, exchanging that same sort of look with Mr. Makeridge that he had when she was at the store.

"Thought I'd can up some preserves, as well," she offered, hoping that she wasn't pressing her luck.

"I'll take whatever you've got," Charlie said, looking around. "Where is everyone?"

"Around somewheres," Olivia said, suddenly uneasy to be entertaining two gentlemen alone. Not that she was entertaining, and not that Charlie Zephin was anyone's idea of a gentleman caller. But that handsome man alighting from the carriage, his trousers just a little too snug, his mustache waxed to a point . . . now he was certainly several women's idea of a gentleman caller if ever there was one.

"Looks like you better get this rose in some water before it ups and dies," Charlie said, picking up the flower that lay on the glider and handing it to her as he walked past her into the parlor. "How many pies you got ready for me?" he asked.

Livvy looked at the rose in her hand and knew that Spencer had left it for her to let her know he was looking after her garden. She'd missed the opening of first bud of the season. And there was so much more she was going to miss.

Her heart sank at the thought.

And then she straightened and brushed the foolish thought from her mind like so much more dirt on the kitchen floor. Bringing her own rose to her as a gift. Now wasn't that just like Spencer Williamson? Like he'd served up her own heart to her on a platter and then said, as it lay there in bloody pieces, that he loved her and weren't they both happy now?

"Lovelier and lovelier," Mr. Makeridge said as he too passed her in the entryway. "I don't know how you do it and still turn out such wonderful pies. Seems to me God gave you more than your share, Mrs. Williamson. Or may I call you Olivia?"

He was looking her over from head to toe, and she couldn't remember when she'd been more a mess. Mr. Makeridge didn't look much better himself. The slight bruise she had seen at the store looked worse. In fact, his jaw was swollen rather badly, the skin discolored to purples and blues, and his smile was decidedly lopsided.

"Whatever happened to your face?" Livvy asked him, tilting her head to get a better look at it.

Mr. Makeridge waved away her concern. "A misunderstanding," he said as if a nearly broken jaw were of no consequence. Livvy guessed some irate husband had taken exception to all those compliments the handsome engineer seemed to dole out to all the ladies. Looking down at her feet, bare from the heat and the floor scrubbing she had been doing, he asked after her ankle.

With her knees bent in an effort to make her dress cover her toes, she answered, "It's fine," feeling herself redden. "Thank you for asking. I'll get you those pies, Mr. Zephin. I've only four, since I wasn't sure just how many you'd be wanting."

She licked her lips nervously, realized that Waylon Makeridge was watching her, and pulled her tongue quickly back into her mouth. He smiled at her as if they had shared an intimate secret. She found herself smiling back out of politeness, wishing she knew what the secret was.

"Four's fine," Charlie said. "Long as you can make me some more tomorrow."

"I'll get them," she said, hurrying to the kitchen, where she tried to shove her hot, sticky feet into leather boots that fought her every inch of the way.

"Appreciate it if you'd hurry," Charlie shouted after she'd been gone a few minutes. "Emma's waiting dinner for us."

"Coming," she called back in response, and was surprised when she looked up and found Waylon Makeridge in the doorway. He put a finger to his lips to quiet her.

"No hurry," he said in a whisper. "I'm not too anxious to get back. Especially now."

She followed the line of his eyes and realized just how far up her dress he must have been able to see as she sat in the chair, skirts hiked to force her foot into her boot. "Oh, my!" she said, quickly dropping the fabric and rising, one foot all the way into a boot, the other at a ridiculous point halfway in, halfway out.

Dragging that foot, she hobbled across to her pies and handed two to Makeridge, who seemed to be amused by the entire situation.

"Haven't you some sort of basket?" he asked, unable to keep the laughter out of his voice. "We wouldn't want them to get ruined by road dust."

She had handed him the pies as if he were supposed to hold them in his lap back to town. There was no doubt about it.

She'd left more than her husband back at the farm. She'd left her mind.

Chapter Seventeen

Why was it, Spencer wondered, as he headed Curly George back toward Sacotte Farm, a wagonload of sleepy children surrounding him, that when he was miserable all Livvy wanted was to make him happy, and now that he was happy, all she wanted was to make him miserable? And she hadn't even taken aim on hitting him with her best shot. He knew Livvy Sacotte Williamson inside and out . . . the thought made him smile . . . and she wasn't about to let him off easy. But, dammit it, she'd loved him her whole life.

Could it really be that she'd finally stopped?

Now?

Now when he was finally ready to give her all the love a woman like Livvy deserved? To build a life with her that included children and whatever else she might want? A life that allowed for hopes and dreams and memories? Would she deny both of them that?

Somewhere an owl hooted and he realized it was later than he thought. Why shouldn't she deny him? The irony was too much for him. Hadn't all those things he was offering her, hoping to share with her, been just the things he himself had denied her?

The truth was, he missed her in his life almost as much as he missed her in his bed, and he rejoiced at the feeling despite the pain. He was alive. And he was in love.

Sacotte Farm, its lamps lit, appeared in the distance. He glanced over his shoulder to find four children sprawled out in the bed of the wagon, all sleeping peacefully under the pale night canopy. He longed to take them back to his own farm, lay them in beds of their own, and crawl in next to his wife.

Instead he slowed George's pace to a crawl and drank in the sight of his wife on the porch glider, rocking slowly, the glass in her hand pressed against her chest.

Her hair was piled loosely on her head, and it glistened in the yellow light of the lantern, telling him she had washed it and it was still wet and no doubt smelled like lilacs. How many nights had he cursed that smell and its ability to draw him in? How many nights had he run from it to the Lucky Clover or anywhere else he could raise a bottle and down a wish?

And what would he give now, just to be allowed to smell that freshly washed hair, let it slip through his fingers, suck the moistness from its ends?

"Evening, Liv," he said quietly after George had come to a halt by the steps.

Her brows came down. "Where are—"

He gestured behind him and put a finger to his lips. "All asleep. Amazing what some fresh air and a little food'll do."

She came to the wagon and looked over the wooden slats at her charges. The stiff shoulders softened, the tight line of her mouth eased into a smile. "Louisa, too, I see."

He nodded. Miss Louisa had been standoffish to start, but he'd given her enough room to come to her own conclusions about joining the fun, and eventually she had become part of the circle on the blanket listening to his ghost stories, Josie on her lap. She'd even accepted a hand-up when the time had come to get back into the wagon.

"Can we talk a minute?" he asked, leading Livvy back up to the porch and standing near her as she resumed her seat on the glider. "Farm's quiet," he said, looking around. "Where is everyone?"

"Remy and Bess turned in early," she said, and even in

the dim light he could see a blush paint her cheeks. "Henry's off with Jenny Watchell somewheres, and Philip promised he'd be home before dark, so I expect he'll be here in another minute or two if he knows what's good for him."

"Bess all right?" he asked, wondering what the blush was all about and surprised to see it return.

"I'd say so," she said, craning her neck to look up toward the bedroom window that sat just above the glider seat. "Yes."

Spencer couldn't help laughing at her discomfort. "But I thought the doctor told her—"

Her face shut down like an old house preparing for a storm, her eyes shuttered, her mouth tight. "We found out in Milwaukee that there are ways," she said, more an accusation than an explanation.

"Not for a good Catholic, Liv," he said, looking up at the window of the room where a lucky Remy was lying next to the woman he loved.

"What about you?" she asked. "What about what you did?" There had been a time when he was almost as religious as Bess, a time when God's opinion had mattered to him.

"I was already in hell, Liv. I didn't have to worry about earning my way in."

Her eyes widened, but she said nothing.

"We'll put it behind us," he assured her, ignoring the slight shake of her head that sent droplets of water out from her hair in all directions only to be caught in the lamplight and look like fireflies surrounding her face. "You're very beautiful," he said, not even meaning to put voice to his thoughts.

She had the beauty of the southern Belgians, the Walloons, they were called, who traced their roots back to the Celts and Romans. It was a beauty that seemed to increase with age, unlike the Flemings, whose fair blond locks faded to gray early like their German ancestors.

She grimaced at the compliment, doubting his sincerity,

and he couldn't fault her. After all, if he'd ever told her before, it had been in the throes of their passion, such as it was. He didn't think he'd ever been speaking of her face.

And what a face it was. Soft, dark eyes rimmed with long black lashes studied him while he examined, as if for the first time, the beauty that had lain beside him every night, eaten across from him every day, and worked beside him week after week for three long years. Her skin was silky smooth, like a child's, her cheeks held a touch of color that made him think of secrets that she kept inside with just a telltale blush to let him know the secrets were about him. Her nose was strong, straight, no-nonsense. But her lips. Her lips were full and no matter how she seemed to set her mouth, he read a smile there.

"Really beautiful," he said, more to himself than her. He moved closer and pulled the pick from her hair, setting it tumbling down in a rush, its weight bringing it to her waist. "It'll never dry all tied up," he explained, running his fingers through it as if he cared whether it ever dried at all, inhaling the lilac scent he was counting on.

"I'd better get the children in," she said, reaching to fasten up the hair once again, twisting it and then realizing that he still held the pick in his hands. She turned her palm up, waiting patiently for him to place the fastener in it.

"What will you give me for it?" he asked. "Is it worth a kiss?"

She let the hair fall once again and shook her head. "I've other clips," she said as she brushed past him to the porch steps.

"Wait." He followed her. While she didn't turn around to face him, she did stand still, one arm on the column that rose to the porch overhang. He lifted the wet hair off her back and twisted it, not well, perhaps, but carefully, and tried to anchor it with the pin. He bent slightly to reach her shorter frame and felt his knees weaken with the nearness of her.

After several moments of fumbling, she reached back and guided his hand until they had, together, fastened the hair off her neck. "Your dress is damp," he said, touching the moist fabric that clung to her back.

Slowly she turned in his arms and her eyes glistened in the lamplight as she stared at him. "Why now?" she asked, one tear escaping and running alone down her cheek.

"Because I almost lost you," he admitted, reaching out to wipe the tear but stopping when she shook her head.

"Not *almost*, Spencer."

"Mama?" A soft voice, thick with sleep, came from the darkness of the wagon.

"Louisa," Spencer told Livvy in a whisper. "She must be dreaming."

"Mama?" she cried again, louder this time.

"I'm here," Livvy said, rushing to the side of the buckboard and reaching out a hand to rub the child's back. "I'm here."

She stiffened as he came up behind her, the starch back in her stance, her anger strengthening her resolve.

"I'll carry them in for you," he offered. "Just tell me where you want them to go."

Her answer was a long time in coming. Long enough to give Spencer hope. But then she lifted Josie in her arms and cradled the child against her. "Louisa and Josie are sharing my old room," she whispered.

Stupid as it was, he was glad Livvy hadn't moved back in there herself. It made him think that maybe all this was only temporary and someday, someday soon, he'd have his family back.

He slipped his arms beneath Louisa and lifted her easily from the wagon. She was surprisingly light for a child that seemed so heavily burdened.

*   *   *

"I don't know, Olivia. I just don't know," Bess said as they prepared breakfast the next morning. "The Good Book says that a woman should cleave to her husband. That Dr. Napheys's book says that lying with your husband without the prospect of children is a sinful act worthy only of paid-for women. The doctor says if I don't take precautions, I'm gonna have three motherless boys."

"I thought," Livvy said as quietly as she could, not knowing who might burst through the kitchen door at any moment, "that the matter was settled last night. And Remy surely looked like cock-of-the-walk this morning . . ."

"It's different for a man, Olivia. A man feels the need in his drawers, while a woman's gotta feel it in her heart. And without the possibility of a baby, I don't feel the same way." Bess flipped the pancakes on the skillet in front of her and carried it with her away from the stove and over to the doorway. "Not that it didn't feel good," she said to Livvy before opening the door with her hip and yelling for the children to mosey their bodies to the kitchen for breakfast. "I'd be lying if I said it didn't . . . and neater. Lord, Liv, so much neater, though I don't suppose Remy thought so." She giggled like a schoolgirl and covered her mouth.

Children came pounding down the stairs, running from every nook and cranny of the house at the sounds of breakfast being served, and Livvy was grateful their conversation had to end. Next thing she knew Bess would be asking her about the marriage bed she shared with Spencer.

She could still feel his breath against her neck as he'd attempted to coil her hair the night before. After they'd gotten all the children in their various beds, he had said the strangest thing. He'd lain Neil down on the couch and covered the boy with a light blanket. *Yours is the first,* he'd said. *Deep blue as the ocean. Just wait a little longer, son.*

When she'd asked him what in the world he meant, he'd cupped her chin and told her that if he had to have patience, so did she. And then he'd kissed her nose and asked how she felt about bluebirds of all things.

"Lord, Thom-Tom," Philip said angrily. "I told you to leave that in my dresser. You got no business going through my things in the first place, but letting that pass, I told you I didn't want it leaving my room."

Livvy turned around to see what of Philip's many treasures Thom-Tom had brought to the table, and hoped whatever it was wasn't alive.

"Wow! Let me see it," Neil said. "Where'd you get it from, anyways?"

"That's a pistol!" Livvy said, stunned to see it passed from Philip to Thom-Tom to Neil. Her brother had owned a rifle as a boy, and she'd even used it once or twice, but a pistol? She didn't even know an adult who owned one. Even the sight of it unnerved her. "Put it down this instant," she ordered.

Neil looked up at her sheepishly and placed the gun down onto the breakfast table. Immediately Josie reached for it.

"No!" Livvy shouted while Bess's chubby hand quickly reached down and plucked the gun from Josie's grasp.

"It's not loaded," Philip said, rolling his eyes at the women. "Do you think I'd bring a loaded gun into *this* house? If Mama didn't shoot me with it, Papa probably would."

"What good's a gun without bullets?" Louisa asked, the usual disdain in her voice.

"It's good for trading," Philip answered as if no one ever understood what he was about, despite his many efforts to educate them. "A gun might be worth a boat to someone."

"Not without bullets," Louisa corrected.

"I could get bullets," Philip said while Livvy and Bess just stood by, eyes wide, mouths wider, and listened to him explain the fine art of bartering.

When he had finished, Bess smacked him rather soundly on the left side of his head. "You untrade this gun today,

Philip Sacotte, or I'll box your other ear so as you won't be able to hear another offer for a week." She opened the highest cabinet in the kitchen and, standing on her toes, placed the gun on the shelf in it. "Until then, it stays up here out of anyone's reach."

"I'm trading it Saturday," Philip said.

"Today," his mother said in her don't-even-bother voice.

"I'm working at Zephin's today. And tomorrow. And Friday I'm seeing old man Yost about his boat. It's got to be Saturday, Ma."

Bess rolled her eyes. "Did you ever see such a household?" she asked Livvy.

"I still don't see who'd want a gun without bullets," Louisa said. "It's like that stupid bike you got without the tires."

"Doesn't anyone around here listen to me?" Philip asked, exasperated. "*You* don't want a bike with no wheels, and *I* don't want a bike with no wheels, but someone with two wheels sure does. And then you trade them for something you do want. Why doesn't anybody but me seem to understand that?"

Livvy checked the time and herded the children out the door. If she hurried she could have a half-dozen pies made before dinner. She could bring those to Zephin's, get a credit toward more supplies—after all, she couldn't keep using Bess's flour and lard and sugar—and get another half-dozen done before suppertime. Charlie had said he wanted as many as she could bake, and she wasn't about to give him time to change his mind.

By noon she was on her way to town, the loaded basket weighing down her arm, her troubles weighing down her heart. Josie pranced along beside her, singing, jabbering, and stopping to pick every third weed and present it to Livvy like some hothouse flower. At the rate the two of them moved,

Livvy's hopes of six more pies were dwindling rapidly to three.

"In you go," Livvy said, holding the door open and letting Josie walk in beneath her arm. "And mind you look with your eyes and not with your hands."

Josie's nose squinched and her top lip lifted to reveal a row of tiny white teeth. "Huh?"

"No touching."

Josie put her hands behind her back and nodded solemnly. Livvy didn't believe for one moment the child would remain that way long, but every second was another small victory.

"Much as I'd enjoy staying and chatting with you, Miss Emma," she heard a man's voice say, "I really must be on my way. I've several sites I must survey if I'm to report to my superiors anytime soon."

The man's back was to Livvy, but she didn't need to see Waylon Makeridge's face to identify the voice. If he wasn't distinctive enough on his own, and in that city dandy suit he surely was, the look on Emma's face would certainly have given him away.

"Morning, Emma," she said, a bit apologetically. She hated to interrupt the couple, but it was that or eavesdrop, which she disliked even more. "Morning, Mr. Makeridge. I've got some more pies and I'm in need of some more supplies, as well."

"Why, Mrs. Williamson," Mr. Makeridge said, twirling on his heel to face her. His gaze traveled from her head to her toes and back again. "Aren't you just a picture?" He shook his head as if he couldn't believe how lovely she looked. It was nearly convincing enough for her to forget she was wearing her old blue dress, the parts that Josie could reach covered in cherry-juice handprints, the bodice sporting only a little less flour than the crusts of her pies.

"A picture?" Emma said, studying Livvy with a somewhat more critical eye. "Of what?"

"Why, of a disaster." Livvy laughed. If she hadn't known better, she'd have sworn that Emma was jealous of Mr. Makeridge's attentions. "I look like a tornado hit Sacotte Farm and I couldn't get to the cellar in time!"

"Then you're still out there?" Emma asked. There was a frown beneath the mustache she had apparently tried unsuccessfully to bleach. Little red pimples joined the short black hairs, and Livvy had to pull her eyes from Emma's mouth before answering her.

"I suspect it's permanent," she admitted softly, searching the store for Josie so that she didn't have to look at the pity in Emma's eyes.

"The man that lets a woman like you get away is the man the Lord himself has branded a fool," Waylon Makeridge said, shaking his head. "What a gay time we had on the way back from Milwaukee. And now you must be racked with loneliness." He came toward her, took the basket from her hand, and put it on the counter. Josie was comparing two rag dolls quietly, and Livvy allowed herself to be led to the stool that stood by the cash register.

Josie began to make her way down the aisle, Livvy noticing for the first time how many delicate items were displayed within a child's reach. "Josie, don't—" she began as the little girl picked up the waxlike ball and brought it to her mouth.

"Eech," the little girl yelled at the taste of the soap, flinging the ball away.

Horror froze all three adults as lamp after lamp went down like a row of children's blocks. With the fall of each glass chimney, Josie's eyes grew wider, her little mouth stretched into a larger O. Glass shattered and tinkled to the floor, sounding not unlike the silver coins it would take to pay for the damage the little girl had caused. Even if she could bake them all, just how many pies could Charlie Zephin sell?

When the last lantern hit the floor, Waylon Makeridge

crunched through the debris and plucked up Josie, carrying her gingerly to Livvy, the girl too stunned to object.

"Are you all right?" Livvy asked, looking her over to make sure that no shards of glass had flown in her direction. "You aren't hurt, are you?"

The little girl shook her head and sucked her bottom lip into her mouth. Like Livvy, she was fighting the tears that were inevitable. Livvy lost the battle first, hiding her face with one hand and sobbing into her palm.

"There, there," Mr. Makeridge said. "It'll be all right." Several hands patted her back. She could swear one of them was little Josie's.

"I should be comforting you," she said to the child. "Some mother I am. How ever am I going to pay for this?" she asked, sweeping the scene with her hand.

Emma looked longingly at Waylon. "You could start at Sacotte Farm," she suggested.

"My thoughts exactly," he agreed. "In fact, perhaps I should accompany Miss Olivia home." He chucked Josie under her chin. "Would you like a ride in a fancy wagon?" Josie looked at the man suspiciously, almost as if she were trying to place him, and then shrugged in agreement.

"Oh, yes!" Emma said. "We could take them home and then take one of Livvy's pies out by the lake and have a picnic."

"A picnic is a wonderful idea," Mr. Makeridge agreed. "I bet you'd like that," he said to Josie, wiping the tears that still dotted her cheeks. Josie nodded, busy trying to get her breathing under control.

"Waylon, I'm sure that *Mrs.* Williamson has too much to do to join us," Emma said, watching the way Waylon was studying Olivia. "I thought that the two of us . . ."

"But the store," he reminded her. "And you've quite a clean-up, my dear."

"Yes, but—" Emma said, stretching her top lip down and

twitching it from one side to the other, not an easy task, considering the size of her teeth. Apparently the damage she had done trying to remove or pluck the hair there was now causing her to itch.

"Now, Miss Emma," Waylon said, and reached out to cup her chin affectionately. "You have work to do and I have work to do. Isn't that right?"

Emma nodded reluctantly.

"And I'll be back this evening for another of your wonderful suppers."

Emma smiled despite her disappointment.

"And you'll see to it that my room is cool, and bring me up some ice, and we'll chat on and on into the night." He scooped up Josie with one arm and extended the other elbow to Livvy. "If you don't mind waiting up for me, that is," he said, the cow bells over the front door clanging as he pulled it open for them. "I'll just take Charlie's rig," he called over his shoulder before taking several handfuls of fancy gum drops and shutting the door behind them.

"I needed to get some supplies," Livvy said, reaching for Josie. "I almost forgot."

"I'll bring whatever you need out later," Waylon said, not letting go of Josie and leading them instead to the carriage and plopping Josie on the seat before turning to assist Livvy. "A shame we don't have a driver again," he said, taking her hand and handing her up.

"I really need to get some things," Livvy said, but she sounded unconvincing even to herself. "I've got pies to bake. . . ." Her voice trailed off.

"And chocolates. Wouldn't it be grand if we had some more chocolates?" he asked.

"I think my wife has had enough chocolates to last a lifetime, don't you?" a voice asked. Livvy's head whipped around to find Spencer standing angrily beside the carriage. His hand reached up toward her face but she pulled back into the confines of the seat. "Have you been crying?" he asked. His voice went from hard-edged to tender faster than Josie could ruin a day.

"I was just taking Mrs. Williamson out to Sacotte Farm," Mr. Makeridge said. Livvy noticed he kept a fair distance between himself and her husband, who seemed to loom over him. It wasn't so much a matter of Spencer's being taller, though he was, but broader, bulkier, so much bigger than the man in the dapper gray suit.

Spencer ignored him. "Were you crying, Liv?"

Oh, she could just imagine the field day he'd have with what the baby he hadn't wanted had just done. She didn't need a lecture on how hard he worked for his money and how a three-year-old child—not his, of course—had, with one sweep of her hand, cost him half a day's work. Especially when the truth was it was more like a whole day's work, or maybe two.

Not that he'd be paying for it. They weren't his problem anymore. Not the children, and not her.

"Come on down, Liv," he said softly, extending his hand to help her. "It's not like I'm the one who left or that I said you couldn't come back. You made a mistake. There's no reason to cry about it."

Livvy couldn't help laughing. Maybe it was the relief that Josie was all right. Maybe it was Spencer's clothes, which hadn't seen the washboard or the iron and were still sporting last night's dinner—or maybe even last week's—something very red. Or maybe it was the fact that her husband still thought that the sun and the moon waited on his moods to rise and set.

"Spencer," she said, shaking her head. "I know it's real hard for you to get this idea, but believe it or not, this had nothing to do with you." She pulled Josie closer to her side and directed her words toward Mr. Makeridge. "Whenever you're ready, Waylon, I'd like to get on home."

She wished that it made her happy to see her husband standing on the sidewalk in front of Zephin's Mercantile with a bewildered look on his face as his wife drove off in the company of another man. She wished it thrilled her to hear the total confusion in his voice as he called her name after the carriage. She wished there weren't new tears tracking slowly down her face, and she wished that both Makeridge and Josie weren't seeing them.

If wishes were potatoes, her mother always said, *then no one would starve.*

"Get your goddamn nose outta my dinner," Spencer told Curly George as he sat on the railing to the corral and ate another of Livvy's cherry pies straight from the tin. "You bit a hole in the last one and I can't even bring it back to Zephin's to get the damn penny deposit back."

Curly George backed up a foot but didn't take his eye off Livvy's dessert.

"You should have seen that guy," Spencer said. "All dolled up like he was going to the goddamn opera."

The horse pawed the ground.

"Don't you be telling me I can't curse all I want to," Spencer yelled at the horse. "Ain't nobody but you around to hear, and you ain't gonna tell Livvy, are you?"

The horse shook his mane.

"Lord, someone would think you understood me. But you don't, do you?"

George shook his mane again.

"Christ, would you stop that?" he yelled.

The horse began nosing Livvy's pie again.

"George?"

The horse ignored him.

"I think I liked it better when I thought you were listening."

He pulled the pie away from George and the horse sauntered away looking for something more appropriate to eat.

Her eyes had been cold when she'd looked down at him from that buggy. Cold and sad and closed as if the chapter were ended. And Josie, who didn't seem to object any to Makeridge picking her up and putting her into the carriage, why, he could swear she'd grown three inches since he'd seen her. Livvy hadn't grown bigger, only more beautiful.

He downed as much more of the pie as he could manage and then whistled over to George, who came running. While the horse worked on the remains of Livvy's fine baking, Spencer took what comfort he could in the animal's company.

"She'll be back," he assured the animal. "She loves me. She's always loved me. That's not something you turn on and off."

The horse nuzzled his shoulder.

"She will," he said again, as if George had told him otherwise.

"What do you say, George? Think Peaches is carrying your foal?"

He couldn't bring himself to say the words, not even inside his heart, but he didn't need to form the thought to know it was there.

He gazed up at the cloudless day, the blue that went on as far as his eyes could see.

He'd been alone before. But then there had been nothing he could do about it.

He eased down from the railing and threw open the barn doors. Neil's bed was cut and sanded and ready for the pounding of the pegs.

And he was ready to pound.

Chapter Eighteen

"Is there some kind of difference between these, Miss Zephin?" Spencer asked as he studied the hairbrushes that were lined up neatly below the glass in the counter. He didn't want to appear stupid, but he wanted to be sure to get just the right one for Olivia's silky mane. And then he wanted to take the brush and run it through her hair for a hundred strokes. And then he wanted to place his hand at the back of her neck and feel the weight of that hair and let it run through his fingers. And then he wanted to . . .

"Well, of course there's a difference," Emma snapped. "That one's twenty-five cents and that one's a dollar." She pointed first to one end of the display and then to the other. A dollar for a hairbrush?

"Well, which is the kind that a woman would use?" A dollar? A dollar was a lot of money. Not that Livvy wasn't worth every penny of it.

"See the ovals?" Emma asked. The cow bells rang out and she nearly jumped out of her skin. "Waylon?" she called out.

"It's just me," Charlie Zephin answered. "You lose him again?"

"As I was saying," Emma continued, her voice quavering slightly, "you'll want an oval. A Florence brush is especially nice." She waved in the general direction of three brushes all with peacocks worked into their backs.

They were centered in the display, so Spencer figured that placed them in the fifty- to seventy-five cent bracket. They

looked a lot fancier than the one on the expensive end, which
was plain aluminum and without any of the cheaper ones'
fancy details. Bargains, he was certain. So it surprised him
every bit as much as he supposed it surprised Emma when he
said, "I'll take the one on the end," and pointed to the aluminum one dollar Cosmeon brush with good Russian bristles, if
one could believe the sign that lay next to it.

"Good choice," Charlie said as he eyed the purchase and
then headed for the stairs up to their living quarters. "Going
for quality is always a good choice."

He hadn't come looking for a brush at all, quality or not.
He'd come looking for Waylon Makeridge, his palms just itching to find the pretty man's face. Not that he didn't trust
Livvy, or that he had any doubt that in another day or two
she'd be back in his house and his bed where she belonged. He
just wanted to make sure that Makeridge had no doubts, either.

But Makeridge wasn't there. And in the hour he had been
waiting, he'd found one thing after another that he'd somehow
never bought for his wife. Things a woman like Olivia should
have, like those side combs for her hair, and cream for her
hands. He didn't know where the money would come from,
especially after he had assured Emma that he'd make good
whatever was owed for Josie's accident or tantrum or whatever it had been.

"Think he'll be coming back any time soon?" he asked,
fingering a pair of dainty slippers and realizing that he didn't
even know what size Livvy wore. When he had her back he
was going to measure ever inch of her. Slowly. Very slowly.

Emma sighed. "If this is the kind of husband he'll make,
I'm not sure I'm really interested," she said, then covered her
mouth with her hand. "My, I didn't really mean to say that. I
suppose I'm just dreaming, after all."

Spencer took a good look at the woman on the other side
of the counter, if ever a look at Emma could be considered

good. She had some sort of red mustache, and that was nearly the most attractive thing about her. Still, she was quiet spoken and intelligent. And her pa owned the only mercantile in Maple Stand and business was good. Add to that the fact that she'd been cooking for Charlie for a long time and he hadn't died or turned into a rail. "The man would be lucky to get you," he said, meaning it as much because he liked Emma as because he didn't care for Makeridge.

"Oh," she said, blushing slightly and waving away his comment with her hand. "And with talk like that it shouldn't take you long to win Mrs. Williamson back."

"Win her back?" he asked. He hadn't realized people knew about her move over to Bess and Remy's. He should have known better. After all, this was Maple Stand.

And then he thought about what he had done to Livvy—and the conclusions Maple Stand had drawn about her and her barrenness—and he wondered if he deserved to ever get her back, after all.

"We all thought that with all those Bouche children . . . I mean, we knew how much your own children meant, but still . . . Well, it's none of my business, but it did seem like a strange time to give up." Emma looked as unnerved as Spencer felt. She busied herself cleaning the top of the counter with her apron. "It's none of my business," she repeated.

If Emma knew, then Makeridge probably did, too. Hadn't he said he was taking Olivia out to Sacotte Farm? Hours ago. He'd said that hours ago.

"I'll kill him," Spencer said. He pulled out his watch and checked the time. "Five minutes. That's all I'll give him. Then I'll kill him."

The cow bells jingled and he spun around.

"Waylon!" Emma said, relief flooding her voice. "Wherever have you been? I mean, I'm so glad you're back!"

"I was doing my job," Makeridge said, pulling at the bottom of his suit to straighten the wrinkles. "I've been measuring all day in that damn sun and I'm hot and tired and I surely don't need an argument from the shopkeeper's daughter.''

"How about from me, then?" Spencer asked. Over his shoulder he said to Emma, "Go on up now and see if your father needs anything. Makebreath and I need to have a friendly little chat."

"Oh, Mr. Williamson, your family already owes enough for broken goods from this morning. . . . And Waylon's chin is still too sensitive to touch!"

The engineer rolled his eyes. "Go on up. I sure could go for some of that lemonade you make." He unbuttoned the jacket to his suit and directed his next words to Spencer. "Olivia makes a good lemonade herself, doesn't she? Between the two of us we must have polished off over a pitcher this afternoon."

"Were you at Sacotte Farm all day?" Emma asked. She was poised at the bottom of the stairs keeping her eyes on both men.

Makeridge shrugged. "Think we got ourselves a nice site for the Ahnapee and Western spur. Tomorrow I'm going to go out there again with my equipment. . . ."

"The hell you will," Spencer said, lessening the distance between himself and Makeridge. "If I hear that you or your *equipment* are within ten feet of my wife, you're gonna wish it was a train that hit you instead of me."

"Mr. Williamson! I'm sure you're misunderstanding—" Emma began.

"Go upstairs!" Spencer shouted at her.

"Do it," Makeridge agreed.

They waited for her steps to reach the upstairs door, which opened and then closed.

"You know, Makebreath, if it wouldn't compromise my wife's reputation, which matters to her, I'd kind of welcome you making a move on her. It'd give me such satisfaction to rearrange what's left of that pretty face of yours."

"Sacotte Farm is not without its treasures," Makeridge said, rocking on his heels confidently. After the punch Spencer had landed in the Lucky Clover, he didn't know what Makeridge had to feel confident about.

"I'm well aware of all the treasures at Sacotte Farm. Especially now. But before you know it, those treasures'll be right back where they belong, and you'll have parts all over Door County."

"I get the feeling you're threatening me, Mr. Williamson. Now, why is that?" He ran a tongue between his teeth and his lip, then began picking at something between his front two teeth. "A bit of cherry pie, I think."

"Better be careful of those pits," Spencer warned. "I've heard a man can choke to death on one small stone."

"What's stuck in your craw, Williamson?" Makeridge asked, using the fingernail on his pinky to continue picking between his teeth. "Think maybe your wife is tired of being treated like kitchen help and is ripe for courting?"

"Anybody going to court my wife, Makebreath, it's gonna be me."

"That so?"

Spencer took one more step toward Makeridge, so that when they drew in deep breaths, their chests nearly touched. "I thought you were interested in Miss Zephin. Isn't one woman enough for you?"

Makeridge laughed. "Emma? You know what Bouche called her? The walrus. You thought I could be interested in her? This store could be a goddamn gold mine and her garden could grow money trees, and even then I'd still need a bag over her head just to manage a poking. If she offered to take it out, wet it down, and blow it dry, I'd still want a buck for my troubles."

For the second time that day glass went shattering to the

floor of Zephin's Mercantile. But this time the glasses came falling down the stairs, at the top of which stood Emma Zephin, tray still in hand while the pitcher and glasses continued to crash toward the store.

"I suppose this means I won't be getting supper," Maker-idge said, still picking at his teeth as if he hadn't just broken the woman's heart.

How women stood men at all Spencer wasn't sure. But how they stood men like Makeridge . . . Spencer picked up the man by his collar and dragged him toward the stairs.

"Now just a second," Makeridge said, raising his hands to shield his pretty face.

Spencer smiled as he sat the man on the fourth or fifth step, where his face would be even with Spencer's fist. The man, Spencer thought as he reached back to deliver the hardest blow he had in him, was a lightweight.

Makeridge crumbled and Spencer looked up past him to Emma, who stood stunned and still.

"Didn't want to break anything valuable," Spencer said, trying to explain why he'd brought Makeridge to the stairs, when the real reason was that he wanted to give Emma the satisfaction of seeing him hurt the man who had just hurt her.

"What's going on out here?" Charlie Zephin said as he opened the door and looked over his daughter's quaking shoulder. "Oh, my Lord! Not Makeridge again, Williamson. We'll never get that spur."

"He insulted your daughter," Spencer said, flexing his fingers and turning to leave.

Charlie came running down the stairs and bent to see to Makeridge. "So?" he said. "Who hasn't?"

Waylon Makeridge was as good as his word. The children hadn't been out of the house for ten minutes when Charlie Zephin's rig was coming up the path.

"Think he'll be wanting any breakfast?" Bess asked, clearing away the children's dishes then pulling off her apron as she headed out to greet the engineer.

Livvy brushed back her hair and smoothed her bodice before following her sister-in-law outside. There was something about the way Mr. Makeridge looked at her—like she was a woman—that made her take an extra moment to glance in the mirror by the door. *Not all that bad,* she allowed herself, trying out a welcoming smile then chiding her ridiculous behavior. It wasn't as if she were interested in Mr. Makeridge. He was Emma's beau, and she was . . .

She refused to finish the thought.

Bess was waiting at the bottom of the steps for Makeridge to alight from his carriage, and Remy was coming in from the field with an arm raised in greeting. But Livvy could tell from the way Waylon bobbed his head about that he was not looking for Bess or Remy.

She pushed out the screen door and watched the smile come to his face.

"My Lord! What happened?" she asked, not even trying to keep the horror out of her voice.

"Oh, this?" he said, pointing vaguely toward his face, which was swollen and discolored and seemed to pain him with each word. "Ran into a door."

"That the same door you ran into when you first came to town?" Remy asked, his gaze flying between Livvy and the engineer, who was easing his way down from the carriage.

Mr. Makeridge nodded and then so did Remy, as if the engineer and her brother had a secret of which she and Bess were unaware.

"Dangerous doors," Remy said with a smirk. "You ever hear how this county got its name?"

"Door County?" Mr. Makeridge asked. "Surely not . . ."

"The Door of Death," Bess confirmed. Mr. Makeridge looked dubious. "Really. Death's Door. *Porte des Morts.*"

Mr. Makeridge swallowed so hard that Livvy could see his Adam's apple fight with his shirt collar.

"For heaven's sake," she said. "It's not as if the doors here go attacking people." She looked at the man's bruises. "Except maybe in your case. It's the waterway between the lake and the bay."

"I see," Makeridge said, completely disinterested. He turned his attention to Remy. "I understood that you might be interested in the spur running right through your farm, Mr. Sacotte." He looked out across the vast orchard of cherry and apple trees that Livvy had grown up around.

"Might be," Remy agreed. "If the price was right."

"Not often we pay for the land," Mr. Makeridge said. "Usually the town's happy enough to get the railroad and all the business it'll bring, that they just grant us an easement."

Remy shrugged while Livvy and Bess exchanged looks. "Not much usual about Maple Stand," Remy said. "Thought you might have noticed that."

"Indeed I did," Makeridge agreed, studying Livvy.

"That is," Remy continued, "no one takes advantage of someone here and gets away with it, if you get my drift."

Mr. Makeridge grimaced and nodded. "Got more than that," he agreed. "Mind if I walk around a bit? I need to get the lay of the land. The rises, the dips." He seemed to be outlining a woman's body as he spoke.

"Take all the time you want," Remy said affably. "Want me to show you around? Born here, right in this house, you know. Livvy, too."

"Is that right?" Makeridge said, turning to Livvy. "I'd hate to take you from your work, Mr. Sacotte. Perhaps Mrs. Williamson wouldn't mind showing me her hills and valleys."

"I—I don't know," Remy said. "Liv's got little Josie to look after and baking to do."

"Josie's still petting those new kittens by the barn," Bess said, gesturing with her head toward the door where Josie sat, a kitten in her lap and another crawling up her chest. "I'll keep my eye on her. You go ahead. I sure don't want to miss this chance, Mr. Makeridge."

"Then shall we?" Mr. Makeridge asked, extending his elbow to Livvy. "Which way would you suggest?"

"That ridge," Livvy said, pointing off into the morning sun and squinting, "hides Lake Michigan. Let's start there."

They walked for a little while in silence, Livvy reminding herself with every step that Bess couldn't manage on the farm anymore and that Mr. Makeridge could solve all her brother and sister-in-law's problems.

"So, you were born here then?" Mr. Makeridge asked as they followed the gradual rise up toward the ridge.

"Born here on this farm and lived every day of my life within sight of my papa's trees. From Marion's and my bedroom we could see Lake Michigan." Well, the lake would still be there, anyway.

"Does the idea of the railroad coming through here upset you?" He slipped out of his jacket and slung it over his shoulder. "You don't mind, do you? It's awfully warm out here."

Sacotte Farm was home, had always been home. When she'd come back to it with the children, she'd felt that she had some sort of right to be there. If the farm was sold, where would she and the children go?

"No," she lied. "Bess isn't very well, you know. And farming is hard work. It would be wonderful if you bought Sacotte Farm."

"Would it?" He stopped in his tracks and Livvy sensed that he would have liked it if she did, too. He would have liked it if she stopped, turned, and let him kiss her, and the knowledge flattered and scared her.

"Look," she said. "There's Lake Michigan. I bet that's what it's like to see the ocean."

"Very much so," he agreed.

"Have you seen the ocean, then?" she asked, turning to him. "My brother-in-law is out west in San Francisco and I imagine him looking out across the water, just blue forever, like the sky, and I think how happy it must make him."

"Have you always wanted to travel?" he asked, keeping pace with her as she followed the line of trees south.

"Oh, no," she admitted with a laugh. "I've never dreamed of being anywhere but here. And even my little dreams haven't come true."

He put his jacket on the ground and motioned for her to sit. "It's a big farm," he said. "And you are a very lovely guide."

She nodded, accepting the compliment graciously.

He dropped to his knees beside her and played idly with the hem of her skirt. "I understand that things between yourself and Mr. Williamson are not going very well."

"How are things going between you and Emma?"

Waylon leaned in toward her and stroked her cheek with the back of his hand, leaving it there while he spoke. "Emma Zephin's wishing something doesn't make it so."

"Neither, sir," Livvy said, pushing his hand away and getting to her feet, "does yours."

Mr. Makeridge shrugged and rose, as well, then leaned back down to retrieve his coat. "I suppose in that way, she is just like the rest of us."

"And I suppose that the problem with wishes is that our own are often in the way of someone else's."

"So only one of us can get his wish?"

"I think that no one gets his wish, more likely."

After all, Bess was wishing that Makeridge would buy Sacotte Farm. And Livvy was scared to death of Bess's wish coming true. For if it did, where would she and the children go?

"Well, we'll see tomorrow, won't we?" he asked.

"Tomorrow? Oh, you mean at the meeting? Will you have made your decision by then?" Livvy looked around her at row upon row of trees burdened with clusters of ripening cherries and knew that Makeridge's mind was already made up. He hadn't even looked at another site and the town council was called for tomorrow.

"I've known the value of Sacotte Farm since the night I came from Milwaukee," Makeridge said.

"And when will things get started?" Livvy asked, wondering how long she had to come up with some plan that would keep her and the children together.

"Oh, not until after the harvest." He brushed back a strand of her hair and tucked it behind her ear. "I wish to be sure to enjoy all the fruits the farm has to offer."

Livvy smiled. She'd just told him about wishes, hadn't she? Some men just never learned. There was one thing about which she was certain. Makeridge would never get what Livvy was well aware he was really wishing.

From now on, her cherries were all her own.

Chapter Nineteen

She knew it the minute he walked into the hall, just the way she had always known when he was around. She didn't have to hear the greetings or, as there were tonight, the whispers. Every inch of her skin prickled and she fought the urge to rub her arms, fearing it would make her look lonely and forlorn. Which maybe she was, but she wasn't about to advertise it.

"This seat taken?" he asked. He stood so close that his leg made a valley in her skirts.

"As a matter of fact," she said, her eyes fastened on the front of the room, "it is."

Something buzzed by her right ear and she tried to ignore it. There was a much bigger pest that was claiming all her attention.

"Don't move," he said, raising his hand to her hair. "There's a June bug that's finding your hair as irresistible as I do."

She stood still while he gently fingered her hair, all the while concentrating on keeping her breathing even and trying to swallow as if his very touch didn't stop her heart from beating.

"Almost got it," he said, tipping her head slightly with one hand as the other trailed up her neck to her loosely coiled bun.

"Spencer, I can . . ." she started when she finally found her voice.

"You can what, Liv? See behind your head?"

She tried to pull away from him, preferring to let a bug burrow into her hair than let her husband burrow into her heart.

"No," he said. "Uh! He got into the knot. You shouldn't have moved."

With his hands on her shoulders, he turned her so that her back was fully to him. This is the man who tricked me, hurt me, made a fool of me, she reminded herself. Despite that, her shoulders still rose and fell raggedly, so raggedly that he had to know what he was doing to her.

"It's only a June bug," someone said. "Nothing to carry on about."

She felt him slip the comb from her hair and felt the locks tumble toward her waist. "What are you doing?"

"I lost it in the coil somewheres," he said, his voice so close to her ear she could feel his breath. "This time don't move."

His fingers slipped into her hair, raising it off her neck, his fingertips just grazing her scalp and sending shivers down her spine.

"There's nothing to be afraid of, Liv," he whispered. "It's only me."

"Spencer, I . . . ." The hair was off her neck again and his breath replaced it. "Spencer," she said, turning her head to look at him.

"Damn," he said to the people that surrounded them. "Lost it again. Hold still there, Liv."

He put an arm around her to steady her. It did anything but.

"So hard to see him against this dark hair," he explained to anyone watching. "Darn smart bug. Try just shaking your head, Liv."

She did, and heard him groan. Dear God, in front of all of

Maple Stand, the man was making love to her hair. And if that wasn't bad enough, she was enjoying it.

Well, not *enjoying* it. She was hating every minute that he was near her. Only her body didn't seem to know what her mind was thinking. Her stupid breasts—which always just hung there, getting in the way when she was baking or hanging the wash—suddenly had thoughts of their own. Thoughts she tried not to acknowledge as they tightened and became acutely aware of the muslin camisole she wore. She could feel the coarse fabric against her nipples with every intake of breath and finally crossed her arms over herself to ease the exquisite pain.

"You scared, Liv?" Spencer asked.

"Of a little June bug? Of course not," she snapped at him.

"I didn't think you were scared of a bug," he said, then lowered his head so that no one could hear as his words brushed her ear. "You're shaking. Is it me, Liv? You scared of me?"

"Forget the stupid bug," she said, pushing her hands through her hair and shaking it. "It's bound to get bored and fly away."

"Don't count on it, Liv," he said, tucking behind her ear the one lock that always escaped her bun.

"The meeting's going to start," she said, taking her seat and looking around for Neil. Where had he gotten to, anyway? Spencer sat down in the seat next to her.

"That seat is taken," she reminded him.

"It certainly is," he agreed.

"Hi, Uncle Spence," Neil said, appearing from nowhere a full five minutes later than Olivia could have used his presence. "See you found her just where I said she was."

"Your uncle has taken your seat," Livvy said formally. *And his thigh is pressing against mine and I may never breathe normally again.* "Perhaps we'd better move."

Spencer put one arm on the back of her chair and then leaned over her, his shoulder grazing her chest, his ear so close to her mouth that if she stuck out her tongue she could trace its pink rim. She blushed furiously at the thought.

"Mind moving over a seat?" he asked the people to her left. His right forearm was grazing her knee as his hand rested on the far edge of her seat. "My wife and I need room for the boy." He gestured with his head toward Neil.

Leaning back put her against his left arm. Leaning forward pressed her to his chest. While she tried not to breathe at all, he inhaled deeply.

"Lilacs," he said with a smile, leaning back into his seat and closing his eyes. "The way you smell, it's a wonder you're not covered with June bugs all over."

From the way she was tingling everywhere, Livvy thought that maybe she was. The people to her left smiled and moved down, and Livvy was relieved to be able to shift over and burrow her fanny into the hard wooden chair. Could she really itch for his touch?

As if Neil were a log and she was being swept away by the current, Olivia reached for her nephew and maneuvered him quickly into the seat she had just vacated, effectively separating herself from her husband.

She'd have congratulated herself on the move if he hadn't looked at the boy and then at her as if she had just given him proof of his effect on her. And if he hadn't stretched his arms up high as if his back were stiff and then come down with his left arm on the back of Neil's chair, his hand in fiddling distance of her sleeve.

And fiddle he did. While beneath the folded hands in her lap, Rome burned.

"Doesn't your aunt look wonderful tonight?" Spencer asked their nephew.

"Sure," he said with a shrug. "You get that wheat in?"

"Could use some help, actually," Spencer said, all the

while inspecting the puff of her cotton sleeve with just his pointer finger.

"Ladies and gentlemen, please," Charlie Zephin said over and over from the podium where next to him stood Waylon Makeridge and Mr. Delisse from the bank. It took several minutes for the crowd to quiet down. When finally the hall became so quiet that all Livvy could hear was her own heartbeat pounding in her ears, Charlie began.

"Well, we got it!" He wiped his brow with a hankie while people cheered, and then waved the cloth in the air for people to quiet down once again.

"And this is the man that did it!" Charlie said, pointing to Makeridge. Livvy looked around for Emma, expecting that she would have been up on the podium or at least nearby, but couldn't spot her. She did, however, see Bess and Remy, who were beaming with joy. She smiled at her brother. His joy was hers, of course. And Sacotte Farm would always be there in her memories. It was just a yellow house and a bunch of trees. That was all.

The dandy came to the podium and was enjoying the cheers for a good long time. Long enough for Neil to get bored and fidgety sitting between his aunt and uncle.

Uncle Spencer was right about how good his aunt smelled. But he wondered if that smile she had pasted on her face was fooling anyone. He was sure his uncle wasn't tricked into thinking she was happy. And his uncle hadn't been there night after night to hear her cry.

"It gives me great pleasure," Mr. Makeridge was shouting, "to be in a position to help towns like yours." Mr. Makeridge looked familiar. He reminded Neil of his father. They wore the same kind of suits and had the same kind of air about them, like their shoes didn't touch the dirt in the road.

He looked down at his boots and the ones that Uncle

Spencer wore, so very much like his own. No matter how they cleaned and brushed them, the farm was there in every crack and crevice of the leather. He smiled up at his uncle. Their picnic had been fun. Even the hard work of helping on the farm was fun.

He smiled up at his aunt. She took his hand and squeezed it gently. She was soft, and warm, and it made him happy to return the squeeze. He loved her cooking, loved her fussing over him and tucking him in, even if he was too old for such things.

He looked from the grown-up on one side of him to the grown-up on the other.

It was too bad that such nice people had to get so stupid. They'd been pretty smart when he and his sisters had come to Maple Stand, but the longer they were there, the dumber his relatives seemed to become. Just take his aunt. She couldn't even make up her own mind anymore. He'd asked her about selling Sacotte Farm, and she'd said it was wonderful. Then she'd cried and admitted that it hurt to see her history swept away by what was the future. Then she'd told Bess how happy she was.

And Uncle Spencer. All he could think about was Aunt Liv. On the picnic he'd wanted to know every detail of her day. Yesterday he'd asked Neil what dress she had on. And he'd been annoyed that Neil hadn't noticed.

But Neil had other things to concern himself with. Like losing his birthright, for one. Sacotte Farm should have been his, at least in part. His and his children's. He'd thought he wanted the railroad to come to Maple Stand, but he hadn't realized it would mean the end of Sacotte Farm. And just when he was beginning to feel like he really belonged somewhere, too.

"There are many considerations," Mr. Makeridge droned on, "that go into the choosing of a specific site for the laying of track as well as the positioning of stations and buildings and the actual routing of a railroad line.''

Next to him, his aunt shivered. Cripes, it had to be eighty or ninety degrees in the hall. His uncle had wet rings beneath his armpits, and Neil was sitting as far forward on the chair as he could to avoid them. His aunt shifted her legs, sort of fluffing up her skirt a little, and his uncle breathed heavily.

He thought about the discussion he'd had with Philip about Philip's older brother Henry, and Jenny, the girl he was crazy about. Philip had described the goofy way Henry just sighed and looked at Jenny with cow eyes. And how Henry found any excuse to touch Jenny, from helping her with her coat to brushing the hair out of her face.

His uncle reached across him to his aunt, twirled a lock of hair around his finger, then tucked it behind her ear.

His uncle was in love with his aunt! Just like Henry was in love with Jenny. Neil felt the heat of his realization flush his cheeks. Philip had told him what Henry was wishing he could do with Jenny. Philip and Thom-Tom and he had even read the details in Uncle Remy's book by Dr. Napheys.

Aunt Olivia brushed imaginary crumbs from her lap and reseated herself. Uncle Spencer uncrossed his legs, recrossed them the other way, and threw his arm across his lap. Lord!

''Are you all right?'' his aunt asked, leaning over and putting the back of her hand to his forehead. ''You're all flushed.''

He was flushed?

''What's wrong?'' his uncle asked, bending so that both the grown-ups' heads were nearly in his lap. His uncle's nose teased his aunt's hair. *Oh, Jeez!*

''I gotta go,'' he said, pushing his way out from between the grownups.

''You want me to come with you?'' his uncle offered.

''No!'' he shouted, horrified. He didn't want to see his uncle. He didn't want to look at his aunt. The words in Dr.

Napheys's book sprang to his mind, unbidden. *Sexual organs. Intercourse.*

He went running from the hall as if he'd said the words he was thinking aloud and someone was after him with a bar of soap to wash his mouth.

Spencer moved over into the seat Neil had occupied. "What was that about?" he whispered in his wife's ear, wishing he could think of anything more to say that would keep him close to her. He didn't suppose she'd sit still for the entire Gettysburg Address.

She shrugged and kept her eyes on the fop at the front of the room. His suit was impeccable and he was handsome in a way that made women swoon. Spencer imagined the man picking his nose and felt better.

". . . And the best site, and I have to say *unfortunately,* now that I've tasted the cherry pies that originate there, is Sacotte Farm."

Beside him, Livvy sniffed, searched in that silly little drawstring purse she carried, and found a hankie.

"I thought this was what you were hoping for," he said. He knew it pleased him, for it had to mean she was coming home. What other choice did she have? But then, maybe that was why she was near tears.

"That's my home," she said to him, a quaver to her voice that he could feel in his chest. "There are memories there, my heritage. How would you feel if you were going to lose your home?"

He considered it for a minute, while around him people shouted and clapped their approval of the offer and Remy's acceptance of it. "I would give up my home, and everything in it," he said as evenly as he could, "to start over again with you. I would give up anything and go anywhere on this earth if I could make you happy."

The most amazing thing to him wasn't the look on her face, nor the doubt he read there. It wasn't even that little flicker of hope she couldn't keep from her eyes. It was the fact that he meant every word he said.

"I'm sorry," she said softly, raising a hand and burning his cheek where she touched him. "It's too late."

Her words hit him like a cold wind, chilling the sweat on his body until it sat like pellets of ice on his skin. In her eyes there was sorrow, not anger, and for the first time since that night in their marriage bed, he thought the unthinkable.

She turned away then, unable, he supposed, to look at him. It was a sign that she was truly and completely done with him.

He felt a tug on his sleeve and looked down. Next to him Neil stood looking every bit as awful as Spencer felt. His face was sweaty and there was vomit on the front of his shirt.

"She's dead," Neil said, his eyes wide and glazed. "I thought she was just sleeping. And I touched her. Touched that big pimple on her cheek with the hair in it. And she didn't move. She just kept smiling."

His voice was without expression, as if he was in a trance. Spencer tugged on Livvy's sleeve. She turned, shaking her head at him, but then saw the boy and crouched beside him.

"What's wrong, honey?" she asked him, cradling his cheeks. "Are you sick?" She raised her gaze to Spencer, her eyes filled with fear.

"She's dead," he said again. "There was blood. A lot of blood."

"Who?" Livvy asked him, crossing herself and saying a quick prayer. "Who's dead?"

"Miss Zephin," Neil said, looking around and fastening his gaze on Charlie. "I better tell her pa."

Spencer picked up the boy as if he were a small child. Neil lay stiffly in his arms. His eyes must have been seeing the scene over and over, for he suddenly shut them tight.

Remy and Bess had made their way through the crowd of celebrators only to find their nephew in Spencer's arms.

"What's the matter with the boy?" Remy asked as Bess reached out and felt his forehead in typical motherly fashion.

"Something's happened to Emma Zephin," Spencer said, unsure how accurate Neil's assessment might be. "Better tell Charlie. I'll take Liv and Neil home."

Livvy looked at him questioningly. Was she wondering if he'd heard a word she'd said?

"We'll be at Sacotte Farm, waiting to hear," he said.

It was a night for misery, all around.

"Hard to believe," Remy said, shaking his head. They were all gathered in the kitchen at Sacotte Farm hovering over mugs of now-cold coffee and going over all the details of Emma Zephin's death.

"Suicide," Olivia kept saying, shaking her head and crossing herself. "And all laid out in the wagon like she didn't want to be any trouble. What could have made her do a thing like that?"

Spencer thought of the look on Emma's face as the glasses of lemonade came tumbling down the stairs. What was it Makeridge had called her? A walrus?

"I don't know," he said softly. Life itself had been an embarrassment for Emma. He didn't see that death should be, as well.

"Charlie said she apologized in the letter for being so hard on the eyes," Remy said. "Said that she'd tried, over the years, to be good and kind and helpful, but that in the end none of those things seemed to count for anything."

"But why *now?*" Olivia pressed. "She looked the same her whole life. Why *now* was that so bad?"

"It's not what you're thinking," Bess said, getting up to get some fresh hot coffee.

"Maybe not," Livvy said. "But if things had gone differently with Mr. Makeridge . . ."

"What exactly are you thinking, Olivia?" Spencer asked. He was weighing whether to tell her what Emma had overheard and how it was that Makeridge's face had come to look like a horse's balls, all black and blue and swollen.

"That she saw Waylon Makeridge as her last chance," Livvy said. "And that he . . . well, he thought that I . . . not that I . . ."

"Put it out of your mind," Spencer said. "It's not your fault that the man found you more attractive than Emma Zephin. Hell, any woman in Door County's more attractive than Emma, God rest her soul. Not that you aren't . . ." He threw up his hands. "They don't come prettier than you."

"But that's not the point," Livvy said. "What difference does it make how pretty Emma was? Did she deserve to die because she was ugly? Look at Charlie. Emma didn't get that face in a box of Cracker Jack. But Wilma married Charlie even if his face could stop a clock. And nobody said he was too ugly to live."

"Nobody said that about Emma, either," Remy said. "Excepting Emma."

"But they did," Bess argued, taking Livvy's side. "By not courting her or marrying her. A woman is on earth for one thing. To bring children into the world. That's what God put her here for, and anyone who stops her——"

Livvy rose abruptly from the table, sloshing the coffee over the rims of several of the cups onto the wooden surface.

"That was thoughtless of me," Bess said, rising and putting her arms around her sister-in-law. "I guess I was just . . ."

Spencer took a deep breath and swallowed hard before interrupting. "No, Bess. It was thoughtless of me. The fact that Livvy and I haven't had any children yet was my fault, not Liv's."

Livvy turned to stare at him, and he realized he'd made some terrible mistake. He just didn't know what it was. She shook her head at him, but he'd let the horse out of the barn and it was too late to shut the door.

"Just how was it your fault?" Remy asked him. Spencer thought if Remy gripped the cup any tighter the handle would crumble in his hands.

Livvy pleaded silently with him. Here he was ready and willing to own up to what he'd done, and her eyes were begging him not to do it.

She bit her bottom lip and looked at the floor. Dear Lord! She was ashamed of her innocence.

"Spencer? I asked you a question."

The last thing he wanted to do was embarrass her. Her innocence was her most precious quality. And he'd trampled it and sullied it and if he wasn't careful, he'd hang it out to dry.

"I stopped praying," he said, watching Livvy for any sign of approval or, better still, forgiveness. "But I can't tell you, Remy, how hard I'm praying now."

Chapter Twenty

"But the way she looked," Neil said again, causing his cousin Philip to cover his eyes and groan. "Her face wasn't all pinched or nothing."

Olivia smoothed back his hair and wet down the cowlick that she thought might look irreverent at the funeral. "Are you all ready to go?" she asked him, her voice gentle and encouraging.

He looked around the kitchen, his heart pounding so hard she could see it through his shirt, his breathing uneven. "Isn't Uncle Spencer coming?" he asked. "He promised, and I thought . . ."

Livvy knew exactly what he thought. He had no doubt begun to believe that the promises his Uncle Spencer made were ones that he could always count on. And as important as any of the promises themselves were, it was even more important that he could believe them, depend on them. Now, in the kitchen at Sacotte Farm, he clearly wasn't so sure.

Livvy, of course, had been there herself. Had hoped and been disappointed and foolishly hoped again.

But if his faith had to be crushed, she wasn't going to be the one running the thresher over his dreams. "I suspect he'll meet us there," she said, bending her knees slightly so that she could look him fully in the eyes.

"But he told me he'd go with me," Neil said, not bothering to hide the fear in his voice.

He'd admitted this morning that the last funeral he'd been

to had been his mother's, and he wasn't looking forward to this one. What if, he'd asked, he closed his eyes and saw Miss Zephin again, like kept happening to him?

"I hear his wagon," Remy said, pulling back the curtains to make sure. "I don't believe you saw this much of him when you were living at home, Liv," he added, watching as she checked her hair one more time in the mirror.

"Do you think they'll fix her hair nice?" Neil asked. "So that she looks pretty?"

"Miss Zephin look pretty?" Louisa said with a laugh. "God can't make an American Beauty rose out of an old stinkweed, for heaven's sake."

"Louisa! It's not like you to be so uncharitable. People's words and actions count far more than their looks, don't you think?" Livvy asked, trying to set a good example.

"Well, he keeps talking about how good she looked," Louisa whined. "Everybody know she was ugly as sin, so how come she looked better when she was . . . you know . . ."

Bess bustled into the kitchen with her hand in her waistband. "Will you look at that, Liv?" she said, holding the skirt away from her body. "Why, I must've lost a good ten pounds, don't you think?"

"I can see it in your face," Liv agreed, despite the look Neil gave her that implied she might be exaggerating more than just a little. "That skirt better not fall down in church!"

"You want my suspenders, my pretty?" Remy asked, pretending to unbutton them for her.

"Why did she look so nice, Aunt Liv?" Neil asked again. No doubt he just couldn't get the picture of Emma Zephin off the insides of his eyelids.

"Because she was with her maker, I suppose," Livvy said for want of a better answer. "And so she wasn't lonely anymore."

"I say hallelujah that her suffering is over," Bess said as

she once again checked the distance between her round belly and the band of her skirt. "She's with God and she knows eternal peace."

"Yes," Philip said, apparently considering what he was being told. "But she killed herself. Isn't that a sin?"

"Anyone home?" Spencer's voice boomed from the porch.

Livvy watched the tension ease out of her nephew's shoulders at the mere sound of Spencer's voice. It was as if just the man's voice from a distance, or his smell when they worked up close, or the sight of him just coming into view, was able to put all their nephew's thoughts in order and helped the world make sense to him.

"In here," Neil yelled, scooting around Olivia and rushing to greet his uncle.

"You all right?" Spencer asked him, bending so that they were nearly eye to eye. "You sleep all right?"

"I touched her," he said, and tears sprang into his eyes. "I thought she was asleep, I swear it! I never would've done it if I knew she was dead."

"No, son," Spencer said softly, his big hand cradling the back of Neil's head and hugging him to his belly. "I know you wouldn't."

"I don't want to go," he said, though the words got muffled against his uncle's shirt.

"Well, I don't suppose anyone really wants to go to a funeral. And unless your aunt disagrees, you don't have to go." He continued to stroke the boy's head as he spoke. "But there's something about saying good-bye—there, with God watching and everyone gathered around for the same purpose as you . . ."

Neil's gaze took in Livvy and he seemed to come to some decision. "I'll go," he said, trying to pull away and end the discussion.

But her husband held him fast and spoke in a dreamy voice

aimed more at himself than anyone else in the room. "It's best to say your good-byes and get them over with and move on. Sometimes you wait too long and then they stick in your throat until they choke you. And you aren't really living yourself anymore, and it takes more will than you think you have, to get it done."

"But I heard you that day," Neil said. "In the cemetery. You told them good-bye."

Livvy couldn't swallow. Truly she couldn't. Panic gripped her throat and lungs, and she spun on her heel so quickly that she caught her hip on the door frame as she rushed back into the kitchen.

He'd told them good-bye. Kirsten and the children were finally at rest for him. She gulped for air and felt the relief flood her chest.

Behind her the swinging door opened, and she didn't have to turn to know it was Spencer that had come after her.

"It'll all work out," she heard Remy say from the parlor where no doubt everyone stood staring in her direction. "Let's head on out to the wagons. I'm sure Aunt Liv and Uncle Spence'll be out here in just a minute."

"It *will* work out, Liv," Spencer said, coming up behind her until she could feel the heat of him against her back.

"It's too late," she said. Though there was more she wanted to add, it was all she could manage before running from the room, grabbing her hat from the peg by the door, and scrambling into the wagon like her tail was on fire. She settled down next to Neil and kept her eyes on the horizon as Spencer followed her at some distance and took a seat on the other side of the boy, then released the brake and turned the horse in a circle toward town.

It's too late. That's what she'd told him the night before, and that's what she'd told him again. It amazed her that he could even think she could forgive him. How could he stand there and tell her it would all work out? Now that his pain was over, did he expect her simply to forget about her own?

"You have Josie tight?" she asked, turning around to check Louisa and the baby, her gaze skimming the top of Neil's head and carefully avoiding Spencer's eyes, though she felt him studying her.

"Of course I have her," Louisa snapped.

The wagon came to a halt. Spencer handed the reins to Neil without saying a word, then shifted in his seat until he was facing his niece.

"I've been patient with you. I've made allowances for you. I know up till now you haven't had it so good. But now that you've got your Aunt Liv, and you've had enough time to see the kind of woman she is, your time's up. You understand me?"

Louisa glared at him but said nothing.

"I asked you a question," he said, making it clear they weren't going anywhere until she answered him.

"Spencer, leave the child alone," Livvy said softly, while Remy pulled his wagon up next to theirs and asked if anything was wrong.

"Miss Louisa?" Spencer asked, not giving an inch.

"I understand," Louisa bit out. Livvy closed her eyes against the hateful stare the child gave first her and then Spencer.

"Nothing's wrong," Spencer told Remy, taking the reins back from Neil and continuing along as if nothing had happened.

Livvy reached back and rubbed Louisa's leg gently, trying to say with her hand what Louisa's deaf ears refused to hear. *I'm here. Let me love you. I'm here.*

To her complete surprise, she felt Louisa grasp her hand and squeeze it, not just with one hand, but with both, like a lifeline she was afraid to let loose.

Livvy knew if she turned around to look at the girl the

moment would be gone, the spell broken. And so she sat, her body twisted, her hand aching, but her heart full in a way she had never known.

When the tears fell, she did nothing to hide them.

"I'm sure Miss Zephin's happy now," Neil said, patting her leg. "You don't have to cry."

Spencer turned and studied her face. *She's holding my hand!* she wanted to shout. But all she could do was study the tips of her shoes and let Louisa cling to her almost as hard as she was clinging back.

The funeral had been brief, embarrassingly so. Spencer thought that the only comfortable person there was probably Emma Zephin, her body resting in a modest coffin, her soul above them all, looking down at all their weaknesses and foibles.

The whole town had failed her, just as the whole town did everything else. They had passed judgment on her and found her wanting in beauty, and that had been enough to condemn her to a life of solitude and sadness.

He thought of Livvy, sitting primly on the wagon seat just a few feet away from him, and wondered how she had managed to cope with the town's judgment of her. They'd branded her barren, excluded her from one thing and another because, they'd told her, she wouldn't be interested.

And he'd let it all happen. Worse, he'd made it all happen. And then he'd turned around with that stupid smile of his and told her he was sorry and expected her to just forgive and forget.

He stared at Curly George's rump searching for the magic words. It seemed as good a place as any to find them. After all, he was a horse's ass if he thought he could erase away all the hurt he'd done her.

"Doesn't seem right to just go back to work," Spencer said, glancing over Neil's head at his wife.

"No," she agreed.

He couldn't tell whether she was wishing he'd just drop her off and leave her be, or ask to spend the day with her, so he hinted again for an invitation. "Sad that there wasn't any gathering at Charlie's, don't you think? Doesn't seem right just going on with the day after burying poor Miss Zephin."

"Why do you think there wasn't any paying of respects?" Louisa asked from the back of the wagon. She had Josie on her lap and the little one was sprawled in the sun with her eyes shut, probably fast asleep. "Because she killed herself?"

Livvy shrugged. "I think Charlie was ashamed. Ashamed that Emma killed herself, ashamed that she wasn't pretty, ashamed that he was ashamed of her."

Spencer supposed she was right, but still he couldn't help but wonder that it could matter so much. "You know, I never noticed that Emma was so burn-your-eyes ugly."

Olivia didn't say anything.

"I suppose there's a lot I never noticed, huh?"

"Doesn't matter now, does it?" Livvy said, picking at a loose thread on her skirt.

"Like what?" Neil asked, and Spencer heard a snort from behind him. That young lady with the sour expression was surely growing up, whether he liked it or not. He felt like he was missing it all—carrying babies to bed, noting an inch of growth, watching Liv braid the girls' hair—things he failed to appreciate that now he missed so much.

"Matters more than anything, Livvy-love," he said as he brought the wagon to a stop in front of Sacotte Farm. She was squinting at him in the sunlight and her skin glowed with just the hint of the summer heat. How women stood those long black dresses in the middle of the summer was beyond him. And they called them the weaker sex? He'd like to see some of

the men in Maple Stand try to do a day's work in those things
their wives traipsed around in.

"Spencer?"

Lord, she was lovely.

"Spencer, are you all right?"

"I'm sorry," he said, trying to recall what she'd asked,
and failing. He could see those soft lips moving, the fullness of
her cheek rise with her smile, but if his happiness depended on
it, and he prayed it didn't, he couldn't recall what she'd said.
"I guess I was daydreaming."

"I guess you were," she agreed. "I asked if you were
hungry. What are you doing about meals, anyways?"

He thought about the fact that she was supplying them. If
anyone would call cherry pie for breakfast, dinner, and supper
meals. "I can cook. I haven't been too hungry lately, anyways." Not for food. What he hungered for sat next to him,
her soft pale skin framed by dark hair and even darker clothes
so that her face seemed to glow like a single pearl against a
jeweler's velvet pad.

"Oh." She seemed disappointed.

"Not that I don't miss your cooking. But I don't want you
to think that your cooking is why I want you back. I'd be
willing to live on . . ." He tried to think of something awful
that he could suffer through just to have her back in their
home.

". . . air," Louisa prompted in a whisper from behind
him.

He smiled.

So did Liv.

Lord, who'd have thought that sharing a smile was as
wonderful as sharing a bed?

". . . air, is right. I'd live on air if you'd just . . ."

The clatter of Remy's wagon drowned out his soft words.

"You all waiting for us before you get down?" Remy
asked, pulling alongside their wagon.

"Uncle Spence was just——" Neil started, but was quickly silenced by his older sister, whom he turned to stare at.

"Aunt Liv was just . . ." Louisa began.

"I was just . . ." Liv said, and then her hand went up as if she were offering something to Spencer and waiting to see if he would accept.

He cleared his throat. "I was just . . ." He didn't know what he was.

Remy tried to stifle a laugh, covering his mouth and exchanging a look with Bess.

"Well, I was just thinking that we ought to gather a few things and head on out to the bay for a good fish boil," Bess said. "I suppose that's what you were all just . . . justing!"

"Be like working on the Sabbath, burying poor Miss Zephin and then getting to work," Remy said, while the boys behind him were gesturing to Neil and Louisa and bobbing their heads up and down in support of the idea.

Spencer was afraid to look at Livvy. There was every reason to believe she would say no to his joining them. And there was no way he would force himself on her.

"Well?" Remy asked, his eyes on Spencer alone. "You coming?"

Spencer took a deep breath and turned his head, pleading with just a look for her permission to accept the offer. Without her nod he would graciously decline and head on home where he would be sorely tempted to find a strong rope and hang himself from the rafters in the barn.

It was a tight smile. Not welcoming, but it was a smile nonetheless. And a nod. Not vigorous, not anything more than resigned, it spoke of not disappointing the children or ruining anyone's day, without even a word being said.

"Tell me what you'll need," he said, relief washing over him like a wave from Lake Michigan itself. "Beyond my skill as the best fisherman in Door County," he boasted.

Philip and Thom-Tom hooted, slapping their father's back.

"My kids and me against your kids and you," Remy said. "Most fish gets . . ." He paused, and there wasn't a sound beyond the slight breeze rustling the leaves in the orchard. Spencer waited for Livvy to remind Remy the children weren't his. He supposed she was waiting for the same thing. Surely Louisa would object to even being called a kid, never mind his.

"A cherry pie," Livvy said quietly. "Winners get a cherry pie."

There was still silence. He'd lived with so much of it lately that he couldn't find comfort in it, but neither could he think of a word to say, nor could he have gotten any past the lump in his throat.

"All right," Livvy said, a shy smile playing at the corners of her full lips. "So do the losers."

"Yeah!" shouted the children in Remy's wagon.

"Yeah!" shouted Neil. Spencer even thought he might have heard a very quiet "yeah" from Miss Louisa, the grump, behind him.

He ventured a sideways glance at his wife. "Yeah," he said, almost a question instead of a cheer.

"Don't know if I've got enough onions," Bess said, not hiding the smile of triumph on her face. "And a few extra potatoes never hurt."

Neil had never seen a fire set right on a beach before. He'd never seen a cauldron as big and black as the one that his Aunt Bess had unearthed in the barn and which was now full of water that was barely simmering.

He'd also never seen his Uncle Spencer so tongue-tied and nervous. Ever since his Aunt Liv had offered to go back to the farm with him and pick up a few things for the fish boil, he'd been jumpier than a frog in a frying pan. He'd insisted that she stay at Sacotte Farm and change into some lighter dress for the shore, and taken off so fast they were all still choking on the dust he'd raised ten minutes after he was gone.

And if he was in such an all-fired hurry to get to the beach, why did he just sit there staring at Aunt Liv like he'd never seen her before when they should have been halfway to Sturgeon Bay? What did it matter whether he'd ever seen her in that dress or not? As far as Neil was concerned, one dress was the same as another. But it was like she was the Blessed Virgin herself, the way Uncle Spencer stared, his jaw dropping and his pipe falling right out.

And when his Uncle Spencer had put his hands on his Aunt Livvy's waist to help her up into the same wagon she'd gotten herself in and out of nearly every day since they'd arrived from Chicago, Neil thought his uncle was gonna be sick. Well, a grown man didn't usually just groan out loud unless he had a bellyache, did he?

He and his cousins had all kicked off their shoes and socks as soon as they'd gotten to the bay, but Uncle Remy and Uncle Spencer had both seen to his aunts' boots before taking off their own. Aunt Liv had insisted she could manage herself, but would Uncle Spencer let her? No, he wouldn't hear of it. Like the best treat in the world was taking off a lady's high-button boots, his uncle claimed it was his pleasure just like he really meant it.

Lord, was Neil ever glad when his aunt refused to let him help with her stockings. His uncle seemed to find it kind of funny, and his shoulders shook as he quickly shucked off his own shoes and walked straight into the water claiming that he needed to cool off.

Neil thought it was pretty cold by the shore, the breeze strong enough to make their clothes flap in the wind. And no one else seemed to need to get wet. Much as he liked him, he still found his Uncle Spencer a strange man.

Neil watched his aunts checking the water in the kettle again and thought it was a good thing they'd both changed out of their funeral clothes. Two barefoot women all in black leaning over a steaming cauldron might just be mistaken for witches, and his uncles would have to defend their wives' honor or see them burned at the stake.

He was imagining again. He did it more and more lately, especially since they'd moved to Sacotte Farm. It didn't take a genius to figure out that there was a real fine line between imagining and wishing. Almost as thin as between wishing and hoping. And if he got tangled up in those lines, well, he'd drown.

"Neil," Thom-Tom yelled to him. "Aren't you gonna help us catch any fish?"

"Hey," Uncle Spencer corrected. "He's on my team. We're gonna win that pie, aren't we, son?"

Something about his question made Philip laugh, but Neil was busy feeling the warmth of his uncle's arm on his shoulder and didn't bother to ask his cousin what the joke was.

"You know how to bait a hook?" Uncle Spencer asked him. Where did he think Chicago was? In the middle of a desert? He'd seen men baiting hooks right at the pier. Maybe he'd never put the squiggling worm on the hook, maybe he'd never even held a pole, still, he wasn't some namby-pamby little sissy who couldn't . . .

The worm that Uncle Spencer held out to him was fat and dirty. It fought to get loose by arching first one way and then another. Neil wasn't afraid of worms. Heck, he found them in the garden and the fields all the time. Still, the idea of sticking that sharp hook through its body . . .

"Get the pole from over there," Uncle Spence said, pointing down the beach a little way to a pole that stood up from the ground about as high as Neil was tall.

It was a boy's pole. "Was this yours?" he asked his uncle

after he waded out to him, careful to keep the pole out of the rising water.

His uncle nodded. "Lines kind of fouled," he said under his breath. "Hasn't been used in a long time."

Neil wondered just how long, but Uncle Spencer didn't say.

"You hold this," he said, forcing the worm on Neil and taking the pole in exchange. "And don't make friends with it. It's some nice whitefish's last meal."

Neil cupped his palm and watched the worm plead for mercy.

"Water's nearly boiling," Aunt Bess yelled out to them. "And so far I've only got two fish to clean."

"You can't hurry the fish," Neil yelled back, and everyone laughed.

Almost an hour later, the fishermen all dry from lying on their backs and letting the sun dry them out while Aunt Bess and Aunt Liv cleaned the fish, Louisa peeled the carrots and onions, and Josie combed the shore looking for stuff and things, the dramatic moment they had all been talking about was at hand.

"Okay, okay," Uncle Remy said, shooing everybody back from the bubbling pot that was filling the whole shoreline with a wonderful smell. "Now stay back. Louisa, you got the little one?"

"I've got her," Aunt Liv said, picking up Josie and settling her on her hip. "Oh, I love this part!"

Uncle Spencer seemed torn between standing with Aunt Liv or helping Uncle Remy. Finally, and Neil thought not so happily, his two uncles carried over something from the wagon and threw it onto the fire.

In all his life Neil had never seen flames jump so fast and so high. With a loud puff and a whoosh of hot air the fire roared to life, sending bubbles of stew over the edge to sizzle back on the flames.

"Burning off the fish oil," Aunt Liv whispered to him when he looked to her to make sure nothing had gone wrong. "Isn't it a sight?"

His face burned from the heat of the fire. He had to squint his eyes to stay as close as he was. So this was why people had cameras. He'd never understood until now. But if he could have, he would have preserved forever this moment, flames shooting around the big black kettle, his uncles smiling and patting each other on the back, the women folk huddled together wide-eyed, and his cousins running along the beach shouting that the stew was ready for anyone who might want to join them.

Life, he thought, as warm on the inside as the fire was making his outside, *was perfect.*

"Liv? You asleep?"

She'd been lying in the sun for quite a while and he was worried about her burning. At least that was what he told the rest of the family when they decided to take a walk along the shore. "Go ahead," he'd told them. "I'll watch over Livvy and make sure she doesn't burn."

Bess had been doubtful. He could read it in the honest woman's face, but thankfully Remy had pushed her along and finally they were all out of sight.

He'd taken up a position that blocked the sun on her face, though if the truth were known he had a real weakness for those little freckles that popped out when she forgot her bonnet for any length of time. And there he sat, guarding her as best he could, watching her chest rise and fall in the late afternoon sun and wondering when being so close to her without touching her was going to kill him.

"Liv?" He ran his hand down her arm so lightly that she twitched in her sleep but didn't awaken.

Like some kind of twisted and demented man bent on

torturing himself, he tried the same thing over her left breast. It seemed to have no effect on her, but he could hardly draw a breath.

"Liv." He said it louder this time, needing to talk to her, to see those eyes, to hear that voice.

"Spencer?" She blinked, raised a hand to shield her eyes from the sun and looked around. Panic gripped her. "Where is everyone?" she asked, coming to a sitting position and scooting away from him as if he were a threat to her very safety. She'd probably rather be closer to the kettle of simmering stew than to him. It hurt him like hell in the pit of his stomach.

"They went for a walk," he said gently. "They'll be back soon."

"How soon?"

"How long can someone carry Josie?" He smiled at her reassuringly.

She didn't appear reassured. "Oh."

"I can't go on like this," he admitted, playing with the sand because he just couldn't bear to look at her and not touch her.

She rose to her knees and said, "I'll go find them and tell them it's time to go."

"No. Please."

She stayed where she was, just the way she was, waiting for him to say what he had to say, to get it over with and let her be.

"Do you know what you're doing to me?" he asked her, her breasts level with his eyes.

"What I'm doing to you?" she asked.

What was that, compared to what he had done to her?

"I'll go find them," she said while he watched her breasts fall and rise, fall and rise.

"Don't go." He reached out and caught one of her hands. "Please. You gave me three years, Livvy-love. I've no right to ask for more, but let me have five more minutes to convince you I'm sorry."

He sank against her, burying his head against her belly, and she allowed it. More, she cradled it there with her hand.

"I know you're sorry," she said, lifting his head so that his gaze locked with hers. "It doesn't matter. Sorry doesn't erase the pain. It doesn't give me back the love you stole, the loyalty you tricked me into giving you, the affection you withheld. You made a fool of me, Spencer, and every time I look at you I see that fool reflected in your eyes."

"No one knows what I did, Liv. And if they did they would blame me, not you. You were innocent and I kept you that way. No one would . . ."

"I would. I do. I was never a wife to you, Spencer. And now you want something I don't even know how to give."

"I want whatever you'll give me Liv. Any morsel of affection. Any seed. I'll plant it and it will grow into a love that—"

She smiled at him, almost laughing. "Isn't it funny," she said, "that you are asking for a seed from me? What was it you withheld from me? When you raised my nightgown and my hopes, what were you planting?"

"I was a fool, an idiot. I was so full of pain I couldn't see that you were my way out." He looked out at the bay and saw the children playing by the canal lighthouse in the distance.

Their voices carried on the wind, laughing, shouting, singing a song he couldn't quite make out. What did it matter? What did anything matter if he couldn't bring her to her senses and make her understand that he was sorry? "Through it all, even when I loved another woman, through my whole life, you've always been there—my lighthouse. The one I could talk to, turn to. No matter how far out to sea I ever went, no matter how lost I became, you were always my lighthouse. Can you tell me now, when I have finally found my way home, that you don't love me anymore?"

He pulled her down so that she lay next to him on the ground. Gently he pulled the pins from her hair and spread it across the grass.

"You love me, Livvy, and I love you." He laid his hand gently just above her breasts. "Look at how hard it is for you to breathe with me near." He grabbed up her hand and put in on his own chest. "See? For me, too. You feel my heart?"

She nodded, and her lips parted ever so slightly. He knew it wasn't an invitation, knew she didn't want him to kiss her, knew it was a temptation she was sworn to resist. But he bent and tempted her anyway, just barely brushing her soft lips with his own. He took her in his arms and waited for her to give in to what he knew from the way her heart pounded she had to be feeling. What he was willing her to feel.

But she lay limp in his arms, refusing to respond.

Backing up just a little, he tried to read her eyes, but she averted them, even after he tilted her chin up so that she nearly had to close them to avoid seeing his face. So she wouldn't meet his gaze. Sight was only one of the senses, and he knew better than most what the other ones could do. How the smell of lilacs could twist a man's insides. How the sound of a sigh could wring his heart.

He touched her as gently as he could, wishing his fingers were half as smooth as the ear whose outline he was tracing. He fingered the pad at the base of her ear, amazed at its softness. Her neck was long and graceful, and he let his fingers follow each other toward the base of her throat.

"Have you lost your locket?"

She shook her head silently.

She was as foolish as he had once been, if she thought that taking his picture away from her heart would erase the place he held there. Still, it hurt to the quick to know how hard she was trying.

As hard as he had tried. But he didn't have the patience

she had. And he'd be damned if he'd waste three more years
of their lives.

"All right, Liv. I won't ask you to love me. I'll learn to
live without it if I have to. But you have to let me love you.
That I can't do without."

He grabbed a handful of her hair and lifted it to his face,
burying himself in it. With his free hand he pulled her closer
against him, fitting her to him, molding her against his hardness. She didn't fight him, yet she offered no encouragement.
Not even when he ran his hands down her back and cupped
her buttocks so that she couldn't help but feel his maleness
pressing into her belly, burning them both with his desire.

"Let me love you, Livvy. Let me . . ."

"It wouldn't be enough," Livvy said quietly. "I've tried
that. Believe me, Spencer, it wouldn't be enough for either of
us."

"Tell me what I have to do, Liv," he pleaded with her.
"I'll do anything you want if you'll just come back."

"There's nothing you can do," she said, pulling away
from him and sitting up to search the shoreline for her children. He watched her straighten her clothing, knowing all the
thoughts that ran through her pretty head, for hadn't he had
them all himself? Hadn't he tried to keep himself from loving
her for three long years? "This isn't the time or the place. For
heaven's sake, Spencer. Emma Zephin was buried this morning and here you are trying to kiss me. And the children not a
hundred yards away."

"And what excuse," he asked her as a cool breeze wafted
over them, "will you find for yourself tomorrow?"

Chapter Twenty-one

It was happening again, and after such a good day, too. Neil tried to bury himself more deeply into the covers, but the night was warm and unless he was willing to suffocate, there was no getting away from the voices that crept under the kitchen door and crawled to his bed on the sofa, strangling his heart.

"You would have thought," his Aunt Olivia was telling his Aunt Bess, "from the way I just lay there, that my heart and my brain had just up and left my body. Like they had no memory of what he'd done and how much it hurt."

He couldn't believe that his uncle would ever take his hand to his aunt, not the way his father had done all those times to his mother. Maybe the man who had been sitting in the house that first night when they had all arrived might have, the man who'd been so angry that he'd frightened Neil. But that man had faded, softened, become his teacher and his friend. A man who could lay his hand on Neil's shoulder and set the world right.

"I don't know how I'm supposed to help you," his Aunt Bess said. Even her sigh reached his ears. "You've never even told me this terrible thing he did. Frankly, Olivia, it seems to me that Spencer has finally fallen in love with you and you're too blind to see it."

Well, that was telling her, and about time, too. Maybe now they could all go home. He pushed the covers further down and let the breeze coming in through the screen door wash over him.

"Things have a way of looking different in someone else's kitchen, Bess. Like your problem with Remy. If a man loved me the way that Remy loves you . . ."

"He does, Livvy. You just don't want to see it all of a sudden. How long are you going to keep this up?"

God bless Aunt Bess. There wasn't a word that Neil could have said better. If she couldn't get his Aunt Liv to see reason, he didn't know what hope there was.

"I'm not going back, Bess. Not ever. I've written to Julian and told him about Sacotte Farm and hinted for some help with the children. I know you'll be moving and I've got to find a place for us to go."

She'd written his father! Neil bit his lip to keep from crying out. His hands balled into fists and he kicked the covers off his legs and then lay rigid in the dark, praying his Aunt Bess could talk sense into Aunt Liv.

"There's no *us*, Olivia. The children will go back to their father and you will move to town and live with Remy and me for the rest of your life. Does that sound like what you want to do? Turn away from a man that loves you and a ready-made family that needs you because a man made a mistake? Every man makes mistakes. It's the nature of the beast. If they were perfect, Olivia, they'd be women!"

Please, Aunt Olivia, he prayed. *Please.*

"Three years of mistakes," his aunt said. "Maybe I could take my share of the money and . . ."

"Your share?" Aunt Bess asked softly.

In the silence Neil began to shiver.

"I hadn't thought about that," Aunt Bess said. "I suppose that only a third of that money will belong to us."

"I—I wouldn't take it at all, you know I wouldn't, if things were different, but I have the children to worry about and when the farm goes there won't even be a roof over our heads."

"Listen to me, Olivia," Uncle Remy said. Until then Neil hadn't even known his uncle was in the kitchen, too. "The way I see it, you've got two choices. You can go back to Spencer, who, Lord knows, seems to have come to his senses just as you took leave of yours, or you can move with us to town and send the kids back to Bouche."

"Or I can—"

"No, Liv, you can't. Not unless in addition to having gone crazy you've suddenly developed a selfish streak, too."

"I'm only thinking about the children," Aunt Liv said, and he could hear the tears in her voice.

"They aren't your children, and I can't spare your share to feed and house Bouche's brood. I never said they could come, *you* did. And I'm not gonna say they can stay. It's not like their father is dead or anything, and I need your share to buy Zephin's, now that he's willing to sell."

"But my share is mine," she said so softly that Neil had to strain to hear her. "Papa left it in thirds if it went out of the family."

"And what are Bess and I supposed to do while you have a perfectly good farm a stone's throw from here that you're too proud or too stubborn to live in? You got options and we got none and that's the truth of it."

The door from the kitchen flew open and Aunt Liv came racing through it, her hand pressed to her mouth as she ran across the room and pushed the screen door so hard it banged against the chair on the porch. He heard one heart-wrenching sob as she went running away from the house into the darkness.

"How could you have said that to her?" Aunt Bess shouted at Uncle Remy. The light from the kitchen flooded the parlor and Neil squinted while his eyes adjusted. His aunt and uncle sat at the table across from one another like two fighters locked in the same ring. He waited for his uncle to rise and lift his hand, a scene that was embedded on the back of his eyelids forever, like so many others that concerned his mother, but instead his uncle reached out and took his aunt's hand tenderly.

"She loves those kids more than anything, Bess. There's no chance she's gonna send them away. If she believes it's the only choice she's got, she'll have to go back to Spencer, where she belongs."

"You better be right, Remy Sacotte. Losing those children would kill your sister, I swear it." She pulled her hand away from his uncle's. "I don't know what he's done, but she can't seem to forgive that husband of hers. She's between the bay and the lake, and either way she thinks she's drowning."

"And you think I just threw her a rock to hold on to. That what you're saying?"

"She loves him. I can see that. It's plain as that pretty nose on her face."

"Sounded like she was panting for him this afternoon, didn't it?"

Neil pulled the pillow over his head. Between hearing about his aunt and uncle's personal business and suffocating, he'd take death. Besides, he had a lot to think about. Like how he was going to get his aunt and uncle back together before it was too late. Once his father got that letter, the smell of money would have him scheming before he opened the seal.

She leaned against the barn and tried to catch her breath. Of course they would need her money. And now, before Charlie started looking for a better offer. It was as if it were meant to be, Mr. Makeridge wanting to buy Sacotte Farm for the railroad, Charlie wanting to sell the mercantile since he didn't need a dowry for Emma anymore.

Poor Emma! What would she think of what Olivia was

doing? Naturally it was easy to condemn her if the facts weren't known. And Lord knew, Livvy didn't want the facts known. Not by anyone who was alive, anyway.

"The man pretended to make love to me," she whispered. "How can I trust him now? How can I believe a word he says when he never told me I wasn't the one at fault?"

"Did you hear something?" a girl's voice said. Livvy thought it came from inside the barn.

"No." The voice was muffled, ragged. "Come back down."

"Henry, I really think . . ." and then a giggle.

"Don't think," her nephew said. "Just feel."

"Oh, Henry!"

Olivia stood rooted to the spot where she leaned against the thin wooden siding that separated her from the young couple. She could hear the rustling of hay, the booted foot that scraped the floor, the sighs and moans of heavy loving. Did Sacotte Farm have to have the only barn in Door County that wasn't built of brick? Was it spared from the fire all those years ago just so that she could hear the sounds of what she would always miss?

She supposed she should stop them. They were too young and many mistakes were made in barns that had to be lived with for the rest of their lives.

"I love you, Jenny," Henry said so loudly it was as if he wanted the world to know.

"Shh!"

There were groans, and the smacking sounds of lips against flesh. Livvy leaned her head back and closed her eyes, imagining herself in Spencer's arms and wishing that her body didn't turn to jelly at the thought. And she wondered if maybe, right now, Spencer was thinking about her and whether his thoughts were running in the same direction.

"Do you really love me?" Jenny asked, her voice raspy and her words interrupted by a deep breath.

"Mm." Boots along the floor, a thud.

"When you move to town you won't have to help out in the orchards any more. You'll be able to get a full-time job, won't you?"

There was a smothered answer that sounded like a yes.

"I heard that Philip is already working at Zephin's."

Another noise that must have been agreement.

"So then you'll be free to work, too, right?"

His foot crashed against the very slats behind Olivia, bouncing her head slightly as it did. Sometimes when Spencer moved in their bed the headboard reverberated just the same way.

"Mm."

"And we'll get married?"

The movement behind Livvy's back stopped. The labored breathing slowed. Her eyes opened to the darkness around her and she hugged herself despite the warm summer air.

"If you'll have me."

There were thuds and scrapes and rustlings, with Jenny demanding to know what Henry was doing. Then a gasp.

"Lord, Henry! Is that for me?"

"I've been carrying it around since that Makeridge fellow settled on Sacotte Farm. It's real gold, too."

The door to the house swung open loudly on squeaky hinges. "Henry? You out there?" Remy yelled.

Poor Neil. It was a wonder how that boy seemed to sleep through all the noise around him. He deserved better than to be sleeping on someone's parlor sofa.

"Henry!"

Olivia came out from behind the barn just as Remy was halfway there. She intercepted him and they stood stiffly looking at each other, one-third of the farm profits standing between them.

"You seen Henry?" Remy finally asked.

"No," Olivia said.

"You been in the barn?"

Livvy nodded. Let the lovers have their moment, she thought. There were so few that could be captured and saved forever, like one sweet kiss behind the very same barn so many years ago. One moment might have to last them a very long time.

"Humph," Remy said, shrugging. "Don't know where that boy gets to. You ready to go in?"

"I think I'll just sit out on the porch awhile," she said, walking back to the house with her brother at her side.

"It'll all work out," her brother said, and she nodded, not believing him, not wanting to hurt him, not wanting to challenge the truth in his words.

He went in and she sat on the porch swing, rocking it very gently and wishing she was still that little girl whose mother would let her fall asleep out on the swing and then cover her with a thin blanket and let the fairies watch over her until morning.

Oh, how she loved this farm. Every inch of ground, every blade of grass, every leaf on every tree. She loved the peeling yellow paint, the dust-coated windows, the rotting second step up to the porch. The house held memories of a loving family in which she was the baby, always shielded from the worries that might have plagued her parents, always coddled against the frustrations her siblings must have known.

She leaned her head on her arm and tucked her legs up beside her, her dress covering her bare feet, and tried to remember just one day—any day—from start to finish, just one in which she was young and happy.

She heard the noise but left her eyes closed. She hadn't been asleep long, she didn't think, and Henry must have been finally sneaking in. But the rustling continued, and then a clanking of sorts until Livvy reluctantly opened her eyes to see what it was that Henry was up to.

A huge ladder leaned against the barn in the semidarkness,

and Livvy's first thought was of an elopement. It was a ridiculous thought, but what with Henry and Jenny getting engaged, and the goings-on in the barn, and then this ladder, and Henry halfway up . . .

What in the world? First off, the man on the ladder was bigger than Henry. Second, the ladder was resting on the solid side of the barn, leading to nowhere. In the dark cover of night it appeared that the man on the ladder was holding a bucket. And a brush. And was smoking a pipe. And whistling.

There was only one man in Maple Stand, probably in all of Wisconsin, who could smoke a pipe and whistle.

She sat up, careful not to set the glider on its squeaky ride, and trod on bare feet down the porch steps. Quietly, aware that her white dress was the most visible thing for miles, she stole her way to within several feet of the ladder.

Above her, in uneven letters that dripped down the side of the wooden barn, was her name. Well, not *Olivia*. Livvy-love, it said. Followed by a fancy dash and then P-l-e.

"What are you doing?" she asked, her voice coming out deafeningly loud in the still night air and startling Spencer nearly off the ladder, so that she had to grab it and steady it with all her weight pressed against the one leg that wanted to throw her husband at her feet.

"Uh, hi." It was too dark to see him blush, but she didn't have to see his face to know he was embarrassed to be caught red handed. Or red-brushed, to be more particular.

"I asked you," she repeated, hands on hips, fingertips thrumming, "what you think you're doing?"

He came slowly down the ladder, and the graceful man who had managed the paint bucket, brush, and pipe seemed to run out of hands on his way down. By the time he reached the ground he had lost his pipe, banged his head trying to reach for it, managed to paint the side of his own face, and left a good-size puddle of red paint not more than a few inches from Livvy's feet.

"Hi," he said again, wiping his hands on his pants.

"Don't 'hi' me," she said, wondering what she must look like to him, barefoot, her dress rumpled, her hair tumbling every which way. She reached up to try to gather it into a bun, searching for the pin that must have come loose in her sleep.

"Oh, don't," he pleaded, reaching a hand up to thwart her, realizing how dirty he was, and stopping. "Leave it loose, Livvy. Please."

"Spencer," she said, crossing her arms over her chest as if he'd caught her naked. "What are you doing here in the middle of the night painting the barn?"

It seemed a direct enough question to her, and certainly the obvious one. He, however, seemed surprised she would ask it.

"Why am I here?"

"Have you lost your mind?"

He nodded.

She looked up again at the letters on the barn. "Is that a note?"

He nodded again. "I saw you sleeping. I didn't want to wake you."

"So you thought you'd just leave me a note?"

He brightened and nodded.

"On the barn?"

He shrugged.

"In paint?"

This time he just lifted one shoulder.

He was insane. That was the only explanation.

"Why don't you just tell me and save yourself the trouble?" she asked, waving at the paint, the barn, the puddle he was stepping in.

"Tell you?"

He was staring at her chest, or was it her neck?

"Spencer!"

Now his gaze dropped to the ground. In a voice that took

her back to their childhoods, he said quietly, "I wanted to ask you to put the locket back on."

She had seen him as a boy. She had seen him through triumph and tragedy. He looked as vulnerable standing in front of her with paint dripping down his face as he had at ten when his dog had gotten caught in a bear trap and there'd been nothing he could do until his father had come to free it.

Her arms spread of their own accord and he raced into them coating her with his paint, smearing her face as he kissed her over and over again. He left his mark every place he touched, her bodice, the buttons of her dress. She imagined the handprints on her behind and smiled at the outrageousness.

"You're grinning! Liv, you're happy!"

Maybe, maybe a little, she conceded silently. Maybe, all things considered, a life with Spencer wouldn't be the hell she had already known.

His eyes glistened in the dark as he took her hand and started leading her toward the trough.

"You're a mess, Livvy-love."

"No worse than you, Spencer," she shot back, beginning to drag her feet as they got closer and closer to the pump. What did he have in mind, anyway?

"Well, this dress has to go," he said, working the last of the buttons and pushing it off her shoulders. "Don't be shy. It's full of . . . Oh, look what I've done now. I've gotten it on your underthings."

He didn't look the least bit sorry.

In fact, he wasn't. He was just disappointed that he had one more layer of clothes to dispose of before he could run his painted hands against her naked flesh. Just the idea had him so randy he could barely move.

"Spencer," Livvy said, looking around her uncomfortably, "I can't just take off everything out here. Even if you did turn around like a gentleman and . . ."

"I'm not turning." Not ever again. No more screens, no more turning down the lamp. He wanted to see in the light of day every perfect inch of the woman who made life worth living. He stood staring at her, then finally shrugged and pulled off his own shirt. "Whew, it's cold," he said as he splashed the water against his chest and up his arms. He unbuttoned his pants and shimmied out of them. He looked down at what she was able to make out in the darkness and guessed it was as apparent to her as it was to him. "Well, I guess you can tell I'm glad to see you."

She didn't answer him, but her eyes were riveted to his summer balbriggans and the tent that the formed between his legs.

"Come on, Liv," he said finally, going around her so that he could help her out of her clothes without being in front of her face. "That a girl. Now the other arm. Good girl. Lift your leg. Here, hold on to me."

"Just the dress, Spencer. And only because I can't go back into the house full of paint . . ." She reached behind her for balance and grazed his manhood without even knowing it as she reached for his arm. It seemed to him he had two choices. Take her then and there, or die.

A light went on in the house and Remy's voice carried down to the trough. "You better have a good excuse for coming in this late," he yelled.

Livvy grabbed up her clothing against her chest and stared at him with wide frightened eyes.

"Come home with me," he begged.

She shook her head and his heart dropped.

"Why?"

"I can't think around you," she admitted, her eyes on her bare toes.

He couldn't hide the smile. "You can't?"

She shook her head.

"Yeah?" He let out a whistle of pure pleasure. "Well, all right!"

"Who's out there?" Remy yelled from the window.

"Go!" she whispered as if her big brother were a threat to his very hide. Didn't she know that nothing could hurt him anymore except her?

"Go!" She pushed his pile of clothing at him, all the while trying to keep herself hidden from his hungry eyes.

"Liv?" Remy's voice boomed in the darkness. His upper torso hung out of the window looking for his sister. "That you?"

"It's me, Sacotte."

"Williamson? What in the . . . Liv? You all right? I'm coming down. . . ." The last of his words were lost as he ducked back into his room.

"Go!" Livvy urged him again. "Please, Spencer."

He grabbed his wife around the waist and pulled her tight to him, her arms in the way, bundled with her dress. He pressed his lips to her in an urgent kiss, one that didn't ask permission, one that didn't apologize.

"I'm leaving, Sacotte," he yelled toward the house. Then he put a finger on the tip of Livvy's nose and whispered, "I'll see you tomorrow," released her, and made sure that she had her footing. He had taken her words, and her breath, away, and he whistled all the way down the path.

But his wet chest was cold now that Livvy wasn't pressed up against it, and his house was dark, and his bed was still empty.

What in hell, he wondered, had he been so happy about?

Chapter Twenty-two

"Don't give me that stuff about how it's supposed to be confidential," Neil said, so angry that he was actually spitting at his cousin Philip as they stood facing each other on the porch. "Tell me what it said. Now."

Philip was bigger than him, maybe by half a foot, and by a good twenty or thirty pounds. Neil didn't care. He didn't care, either, that it was against the law for Philip to tell him what was in the telegram his father had sent to his Aunt Liv.

What scared him wasn't Philip's size or his strength. It was that Philip wasn't gloating or lording over him the fact that he knew something that Neil didn't. If anything, Philip seemed uncharacteristically sympathetic, laying a hand on Neil's shoulder, which he quickly shrugged off.

"Is he coming back?" Neil demanded, his chest heaving with each heavy breath he tried to take.

Philip shook his head.

"Then what?"

Philip gestured beyond him toward the screen door. "Louisa in there?"

"I don't know where she is," Neil said, "and I don't care."

"I don't want her coming out here and trying to kill me," Philip said, looking over Neil's shoulder and cupping his eyes to see into the darkened room. "You know what Aunt Liv always says about confusing the bearer with the news."

"Well, Aunt Liv's full of stupid thoughts these days,"

Neil said, letting his annoyance with his aunt get the better of him. All of this was her fault, and if she really loved him and his sisters the way she claimed, they'd all be back at Uncle Spencer's, where they belonged. And there probably wouldn't even be a telegram from his father to worry about. "What did he say, Philip? Does he want Aunt Liv to send us out to him?"

He doubted that possibility, for there wasn't any profit in it for his father. But the thought frightened him so much that he had to ask.

"He said that after the farm is sold Aunt Liv should send him her share and his share and then come out to California." Philip looked at the ground and chewed at the inside of his lip.

"Just her?"

"No, he said all come out, I think."

"Who's all? Did he say? Did he mean to visit? What exactly did he say?"

Philip raised his eyes then, sad eyes that glistened with the warmth that Neil knew the older boy felt for him, and which, despite their bickering, he returned.

Philip swallowed hard and then spoke quietly, repeating the words he must have memorized from the telegram. "Perhaps your separation from Williamson for the best. Your share and mine could start a business up North. You and the children could join me. Have always felt deep affection for you just as I had for your sister."

Neil felt the bile rise in his throat. He sat down on the porch settee and stared off at the orchard that would be destroyed by the railroad's coming and wondered why nothing was ever the way it should be.

"I took down the words myself," Philip was saying. Neil heard him, but the words seemed to have no meaning. "Mr. Zephin called out the letters as they came over the wire and I wrote them down."

Neil nodded.

"You all right?" Philip tried to sit down next to him, but

Neil had plunked down in the middle of the bench and there was not enough room on either side.

"Stop it, Louisa," Aunt Liv yelled from inside the house. "Stop it right now."

"I hate him," Louisa shouted. "He had no right to go through my things."

"What are you hiding, anyways, Lou Lou?" Thom-Tom said.

"Don't call me that! I don't have a stupid name like yours." He heard his sister's feet on the stairs and then her parting words. "And I hate living here."

"Well," Aunt Liv yelled up after her, "have some patience. We won't be here much longer."

A chill ran down Neil's spine. He looked at Philip, who suddenly found a knot in the porch floor of keen interest. He thought about what life with his father had been like and wondered just how Aunt Liv's presence would change things.

There had been women in his father's life after his mother's death, women who had babied him and women who had ignored him. Neil had seen them let his father touch them, fondle them. He'd seen them do things in the darkness with his father that even with the distance of time still made his skin crawl and his stomach turn.

He thought of his Aunt Olivia, soft, kind, and he knew that his Aunt Bess was right about her. She was in love with Uncle Spencer. She had to be. She just had to realize it. Before it was too late.

Voices droned on inside the house, his sister's joining the others once again. The talk had moved on to Emma Zephin, as it had over and over in the past few days. Neil was sick of hearing about how happy Miss Zephin was now that she was dead. If his sister wasn't snapping at someone, she was turning Emma into some sort of saint. And there was too much talk about womanhood, too. And Louisa being on the brink. Aunt Olivia had even asked him to make allowances for his sister and her sudden bursts of temper, bringing up her being a young woman as if that gave her license to be mean to the very people that loved her.

Aunt Olivia forgave her every outburst. Somehow, despite his sister's abominable behavior, his aunt had come to love her. It shouldn't have surprised him, for didn't she love Josie, who'd nearly decapitated her on the night they'd arrived? And he had no doubt that his aunt loved him, as well. She'd do anything for Louisa and Josie and him. . . .

The idea came to him all at once, like the Lord himself had put it into his head. He grabbed Philip's hand and ran off the porch, half dragging his cousin behind him until they were far away enough from the house so that there would be no chance they were overheard.

"What bee's up your behind?" Philip asked, loosening himself from Neil's grasp and squinting in the late afternoon sun.

"You could get more of that telegraph paper, couldn't you?" Neil asked.

"Sure," Philip answered, not catching on. "Why?"

Neil felt the smile crawl slowly up the edge of his mouth until his grin was wide enough to split his lips. "What do you think Aunt Liv would do if she thought Uncle Spencer agreed to send us back to our pa?"

"Looks like we're gonna see, doesn't it?" Philip asked.

Neil shook his head. "I don't mean her, too. I mean what if she thought that she'd be staying here and just us kids would be going back?"

Philip scrunched up his face as if to say the idea was ridiculous. "Aunt Liv wouldn't just let you all go. I think she'd go back to Uncle Spencer before . . ." His smile mirrored Neil's own as the idea dawned on him. "Ma," he yelled toward the house, "I gotta go back to town. I promised Mr. Zephin I'd watch things this afternoon."

Neil spit into his hand and extended it. Philip did the

same. Solemnly they shook hands and then let out a whoop of unadulterated joy. He might not be able to live on his grandfather's acres and tend his orchard, that might be out of his control, but he and his sisters could surely find a home with Aunt Liv and Uncle Spence once they made both of them realize the alternative was either Uncle Spence losing Aunt Liv or Aunt Liv losing the three children she loved.

"Take the pies as long as you're going," Aunt Liv yelled from the house. "And tell Charlie he can apply the seventy-five cents to what I owe him for the breakage from the other day."

"Uncle Spencer paid him for that," Philip said as he and Neil passed their aunt on the way to the kitchen to get the pies.

"What?" she asked, grabbing Philip's sleeve and spinning him around.

"Uncle Spencer told Mr. Zephin to put it on his bill," Philip said with a shrug.

Aunt Olivia, her mouth forming a small O, let him go and said something about having to go over there and pay him back. "I suppose I could do his laundry," she said absent-mindedly. "Lord knows he isn't doing it himself."

"I asked you if you thought that Emma Zephin is in hell," Louisa said to their aunt with apparent exasperation at being ignored.

Neil sighed loudly and Philip gave a snort. They were both sick of the subject of Emma Zephin and raced each other to the kitchen door.

"No," Aunt Liv said, and Neil backed up slightly to hear her reasoning. After all, Miss Zephin had killed herself. Neil thought that surely she would go to hell for doing that.

"I don't really believe so. Emma was a good woman who lived a good life and had a weak moment. I think the Lord, who made life so difficult for her in the first place, would have to forgive one moment in favor of a lifetime of bearing what turned out to be the unbearable.''

"Really?" Louisa said very skeptically. "Then she's in heaven? Even after killing her own self?"

Aunt Liv looked over at Louisa distractedly. "I don't suppose we'll know for sure until we die ourselves, Louisa." She reached for her bonnet beside the door and fastened it beneath her chin. "Would you mind watching Josie for a little while?" she asked.

Louisa shook her head. Aunt Liv rushed out the door and was halfway down the path by the time the boys looked out the kitchen window after her.

"Let's go," Philip said, picking up the basket of pies and then laughing.

"What's so funny?"

"Aunt Liv should have taken these with her. Uncle Spencer's bought every pie she's baked!"

"You mean he's paying a quarter for . . ." Neil began to laugh himself. Aunt Bess was right. They loved each other, they just needed someone to give them a push back in the right direction. And he and Philip would provide that little shove with one slightly yellow piece of telegraph paper.

They were still laughing as they poured out the front door and nearly ran smack into Aunt Liv, on her way back in.

"Maybe I'll just take one of these to your uncle," she said, reaching into the basket that Philip was holding. "I suppose I owe him something for paying my debts."

Neil tried to keep his giggles under control. He could see Philip struggling just as hard, maybe harder.

"Something tickling your funnybones?" Aunt Liv asked, looking at them suspiciously. Her cheeks glowed with the heat and, Neil was beginning to think, the prospect of seeing his uncle. This was going to be a piece of cake. "Your uncle ought to appreciate this pie," she said as she dismissed them and hurried down the steps. "I bet he hasn't had a decent meal in weeks."

Holding their breaths until she was far enough down the path to be out of earshot, they hoped, the boys convulsed with laughter.

This was a good place, Neil thought, sobering for a moment. He would truly like to stay.

The most beautiful woman in the world was sashaying down his path. For a moment Spencer thought she was just a mirage, a product of his wishes or a memory from the previous night. Just in case she was real, he hurriedly wiped his hands on his pants and ran down to close the barn door, where the last coat of paint on Neil's bed was drying. Another week and they would all be done. Could she resist him then and turn away from a home for them all?

He stood by the fence, Curly George nuzzling him and nosing him encouragingly in his wife's direction. When she was close enough for him to see her face, she smiled tentatively. "Hello," she said, looking shy and girlish and holding out to him . . . Lord, no! A pie.

"What's this?" he said, forcing a smile as he took the all-too-familiar tin plate from her hands. "Don't tell me it's a pie!"

George snickered and backed away, sauntering over toward Peaches with a quick look back that seemed to Spencer to be full of amusement. Damn horse was getting too human for Spencer's comfort. It must be all the hours they were spending together, Curly George listening to Spencer's troubles and his plans.

"I've been selling them, you know," she said proudly.

"You don't need to, Liv," he said, and watched her smile fall. "But if it makes you happy . . ."

"I'm contributing, Spencer. Not quite pulling my own weight, but I'm not just a burden on someone else."

"You've never been a burden, not to anyone. Especially not to me."

Women. They carried the whole world, one way or another, and they still felt like they weren't worth a hill of beans unless they got paid for their troubles. And troubles they had plenty of.

"Well," Livvy said, "I wanted to thank you for taking care of the bill at Zephin's." She was squinting those big brown eyes into the sun and he shifted slightly, placing her in his shade. "Oh, thanks." She lowered her hand from her eyes and flailed it around a bit before finally clasping it with her other one.

"Have you ever known me to shirk my responsibilities?" he asked, offended that she doubted he would pay their debts. The shock on her face made him repeat the question in his mind, and he closed his eyes and winced. "Financially," he amended, wanting to smack himself.

He thought perhaps he should start stuffing his mouth with sheepskin. That way if he managed to get a word out around the stuff, he knew that at least his foot would be comfortable in its inevitable home.

"Well," she said awkwardly. "I just wanted to thank you." She looked around, her eyes taking in all the things he had let slide in the effort to get all the furniture ready before Sacotte Farm was sold. He wanted her to be sure she and the children were the most important things in the world to him, and he didn't think just his words would do it.

"I've been kind of busy," he said, kicking the spoiled bucket of milk he'd forgotten to bring in after he'd milked Miss Lily. Liv winced at the smell.

"Animals all fine?" she asked, peering beyond him at George and Peaches.

He nodded. "Looks like Peaches is in foal," he said,

quickly moving to place the pie on the porch, thereby avoiding looking at her face. Being in the family way was a delicate subject between the two of them. He thought that maybe he'd better make room in that mouth for his other foot.

"Really?" she asked, her voice full of the wonder that always made her seem younger than she was. "Are you sure?"

He whistled to the horses and they sauntered over, hoping for a handful of oats. Patting Peaches's side gently, he told Liv that she hadn't gone into heat again, and left it at that. In the moments of quiet he thought about how each day when he checked Peaches he hoped that there was still no sign of her time.

An image of shoes outside his bedroom door came to mind unbidden, and he remembered the tears in his wife's eyes when month after month her time came again and again.

Will you ever forgive me? he wanted to ask her, but didn't dare. He had been so lost in his own pain that he had had no room for hers. And what had all his careful protection brought him, but a pain even greater than his own—the sight of her hurting.

"Have you gotten any of that laundry done?" she asked, looking at the empty washline accusingly. In truth, he had rinsed out a few underthings so that at least they didn't offend his nose. But the thought of seeing her touching his belongings, hanging things on the line, as if life were normal, was a temptation too great to resist.

He gave her his guiltiest look and a weak smile.

"I suppose I could do a few pieces this afternoon," she said. "After all, I do owe you for—"

He cut her off. "You don't owe me, Liv. Not for anything. But if you've a mind to see me in a clean set of clothing, I'd appreciate it."

She nodded and turned toward the house. "I'll just get you a fork for the pie and then get to it."

He jumped in front of her, blocking her way. All she had

to do was step foot in that house and she'd know that all he'd eaten for as long as he could remember at this point was her cherry pies. The kitchen was stacked with tins. The table held every plate they owned, each smeared with the remains of her no longer appreciated pies. "It's a mess in there," he said, putting his hands on her shoulders and holding her at arm's length. "Me living alone, and all. And hot. It's real hot in there." That was the truth. The dirty remains of the pies had attracted every fly in Wisconsin, and he'd had to keep all the windows and doors shut or the buzzing drove him crazy.

"Well, I've got to get the laundry, even if I'm going to wash it outside. And I would like to see you enjoy some of that pie."

"Yes," he agreed. "Absolutely. But, please, let me get a couple of plates and forks and bring out the laundry. I don't want you lifting and carrying all that stuff."

"Spencer, I've never seen you like this. I'd swear you were nervous." She blinked those big eyes at him a couple of times as if trying to get him into focus.

"Embarrassed is more like it," he lied. Pretty wasn't even the word for her, standing there in that pink dress, the bodice all covered with little embroidered flowers, and her old bonnet covering her hair. Beautiful didn't even do her justice. "You just wait outside, okay?"

"Well, I could go check on Miss Lily," she said.

The barn! "No!" he shouted, startling her. "Hot. Very hot. Don't go in the barn."

"Well, if it's so hot in the barn, I'll bring her out. Are you hoping for more spoiled milk?" She tried to pass him, but he grabbed her arm. Soft flesh gave way under his fingers and his knees nearly buckled.

"Will you just wait right here?" he begged.

"You are acting very oddly," she said, crossing her arms and nodding at his request.

"Me?"

"No, Curly George," she said sarcastically.

He smiled the crooked smile that used to melt her heart when they were younger. "Must be expectant father stuff."

"Spencer, you don't think I'm . . ." she pointed toward the house with a bewildered look on her face. "The heat? Lifting and . . ." She shook her head sadly. "Spencer, I'm not . . . that one time didn't . . . if you thought . . ."

"No, no," he said quickly, realizing what she meant. "I didn't think you . . . I meant Peaches . . ."

He hadn't realized until that moment how much he had been hoping that perhaps she was in the family way. Lord knew, it only took one time. He patted her shoulder and then climbed the steps to the porch slowly. And they'd only had that one time . . .

It didn't take long for him to set up the wash kettle outside just where Livvy had always done their wash in the summer. A few more minutes and she was shooing him back to the fields and holding his clothes at arm's length with her head bent away from the smell as she tossed his clothing into the big tub.

He dragged himself only as far as the closest of his fields, not wanting to risk missing her go toward the house or the barn. He hadn't even hooked up the hay rake yet and the day was nearly over.

A fine job he was doing. He'd win her back and then they could all starve together. And those little ones never seemed to have far to go, starting out so thin and frail.

He wondered how they were doing. His Miss Louisa was changing daily, her figure becoming harder and harder for her to hide, though he noticed that she hadn't given up trying. And soon he suspected there would be shoes outside her door, too, if he didn't miss his guess.

And Neil. He came over nearly every day to help Spencer with what little farming he was doing. It had gotten so that

Neil was doing a better job than Spencer, and considering how poor Neil was at raking, it was amazing there was any hay left to haul.

Spencer began to make his way down toward Livvy, thinking how all that was needed to make perfect the picture of his wife hanging up his laundry was Josie to hand her up the pins and the sound of their voices on the breeze.

She must not have heard him come up behind her, because she jumped sky high and clutched the wet clothes to her body when he spoke her name. "My word, Spencer!" she said, catching her breath and pulling the dripping balbriggans away from her chest. "You scared the living daylights out of me!"

She had taken off her bonnet and a good portion of her hair had slipped out of its bun, trailing down her chest like arrows pointing the way to two dusky nipples that showed faintly through the wet pink fabric of her dress. He swallowed hard and tried to find his tongue, but had the terrible notion it was hanging out of his mouth.

"Did you want something?" she asked, all innocence.

He tried to talk and found frogs had made a home in his throat. They went well with the butterflies in his stomach.

She reached up to hang his underthings on the line and he fought to keep his eyes on her face instead of her breasts, which changed shape before his eyes as she stretched. "I was wondering," he said after clearing his throat, "how the children were."

Her features, already soft and misted with the dew of hard work, softened even more at his words. A smile graced her full lips. A dreamy look came into her eyes. "They're fine," she said as if she were embarrassed to gush over them.

"Louisa's not giving you any trouble?" The girl had proven to be the biggest handful of all, rather than the most help.

"It's not easy being twelve, especially in a house with boys around the same age."

"Well," he said, remembering how his Miss Louisa enjoyed her privacy, "that'll be over soon."

"And Neil, poor thing, is on the sofa, and at Sacotte Farm that seems to put him smack in the middle of everything that's going on."

"He won't be on the sofa long, Liv." He thought of the blue bed that was just the way Neil wanted it, just what he had asked for. He was only sorry he couldn't give him Sacotte Farm, too. A boy like Neil had an appreciation for his heritage and the land of his ancestors. "I'm just sorry the boy can't have everything he wants."

"I got a telegram from Julian," she said, looking at the ground. "He's asked me to bring the children to him."

Julian? It took him a minute to realize who she even meant. He'd thought Julian out of their lives, had begun to think of the man's children as his own. To him Julian was dead and the loss had gone unnoticed.

Now he felt like he'd been smacked in the gut with a two by four.

"I don't have too many options," she said quietly.

"You have a home, dammit, Livvy, right here. You belong here, in my house and in my bed, and I've been damn patient up until now, but I'll be dead and buried before I let you go off to the likes of Julian Bouche."

"But the children—" she began.

"Damn them, too," Spencer said, his patience coming to an abrupt end in the hot afternoon sun. "I want you, Livvy. Look at yourself—" He pointed to her bodice, soaked through and plastered to her skin. "How much do you think I can take? I've told you I'm sorry. I've done everything I can to show you I was an idiot. And now you come waltzing in here looking like that and telling me that Bouche is making some kind of claim on what's mine?"

She was looking for something with which to cover herself, her gaze darting around only to settle on the front door. She took a step in that direction and he grabbed her from behind and hugged her against his chest.

"Tell me you're not going, Liv. Tell me so I can breathe again."

She tipped her head back against his chest and her body seemed to melt against his. "I'm not going."

His breath ruffled the few hairs that weren't plastered to her head by soap and water and sweat. "No matter what?"

"Things will have to be different," she said, but her voice was as husky as his and he knew from the weight of her against him that he'd won.

"They will," he promised, tipping his head back with relief and dragging in a gulp of air. "You can bet they will be."

He let his hands begin to wander, cupping her breasts, riding her ribs, touching her belly.

"Not just in bed, Spencer," she warned.

"Wherever you want," he said, his hand reaching down lower to cup her femininity.

Her hands reached up to cover her burning cheeks. "I didn't mean . . ."

He laughed. It had been a long time since he had laughed so heartily and so well.

"It has to be different with the children," she said seriously.

"I promise you that," he said, imagining Josie on his shoulders and the bigger ones, polished and pressed, between himself and Olivia as the strode down the aisle at church for St. Anne's Devotion. "You can count on everything being different than when they came."

"What about Julian?" she asked, pulling the damp telegram out of her pocket. "He wants them back."

Spencer let her go reluctantly and took the telegram from

her hands. Reading it quickly, he was convinced that Julian clearly didn't want the children. He wanted the money. And Livvy. It dug at him even to consider it, but if they sent Julian his share from the sale of Sacotte Farm, perhaps that would satisfy his greed. Amazing how quickly the man had managed to respond to the smell of profit and to the scent of a woman alone. Spencer's stomach churned.

"You never ate your pie," Livvy said, mistaking the rumblings in his stomach for hunger.

"When did you get this?" he asked, trying to remember something that seemed to elude him.

"The pie? I made it this morning, just before Philip came home with the telegram."

"Not the pie," he said. "The telegram." He realized she'd inadvertently answered him. "Oh. This morning."

"Yes, this morning," Livvy repeated, looking around for the pie and pointing to the porch steps. "Oh, there it is."

She took his hand and led him to the steps, sitting and uncovering the pie.

"Why?" she asked, searching for a fork and then shrugging and picking out a cherry with her fingers. Watching her, he almost forgot his train of thought.

She popped the cherry into her mouth and licked her fingers, shrugging apologetically. "Just testing it. A couple didn't come out all that well."

"Maybe you had your mind on something else," he suggested, and couldn't help laughing at her blush.

She looked around again for a fork and then, biting gently on her bottom lip as if she were fighting with herself, pulled out another cherry and offered it up to his lips with her fingers.

Livvy made good pies. Great pies. Extraordinary, exceptional pies. And he'd had enough of them in the past week to know. Still, not one had tasted as close to heaven as the morsel she had placed on the tip of his tongue. It made him forget, for a moment, the business at hand.

"Wait a second," he said, swallowing one cherry and anxiously awaiting another. "Just when did you write to Bouche?" He captured her fingers and let them slip only reluctantly from his mouth as he waited for her answer. How had he ever managed to stay away from this woman for so long? Now every second that went by without touching her, taking her, seemed as long as a century.

For want of anything on which to wipe them, she licked her fingers before answering him. At first he just didn't hear what she said.

"What?" he asked, almost dizzy with need.

"That's the amazing part," Livvy said, fishing out still another cherry for him. "Only the day before yesterday. And my letter got all the way across the country."

He opened his mouth for the cherry, willing to take all she would feed him no matter how much pie he had already consumed. She looked at the dark red goo that coated her fingers, and before she could stick them in her mouth, he took her hand, meaning to lick the fingers himself.

Instead a memory flashed across his mind. A pie-covered finger . . . Spencer reaching out for a wrist . . . Makeridge.

Of course! Pieces of the puzzle fell into place one after another. And Makeridge was the centerpiece.

Just maybe he could have it all. Livvy, the kids, the farm.

He kissed her neck, her collarbone, and began trailing kisses toward her sweet wet breasts, kissing and suckling right through the wet fabric and leaving cherry stains everywhere his lips alighted.

"Spencer," she said, an embarrassed giggle in her voice as she looked around. "We're outside where anyone could see. Can't you be content with your pie?"

"I'm not hungry for pie, Livvy-love," he said, wishing he could do more than ogle his wife and steal a kiss or a feel.

But he couldn't take her in the house. He couldn't take her in the barn. And he wanted to do it right this time, wanted everything perfect for his Livvy-love even more than he wanted the blessed relief of burying himself inside her. He set her away from him and let her right her garments.

In his head he did the calculations. How many hours to finish carving their bed, then painting the beds, letting them dry. "How's Tuesday?" he asked.

"What?"

"Tuesday. Would you consider moving back home next Tuesday?"

She buttoned the top button of her dress and looked anywhere but in his eyes. "Tuesday? I thought you couldn't wait."

"I can't," he said, feeling the strain in his loins and knowing that if he wanted her, he could have her back in his bed tonight. But it was a bed from another lifetime, and he wanted her to have her own, hers and his, a brand-new start. And if things worked out the way he thought they might . . . Well, this just wasn't the time to be ruled by his pants, or even his heart. That could wait a few days. "I've got to get ready for you," he said, lifting her chin with his forefinger. "I've got to make it perfect."

They rose from the porch and stood awkwardly just feet from each other.

"Tuesday?" she asked again, squinting up at him and biting that luscious bottom lip. Damned if she wasn't just as randy as he was!

"If it doesn't rain," he added, praying that the hot dry weather would hold and the paint would dry fast enough for him to bed her before he burst.

What he wouldn't give to sweep her in his arms and take her inside and make love to her until neither of them could move a muscle. But were his needs any more important than her pride? He'd nearly killed that pride once, when he'd been so obsessed with his needs. He wouldn't do it again. One look at her kitchen and she'd know he was the one buying all her damn pies.

"If it doesn't rain?" He silently cheered the disappointment and confusion on her face. Heck! She wanted him now!

But he had to see to a few little details if everything was going to be as perfect as he hoped. One little trip to town, a word or two with Makeridge, and even Remy Sacotte, hard as he was to please, might be happy.

"I've got some things I've gotta take care of," he said.

"Things?"

"You don't have to know every blessed thing, Livvy-love," he said, touching the tip of her nose. "Leave a man his secret machinations, will you?"

Reluctantly she gave him more of a shrug than a nod.

"Just think," he said, trying to placate her. "In less than a week you'll be right back where you belong and life will be perfect."

"What's wrong with now?" she asked shyly, kicking at the dirt with her booted toe.

"Can't wait?" he teased. "Maybe this'll hold you." He took her up against him, his arms cupping her round bottom and raising her to her toes. Just the briefest touch of her against his manhood and he was hard with longing. His ragged sigh brushed her lips and he attempted a chaste kiss, but his mouth was having none of it. His lips pressed against hers until he managed to ease them apart and slide his tongue into the warmth of her mouth. His tongue danced with hers until kissing was not enough, and he maneuvered her toward the fence post, hoping to lean her against it and roam her body with his hands.

One eye on where they were headed, he saw something moving in the distance. *Not company,* he thought. *Not now.*

The small arm waved and Spencer couldn't keep the curse from escaping his lips.

Livvy's eyes widened as he reluctantly pushed her away and straightened her dress for her yet another time.

"What's wrong?" she asked, still having trouble getting her breathing under control.

Tuesday? Had he said Tuesday? Maybe if he only gave the bed one coat . . .

He nodded with his head out toward the path that led to Sacotte Farm. He couldn't hide the grimace. The boy couldn't have had worse timing.

"Isn't that Neil?" she asked, waving at the child.

"For Christ's sake, Liv. Don't encourage him." He looked down at his pants and willed the telltale bulge to subside. The tent remained. "I think I'll get going on my errands now," he said as Neil got closer.

"Will you be by later?" she asked him, reminding him of when they were very young and she would stand right by this fence and ask him if he'd be dropping by Sacotte Farm.

"I might," he said, the way he always used to, giving her that crooked smile.

"There's the eclipse at suppertime," she reminded him.

"I know, but there are an awful lot of people over at Sacotte Farm," he said, amazed that while so many things had changed, some things still remained the same. "Maybe you could slip away and . . ." He buried his face in her hair and nipped gently at her ear.

Neil was nearly there and, if anything, the tent in his pants had gone from a tepee to a full longhouse.

"I'll be waiting in the field," he said, patting her bottom and hurrying down the road toward town before Neil could get a good look at his randy old uncle.

"And you," he yelled at the boy over his shoulder, "could learn a little about timing!"

Livvy put her arm around the boy and shook her head in answer to whatever it was Neil was asking.

Neil would see her home. He could leave Livvy safely in the boy's hands.

Chapter Twenty-three

Olivia sat on the porch swing at Sacotte Farm twirling one loose strand of her hair around her finger and wishing away several days of her life. Tuesday. Lord, it couldn't come fast enough. *Everything will be perfect on Tuesday,* he'd said.

As far as Livvy was concerned, perfect had already started with his kiss and the plea for her to stay with him always. *If you wish long enough and hard enough,* her mother used to say, *all dreams come true.* Who'd have thought her mother would be right?

The boys came out of the barn, Neil pushing Philip, who was dragging his feet. They were arguing about something, but when they saw her sitting there, they stopped. Grateful her services as a referee weren't going to be required, she got up and stretched, considering maybe taking a quick bath before supper and the eclipse.

"Ask her," Neil said, shoving Philip forward so that he tripped up the steps and nearly sprawled at his aunt's feet.

"Clinchpoop!" he yelled at his cousin.

"Ask me what?" Livvy said, feeling as if they could ask her for the moon and she could give it to them. And tonight was the night for it, wasn't it, what with the eclipse and all? She bit her bottom lip to keep from crying out with joy. Spencer Williamson, the only man she had ever loved, loved her in return! And maybe it had taken twenty years or so, and maybe they'd both had to walk through the fires of hell to get there, still . . .

"I got some mud on my pants down at the store," Philip said, looking at Neil instead of her. "And Ma'll kill me. Think you could help me get it out?"

"Your ma will kill you?" Livvy asked skeptically. "Seems to me she's been washing your clothes for twelve years and I see you're still in one piece."

"But these are new," Philip said, shooting arrows with his eyes at his cousin.

"Do you have something to do with this?" she asked Neil, fixing him with a stare.

"Me?" Neil asked with a gulp that announced his guilt.

Livvy sighed. Boys, she supposed would be boys, even on heavenly summer nights when the moon would block out the sun and her own face would finally replace Kirsten's in Spencer's eyes. "Go in and take them off and give 'em to me," she said, ruffling Philip's hair. "But hurry now. I've things I want to do."

The boys hurried in and Livvy followed them, then veered off to the kitchen to find an old potato to rub on the mud on Philip's new black pants. Finding Bess busy preparing supper, Livvy was overcome with guilt.

"I should be helping, at the very least," she said.

Bess smiled and pointed to Josie, who was mashing potatoes with a vengeance. "Got a helper," she said.

"You are such a good girl," Livvy told Josie. "You sure have made yourself at home here."

"This is home," Josie said, her pale eyebrows coming down in question. "Isn't it?"

"For now," Livvy agreed, kissing the top of her head. "For now." She grabbed up a slice of the raw potato from the bowl beside Josie.

The kitchen door swung open. "Here," Neil said, thrusting the pants at her and running like a thief from the room.

"You're welcome, I'm sure!" Bess shouted after him,

making Livvy laugh. Her eyes narrowed. "Those look like Philip's new pants."

"Mm," Livvy said, examining them for the stain. "Seems like Neil managed to mess them up for him somewheres."

Bess reached for them. "Well, I'll . . ."

"Oh, no," Livvy said, whisking them out of Bess's reach. "You're doing quite enough. I can . . ." She reached down to pick up the paper that had fallen out of Philip's pocket as she spoke.

"What's that?" Bess asked.

"Looks like a telegram," Livvy said, flattening the paper. *Signed, Spencer Williamson,* caught her eye. "It's from Spencer," she said, trying to make out the light pencil writing of what appeared to be a draft of a telegram from Spencer to Julian.

It was dated and timed late that afternoon, and sent to San Francisco. Livvy found the chair with the backs of her calves and sat down slowly. She read the message once, sure she was misunderstanding it somehow, and then read it again.

Sacotte Farm to be sold on Tuesday. Children will be sent on train at 11:00 a.m. Will arrive San Francisco 2:00 Friday. There was no way to put the words together to mean anything else.

"Olivia? What is it?" Bess had stopped wrapping the slices of ham around the endives sprinkled with Gruyère and slathered with cream, and was staring at her.

"Fool me once, shame on you," Livvy whispered, dazed. "Fool me twice, shame on me."

"What, honey?" Bess asked, coming to pull out a chair by Livvy's side.

"I told him that Louisa was having trouble living with the boys. . . ."

"So?"

"What did he say?" she asked herself, her mind racing, her gaze darting around the room. "What did he say? *She won't have to do that much longer?* Was that it? Or was that what he said about Neil?''

"Livvy, honey, you're gonna break that chair, grasping the seat like that. Look at your knuckles!"

"I'll break the chair, all right," she said, rising and glaring at Bess because she was the handiest target. "I'll break the damn chair over his stupid skull." She needed to throw something, anything. She needed to pound a wall, or break a window.

"Spencer?"

She whirled on Bess, shaking the slice of potato in her face. "Don't you ever, ever, say that name to me again, you hear me?"

"Livvy, what in the world?" Bess said. "Get a hold of yourself. I don't know what the telegram says, but Spencer loves you and . . .''

Livvy put her hands over her ears and ran from the room, Bess on her heels.

"Tell Louisa to get in the kitchen and see to the baby," Bess shouted at Neil as they raced past him.

"Is Uncle Spencer coming over to watch the eclipse?" Neil shouted after them.

Bess shook her head. *Uncle Spencer coming over?* Livvy laughed, maybe hysterically, all out of control. "I don't think so," Bess said, and Livvy laughed harder as she ran down the steps.

"*Meet me in the field,* he said. Tuesday he wanted me back. God, I am a fool."

"Slow down, Livvy. I can hardly breathe." Bess was gasping behind her.

"I'd rather be a fool than a liar," she said, kicking a tuft of grass clear out of the earth. "And I'd rather spend the rest of my life with no man than with one plying me with pretty words when all he wants is clean balbriggans and a place to ease his needs."

"You go on, Liv," Bess called out from several yards back. "Get it out of your system."

"I would have lain with him tonight, in the grass, I know I would."

"Should I get Remy?" Bess yelled.

"A man? What in hell would I want a man for?"

"Olivia! You watch your tongue! You're not so old that—"

"Oh, yes I am. I am the oldest damn woman you've ever met. I'm old and I'm done and I've half a mind to take Julian up on his offer."

"I'm getting Remy."

"I will not be made childless twice!" She reached around her neck and ripped from it the locket she had returned to her neck only that very day, the chain breaking easily with the force of her tug.

"Oh Liv, don't," Bess whined as Liv cocked her arm back and let the necklace go as far as she could throw. "Liv!"

"Remember when the children first came?" she asked Bess. "How Neil called Spencer Uncle Die?"

"Don't say it, Liv," Bess warned.

"Oh, I don't wish him dead. It's too late for that. He is dead. He died along with Kirsten and the children. I was just too stupid to see it. Stupid. Stupid. Stupid." She punctuated each accusation with a smack to her forehead with the heel of her hand.

Somewhere in the vicinity of where Livvy had thrown the locket, Bess was rooting in the grass like a warthog. "Come, sweetie, help me look," she said gently. "You'll be sorry later."

"No," Livvy said. "I've been sorry and I'm sick of it. I'll never be sorry again. I gave him that power, and I'm taking it back."

Bess sighed and stood up, arching her back to get out the

kinks. "I don't see it. It'll be easier in the bright sunshine tomorrow."

"Forget it, Bess," Livvy said, heading back toward the house. "It's over. My new life starts tomorrow and no one's gonna stop it."

"It'll look different in the morning, honey. You'll see."

She looked over her shoulder in the direction of Spencer's land. He was never, never going to hurt her again. "I don't doubt it for a minute," she agreed with Bess.

"Hey," Philip yelled as he reached the top of the stairs a step or two in front of Neil. "What do you think you're doing?"

Neil tried to peer around Philip's legs, but couldn't tell what was going wrong now. He didn't like the way his aunts had gone running from the house. He had a real bad feeling that things might not be going quite the way he had planned.

"I wasn't doing anything," Louisa answered, slamming a door.

"You were in my room," Philip bellowed. "You're not allowed in my room."

"Says who?" Louisa said, pretending that Philip didn't scare her.

"I says," Philip answered, reaching Louisa before she could escape back into her own room and grabbing her by the arm. "And it's my house."

"Yeah, I know," Louisa said more softly than Neil would have expected. "So?"

"So you can't go in my room. I've got things, *private* things." He looked at Neil as if Neil could do something to help him. If he hadn't "borrowed" that book by Dr. Naphreys, he wouldn't have to worry about Neil's sister nosing around in his room.

"Yeah," she said, smiling at him. "I saw them all."

"I'm telling," he yelled, turning to go down the steps.

"Go ahead," Louisa yelled after him. "And I'll tell what you've got."

The front door slammed and Philip lowered his voice. "Tell and I'll tell everyone at school you've started your monthly."

Louisa turned three shades of red, and Neil supposed that his cheeks, too, must have pinkened. But what was going on between Louisa and Philip paled when Aunt Liv stomped up the steps like she was going to war.

She stared at the three of them, her hands on her hips, her chest rising and falling like she'd run a mile.

"Where's Josie? Who's watching her?"

"She's in the kitchen, I guess," Louisa said with a shrug.

"You guess?" his aunt screamed, her voice cracking. "You guess?"

Louisa backed away slightly, shrinking from her aunt's rage, and they all exchanged glances as Aunt Liv turned and went running down the stairs calling to Josie to reassure herself that the baby was all right.

"I can't believe you just left her," Philip said.

"Oh, like you've ever watched a three-year-old," Louisa complained.

Neil hardly paid attention to their bickering. His aunt wasn't reacting quite the way he had planned. And how was she going to beg Spencer to take her back if he wasn't even coming over to watch the eclipse? A sick feeling swirled in his stomach and crawled up his torso toward his head. He didn't think he could feel so cold in July.

"You'll be sorry," Louisa said, "talking to me like that."

"It's starting," Uncle Remy shouted into the house. "Get your back porches out here now."

"You're not supposed to look at the sun," Thom-Tom

said, strolling out of Louisa and Josie's room fanning himself with a composition book.

"Oh, my God!" Louisa shouted, blanching and grabbing after Thom-Tom and the book like a circus juggler.

Philip caught her skirts and she couldn't make any progress except to scream as if she were being attacked by banshees.

"You stop that this minute," Aunt Bess yelled from the foot of the stairs. "Supper's on the table. Get down here and wash up."

"You coming?" Uncle Remy yelled, banging on the screen door with his fist.

"No, they ain't coming," Aunt Bess yelled back.

"But they're missing it."

"I don't care," Bess said, beginning to climb the stairs, threateningly. "What in blazes . . . ?"

"Give it to me," Louisa demanded of Thom-Tom, who flipped her the book and then ran past everyone and down the stairs passing his mother and patting her gently on her shoulder.

"They're such babies," he said to his mother and then yelled toward the door, "I'm coming, Pa."

"I hate you all," Louisa said, pulling her dress from Philip's clutches and stalking off to her room.

"Downstairs, young lady," Aunt Bess said. "Now. And you too, boys."

When everyone had been served, Uncle Remy instructed them to take their plates outside. "We'll sit on the porch and watch this miracle of nature."

"You want a miracle?" Aunt Bess shouted at Uncle Remy. "A miracle would be anything good coming out of your stupid plan." Neil expected her to turn and point at him, but she didn't. Apparently he wasn't the only one with a stupid plan.

"And until it works out for your sister, don't plan on any favors from me, if you know what I mean!"

Neil thought he did, especially from the shocked look on Uncle Remy's face.

Just as they were on their way out of the kitchen, each of them carrying their plates and grumbling at each other, Henry came through the front door. Anyone would have thought that he had been there for all the fighting, what with the life-just-smacked-me-between-the-eyeballs look on his face.

"Where the heck have you been?" Uncle Remy shouted.

Aunt Bess balanced the plate she was carrying in one hand and bashed the back of Uncle Remy's head at his words.

"Don't you use that language in my house," she yelled.

Uncle Remy glared at her and stepped deliberately through the open doorway onto the porch. "Where the heck have you been?" he said again, daring Aunt Bess to claim the porch was still in her house.

Henry looked down at his shoes as if he were gathering his courage, then took a deep breath and looked his father in the eye. "I'm marrying Jenny on Sunday," he said. "And we'll be moving in with her folks."

There was total silence, and then Uncle Remy said, "The hell you are," and Aunt Bess just gasped and covered her mouth.

"I thought you were gonna get married at Christmas," Philip said.

Henry seemed to be cleaning his teeth with his tongue. Finally, his eyes avoiding everyone's, he said, "We can't wait."

"Oh, my God, not again," Aunt Bess whispered. "Like father, like son."

Aunt Livvy's eyes got bigger than Neil had ever seen them get as she stared at Aunt Bess and Uncle Remy and her plate clattered to the ground, peas and potatoes flying everywhere, spots of them clinging to her bare feet.

"Can't wait?" Uncle Remy said, slapping his son with enough force to stagger him. Henry's eyes watered but he stood there, and Neil thought that he looked quite the grown man.

Aunt Livvy tried to say something, but no words came out and she pushed her way past everyone and looked to be going toward the barn.

"Go after her," Uncle Remy said to Aunt Bess, rubbing his reddened palm on his pants and trying to pretend that it didn't hurt.

"Liv?" Aunt Bess called, unsure what to do.

Aunt Livvy shook her head and put up her hand. "Just let me be," she said, barely loud enough for them to hear. Then she walked into the barn and closed the door.

"When does the miracle happen?" Josie asked when everyone just stood there staring at Henry's cheek and watching it turn redder and redder.

"Go back inside," Aunt Bess said softly, nudging the baby and Louisa and Thom-Tom through the door. "There isn't going to be any miracle tonight."

Spencer lay back on the grass in the meadow, chewing on a long stalk of hay and every now and then glancing at the setting sun as, little by little, the moon took a bite out of it. Mostly he kept his eye on the path between his place and Sacotte Farm, imagining Livvy getting the children all settled and then sneaking off to meet him.

In some ways he wished he could join them all, but he and Liv needed this time alone. Every time he got within ten feet of her, his desire raised a flag in his pants. Even thinking about her had an effect on him.

He closed his eyes to blot out the sun and thought about what a good day it had been. Not just good. Great. Wonderful. He yawned widely and felt himself drifting closer to sleep. Just wonderful?

No, he thought, smiling and enjoying the last strains of the sun as they played on his face, *miraculous*.

Chapter Twenty-four

Olivia had no idea how long she'd cried before she'd finally fallen asleep in the barn. She only knew that at some point someone had come in and thrown a blanket over her, and that now it was time to get up and get on with her life. There were children to get off to school, pies to be baked, belongings to be packed—Sacotte Farm would soon live just in her memory—and there was no time for shedding tears or drying them.

Pulling hay from her hair as she made her way to the house, she thrust back her shoulders and tried to find the bright face she made it her business to present to the world. In some ways, she told herself, it was all for the best. In all likelihood she could never have forgiven Spencer for what he'd done to her in their bed, even if it was true that she did love him—always did, and, she supposed, shaking her head at the notion, always would.

No, she forced herself to counter. Love grew side by side with trust, like two vines intertwined. And deception and indifference had grown like weeds among them, choking out anything good that could have grown between the two of them. Just as well to be done with it altogether.

Maybe there was something wrong with her that everyone she knew lied to her. Bess and Remy had needed to get married and she'd never known. Of course, she'd been ten at the time, but in all the intervening years someone might have seen fit to tell her, not leave her to be as shocked as the children at

Bess's admission. Maybe she should consider Julian's offer one more time. He wasn't any more dishonest than every other adult she knew. Water under the bridge, all of it. Time to start fresh with Louisa and Neil and Josie and put the rest of it aside.

She saw to her needs and washed up and at the pump, still searching for her illusive smile. By the time she got to the house, she'd abandoned hope for a smile and would have settled for anything short of a grimace complete with gritted teeth.

"Up," she said to Neil, wiggling the boy's toes beneath the light sheet that covered him. It was bad enough that he had to sleep on someone's sofa in the parlor. Come Tuesday night, where in the world would he be sleeping? The deal for Zephin's was done. Remy had signed all the papers the day before. And Livvy supposed there would be no room above the store for four extra human beings, even if one was only three feet tall.

All she knew, with a certainty so final that her very bones rang with the truth of it, was that those three children were not going to be torn from her by her husband, by their father, or by the threat of poverty looming over her head.

Neil rubbed his eyes and blinked at her. "They wouldn't let me see you last night," he said. "Uncle Remy stood in front of the door like some big she-wolf was after his chickens."

"Well, I'm here now," she said, checking the clock on the wall and realizing that it was getting late. "And all's right with the world. So rise, young man, and shine." She forced a smile. It wasn't so hard after all when she looked at the sweet face studying her own. "We'll be just fine," she reassured him.

"What about Uncle Spence?" Neil asked, sitting up now and getting his bearings.

Any man who could resist such hero worship, such unselfish devotion, didn't deserve a boy like Neil in his life, and Livvy was glad—yes, glad—that Spencer wouldn't get to share this child's life. Why, Spencer wasn't worthy of walking behind the same plow, hoeing the same row, mucking the same stall.

"Get ready for school now," she told him gently. "I've got to get your sisters up."

"Aunt Liv?" Neil called after her plaintively. "There's something I have to tell you."

She turned, her foot on the bottom step, and looked at him encouragingly. Something in his voice made her expect that he would admit that he loved her, and she waited patiently while he swallowed and bit at his lip. Boys and men—the word love just seemed to stick in their throats. *Need* and *want* came out loud and clear, but *love*? "Yes?" she prompted.

"If you do something you think will go one way—that is, if you do something that you mean to be good . . . to turn out good, and then, well, it might not . . . Do you think that God, or anyone, knows that if you didn't mean for it to . . ."

Livvy glanced again at the clock. It was too late for theoretical discussions. "Haven't you ever heard that the road to hell is paved with good intentions?" she asked. "Best to stay out of other people's business, young man. You've quite enough on your plate just handling your own. Does that answer your questions?"

He seemed to be considering her advice, so she headed up the stairs to wake up Louisa and Josie. The baby lay there with long lashes resting lightly on chubby cheeks, the picture of innocence. To Livvy's surprise, Louisa's bed was already made. Well, this was a first. Louisa up and ready without their usual argument over whether she belonged in school or not.

"Up and at 'em, sweetie," she said, placing a light kiss on Josie's forehead. "Go take care of your business and then come find me in the kitchen."

Groggily Josie reached up and put her arms around Livvy's neck, giving her a squeeze. The little girl's body was sweaty with sleep and smelled like yeast and soap and heat. Livvy breathed in deeply and rubbed the child's back through her muslin gown.

"Whose girl are you?" she asked, reveling in the moment.

Josie backed away slightly, then pointed a small stubby finger at Livvy's chest. "Yours," she said simply, as if the question were a foolish one.

Livvy blinked back tears that fought to loose themselves from watery eyes. "Mine," she said, her voice hoarse and uneven. "All mine."

Josie squirmed and Livvy let go of her, rose and gave the little girl a hand up.

"Off you go," she said, wiping at her cheek with the corner of her dress. "And if you run into your sister, tell her I'm very proud of her for getting herself up and out."

Josie bobbed her head and then scampered from the room without looking back. Livvy followed her and passed Philip in the hall. "Louisa in there?" he asked angrily.

She sighed. "What now?"

"She has something that's mine," he said, then shouted over her shoulder in the direction of the girl's room. "And I want them back. Now!"

"She's not there," Livvy said, one hand on Philip's chest. "Get ready for school. You can threaten her at breakfast if you like."

Philip went off in a huff and Livvy hurried down to the kitchen, anxious to see to breakfast before Bess managed to get everything done without her. If they were going to live to together awhile longer—and Lord knew, it appeared that somehow they would have to—she was going to have to carry her own weight, and that of the children.

Naturally, Bess was already at the stove. "Morning,

lovey," Bess said without turning around. "You all right this morning?"

"Just perfect," Livvy said, rolling her eyes behind Bess's back. "Everything is just peachy keen." It felt odd to take her place next to the woman she thought she knew so well and find she didn't really know her at all.

"You don't look so good," Bess said as if nothing between them had changed.

What? Did she have eyes in the back of her head, like her children claimed?

"Okay," Liv admitted with a shrug. "Not so peachy keen." She didn't have any desire to discuss it with this stranger in Bess's clothing. "You seen Louisa?"

"Note on the table," Bess said. "That girl is a strange little one."

Livvy pulled the bacon from the icebox and sliced it, put it in the pan one piece at a time, turned the fire up slightly, and then wiped her hands. "A note, huh? Where could she be off to so early? It's not like her to get to school before Mr. Langford is ringing his bell." She looked over at the table expecting to find a scribbled note, but instead there was a fine blue envelope with the words *Aunt Liv* written in Louisa's neatest script.

She didn't like the looks of it at all.

"You see her before she left?" Livvy asked.

"Uh-uh," Bess said. "You gonna see to this bacon?"

"In a minute," Livvy said, and flipped over the envelope without picking it up. "It's sealed."

"The bacon, Liv?"

Livvy touched the envelope as if she could divine the message without opening it. A note like that couldn't be good news. A note like that didn't say *see you later*.

She was being ridiculous.

"Where is she?" Philip demanded, bursting through the swinging door.

"She *loves* us," Thom-Tom said, coming in behind his brother and nearly drooling the word *love*. "Says so in that journal of hers."

"Bacon's burning," Bess said matter-of-factly.

"What journal?" Livvy asked.

"Oh," Thom-Tom said with great authority. "She writes everything in this little book. You should see . . ."

He stopped when he caught the glare his mother was giving him.

"It fell open," he swore, his eyes wide with feigned innocence. "I just saw a few words. Said she loved Aunt Liv and Uncle Spencer and some stuff about missing them."

With a dread that knotted her stomach, Livvy opened the pale-blue envelope and pulled out the letter.

> *Dear Aunt Liv—I thought that you loved me. I was wrong, I guess, but I know that you do love Josie, so I'm begging you, with my last words, that you don't send her back to our father. I will miss you but I'll be waiting for you on the other side where I won't be lonely anymore. Love, Louisa.*

"The other side?" Livvy whispered. "Oh, Lord in heaven, no!"

"What is it?" Bess asked, grabbing the note from Livvy's hand and reading it aloud.

Philip fell into a chair. "She took the bullets," he said, putting his hand to his head. Then, seeing his mother's horror-stricken face, he added quickly, "I hid them in my top drawer. I didn't think anybody was going to . . ."

The gun was gone. Livvy stood on her tiptoes and felt for it in the cabinet where Bess had put it for safekeeping. Finding nothing, she dragged over a chair and stood on it. Still nothing.

"Oh, no," she said, shaking her head and nearly leaping

from the chair. "No, no, no. This can't happen," she shouted, running for the door.

The screen door stopped halfway, smacking into something hard.

"Whoa," Spencer said, holding his head and reeling slightly from the blow. "You're a little late. I waited the whole damn night in the field."

"She's gone," Livvy said, choking on her tears. "Louisa—she's gone and she took the gun." She was running down the path, but when she got to the fork, she stopped, not knowing which way to turn.

Spencer ran after her, spinning her around and demanding to know what in the hell she was talking about.

As quickly as she could, between sobs and gulps and false starts in one direction and checking the barn, she related the note, the missing bullets, ending with Thom-Tom's revelations from Louisa's diary.

"This way," he said, running toward his farm and then cutting across the field to the small pond. "Secret spot," he shouted over his shoulder. "Book. That day." All his words were interrupted by gulps for air as he ran, putting more and more distance between them with his long legs. Philip passed her. Neil, as well.

Her side ached with each step and she clutched it as she ran, ignoring the burning in her throat and chest. Pebbles cut at her bare feet, branches lay in wait stubbing more than one toe. None of it mattered. If anything, *anything,* happened to Louisa, Livvy would never forgive herself. Children were a sacred trust, and somehow she had failed. She had let something threaten her child.

Her child.

Maybe she hadn't given birth to them, but those children were ensconced in her heart and her womb as surely as if they had begun there.

And if something happened to one of them, it wouldn't

just rip a piece out of that heart but tear it asunder, never to be whole again.

A shot rang out, setting the echoes ringing and drowning out the sounds of their feet hitting the ground, their lungs sucking the air, their hearts beating against their breastbones.

It took a moment for them to stop, for the stillness to envelop them and leave them in silence as if not a one of them was breathing, not a heart was beating.

"You wait here," Spencer ordered, turning and fixing all of them with his stare.

Livvy didn't bother to argue, didn't shake her head, didn't push him out of her way. She just went around him and continued through the undergrowth, letting some distant memory from her youth guide her toward the pond. How fitting that this daughter of her heart should have sought out the same hiding place to heal her hurts.

"There!" Spencer said, his voice just above a whisper, his arm outstretched over her shoulder and pointing toward Louisa, who stood crying silently by the small pond, her hand pressed against her mouth.

Livvy crossed herself and shut her eyes, mumbling a quick thank you to the Lord, before running into the tiny clearing and stopping awkwardly just a few feet from Louisa.

"You scared us"—Livvy said, her voice a mere hush on the wind—"half to death."

"Where's the gun?" Spencer didn't hesitate to go straight to the girl, put his hand on her shoulder, turn her into him, and hug her to his chest as if there had never been anything but love between them.

"I dropped it," Louisa said between sobs. "And it went off. I was never so scared in my life."

"Then you didn't . . . ?" Spencer said, leaning back and tipping up the girl's chin.

She shook her head. "I couldn't." She stiffened and

pulled away from Spencer, glaring at him. "But I won't go back. You can't make me. I'll run away."

Livvy stepped forward, petting Louisa's soft silky hair. "I would never let you go back, don't you know that?"

"But Uncle Spencer . . . the telegram . . ." she started, her words muffled against his chest.

"Uncle Spencer be damned," Livvy said, prying the girl out of his arms while he stood there with a shocked look on his face. "I said you aren't going back, and you will not, no matter what Uncle Spencer wants."

"Are you crazy?" Spencer shouted, looking from one of them to the other and then settling on Livvy. "Send them back to Bouche? Don't you think he's done enough to them?"

There were tears in his eyes, but Livvy wasn't going to be taken in again. His plans had nearly cost Louisa's life. "Come on," she said to Louisa, her arm tightly around her. "We'll go back home now."

"Wait," Spencer called after them. Out of the corner of her eye she saw him bend and pick up the gun, then toss it more than halfway across the pond. They heard the *plunk* as it hit the water and she and Louisa turned at the sound.

There was a tear making its way down Spencer's cheek. "What did I do? What's happening here?"

"Philip brought home the telegram last night," Livvy said. "We know what you were planning, but it won't happen. I won't give them up."

"But I thought it was what you wanted. You said you hated to see Sacotte Farm sold. It made such good sense. I buy the mercantile from Zephin and trade it for Sacotte Farm. The railroad'll go right through my failing fields while we're busy picking cherries at Sacotte Farm. It's all arranged with Makebreath. Isn't that what you wanted?"

She stared at him trying to make sense of what he was saying about the farm. "But Sacotte Farm'll be sold. And why would I want the farm without the children?" she asked.

"Why would I want . . . Oh, what difference does it make? Did you think my family farm would make up for my family?"

"Livvy," he said, staying her with one hand while touching Louisa gently with the other. "Louisa. I love you. I love you all. I thought I was making you all happy."

He looked so confused, so lost, it was hard to believe that he had really planned to send the children away. "We saw the telegram," she said.

"And it didn't make you happy?"

"Happy?" she shouted. "Make me happy? Sending the children back was supposed to make me happy?"

"Who said anything about sending the children back?"

By now Philip and Neil had shown up, and Neil fell to his knees hugging himself until finally he began to retch in the grass.

"You did," Livvy said to Spencer as she leaned over Neil, holding back the hair off his forehead and pressing a cool hand to the back of his neck. "She's all right," she told the boy. "It's all over now."

"Me?" Spencer asked, fishing for a hankie and leaning over to wipe the boy's mouth. "You think *I* wanted to send the children back? It was *you* who said that Bouche wanted you to bring them out. *You* were the one considering it, not me. I made you promise not to. For the love of God, Olivia. I've already lost two of my children. Do you think for a second I'd be willing to let any more of my children go?"

Neil's heaving was the only sound on the meadow where they all stood. "My fault," he said, gagging and coughing and throwing up his insides. "All my fault."

"And mine," Philip said softly.

Slowly, reluctantly, Philip pulled from his pocket several yellow pieces of paper, a different message scribbled on each one as if he had been practicing sending a telegram.

Livvy covered her mouth with her hand. "But why?" was all she could manage to get out before she fell to her knees, picking at the papers and handing them up to Spencer, one after another after another.

"We thought—" Philip started.

"If you thought you'd lose us . . ." Neil added, his voice shaking so much he was hard to understand.

"Ma said you loved each other," Philip explained, shaking his own head.

"I don't know," Neil admitted weakly. "It seemed so simple when we started. I thought you'd go ask Uncle Spencer to take you back and . . ."

"We're sorry," Philip said. "We're so, so sorry."

"Do you realize," Spencer whispered, pain raw and naked in his voice, looking at Louisa with nothing but pure love in his eyes, "what you might have done?"

Louisa stood off to the side, watching faces and looking unsure. But when Spencer opened his arms and motioned to her, she hurled herself against him and burrowed into his chest.

Neil nodded, and gagged again.

"So you didn't mean to send them back?" Livvy asked, the tentative beginnings of a smile breaking across her face.

"Oh, God, Liv!" He shook his head. "Never."

"But you sent a telegram. To who?"

Spencer jaw tightened. "It was supposed to be a surprise," he said, glowering at Neil.

Livvy tried to put together the things Spencer had said about Sacotte Farm and Zephin's and to figure out what it all had to do with Waylon Makeridge. But it didn't matter. None of it mattered.

Olivia Williamson had it all.

"You can keep your secret," she said, tears streaming so freely down her face that they were wetting her bodice and making her hiccup. "I trust you."

Chapter Twenty-five

On Sunday, Spencer picked his family up at Sacotte Farm for church and Henry's wedding, which would follow the service. He had scoured his skin to be sure that there was no telltale trace of paint that would give his very last secret away, but the hours of sanding and carving and painting had taken their toll and his hands could barely grip the wagon reins.

He had promised her perfection on Tuesday, and come hell or high water, he would deliver. If ever he had to see disappointment cloud Olivia's eyes again, he wanted to be sure he was the one to lift it, not the one to put it there.

They were waiting on the porch, his girls all decked out in their Sunday finery; Neil in a suit that so closely resembled his own he had to smile. Livvy shone there, the beacon of love and faith he would be coming home to for the rest of his life. Surrounding them were stacks of crates waiting to be moved to Zephin's Mercantile, soon to be renamed Sacotte and Sons.

Without even waiting for the wagon to come to a full stop, Neil began to climb up onto the seat next to Spencer, hoping to drive old Curly George to town.

"Hold these, son," Spencer said, then jumped down to assist the girls into the back of the wagon. Josie was soft in his arms, and her kiss knocked his glasses off kilter. Louisa was soft, too, in her own way, no longer stiff and unyielding in his arms.

But nothing felt as soft to his scraped knuckles as his

Livvy-love's cheek, which he barely grazed as he sought to tuck an errant tendril behind her ear.

"Oh, Jeez," he said, his eyes closed, his balance suddenly in jeopardy. He took a deep breath to steady himself. Instead of stemming the rising tide, it only made things worse. "Lilacs. I should have known. Livvy-love, you'll be the death of me, for sure."

His knees were buckling.

"It's just two more days, Spence." His goddess in a white blouse with a piece of lace that ended just above the breasts he was itching to touch reached up and stroked his cheek. Struggling to swallow, he was almost embarrassed by the effect her face had on him. Just looking at the love in her eyes brought him close to tears. "You got a good shave," she said, smiling up at him.

"Were you always this beautiful?"

"Oh, I'm hardly that," she said, dismissing his compliment with her hand as if he had uttered sheer foolishness. It had taken him long enough to see her strength, her warmth, her earthiness, as beauty that would endure whatever life might chose to throw their way. If it took him the rest of their lives to convince her, so be it.

"If ever there were eyes that lovely," he said, looking deeply into them and knowing if he got to see them every day for the rest of his life it wouldn't be often or long enough, "I've never seen them."

"Spencer!" she said, clearly flustered by his attention, the forthright way he was staring, the words he had waited so long to say.

"Do you know why they're so beautiful? Because I can see your love in them, Liv. Your love and maybe even your trust."

"We're going to miss the wedding," Louisa complained to Neil in the wagon. "And I've never been to one."

"We're coming," Livvy told her, taking the arm Spencer offered and lifting her good dress up off the ground. As soon as they had some extra money he was going to take her to Sturgeon Bay and buy her some fancy clothes. A woman as pretty as Livvy, he thought, and then changed his mind mid-stream. A woman as pretty as Livvy didn't need fancy clothes. Her beauty wasn't dimmed by muslin nor enhanced by lace.

He watched as she settled herself in the wagon and looked around her at her family. Perhaps it was love that made his wife beautiful, for she was surely surrounded by it and had never looked more radiant.

The service was interminable, but so had every moment been since she and Spencer had agreed to wait until Tuesday to begin, once again, their life as husband and wife.

In church, she'd positioned Josie between them, hoping that the child would cool the heat she'd felt when her leg had been pressed against Spencer's in the wagon while Neil drove them to church. Spencer, apparently one to enjoy torture, had taken the child onto his lap and scooted closer to Livvy, with the weak excuse of sharing her prayer book.

His breath fanned her hair, seeped easily through the lace insert in her sheer batiste blouse, heated her everywhere it touched. And several places it didn't. In two days she would be back in Spencer's house and his bed, and while she'd miss Sacotte Farm, no piece of land could hold a candle to the piece of her soul that Spencer possessed.

In her heart of hearts, where her hopes and dreams had for so long been buried, she thought she knew what Spencer's secret was. He'd almost given it away by the pond that day when she'd nearly had to learn the hard way just what losing a child could do to a parent's heart and mind and soul. But even if he hadn't managed to save for her a small piece of Sacotte Farm—the part, she supposed, that abutted his land—she could live with the disappointment.

What she couldn't live without were all the people around

her who were now all coming to their feet for the joining in holy wedlock of her seventeen-year-old nephew, Henry Charles Sacotte, and pretty little Jenny Wachtell. Spencer placed Josie's tiny feet on the pew and guided her toward Louisa, whose arm went around her easily. Then he twisted Livvy slightly and pulled her to him so that her back rested against his broad, hard chest.

"I don't suppose they'd fall for the bug in your hair again, huh?" he whispered, and had to stifle a laugh when she turned her shocked face around to him.

"And I thought I could trust you," she chided, pretending to be angry.

"Trust me to love you, Livvy. Always."

Her answer was to lean back against him, rubbing the back of her head gently against his chest. The effect was immediate, and he could tell from her sudden jump that she was aware of his desire.

"Don't move," he whispered in her left ear. "Or it could prove awfully embarrassing."

Obediently she stayed exactly where she was, driving him wild every time she as much as shifted her weight.

Father Martin asked if there were any objections to the marriage and then got down to the *I dos.*

Spencer leaned down slightly and, along with Henry, said that he did. Apparently she liked that because she reached back and squeezed one of his sore hands, and painful as it was, he didn't think he'd ever felt anything as reassuring as that firm hand within his own.

That is, until she suddenly twirled in his arms, her skirt slowly following her, and said, "I do," along with Jenny, then raised her lips to let him kiss his bride.

"Tuesday be damned," he muttered, wishing he could finally do just once what he figured his nephew and Jenny would be doing all night.

*   *   *

The wedding was a lovely affair, Jenny's parents apparently so relieved at Henry's eagerness to do right by their daughter that they invited the whole of Maple Stand to share in their happiness. Spencer spoke to Henry privately and then told Livvy that he had made arrangements to give Henry and Jenny their wedding present on—when else?—Tuesday.

Waylon Makeridge, who, Livvy hadn't seen since Emma's funeral, stopped in to wish the newlyweds well and have a private moment with Spencer. She had no idea what the two men could possibly have to say to one another, but Spencer seemed more than satisfied when the conversation ended and Makeridge had been shown to the door.

Merely waving at Livvy and giving her a smile on his way, Spencer went directly from Mr. Makeridge to Remy. Livvy had only made it halfway across the room to join them when her brother let out a yelp and called for more beer.

Just as she reached them, she heard Spencer say, "She doesn't know yet."

Whatever it was, it had made Remy happy as a clam, and he beamed at her right along with her husband. And suddenly it didn't matter anymore what she didn't know, only what she did—that Spencer Williamson loved her, loved her as deeply and as fully as she had always loved him.

"Your husband is top shelf, Livvy. Top shelf," Remy boomed, slapping Spencer on the back. "He's one fine man. I gotta find Bess. Bess? Bess!" He ran off, beer on his lips and his wife on his mind.

"What makes you such a fine man, Spencer Williamson?" she asked, not doubting her brother's assessment for a minute. "How come you're top shelf?"

*   *   *

He was determined to wait. Then he and Livvy could start over, fresh and new, in the home she cherished, on land that would one day be worked by Neil as well as any sons that he and Livvy might have. And daughters, daughters weren't out of the question, either.

But she smelled so good.

And her eyes were shining.

And her pulse was racing just as fast as his.

"Shit," he said, and then covered his mouth. "Sorry. Could you wait here, just one minute?" he asked, starting to leave, coming back for a quick kiss, and starting to leave again. He could just kick himself. Didn't he have any self-restraint? Couldn't he wait just a matter of hours? Her tongue came out and moistened her top lip. He couldn't. "Just one minute, okay?"

She nodded and he bent down and whisked up Josie, who had been clinging to Livvy's skirts, taking the baby with him. It took him only a moment to spot Bess, now dancing the two-step with Remy, and to be sure that her husband had filled her in on the plan. Wheezing from the exertion, she came and laid a big kiss on his forehead, her bright-red cheeks moist when they came in contact with his skin.

"You think you could take the kids home with you?" he asked, a small part of him wishing that Bess would refuse and he would be forced to wait until Tuesday to tell Livvy; a more personal, more immediate part praying she would say yes. Which, of course, she did.

"You're a fine man, Spencer Williamson," Remy said again, this time picking up Josie and giving her a twirl. "I don't care what anybody says about you!" He threw his head back and laughed heartily at his own joke.

"Listen to me," Spencer said, trying to quiet the man down. "It's a secret, remember?"

Remy put his fingers to his lips. "Yeah, Yeah. A secret."

* * *

Dusk was falling when they pulled up to the farmhouse. Curly George nickered at Peaches, who stood just on the other side of the fence. The chickens cackled as though they recognized Livvy. Miss Lily mooed long and low.

On the porch were piles of pie tins Spencer had washed out before the wedding. Livvy looked first at them and then at him accusingly. He could have smacked himself for leaving them there, but he'd never expected to bring her home.

"I couldn't let you share your cherries, Liv," he said, sounding pathetic even to himself.

"You bought all those pies?" There was utter disbelief in her eyes, but at his nod, the open mouth of surprise turned into a wide grin. "You did?"

"You're not mad?"

"No," she said, shaking her head. "I'm touched."

Women! He'd never understand them, but he'd never give up trying when it came to his wife.

"You want to get down?"

She lifted a shoulder and said, "I guess."

"No rush," he said, sitting with his hands in his lap and his heart in his throat. Beside him, despite the warm night, she shivered. "You cold?"

She shook her head, but he slipped out of his jacket and placed it over her shoulders anyway. She looked like a newly-wed, frightened and eager all at the same time. And even more pressing than his need to satisfy her—not to mention himself—was his need to reassure her that she was safe with him. Her heart was safe in his keeping.

"Nice night," he said, leaning back and crossing his ankles. She looked at him suspiciously. "Don't you think?"

"Oh, yes," she agreed, her head bobbing with enthusiasm as if either one of them cared about the weather.

"Smells good, too," he said. He inhaled so deeply he

could almost taste her on his tongue, feel her creep into his lungs—but then that wasn't all that far from his heart, where she already resided.

"My roses," she said, gesturing over her shoulder.

"Smells more like lilacs to me." He reached out and touched the pin that held her hair tightly to the nape of her neck. "All right?" he asked, pulling gently on the pin.

She gave the tiniest little nod and turned so that he could reach it easily. As her hair came tumbling down she said something, but the blood thrumming in his head drowned out the words.

"Spencer?"

He had a handful of her hair held up to his nose, and it was doing what it always did to him. His breathing was more ragged than he would have liked. "Hm?"

"Why are my roses all balled up?"

"You do know we're moving, don't you?"

"Moving?"

"This isn't the way I was going to tell you. See, it was all supposed to happen on Tuesday . . ."

She crossed her hands over her chest. "What was?"

The moon was rising, shining on her skin and dancing in her eyes, and she was close and the future was just around the corner and he couldn't help himself. "Could I kiss you?"

"Maybe you better tell me this plan," she started, but he put his arm around her and brushed her lips with his, saying a word, kissing her, saying another.

"You're gonna"—he pecked at her lips—"like it."

"I am?" she said dreamily, melting against him and returning his kisses tentatively.

She had the softest lips he could imagine, full and warm, and he could taste a touch of wine on them still from the wedding.

"Well, I"—he kissed the corner of her mouth, touching it with his tongue—"hope so."

"Why don't you"—her chest rose with her breath and then she let him pull her against him, closer and closer until there was no space at all—"tell me?"

He loosened the tie that was strangling him and found that it wasn't any easier to draw a breath without it. Careful not to let go of her or break their kiss, he wiggled his way to the edge of the seat, taking her with him.

"A second," he said, dragging in a gulp of air and then jumping down from the wagon. "Easy, boy," he said to George, setting the brake from the ground and then reaching up for Livvy and taking her in his arms like a baby.

"Spencer, put me down," she said, but when he didn't, she just put her arms around his neck and rested her head against his chest. "Then take me in the house," she said, and there was no mistaking her meaning.

He shook his head and headed for the barn, kicking the door open with his feet. There, awaiting a second coat of paint, was the bed he had been working on so lovingly, a big white headboard into which an *O* and an *S* had been carved and the letters connected with ribbonlike swirls and curves.

She stiffened in his arms and pushed against him, trying to regain her feet. Gently, reluctantly, he set her down.

"Oh, Spencer!" She ran her hand just inches above the wood, not touching it with her body but fondling it with her eyes. He lit the lantern that hung by the door and held it so that she could better examine his handiwork. "Oh, but it's beautiful!" Wiping with the back of her hand the tears that gathered at the corners of her eyes, she took in the other three beds that stood behind their own.

Neil's was blue, just as he had requested, with waves cut out in the wood and a white sailboat painted above them. Josie's was a pale pink, with hearts painted on either side of a carved-out *J*. Louisa's was simpler, more elegant, with one heart carved in the center of the headboard and a matching one in the footboard.

"When in the world did you do all this?" she asked when she could catch her breath.

"I had a lot of energy to work off," he said, thinking about how much he wanted to take her, then and there, and how wrong it was, wanting to make love to his wife in a barn in the semidarkness. But there was no helping it.

"Want to try it out?" he asked. At her blush he could have kicked himself. What kind of idiot asks his wife if she wants to try out a bed frame filled with straw in the barn when it wasn't even quite night and . . .

"Yes."

"Yes?"

"I'm sorry, Spencer, that I'm so shy." She stared at the ground and bit at a fingernail.

"Sorry?" he asked, cupping her chin and lifting it to search her eyes. "Livvy-love, you've nothing to apologize for. You're perfect."

"No," she said, shaking her head and sending waves of hair dancing across her shoulders and breasts. "I'm hysterically shy, and repressed, and—"

"That's the stupidest thing I've ever heard," Spencer said, closing any distance between them and hugging her to him. "You are perfect," he repeated.

"But Dr. Roberts—" she began.

"The doctor in Milwaukee? The one Bess saw?"

Guilt colored Livvy's face scarlet.

"She said you were what?"

Livvy mumbled something about River Street that was lost in his chest. How could he listen to her when her warm breath was teasing his nipples and it took all his concentration just to breathe?

"I said," he managed to get out finally, and with a certain authority, "that you are perfect. And you deserve better than this, Liv."

She took a deep breath and then she crawled over the side

rail and lay on her back, her arms out to him, reaching, beckoning. "Do you really think I'm perfect?"

He fought to swallow and had to settle for merely nodding.

"Then don't leave me here alone." She rolled over in the fresh hay until she was on the far side of the bed and looked up at him. Her eyes were almost closed. Her chest rose and fell. A small sigh escaped her lips.

Dear God! She wanted him.

It was why he'd brought her back to the farm, after all. To take her to his bed and make her his own. But now he stood beside the bed ashamed of himself and humbled. He hadn't made her his, at all.

It was she, with her soft ways, her patience and her love, who had made him hers, forever. And all he wanted was to make her world as wonderful as she had made his. And that didn't mean a hay bed in a barn with a cow and a couple of dozen chickens there to watch.

She reached out her arms again, and he was undone.

"But it'll be perfect on Tuesday," he said, forcing himself to wait. "You don't understand. I've got you—"

"Spence, shhh. It's perfect now." She began unbuttoning her dress, her eyes fixed on his.

"Livvy, I've gotten you Sacotte Farm." He hadn't meant to blurt it out, but his brain couldn't function any better than his lungs, which were having trouble taking in air, or his tongue, which was hanging from his mouth, or his heart, which had ceased to beat at the sight of his wife's creamy skin being revealed inch by precious inch.

Her eyes widened, but she only said, "That's nice," and worked at pulling the tails of her blouse out from her skirt and easing out of it until only her camisole covered her breasts, as if being there with him at that moment was more important to her than her family farm.

But that couldn't be. So he continued.

"I figured out that Makeridge was in cahoots with Bouche from the very beginning. Seems they met on the train to Milwaukee and Bouche offered Makeridge a piece of the profit if he bought Sacotte Farm, and . . ."

She was having trouble with the button at the waistband of her skirt. He came to the edge of the bed and got down on his knees to help her.

"Waylon and Julian?" she asked. "Oh. Uh-huh," she said distractedly, working the rest of the skirt buttons with less trouble.

"And I threatened to expose him if he didn't buy our farm, instead."

She eased the skirt down over her hips. White cotton with lace edges framed her like some sort of doll.

"He bought our farm?" She seemed only mildly interested. He was rapidly losing interest himself.

"Mm. He did." He reached out and ran one finger down her arm, watching the gooseflesh rise in his path.

She reached up and pulled on the tie that hung loosely around his shirt, drawing her to him.

"Wait, Liv," he said, knowing that once he joined her on that bed, he would be lost. "Then I bought Zephin's . . ."

She was getting cold, he could see, lying there alone in just her underthings, and she crossed her arms over her chest for warmth.

It worked. He felt the sweat begin to gather on his forehead at the sight of her ample breasts pressed together.

A gurgle came from his throat. He eased himself down onto the hay next to her. "You're so beautiful," he said, untying the ribbon on her camisole and fighting with the buttons.

"So then," she said, twisting so that she could reach his shirt buttons and working on them while he fought for breath, "we're going home?"

He nodded, unable to speak, running his hands everywhere, looking for skin to touch as if he needed to reassure himself that she was real and in his arms again.

There was still one thing he hadn't told her. Bouche had given up merely hinting and asked him for two hundred dollars to make his stake in the Klondike. He'd guaranteed that Spencer would never hear from him again.

"Liv?" he said. "There's something . . ."

But she was fighting with the buttons on his shirt, and when she mastered them, she struggled to free his shirttails from his pants.

"Liv . . ."

"I can't . . ." she said, fumbling beneath him. He lifted himself slightly from the hay, trying to see if her hands could be doing what it felt like they were. Dear God! They were! She was unfastening his suspenders! He rolled onto his back and gave her access to all of him.

He and Remy had taken the first two hundred dollars from the sale of Spencer's farm and wired it to Bouche. It meant they still owed some money to Zephin, but with a good crop . . .

He swallowed hard.

How was he supposed to keep his head when she was tugging at the waistband of his pants? The strap to her camisole fell off her shoulder and she pushed it back up, returned to her struggles, and repeated the gesture twice more.

"Liv?" he said, fighting for breath and trying to remember what it was he wanted to tell her.

"What is it?" she said, a little impatiently, he thought, stopping to look up at him and brushing the hair away from her face in a fluid, graceful motion.

"Leave the strap alone," he said, easing it off her shoulder. He could tell her tomorrow that he had to guarantee the rest of the money to Zephin. Or the next day.

But there were to be no more secrets, he reminded himself. "Liv?" He could hardly get the word out. Not that he was worried about money. After all, Livvy's pie sales alone would probably cover what they owed. And what choice did they have when it came to their children? Still, he felt he ought to tell her. "Liv?" he said again.

"Spencer?" she asked, pausing in her ministrations. "Are you nervous?"

The question was ridiculous. He snorted in response. She was the one who was shy. Repressed.

"Do you not want to do this?"

He snorted twice, for emphasis. Of course he wanted to do this. But he wanted it to be perfect.

"Then, Spencer?" She went back to work on his clothing with a diligence she usually reserved for dirty necks on little girls. "Shut up!"

He wanted to tell her he was shocked, tease her about her sudden loss of shyness. But just then she lowered her head to his now bare chest and lay one sweet perfect kiss just inches from his nipple. A charge coursed through him unlike anything he had ever felt. Like lightning hitting him. Like holding two of those new electric wires.

Her lips tentatively explored his chest, and it felt as though she were tracing his Adam's apple with her tongue. For a brief moment, he wondered if he had died and gone to heaven.

He lay there, flat on his back, straw tickling him behind his knees, the smell of her lilac hair filling his nostrils, and let her kiss him.

She paused and raised her head to him. "Do you really think I'm perfect?"

His answer was a low groan. How could she doubt it? His hands rested on her shoulders, and he let them slide down her arms, dragging her camisole straps with them until he could see her perfection for himself. "Oh, God!"

There were things that had happened in his life that he hadn't deserved. He'd always thought those were the bad things. Now, next to him, was one more thing he didn't deserve. But this one he vowed he would be worthy of.

"This inch is perfect," he began, kissing the small beauty mark he was surprised to find on her shoulder. After tonight he expected there would be nothing about her body he wouldn't know. "And this inch," he added, kissing her collar bone. "And, oh my Lo—"

Her breast was silky against his tongue, and he latched on to the nipple like an infant seeking sustenance. From her he would draw the strength he needed for whatever they should face. His hands traced the hourglass figure he had denied himself for so long, felt the swell of her hips and the soft expanse of her belly.

As good as she felt, warm and supple and satiny smooth, nothing felt as wonderful, or sent waves of excitement through him, as much as when he felt her timidly begin to explore him. Her hand played across his chest, tangled in the hair she found there, followed that hair down his torso and pressed against his belly just inches from his manhood.

And then her hand dipped lower.

"Shy?" he whispered against her temple when he could finally get the word out. "She said you were shy?"

The hand stilled.

"What did I tell you?" he asked her, not moving an inch.

"Perfect," she said softly, and he felt again the tentative movements of her inquiring fingers.

"I love you, Olivia Williamson," he said and rolled her to her back. "My perfect Livvy-love."

And when they couldn't stand the sweetness of just touching and kissing any longer, he took his love home.

She rose long after he was asleep and slipped from within the shelter of his arms. A piece of hay teased his nose, and she moved it away before rising from the bed he'd built for them to share. On bare feet she tiptoed from the barn and made her way toward Spencer's house, a house that had never quite belonged to her.

Inside, it was eerily quiet, and with the utmost care she climbed the ladder to the loft where Peter and Margaret's belongings awaited their return. Tenderly she plucked each bird from the shelf on which it rested and placed one after the other within the folds of her skirt. When she had them all, she gathered the edges of her skirt into one hand and held them tight, careful that none of the birds could escape their soft nest.

On her way back toward the steps she picked up Margaret's doll and added her to the cache. "We're moving, Winnie," she said softly. "And I wouldn't want you left behind."

Down in her kitchen she looked around her in the early light of dawn. It would be harder, she realized, to say goodbye to the old house than she thought.

But then again, everything that mattered would be coming with her.

There was a crate on the table, and she put the doll and carvings into it, nestling them right next to the carving tools and blocks of wood Spencer had already packed. Then she carried it to the porch to be sure it went with them to Sacotte Farm.

The sun was just rising over the hill when she reentered the barn and tried to slip back into the makeshift bed in which Spencer was snoring lightly.

"Liv?"

"Mm?"

"Are you happy?"

His eyes were still closed, so he couldn't see the smile that split her face, or the tears that spilled down her cheeks, or even the nod of her head. And so she answered aloud the question he had never asked her before.

"Yes," she said softly, guessing he had already fallen back to sleep again. "Completely."

"Good," he said, surprising her. "That's all I needed to know."

He shifted to accommodate her, pulling her into the curve of his body and pressing her bottom against his resting manhood. Outside the barn the crickets chirped, and a cool breeze sent chills across Olivia's scantily clad body. She should have thought to bring a blanket back to the barn, but from the stirring behind her she doubted she would be cool for long.

And he proved her right, once again.

Later, much later, he tucked his discarded shirt around her. "Do you think we might have made a baby?"

"I—I don't know," Olivia said, and she felt his hand cradle her flat belly and she covered it with her own.

"I think we did," he said. His voice was sure and hopeful, as if a union so perfect had to have produced a miracle.

"It doesn't matter," she said, no doubt surprising him as much as herself. "The truth is, I have everything I want right now. Everything I've always wanted."

He snuggled her closer to him, his contented sigh chilling her sweaty skin, a kiss warming it again.

"Still," he said, playing with her hair and teasing the skin on her arm with it, "I bet we did."

She twisted around to look at him and asked, "Does it matter so to you?" After the years of disappointment, she hated the thought that he might be disappointed again.

"Only," he said, seeking out her breasts and teasing a nipple, "that if I'm right, we've got ourselves one more child to love. And if I'm wrong . . ." His hand inched down her belly and found the still-moist curls of her womanhood. "We'll just have to try again . . ."

He kissed the top of her head softly.

"And again . . ."

His lips kissed her eyelids and moved down her face to find her lips.

''And again . . .''

Then he finally shut up and made good on his promise.

Author's Note

I found George H. Napheys's Book, *The Transmission of Life, Counsels on the Nature and Hygiene of the Masculine Function,* in a small antique shop in Cambria, California, a quaint oceanside town where my husband and I spent our twenty-fifth anniversary. It was published in 1878 by David McKay Publishers, Philadelphia, and contained all sorts of interesting information, such as women's inability to enjoy the sex act, in addition to the fact that if a disabled man fathered a child, whether his disability was caused by an accident or not, the child might inherit the disability.

I'd like to challenge another of Dr. Napheys's claims—that a largely or exclusively vegetable diet would result in loss of sexual function. Being a vegetarian myself, I would like to go on record as disputing *that* claim along with nearly all his others!

I thank you for reading *The Marriage Bed.* It was a joy to write, and Olivia and Spencer now join my other characters as active members of my fictional family.

I would be very happy to hear from you. Your comments and suggestions are always welcome, and on more than one occasion I have been caught dancing and singing in my kitchen as I celebrate the receipt of an enthusiastic letter from a reader! Please write to me at *Stephanie Mittman, c/o MLGW, 190 Willis Avenue, Mineola, NY 11501.* Please enclose a stamped self-addressed envelope for reply.